TO BEGIN AGAIN

By the same author:

The Best of Times

TO BEGIN AGAIN

A Novel of Love and War

much love, Aunt Louise

TERRY

Sept 2006

Terence T. Finn

www.ivyhousebooks.com

Map of Korea from *In Mortal Combat* by John Toland.
Copyright © 1991 by John Toland. Reprinted by
permission of HarperCollins Publishers.

PUBLISHED BY IVY HOUSE PUBLISHING GROUP
5122 Bur Oak Circle, Raleigh, NC 27612
United States of America
919-782-0281
www.ivyhousebooks.com

ISBN: 1-57197-462-8
Library of Congress Control Number: 2005910592

Printed in the United States of America

For Joyce, with love

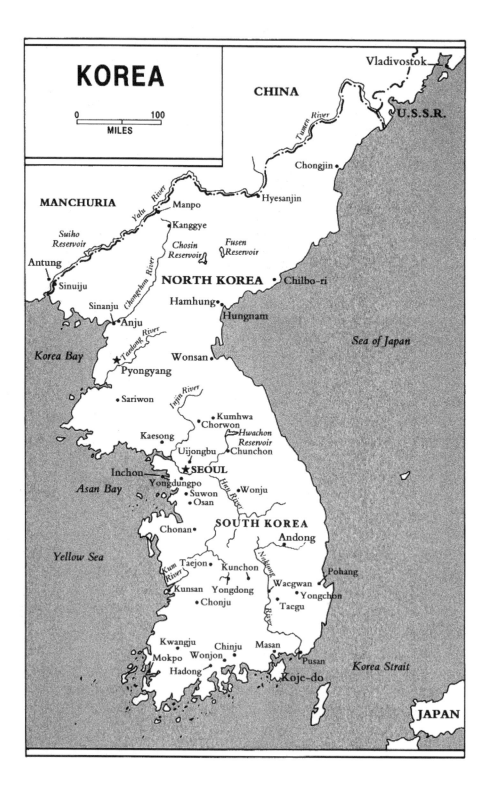

PROLOGUE

The Korean War was fought for three years, one month and two days, from June 25, 1950 to July 27, 1953. Losses in the conflict were high. American dead numbered 33,629. Nearly twice that number were wounded. Over five thousand Americans were declared missing. Korean losses were much higher. At least a million people died. Loss of life among the Chinese also was substantial though difficult to estimate precisely.

How the war began can be traced to the defeat of Japan in 1945. Throughout its history the island nation had coveted its neighbor, finally annexing Korea as a colony in 1910. With the end of World War II the peninsula was divided arbitrarily along the 38th Parallel. To the north lay the communist regime of Kim Il Sung, a totalitarian state established and supported by the Soviet Union. This Democratic People's Republic of Korea was a disciplined, efficient society in which devotion to the nation and its leader outranked individual choice. To the south lay the Republic of Korea (RoK), a country recognized by the United Nations and led by Syngman Rhee, a fiery Korean nationalist educated in the United States. America backed Rhee's regime as a bulwark against communism, hoping that he might eventually improve the economic conditions of a people still suffering from years of harsh Japanese occupation.

Kim Il Sung was ruthless, cruel, and ambitious. Syngman Rhee was corrupt, devious, and intolerant. Both men saw themselves as the legitimate ruler of the entire Korean peninsula. Each was intent upon destroying the other.

Kim Il Sung struck first. Early on Sunday morning, June 25, 1950, after a thunderous barrage of artillery, the North Korean army crossed the border. Kim's goal was a quick victory, before assistance to Rhee could be rendered. A worker's paradise would be imposed upon a largely agrarian south. Well trained and well equipped, especially with Russian T–34 tanks, the North Koreans overwhelmed their outnumbered RoK counterparts who, in most instances, fought poorly. What began as an assault soon became a rout. Seoul, South Korea's capital, was captured in three days. Rhee's army lacked competent generals. It also lacked heavy artillery and tanks, purposely so, for the United States feared that a well armed Syngman Rhee would start World War III by attacking Stalin's puppet regime in the north. To the contrary, as the North Koreans pushed farther south, Kim's goal seemed within reach.

By June 27th the Americans in Seoul had been evacuated. Most left by ship via Inchon, a port city just south of the capital on the western coast of Korea. They sailed to Japan, from where U.S. air force planes soon flew missions in support of the disintegrating South Korean army. Several leaders in Washington saw the North Korean attack as an assault upon Western Democracy orchestrated by the Soviet Union. The object was to either test American resolve or to stretch American military resources thereby making conquest in Europe much easier. Thus, as President Truman was reviewing options, consideration was given to nuclear strikes upon Soviet air bases in the northeast, where the border of Korea met that of Russia. The president chose a less drastic approach. He ordered U.S. ground troops into Korea.

Truman's decision was made easier by a United Nations' resolution authorizing member states to provide military assistance to the Republic of Korea. This passed the same day the Americans left Seoul and was made possible by the absence of the Soviet Union in the Security Council. Stalin's regime was protesting the exclusion of the

Chinese communists from the U.N. Most Americans supported the presidential decision. Those that did saw the need to confront communism when challenged. Those that did not thought that Korea simply did not matter. After all, had not Secretary of State Dean Acheson, in a speech on January 12, 1950, excluded Korea from areas vital to American interests?

The first American ground troops in Korea were a small combat team of 450 men. Named Task Force Smith, after its commander, the team arrived on the peninsula on July 1, 1950, and soon engaged the enemy. Task Force Smith has since become legendary, but for unhappy reasons. To the shock of many, the North Koreans quickly disposed of the Americans. Smith's bazookas could not stop T–34 tanks. More importantly, his soldiers were not the equals of Kim Il Sung's. With many casualties, the team withdrew, joining the RoK forces in full retreat. For the Americans the news would get worse before it got better. Additional U.S. troops were thrown into battle. These too failed to do well. One unit in particular, the army's 24th Division, performed miserably, with its commander, a major general, allowing himself to be captured. The reality was that in 1950 the U.S. army was hardly the armed force that had defeated Hitler's army. American soldiers in the Far East were occupational troops, ill suited for combat.

As the situation in Korea deteriorated, the United States sent in more troops. Among the arrivals were U.S. marines, and soldiers willing to fight. These were joined by a brigade of British troops. As other nations provided small symbolic contingents the U.S. effort became, and called itself, a United Nations command. Still, the bulk of the forces opposing the North Koreans were American, specifically the United States Eighth Army led by Lt. General Walton Walker. By early August these forces had been pushed back to a small perimeter surrounding Pusan, a port at the southeastern tip of the peninsula. Expulsion from Korea was a distinct possibility. For six weeks fierce fighting took place. Mindful of Walker's call to "stand or die," the Americans repulsed determined North Korean attacks. The perimeter held. Pounded by U.S. aircraft and U.S. artillery, the communists were unable to reach the sea. There would be no Dunkirk in Korea.

Despite the successful defense of the Pusan perimeter, the reputation of the American military had suffered. North Korea had defeated the U.S. Eighth Army, though it had not destroyed it. Yet at the moment of greatest danger to Walton and his troops, the United States would conduct an audacious maneuver that would shatter the overextended North Korean forces, reminding the world of how capable America's military was.

The maneuver was an amphibious landing at Inchon, well up the western coast of Korea, deep behind enemy lines. Conceived by General Douglas MacArthur, the supreme commander of U.N. and U.S. troops, the operation was considered risky by the Chiefs of Staff in Washington. Yet the general prevailed. His reputation was such that the operation took place as planned. On September 15, 1950, U.S. marines and the army's 7th Division landed at Inchon. The landings were a complete success. By September 27, Seoul was retaken. In the south the day after the landing, Walker's army attacked. Now outnumbered, the North Koreans gave way. The Eighth Army advanced, linking up with the Inchon forces on September 26. Badly beaten though still intact, Kim Il Sung's army retreated, crossing back over the 38th Parallel from where, four months before, it had started the war.

Now came a decisive moment. Would the U.N. forces cross the Parallel seeking to destroy Kim's army and with it his regime? The original purpose of the largely American effort had been met. The Republic of South Korea had been saved. Crossing the 38th meant expanding the war.

MacArthur wanted to proceed north. He argued that if the North Korean forces were not destroyed they would be in a position to attack once again. Moreover, he believed the war to be a part of a Soviet-led communist conspiracy to destroy the West, an assault upon democracy that must be stopped.

Syngman Rhee also wanted U.N. forces to cross the Parallel. He viewed the conquest of North Korea as a means to unify the country under his control. Many people believed that Korea should be a single entity, though not everyone thought Rhee should be its ruler.

America's allies were torn. They worried about further casualties, but they worried more about the reaction of the Chinese government in Peking, which had warned against an American "invasion" of North Korea. Yet the allies wanted to show support of the United States. In Europe and in the Pacific they were dependent upon America in countering the political and military threats posed by the Soviet Union. Abandoning the Americans in Korea was hardly the way to secure American backing elsewhere.

Everyone—MacArthur, his troops, the allies, Syngman Rhee and the leaders in Washington—was caught up in the euphoria occasioned by the success at Inchon. A great victory had been achieved. The North Koreans were in disarray. The war would be brought to a successful and definitive conclusion. The troops would be home by Christmas.

Late in September, MacArthur received permission from Washington to cross the 38th Parallel and to continue with the destruction of the North Korean army. Pointedly, he was told to watch for evidence of Chinese or Russian intervention. Under no circumstances was he to advance beyond the Yalu River into Manchuria or the Soviet Union. Having vast influence at the United Nations in 1950, the United States was able to secure passage of a resolution supporting what MacArthur wished to do, in effect approving a military advance into North Korea.

On October 9, 1950, the Eighth Army moved north. That it had been preceded by RoK troops mattered little. The United Nations was now committed to the liberation of North Korea. A momentous chapter in the history of Korea was about to be written. And the United States Army would soon receive a most unpleasant surprise.

At first the campaign went well. While meeting resistance the Eighth Army nonetheless readily advanced along the western side of the peninsula. By October 19, the army had captured Pyonyang, the capital of North Korea. Earlier Kim Il Sung had fled to Sinuiju, a city on the Yalu River across from the Chinese city of Antung. By

November 1, Americans were eighteen miles south of the river. In the east U.S. marines landed at Wonsan and, joining army troops, proceeded north to the Chosin Reservoir. The army's 7th Division reached the Yalu itself from where it could peer into Manchuria.

However, Chinese troops in large numbers had deployed into North Korea. The regime in Peking was alarmed by the approaching "imperialist" forces. Four field armies, each with thirty thousand men, had been sent across the Yalu and were in position, soon to be joined by two additional armies. Remarkably, the Chinese went undetected. MacArthur and his officers did not believe the Chinese would enter the war. The evidence that they had was ignored. Moreover, the Americans believed that if the Chinese were to join the battle the United States easily would defeat them.

On October 25, 1950, the Chinese struck. At first they attacked RoK troops. Six days later they hit the U.S. forces. Both the South Koreans and Americans were vanquished, and easily so. Loss of territory, though, was limited. Surprisingly, the Chinese soldiers did not follow up these initial victories. Instead they withdrew to the hills and waited.

Why did the Chinese not continue? Were they sending a message to General MacArthur and President Truman? Were they warning the U.S. not to remain at the Yalu? If so, the Americans did not listen. They chose an alternate message. MacArthur believed the Chinese had made a face-saving gesture. He expected them to withdraw. He thought they had done their best and no longer were a threat.

On Thanksgiving Day, 1950, Americans throughout Korea enjoyed their traditional turkey dinner. The next day General Walker, in command of troops in the west, launched an offensive he and others believed would soon end the war. The Eighth Army moved out, expecting to finish off the North Koreans and any Chinese it encountered. However, the Chinese were the better soldiers. They inflicted a humiliating defeat upon the U.N. command. A few Allied units fought well. Most did not. The U.S. Army's 2nd Division failed totally. Only the marines at the Chosin Reservoir upheld the honor of American arms.

They retreated, but the marine formation brought their dead with them and were evacuated by the navy at Hungnam.

By December 5, the Chinese had recaptured the North Korean capital. A month later they had retaken Seoul. North Korea no longer was in U.N. hands. The Eighth Army had been routed. Its soldiers, to use the phrase of the day, had bugged out. But the Chinese advance, extensive as it was, began to run out of steam, hampered by now lengthy supply lines. It came to a halt just south of the Han River, roughly along the 37th parallel.

Two days before Christmas, Walton Walker was killed in an automobile accident, his Jeep colliding with a truck. His replacement was Lt. General Matthew Ridgeway, a soldier with a distinguished combat record in World War II. Ridgeway energized the U.N. command. He rebuilt the Eighth Army. He commanded all troops in Korea whereas Walker had not. Previously, American troops in the east had been commanded by Major General Edward Almond, a favorite of MacArthur. Most importantly, Ridgeway brought to Korea skill and leadership, attributes that in Almond and Walker had been lacking.

When Ridgeway's forces attacked late in January 1951, they were well prepared. The troops soon pushed the Chinese back across the Han. In the east, the Chinese themselves launched an attack. But this time the Americans held, with the reconstituted 2nd Division redeeming itself. Supported by massive air power, the U.S. soldiers shattered four Chinese divisions.

All across Korea, Chinese commanders held a low opinion of G.I. Joe. In the months of January and February 1951, this began to change. Under Ridgeway, U.S. troops fought well. And they fought successfully. By mid-March, Seoul—by now a city in ruins—was again in U.S. hands. Thirteen days later American soldiers crossed the 38th Parallel. Reaching the Imjin River, some thirty miles north of the city, they dug in.

Ridgeway expected a new Chinese offensive. This he received, but before the attack materialized the general was given a promotion he had not expected. On April 11, Douglas MacArthur was fired and

Matthew Ridgeway became Supreme Commander of all U.N. forces in Korea.

MacArthur had issued several statements on the war that were contrary to U.S. policy. President Truman, Secretary of State Dean Acheson and the Joint Chiefs of Staff all wanted to limit the conflict to the peninsula. General MacArthur sought a wider war. With support from influential Republicans in Washington, he advocated attacks upon China and saw no reason not to employ nuclear weapons. Moreover, he felt that as supreme commander in the field he, not Mr. Truman, should determine the course of action. Truman, whose standing in the public was as low as MacArthur's was high, reacted to the general's insubordination and sacked him. MacArthur left Tokyo and returned to America, receiving a hero's welcome. He then sought the Republican nomination for president in 1952, but failed. The GOP delegates chose instead another general, one by the name of Eisenhower.

On April 22, 1951, the Chinese launched yet another major offensive, throwing 250,000 men at the Eighth Army now commanded by Lt. General James Van Fleet. The goal of the offensive and that of another one in May was, once and for all, to evict the Americans and their allies from Korea. The communists were aiming for a decisive victory. They were willing to expend thousands of lives to achieve it. They achieved the loss of life but not their goal. U.N. soldiers fought tenaciously, retreated a few miles, and held. Then they themselves attacked and pushed the Chinese back several miles.

And there for the next two years the battle was drawn. The war in Korea continued with heavy casualties but little exchange of territory. Peace talks first began in July, 1951. They concluded only in July 1953. During that time the front lines, with trenches and fortified bunkers, resembled those of the First World War. Fighting was extensive. Individual hills were contested. Names such as Pork Chop Hill became legendary. But military gains and losses in any strategic sense were minimal. The Chinese could not drive the Americans into the sea. The Untied States was unwilling to accept the consequences of pushing the Chinese back across the Yalu.

Thus the war ended as it had started. Korea was cut in two, roughly along the 38th Parallel. In the north Kim Il Sung remained in charge of a totalitarian state that still exists today. Then and now, its citizens lack material comforts and are deprived of political freedom. In the south the Republic of Korea continues. Now it is economically prosperous and a democratic society. Nevertheless, fifty years after the Korean War, armies confront one another halfway down the peninsula. One of them is the United States Eighth Army. This time it is well trained and well equipped. It serves as a deterrent to war and a reminder of a bloody conflict now largely forgotten.

For the United States Air Force the war in Korea was no small affair. During three years of conflict, it flew 720,000 sorties and lost over 1,400 aircraft. Increases in personnel were substantial, from 411,277 in mid-1951 to 977,583 at the war's end. Moreover, the full array of combat missions were flown. Employing a variety of aircraft, air force pilots flew close air support, interdiction, reconnaissance, strategic bombing, anti-submarine, and air combat missions. Hardly a day went by when the air force was not engaged in the skies above Korea.

The war also brought new developments in air warfare. Helicopters saw their first employment in combat, as did American and Russian jet-powered aircraft. Air-to-air refueling had its wartime introduction. Each of these developments pointed toward the future. To its credit, the air force recognized their importance and invested heavily in them.

Nearly half the missions flown in Korea were for the purpose of interdiction. This meant the disruption and destruction of enemy supplies and troops well behind the battle line. Having just gained independence from the army, the air force had little interest in focusing upon close air support. As strategic bombing targets were limited, the air force concentrated on interdicting the flow of men and material. In this it achieved considerable success. Yet given the manpower available to the North Koreans and Chinese, as well as their willingness to accept casualties, interdiction did not achieve its goal of collapsing the enemy's ability to wage war.

Where the air force did much better was in air-to-air combat against Russian-built MiG–15 fighters. The MiGs were first-rate aircraft. Yet against them, America's best fighter, the F–86 Sabre, excelled. Sabre pilots claimed the destruction of 792 MiGs, a number now generally accepted as too high. Of the 110 Sabres lost in Korea, 78 were shot down by MiGs. The others were lost to ground fire or for reasons unknown. Success of the F–86s was due largely to their pilots, who were experienced and well trained. Sound tactics and a superior gunsight made the difference as well. Most of the time MiG pilots were outmatched. A few did well, particularly a number of Russians, but the majority of those who flew from Antung and the other bases in Manchuria crossed the Yalu at their peril. In July, 1953, when an armistice was signed at Panmunjon, one fact was indisputable: above North Korea, Sabres owned the sky.

ONE

She had Irish red hair and green eyes, much like Rita Hayworth's. Her skin was pale and her figure was of a shape that men invariably noticed and admired, again like that of the movie star. McGrath was convinced she was the most beautiful girl he had ever seen. But it was Catherine Caldwell's face that forced him to stare, against his wishes. Her features were angular. Considered separately, they seemed too prominent, yet combined they fit together as if mocking traditional concepts of beauty. McGrath found the resulting image compelling. This, he realized, would complicate the situation, for they both were in a classroom at Georgetown University. Catherine was one of seventeen students in the class. McGrath was their teacher.

Entitled *America Enters the Twentieth Century,* the class met every Tuesday and Thursday. McGrath lectured on the former, devoting the second day to classroom discussion. Already he had covered the Robber Barons, the Social Gospel, and the wave of immigration. For this last subject he employed Ellis Island as the focal point, noting that from 1892 to 1907 over fourteen million people passed through this gateway to America. As intended, this number impressed the class, though McGrath noticed they seemed more impressed that among these immigrants were Knute Rockne, Irving Berlin, and Felix Frankfurter.

Next on the syllabus was World War I. McGrath intended to spend one week on America's entry into the war and one week on the conflict itself. The first two classes would be devoted to Woodrow Wilson. The next two would cover how the battles were fought on land and sea, how Germany came to lose a war it might have won, and what the war meant to the United States both before and after 1917. In addition, in the second week, McGrath planned a quick look at the poetry of World War I, this for the benefit of the girls in the class. They would read Sassoon and Owen. For the boys, he would have them read about aerial warfare. They would learn, as he once had, of the exploits of Mannick and Bishop, Richthofen and Rickenbaker.

Regarding Wilson, McGrath would discuss the president's domestic agenda followed by the steps Wilson took, and did not take, that resulted in war with Germany.

The first lecture began well. McGrath was discussing the Federal Trade Commission when a student—not Catherine Caldwell—politely interrupted and asked a seemingly simple question.

"Professor, I'm somewhat confused. I know Woodrow Wilson was president during World War I, but later on, at Versailles, he's always talking to prime ministers and I'm not sure I know the difference. That is, between a president and a prime minister."

McGrath considered the question legitimate, but out of place. Better to answer it another day, and at length. At least that was his initial reaction. But then he noticed that Catherine Caldwell was staring at him with an expression that seemed unrelated to the subject at hand. Ignoring the other student, he focused on Catherine. He had seen her before and found her compelling. McGrath imagined her elsewhere, at the beach, at a picnic, at a dance, each time with him. A moment passed, then another. *Pay attention to what you're doing, which is teaching a class.* And he did so, but not by excluding the subject of his pleasant diversion.

"Miss Caldwell, the question is a good one. Might you be able to provide us with an answer?" McGrath was attempting to be both friendly yet distant, as first-year Assistant Professors of History were expected to be.

"Yes, sir, I think I can." *He does know my name—I thought so and now I'm sure.* Then she too paused. Her mind imagined a time and place beyond the classroom, where she and this intriguing man might be alone, enjoying the company of the other. The interlude lasted but seconds, for someone coughed and Catherine Caldwell quickly returned to where she was: inside a gray stone building at the college quadrangle. She was pleased though that she had this flight of fancy. She also was pleased she knew the answer to the question.

"Presidents, at least those here in the United States, are the head of a separate branch of government—the executive branch—and are elected by the people. Prime Ministers are part of a legislative branch, like parliament. They're the leaders of the majority party in a parliament. Presidents aren't in the legislature. They have a fixed term of office, whereas prime ministers can be in office as long as the majority of the party members want them to be. The main difference is that presidents are separate from the legislature."

"Exactly so, Miss Caldwell. Nicely done." McGrath had hoped she would know the answer, concerned that she might not. After all, this was a history class, not a class in government. "Perhaps we'll talk about this later on, or better yet have Father O'Boyle trek over from Political Theory 101 and reveal to us the mysteries of democratic leadership."

What McGrath had just said was not utmost in his mind. His attention again was focused on Catherine Caldwell. *How very interesting. She's not only lovely to look at; she's also an intelligent young woman.*

Catherine was a senior at Georgetown. Born in Montana, she had come east when her father and mother had moved to Washington. George Caldwell, a graduate of the Naval Academy, had made admiral in 1939. He was deputy commander of the Bureau of Ships when he died three years later. Illness then claimed her mother, who passed away in 1947, a year after Catherine started college. She moved into the home of her uncle, who also was in the military. He and his wife Laura lived in Washington, not far from the National Cathedral. Each day he drove to the Pentagon, or rather was driven by his air force chauffeur. Catherine also used an automobile. In 1948 her uncle had bought her a brand new Ford convertible. The car was baby blue and Catherine loved it.

"Oh Uncle Mike, it's beautiful. Is it really mine?"

"Yes, my dear, it is. Enjoy it, and just remember that your Aunt Laura and I love you."

"I will, Uncle Mike. I will."

Initially, Laura had thought the automobile was extravagant. But she knew her husband adored their niece and wanted the girl to be happy. So she raised no objection when he wrote a $1,040 check to Arlington Motors. Laura reasoned that Catherine had experienced her share of grief. She deserved a bit of joy.

On the day that McGrath had lectured on Wilson's leadership, Catherine was dropping off her books in her car prior to having lunch. As she closed the door of the Ford she saw McGrath walk into Max's, a delicatessen four blocks from campus. There and then Catherine Caldwell made a decision that would alter her life. Later, as she would recall that moment in time, Catherine marveled that she had acted instinctively, without debate, not caring about consequences or what others would think.

McGrath had not reacted at all. He wanted simply to have lunch. He was hungry and he intended to continue his quest. McGrath was searching for the perfect egg salad sandwich. Max's served a good one. Egg salad sandwiches required four or five slices of tomato, no lettuce, several shakes of pepper, and genuinely fresh bread. Even then, the sandwich would fail if the mayonnaise in the egg salad was overdone. In McGrath's experience this usually was the case. Mayonnaise had to be employed sparingly. And the bread itself had to be free of the spread. Since McGrath had entered college he had sought the perfect sandwich. Once, as a graduate student at Notre Dame in 1948, he had come close. Max's was not that good. But it was one of the better ones. As he looked at the sandwich, McGrath contemplated with satisfaction what he saw. The sandwich sat appealingly on the plate. Next to it were a pickle and a spoonful of coleslaw. The Coke McGrath had ordered stood nearby, the glass full of ice as he had asked. Lunch was on the table and he was ready to eat.

Though he enjoyed the sandwich, McGrath never finished it.

"Excuse me, Professor McGrath, I've got a question or two about the class. Would this be a good time to ask them?" Catherine had no idea what questions she would ask, but could think of no other way to initiate a conversation with someone she hoped to know better.

"Certainly, Miss Caldwell." As he spoke, McGrath stood up. His mother had taught him to rise whenever a female came to the dinner table. Granted, this was a more informal venue, but McGrath knew his mother would approve. Eleanor McGrath was a woman of strong opinions and she felt good manners were necessary at all times and in every instance.

"Here," McGrath motioned to the other chair at the table. "Please sit down."

"Thank you." Catherine slid into the chair.

McGrath noticed she was looking at his sandwich. "Can we order you a bite to eat? It is, after all, lunchtime."

"Yes, if you don't mind." Catherine took the menu McGrath had proffered. She appeared to him to be studying it intently. In fact, she was frantically thinking of history questions she might ask if called upon to do so.

"So what will it be?"

"Oh, I have a question about Woodrow Wilson." At the moment she spoke Catherine Caldwell had no idea what she would say next.

Unwittingly, McGrath came to her rescue.

"No, I mean for lunch."

"Oh. I'll have a BLT on toast, but with just a dab of mayonnaise."

McGrath reacted with a smile. "Sounds good. Let me go find Max and order it. Want something to drink?"

"Yes, a cup of hot tea would be nice."

McGrath excused himself and went up to the counter. There he waited until Max was free. Then he asked the proprietor for one bacon, lettuce, and tomato sandwich and a cup of tea. "And Max, make it on toast and go easy on the mayo."

"Yes sir, Colonel." Max always addressed McGrath by his wartime rank. He too had served in the Eighth Air Force, though not under McGrath's command. Maxwell Hopkins no more could call the former C.O. of the 27th Fighter Squadron "Professor" than he could Dwight Eisenhower, once president of Columbia University, "Mr. President." At first McGrath had tried to have Max use the academic title, but the former technical sergeant couldn't and wouldn't.

"Doesn't seem right, Colonel, just doesn't somehow," proving that indeed old habits die hard.

"Well Max, the war is over and we are now different people. I'm a history teacher at Georgetown, which suits me just fine. What you and I did in England doesn't matter right now. That time is past and what's important now is what we're doing today, and tomorrow, and down the road."

"Maybe so, Colonel, but what we've been is part of who we are. And in your case, well sir, you were in charge of an Army Air Corps fighter squadron, in the best air force the world has ever seen. And that's something no one should forget."

"All true, Max, and we won't forget. But it's not the life we're living now. That was then, and now is now. I'm getting on with my life and that's what we all should be doing. Heck, you are. You own this delicatessen; you're a man of business and making a success of it. Fact is, I'm real proud of you."

"Thanks, Colonel. But like that movie with Dana Andrews, I think the time we had in England were the best years of our lives."

"Maybe so. We'll see what the future holds." McGrath hoped that Maxwell Hopkins was wrong. He wanted to believe that at age thirty, life was starting over. He had a new career. True, time in the air corps had been wonderful. He enjoyed flying, and still flew as part of the D.C. Air National Guard. Command of the 27th had been an honor, a time of triumph. But he wanted to live in the present and found it sad, if not pathetic, when men did not move beyond their time in uniform.

University life suited McGrath. He enjoyed the intellectual atmosphere. Now, instead of helping young men to fly and fight, he was teaching youngsters how to think, how to examine past events, how to draw conclusions despite conflicting evidence. The work was satisfying. Particularly gratifying was to see a student reach new levels of understanding.

Yet doubt had not vanished completely from McGrath's mind. He knew how important victory in Europe had been. He knew too that the Eighth Air Force had made possible Germany's defeat. He had contributed to that outcome and felt proud of what he had accomplished. During his time in command, the 27th Fighter Squadron had destroyed 209 German aircraft. He himself had downed eleven planes. Maybe Maxwell Hopkins was correct. Maybe the fourteen months in England were the crowning achievement of his life. Could anything else be that significant? McGrath hoped so. He thought life would be grossly unfair were the high point to be reached at the age of twenty-four.

Returning to the table, McGrath placed the sandwich in front of Catherine as he sat down. "Here it is. One BLT. The cup of tea is on the way."

"Thank you," said Catherine. To her surprise, her first reaction was neither to think about McGrath nor to consider what she would say next. She wondered whether this man had paid for the sandwich. Catherine had planned to pay the forty-five cents herself, but quickly decided not to object should McGrath treat her to lunch. He did so, and much later would tease her that she had been a cheap first date.

Catherine's next thought concerned Woodrow Wilson. From payment for a BLT to Wilson's initial desire for neutrality covered quite a distance, but Catherine's mind traveled far and quickly. She was ready to respond should McGrath act like the professor he was.

He did not. "I've had enough of Woodrow Wilson for today, Miss Caldwell. Tell me a little bit about yourself."

Pleased that the conversation would have a personal flavor, Catherine spoke nonstop for the next fifteen minutes, doing so in part out of nervousness, in part out of a desire that he learn about her so that she in turn might learn about him. She told McGrath about growing up in the west. She recounted how she had come to Georgetown rather than attending Vassar. She recited the events surrounding her mother's death. She revealed her desire to visit Europe, especially Italy.

"I've never been to Italy," said McGrath. "And I would like to, especially Venice. I'm told it's a lovely city."

"Yes, I'm sure it is." Catherine had heard Venice must be visited with someone you love. The thought that someday she might do so with McGrath crossed her mind. That would be special, very special. The idea was insane of course. She hardly knew the man. Still, if mad, the thought was not unpleasant. Rather sweet, in fact. Time to shift the conversation. The images in her mind were dangerous. "I've talked long enough. Now tell me a little bit about yourself."

McGrath paused, considering what he might say. He had divided his life, like Gaul, into three parts. The first part was growing up and going to college. The second was his service in the air corps. The third part was the present. This consisted of Georgetown, the Air National Guard, and a social life he believed needed improvement. McGrath chose to discuss the first one.

He relayed to Catherine his childhood on Long Island. He told her about the Quaker prep school in Locust Valley and about going off to college in 1938. He mentioned that Amherst had been intellectually rewarding and thus responsible for his decision to pursue a Ph.D. He did not mention the death of his friend Jimmy Rodgers.

Catherine interrupted with a question, the answer to which she already knew. She did so because she had learned from her aunt that most men liked to talk about themselves and did so more easily if responding to a question.

"And where did you get your Ph.D.?"

"I spent several years at Notre Dame, and finished just last year."

"And what, if I may ask, was the subject of your dissertation?" For this question, Catherine did not have the answer.

McGrath smiled. He was recalling both the pleasure and agony of producing that first piece of scholarship. "I wrote about the War of

1812, about how the United States gained much from a war it essentially lost."

Catherine Caldwell knew little about the subject, but was willing to hear more, as long as McGrath shortly returned to what she considered important, which was the story behind the man who wrote the dissertation.

McGrath obliged. He said simply that the war established a naval tradition that has served the country well and that by at last removing the British presence from the Ohio Valley, the U.S. could expand westward and not be simply a coastal nation.

"And what happened next, after college? Someone told me you were a pilot during the war, in England."

"Yes, that's true. I was." McGrath did not wish to discuss P–51s and the 27th Fighter Squadron with Catherine Caldwell. He wanted her or any female to like him for what he was and might be, not for what he had been. He thought too that she might find wartime stories boring, or worse, that he was full of himself. In McGrath's view fighter pilots tended to be extremely confident and self-absorbed. They needed to be the former but the latter he felt was unattractive and not a characteristic he wished to claim.

"Here is your tea, young lady." Max had arrived and put the cup upon the table.

Aware that Hopkins had heard Catherine's last remark, McGrath gave him a visual command: *Do not talk about England. Do not discuss aerial exploits, mine or anybody else's. Leave the tea and depart.* Maxwell Hopkins obeyed, but not before winking to the pretty girl opposite the colonel.

Max's interruption provided McGrath the opportunity to continue, which he did, essentially skipping 1942 through 1945.

"Some dissertations take a while to write, some go more quickly. I finished mine last year and here I am. First job and on my way. Though at age thirty I'm a bit old to be a rookie professor."

"I think you're doing splendidly." Catherine answered a question McGrath had not asked. He wanted to know how she thought he was doing. He was pleased to learn Catherine Caldwell considered him a fine teacher.

Catherine also considered McGrath attractive. As he spoke about Notre Dame and the War of 1812 she remembered how struck she had been when he first entered the classroom, four weeks earlier. Then, as now, he was well dressed, in tie and jacket and well-spoken, in command from the very start. Catherine estimated his height to be just under six feet. His hair was light brown, on the short side but combed and clean. Despite fair skin and a lean torso he appeared fit, even robust. Most noticeable, however, were his eyes. Slate blue, they conveyed a strength and sternness that lessened when he spoke, for his voice was soft and his manner informal. Having a sense of humor, he could laugh with others and, if need be, at himself. Yet no one who met him, be they students or air corps officers, doubted his seriousness of purpose. McGrath was not someone to trifle with. His standards were high. His tolerance for mediocrity nonexistent. Catherine sensed this. To some this made them fearful of the man. She found it appealing.

They talked for several hours and found out more about the other. McGrath learned that the young woman across from him liked to shop for clothes and go to the movies. He discovered she did not like to cook or ride the bus though she enjoyed a good book, followed current events, and considered Georgetown far less difficult than expected. Catherine learned that McGrath had interests other than history, was fond of Amherst, and would not discuss his wartime service. The only military experience he mentioned was that of Lord Jeffrey Amherst, commander of British forces in North America during the French and Indian War, for whom his college was named. Catherine was pleased to hear that McGrath too enjoyed reading and liked motion pictures. Another pleasant discovery was his fondness for musicals. She adored them, *Showboat* and *Oklahoma* being two favorites.

One subject upon which they differed was baseball.

"It's just so boring."

"No, it's not," said McGrath. "Baseball is a game of great skill and complexity. Youngsters can enjoy it. Old timers too. There's no better way to spend an afternoon than at the ballpark."

"But nothing happens. And it takes forever."

"That's part of its charm, Miss Caldwell." McGrath wanted to call her "Catherine" but did not. "Baseball is not instant gratification It's a game to be savored."

"It's a bunch of men in silly clothes running around and trying to hit a ball with a stick."

"Hitting that ball is quite difficult. The best players in the world can't do it four times out of ten."

"I'm not impressed."

`"You should be. Hitting a baseball is one of the most difficult things to do in all of sports."

"Why is that?"

"Because it's coming at you very fast, almost ninety miles per hour. And sometimes it curves and sometimes it sinks."

"But the game is so slow. It takes forever."

"That's part of its attraction. It's slow at times but then all of a sudden becomes fast and exciting. Besides, going out to the ballpark and spending a few hours relaxing, having a hotdog and a beer—or in my case, a Coke—is one of life's great pleasures, part of Americana."

"But the Senators aren't that good. Don't they lose most of the time?"

"True, but so what."

"Doesn't that upset you? Don't you want them to win?"

"Not really."

"But I thought you'd root for the home team."

"No, I don't. Actually, I'm a Yankee fan."

"Oh no. I think that's terrible. Don't they win all the time? Seems unfair to the other teams."

"That's part of their attraction. Besides I'm from New York and grew up with Gehrig and DiMaggio. They and the Yankees, well they're all part of who I am."

"I'm sorry to hear that. Even though I'm not a baseball fan, I just don't care for the Yankees. No one team should win all the time."

McGrath was smiling when he spoke. "Well, that means only one thing."

"Which would be?"

"I shall not be taking you to a Yankee game."

This remark caught Catherine by surprise. She did not know if McGrath was teasing or whether he might have taken her to a game. She suspected he was not serious. College professors do not take students to baseball games. To historic sites perhaps, but not to sporting events.

However, both sensed that McGrath's remark, whatever the intention, had caused a boundary to be crossed. Both were aware of the boundary. It was a line clearly delineated, and central to the university's integrity. McGrath understood that he had spoken too soon. He was afraid Catherine would react negatively and draw away. She did not. His remark intensified her intention to know this man better. It reinforced her desire to see him again. She knew that danger lay ahead. Yet, despite the risk, she felt compelled to proceed. Romance often conflicts with propriety. At a small table in Max's delicatessen not far from the Georgetown campus, Catherine chose the former. She wondered if McGrath would do the same.

He already had. Ordinarily McGrath was not reckless. He had proven that in England. Reckless pilots get themselves killed. McGrath had done well in combat. With skill and courage, he had calmly calculated when to attack and when to withdraw. Each day, in each aerial contest, he had remained in control of himself and of his squadron. McGrath now believed he could control the situation with this young woman, his student. Acknowledging the risk, he told himself he would proceed discreetly. He was certain he could pursue Catherine Caldwell without endangering her or himself. At Max's, after a casual remark that changed their relationship, McGrath too chose romance.

Lunch continued for another twenty minutes. Conversation was easy. Catherine Caldwell and her teacher felt connected to one another.

Neither wished to say something that might cause the other to back off. Each searched for a comment from the other that gave permission to continue to delve into personal matters. Both found them.

McGrath learned that Catherine did not have a boyfriend. He could not understand why. How could such an attractive, intelligent female be unattached? The answer was simple. Catherine had not yet found someone she loved. She enjoyed the company of men and did not lack opportunities to date. Several boys at Georgetown had tried hard to win her over. But she found them too serious or not serious enough. Catherine was waiting for someone special. She was convinced he would appear and that she would recognize him when he did.

Catherine's permission to continue came twice. The first arrived when she learned that McGrath was not married. "No roommate, no wife, no girlfriend. I'm pretty much alone. I don't even have a dog or cat. It's me and my books. I like to read and spend time by myself."

In college McGrath had led an active social life. He was attracted to the opposite sex and they to him. At Amherst he had several pursuits other than intellectual. He became especially fond of a Mount Holyoke junior but she drifted away once McGrath left college to enter flight school. During the war he ignored women. There was too much to do. Personal matters were put aside. Despite several opportunities, including the daughter of an Earl who showed considerable interest, McGrath led a hermitic life in the U.K. The only diversion from the war was an occasional good book. Once back home that changed. In succession, he dated a local high school teacher, a fellow grad student, and an airline stewardess. But none of these women held his heart. So midway through studies at Notre Dame, he put females aside and focused on academics. The concentration paid off. He earned his Ph.D. in 1949, graduating with high honors.

The second time Catherine received permission to continue came toward the end of their lunch. McGrath's remark was casual. He said simply that, "We should do this again." He did not say where or when, just that what had occurred should not be a one-time event. Trying not to appear forward, he kept his words and tone low-key. McGrath wished to have Catherine understand that he'd like to see her again. Fortunately for romance, Catherine received the message. But, sitting at the table, she wondered how they would get together.

McGrath left Max's before his student. He was late for a meeting with Roger O'Boyle, his Jesuit friend and university colleague. O'Boyle had asked him to serve on an academic committee that was to review foreign language requirements at Georgetown. McGrath believed graduate students at the university should be fluent in such a language. O'Boyle agreed, though McGrath would tease him that it would not be Latin.

Catherine remained at the delicatessen. She was recounting in her mind what had just transpired. She sensed that it was important, that life was never to be the same. This made her excited, uncertain, and, she admitted to herself, slightly afraid. To calm down and to fiddle with something while she reflected on her life both present and future, she ordered another cup of tea.

"It's on the house, miss," said Maxwell Hopkins as he set the cup down upon the table.

Max then walked back toward the kitchen where he was to prepare tomorrow's salads. Reaching the lunch counter he turned around, smiled, and spoke to Catherine.

"Oh, miss, the Colonel has lunch here every Tuesday and Thursday, after class."

TWO

When the aircraft reached 128 mph McGrath gently pulled back on the stick and the nose of the F–84 began to rise. Seconds later, the aircraft left the ground. Wheels up, flaps up, radio check with the tower, and the Thunderjet headed north. Gaining altitude, McGrath could see Baltimore, its harbor easily recognizable from the air.

The F–84 was the air force's second jet fighter. Built by Republic Aviation, the aircraft was a straight wing, single engine fighter plane. McGrath was piloting an F–84 that, powered by an Allison J–35 axial-flow turbojet engine, would achieve 521 mph at sea level and had a service ceiling of 43,200 feet. Later models could fly faster and higher. They also cost slightly more than the $147,699 the U.S. government had paid for McGrath's airplane.

Early Thunderjets had several deficiencies that caused concern to the air force and financial difficulties for Republic. Yet both organizations persevered. The result was an aircraft that served the country well. The F–84, while no match for MiG–15s, became the principal fighter-bomber of the air force and was widely employed during the Korean War. Pounding the enemy, Thunderjets played a key role in the application of air power during the three-year conflict.

McGrath and his airplane belonged to the 121st Fighter Squadron, a District of Columbia Air National Guard unit based at Andrews Air

Force Base in Maryland, a few miles southeast of Washington. The 121st was the first ANG unit to equip with the F–84. McGrath liked the Thunderjet. Below fifteen thousand feet it was highly maneuverable. True, its rate of climb was abysmal and it took forever to get airborne, but the F–84 was a stable weapons platform, had decent range, and could outdive most aircraft. However, McGrath did not like the guard unit. To him it seemed more like a flying club than a military organization. Discipline seemed slack and training casual. Pilots were weekend warriors who came out to Andrews for a round of flying rather than of golf.

At times McGrath could hardly blame them. Flying a high performance fighter in a non-threatening environment was exhilarating. Soaring across the sky, caressing the clouds, and peering down at the land were unforgettable experiences. Images of beauty and three-dimensional control made flying a form of artistry as well. Of course there was a technical side to flying. It was far more complicated than driving a car or sailing a boat. McGrath was a good pilot. He understood the mechanics of flight and recognized the danger inherent in military aviation. But on days such as this, when the November air was crisp and cloudless and the sky a deep blue, he also recognized the sheer fun of flight.

Heading northwest, McGrath soon reached the Patapsco River, entrance to Baltimore's fine harbor. From fourteen thousand feet, he could peer down to the left and see the plant where Martin Aircraft Corporation had built its Maryland and Marauder bombers. Near the water he could see the seaplane ramps the company had used for its prewar clippers. Still climbing slowly, for the F–84 was no interceptor, McGrath passed over the several rivers north of the city. To avoid Aberdeen Proving Ground, he turned directly north. Crossing the Mason-Dixon line, he turned east. Above the Susquehanna River at 22,000 feet, he could see Wilmington and, to the northwest, Philadelphia. He continued east for two minutes, still climbing, then turned south, soon passing over Chestertown on Maryland's Eastern

Shore. Alone in the sky, he eased back on the throttle, retrimmed the aircraft, and took in the magnificent expanse of the Chesapeake Bay.

How different this flight was from the aerial journeys over Germany. McGrath had no bombers to escort, no squadrons to direct, and no enemy aircraft to engage. Here there was superb scenery to view and simply one's own instruments to monitor. All was peaceful, and he took pleasure in the serenity of his surroundings. If the D.C. Air National Guard was a flying club, it certainly was a good one.

Proceeding south, he overflew Kent Island. To his right McGrath could see Annapolis. To his left, in the distance, he saw the Atlantic Ocean. Then his mood changed. He became more alert. Instinctively he advanced the throttle and the Thunderjet picked up speed. McGrath again recognized the F–84 for what it was, a weapon that, with six .50 caliber machine guns, could wreak havoc upon targets both on the ground and in the air.

McGrath's alertness paid off. Approaching the mouth of the Patuxent River, he spotted a navy F9F Panther jet, an aircraft comparable to the F–84. The pilot of the naval plane had not seen him. Coming out of the sun, McGrath took his Thunderjet down, picking up speed quickly. His goal was to achieve a firing position on the Panther. With an airspeed of 610 mph, he soon was upon his unsuspecting target. His position was ideal, behind and slightly below the F9F. Murmuring "Gotcha," McGrath slammed the Thunderjet's throttle forward to full power and zoomed by his friendly adversary. Rattled, the navy pilot chose not to give chase. He continued his mission, which involved calibrating several ground radar stations.

Still at high speed, McGrath continued south. At the mouth of the Potomac he pulled a 6–g turn to the right. He then flew upriver, bleeding off speed and altitude. Well south of Washington he checked in with the Andrews control tower and received clearance to land. Continuing his descent, he soon had the airfield in sight. Coming around on final, he lined up the F–84 with the runway. McGrath came "over the fence" a bit fast but with great skill he set the airplane down gently, first on its two main wheels then on the nose wheel. Rolling out, he used the entire runway. Taxiing toward the flight line, McGrath looked at his watch. He had been airborne for fifty-three minutes.

While McGrath was landing the Thunderjet, Hoyt Vandenberg was sitting alone in his Pentagon office, awaiting the arrival of a fellow air force general. Vandenberg was chief of staff, the top job in the air force. Considering his rank and position, the office, while large, was simple in decor. His desk was wood, solid in appearance and construction. In front of the desk were a comfortable sofa and two chairs separated by a handsome coffee table. The chairs and sofa were covered in matching raspberry-colored fabric that gave this office a soft, pleasing look. The home-like impact was muted, however, by a standard wooden Pentagon conference table and chairs, which sat to one side of the room. Here Vandenberg met with aides and others on utilitarian air force business. The sofa and chairs were used for more prestigious visitors or when the general wished to have lengthy, informal conversations. Vandenberg's secretary, a Mrs. Langston, could tell the nature of a meeting by the location of the visitor.

Behind General Vandenberg's desk were two flags. One was the national emblem, the Stars and Stripes. The other was blue with an official seal in the middle. This flag was new, as was the air force. Just three years earlier the service had become a separate entity, independent of the army. No longer the Army Air Force, the service was now the United States Air Force. Army brown had given way to air force blue. Vandenberg and other senior leaders in the air force were determined to have the newly minted force become the principal American weapon to counter the threat of Soviet-led world communism.

On the wall to the left of the flags were four photographs. The first was of a more youthful Vandenberg in the cockpit of a P–47. The P–47 belonged to the 9th Air Force, which Vandenberg commanded during World War II. The second photograph portrayed Sir Arthur Harris. Sir Arthur had led Bomber Command, the RAF unit that struck Nazi Germany night after night. The third was of the *Enola Gay*, the B–29 that had dropped the atomic bomb on Hiroshima, thereby accelerating the surrender of Japan. Vandenberg much admired Colonel Paul

Tibbets, who had piloted the B–29. The fourth photograph was the obligatory portrait of the president, Harry S. Truman. Along with many in the Pentagon, Vandenberg disliked the president. In his view, Truman had allowed the air force to wither. From an authorized strength of 2.2 million individuals on V–J Day, the service had just over four hundred thousand men when the war in Korea broke out. The chief of staff believed the air force could not now meet its responsibilities and he blamed Truman.

The blame was misplaced. No president could have bucked the mood of the American people in 1945. The Second World War had been won. The fighting was over. For 150 million men and women it was time to enjoy life and spend dollars on houses and cars, not military hardware.

Vandenberg believed his mission was to rebuild the air force, with new people and new equipment. Central to his strategy was the ability to hit the Soviet Union with nuclear weapons. Central to this ability was a new bomber, Convair's B–36, a model of which sat on Vandenberg's desk. There were no models of fighter jets. Vandenberg believed their role would be limited in the next war. Their primary job was air defense. They would destroy incoming Soviet bombers while the B–36s hit every target in Russia and Red China.

Vandenberg looked up from his desk as Mrs. Langston quietly slipped into the room. He appreciated the procedure she always followed. She would knock gently on the office door three times, then slowly push the door open and take three steps into the room. She thought little about this routine, but Hazel Langston was the only person in the country with standing permission to enter unannounced the office of the air force chief of staff.

"General Vandenberg, General McCreedy is here for your eleven o'clock."

"Thank you, Mrs. Langston." Vandenberg looked at the clock on his desk. It was 10:59. Vandenberg smiled to himself. Like most military officers, McCreedy was never late for a meeting. The chief of staff appreciated punctuality and Lt. General Michael McCreedy had never disappointed.

McCreedy was the air force's director of Policy and Plans. Though a staff job, Vandenberg considered the position one of the most important in the service. The job required someone who could think analytically, someone comfortable with ideas who could see problems and solutions not readily visible to others. The chief of staff thought the P&P director needed to be the smartest general in the air force, and he believed he had found just that in Michael J. McCreedy.

McCreedy loved the job. And he was very good at it. But as with most officers who wore wings on their uniform, he missed the thrill of flying combat aircraft. And like most three star generals, he hankered to command an air force in battle. Vandenberg understood this desire. But he valued McCreedy's brain too much to let him go. Most generals, Vandenberg believed, could direct a combat organization. Very few, he felt, could think through how the entire United States Air Force should be employed.

"Please have General McCreedy come in."

Seconds later the director of Policy and Plans entered Vandenberg's office.

"Good morning, General," said McCreedy.

"Morning to you, Mike." Vandenberg rose from his desk, where he had been reading reports on B–36 production, and moved to the sofa, gesturing with his hand that McCreedy should sit in one of the chairs, which he did. "Three topics to discuss today: nuclear strikes, Korea, and MiGs."

"An unholy trinity."

"To be sure. Let's start with the first. What do you have for me?"

For the next twenty minutes General McCreedy discoursed on how, in the event the Chinese pushed American troops in Korea back once again to Pusan, thereby threatening the entire U.N. presence on the peninsula, the air force could deliver six tactical atomic bombs onto the massed Chinese formations. McCreedy also reviewed how, if necessary, nuclear weapons could be dropped north of the Yalu River on

China proper. The director of Policy and Plans reviewed possible targets, operating requirements for the bombers that would execute the plans, and possible military reactions by the Russians both in Asia and elsewhere.

"How many of the Reds will we kill if we target Manchuria?"

"My estimate is about two million Chinese."

"And if we limit the attacks to Korea?"

"If we're to stop the Chinese from pushing us into the sea, if General Walker and his Eighth can't stop the Reds' advance with conventional forces—which they ought to be able to do given the close air support we're providing—then six Class B devices should pulverize eighty thousand front line troops. Even the Reds can't take that kind of punishment."

"That's true, Mike. So far they're knocking the hell out of Walker, but even the Chinese can't lose three field armies in one day and continue to fight."

"I believe that's correct, General."

"Let's hope you're right. I don't want to start World War III and I certainly don't want to start it in Korea."

"Nor do I. But as you've said more than once, U.N. troops in Korea cannot be allowed to be kicked out of Korea. The message that would send to Moscow is not one we can afford to have them receive."

"I don't think Korea is where the communists will strike. Stalin doesn't give a damn about Korea. He's interested in Europe. If war breaks out, if war is to come, it will be on the European continent. Korea is a sideshow. Stalin's letting the Chinese stir up the pot and distract us from the main arena."

"But Korea is where the fight is right now, General. And so far we're not doing all that well."

McCreedy then reviewed the situation in Korea. As he had just indicated, the news was not good. After defeating the North Koreans in September 1950, U.S. forces crossed the 38th Parallel in October, advancing north to the Yalu. Alarmed, the Chinese moved into Korea in large numbers and, in November, attacked the Americans, achieving great success. For U.S. troops what began as a retreat soon became a rout.

"So the U.S. Army is withdrawing."

"Actually, General Vandenberg, it's far worse than that. They're calling it the Great Bugout. Many of our soldiers are simply throwing away their rifles and running, or just giving up. The Chinese are rolling over us."

"Jesus! What a disgrace."

"The only exception is the marines. On the east coast they're in retreat too, but in a disciplined way. The navy's going to pick them up at a place called Hungnam."

"How is our air support?" By the word "our" Vandenberg meant the air force, although the U.S. Navy was assisting ground forces using carrier-based aircraft.

"We're flying over two hundred sorties a day. We're hitting the Reds herd. The problem is that they've got over one hundred thousand troops committed, more in reserve, and don't seem to mind taking casualties."

"What's the likely outcome?"

"One outcome, a scenario that's not farfetched, is that MacArthur does not recover and the 8th is pushed into the sea."

"An American Dunkirk."

"Exactly. In which case we will have to be prepared to go nuclear. But I don't think it will come to that. There's a very good chance the Chinese offensive will run out of steam. Winter's arrived, making movement in Korea more difficult. Chinese supply lines are stretched thin and are vulnerable to our strikes. We're using Mustangs, F–80s, and B–26 Invaders. We're hitting everything that moves. The Reds are losing lots of trucks and lots of men."

"And the B–29s?"

"The irony of it. Here's our best bomber of World War II, a strategic weapon now flying tactical missions. We're hitting the Chinese everyday, with everything we've got. I don't believe they will make it to the sea. They're taking a terrific pounding."

"Let's hope you're right."

"But the alarming news is not on the ground. It's in the air."

"The Reds have a new fighter. I've read the intelligence report you sent me."

"Yes, General, they do, and it's better than anything we have over there."

The aircraft was the MiG–15. This was a single seat, swept-wing Russian fighter that first appeared in November 1950, in Korea. MiG was an acronym formed by the last names of the two men responsible for the plane's design, Artem Mikoyan and Mikhael Gurevich. Extremely fast, the MiG had a power plant derived from advanced Rolls Royce jet engines that the British government, desperate for cash, had sold to the Soviets, despite objections by the Royal Air Force. The appearance of the MiG–15 stunned and alarmed the Americans. And with good reason. Unchecked, the MiG would mean loss of air superiority in Korea. More ominously, it could mean that in a future European war, control of the air would not reside with the West.

"I gather that we don't know much about this MiG."

"Not really," responded McCreedy. "Except that apparently it's a damn fine airplane. It's faster than our F–80. It can turn inside a Thunderjet, and from what I know it can outclimb both of them. Unless we do something soon, we will lose the air war in Korea."

"If we lose the air war, we lose the war."

"That's right, and that would leave us but one option."

"Which I do not want to go with, at least not in Korea."

"Then," said the director of Policy and Plans, "we have but one choice."

"I know what you're about to say, Mike. Let's hear it."

"I recommend we immediately send two wings of F–86s to Korea."

"I can't do that, Mike."

"The Sabre is the best we've got, General. The Russians have fielded their best. It's time for us to do the same."

The F–86 was America's newest, most advanced jet fighter. Entering service in 1949, the F–86 outperformed the F–80 and the F–84, both straight winged aircraft. The Sabre, like the MiG–15, featured wings that were swept aft. This configuration, an aeronautical design that reduced drag, translated into increased speed. In November 1950, when McCreedy was meeting with Vandenberg, F–86s were relatively few in number. How and where they were deployed was thus an issue for the air force. Commanders everywhere wanted the airplane. Not all of them would get it. Those that did received a remarkable machine, one that would become legendary in the skies above Korea.

"Mike, the 86s are just now beginning to equip our air defense squadrons. I've got to give them priority."

"General, there's a battle going on now, and it's in Korea. That's where, for now, we confront the communists. If we don't stop the Reds there, we send Moscow exactly the wrong message."

"True enough, but we can't spare two wings. And since you knew that's what I'd say, tell me your real recommendation."

Mike McCreedy smiled. He liked Hoyt Vandenberg and much admired the chief of staff, especially when he anticipated what others would say. "Here's what I think we can and must do."

McCreedy then outlined his plan. Two fighter wings would go to Japan, but only one of them would have F–86s. The 27th Fighter Escort Wing flew F–84s. Once in Korea, it would fly reconnaissance and close air support missions. The other group, the 4th Fighter Interceptor Wing, would take its sixty-six Sabres and secure air superiority. Both wings were to be sent at once. They needed to be in Korea as soon as possible, for the Chinese were pressing home their attack.

"How do we get the aircraft to Korea?" queried Vandenberg.

"We fly everyone and everything to California. Then the navy transports them across the Pacific. Admiral Flowers says just give him the word and he'll get our planes to Japan. They then fly over to Korea and begin to make a difference."

"Okay, Mike, cut the orders. Our air defense commanders will have to wait a little while longer."

"Yes, sir."

On November 8, 1950, the two fighter wings began their move west. Aircraft were ferried to San Diego and placed aboard two navy ships, one an aircraft carrier and one a tanker. Two weeks later they were in Japan. By early December both wings had detachments in Korea, ready for combat. The 27th Fighter Escort Wing flew their first mission on December 6th. The 4th Fighter Interceptor Wing took to the sky on December 15th. On the 16th it snowed, grounding the Sabres. The next day, on an afternoon combat air patrol, the fighters went looking for the enemy and found them. The results were good. An F–86 shot down a MiG. It would be the first of many.

There was no model of a B–36 in the office of the Reverend Roger Frances O'Boyle, S.J. He was an associate professor of government at Georgetown and his office, like those of many who teach, was small and crammed with books. Yet in one way, O'Boyle's office was similar to that of Hoyt Vandenberg. Four pictures hung on the wall. One was an image of Christ. Another was of Santa Maria Maggiore, O'Boyle's favorite church in Rome, where as a young prelate he had spent two happy years of reflection and study. The third was a photograph of the O'Boyle family, taken in 1934 when Roger was a teenager. In the picture O'Boyle and his four brothers are surrounding their mother and father. The latter was smiling. Mary O'Boyle, responsible for the discipline in the family, was not. The fourth picture was like the first, a painting—or rather a good print of a painting—by an unknown artist. The subject's face looked similar to that of Christ though much older. Oddly, the man was a soldier, one of Dumas' musketeers. O'Boyle knew what few did, that in the final sequel to the book about D'Artagnan and his three companions, Aramis becomes Governor General of the Jesuits.

McGrath was sitting in one of two chairs that faced O'Boyle's desk, behind which the priest himself sat. The two men liked and respected each other. Their conversations, at dinner or in their tiny offices, covered every conceivable subject.

The week before, they had talked about one of their favorites, the Catholic faith. McGrath had been raised a Catholic but had stopped attending church. O'Boyle was hoping to bring his friend back into the fold.

"Roger, what I have trouble with are the core beliefs of the Church."

"So you've said. I sense, my friend, you want to believe but don't."

"That's true I guess. Religion offers great comfort to people but part of the deal is that we accept what the Church preaches."

"The Church preaches many things. One is the necessity of faith."

"And tell me again what faith is."

"You need to read your catechism. When God speaks it is revelation. When man listens, it is faith."

McGrath was struggling spiritually. He questioned the need for a hierarchy of priests to explain the will of God. And he doubted the divinity of Christ. O'Boyle reacted calmly to this. He did not chastise or condemn. Instead, he explained. He attempted to reach McGrath through reason and logic. God, he said, so loved his flock that he created a son to show the world how to live and how to obtain eternal salvation. And God's will and the teachings of Jesus required interpretation.

"We know," said the Jesuit, "the meaning of what God has revealed by what the Church tells us, through Peter and his successors."

"So the Church tells us what to believe."

"The Church, my friend," said O'Boyle, "helps us to understand the revelations of God. Through wisdom and tradition, through intellect and experience, it shows how to lead a life that results in good works here on Earth and eternal life in heaven."

"So good works are important."

"Yes, indeed."

"But they are not by themselves enough?"

"No, as you well know, faith is necessary for salvation."

"And tell me again your definition of faith."

36

"Faith is the belief in and obedience to God. In faith you accept the will of God and the teachings of his Christ."

"And that is where my problem lies."

They had had this conversation before, or ones similar to it. And they would cover the subject again. McGrath was seeking a faith he intellectually could accept. O'Boyle was offering answers and a doctrine many had embraced.

Today, however, they were not talking about the Church. They were discussing a problem McGrath had brought to his friend. The problem involved a female, a student at the university.

"Her name is Catherine Caldwell," McGrath had begun the conversation.

"I think I know her. She's in one of my classes. Pretty thing."

"That's part of the problem."

"How so?"

"Well, I find her immensely attractive and I think she has some feelings for me."

"Go on." O'Boyle's demeanor was changing to one of concern.

"Well, we've seen each other several times now, at Max's deli. It's all been on the up and up, so far at least. Just a professor and his student having lunch. But I think, actually I feel, there's more to it than that. We just seem to click. Conversation is easy and we've been meeting at Max's on purpose, though we don't schedule a get-together. At least not out loud. We just know that on Tuesdays and Thursdays, that's where we'll be."

"Do you have feelings for this girl?"

"Yes, I do. She's special, not like my other students. And it doesn't help that she is absolutely lovely. The truth is, I can't keep my eyes off her."

"You're on dangerous ground, my friend."

"I know, I know. But I feel like there's a force bigger than me, bigger than the both of us, that compels me—us—to proceed."

"What do you want to happen?"

"I want to spend time with her. I want to get to know her better."

"Anything else?"

"Yes, I want to touch her and take her to bed."

"You need to be very careful here. I don't need to remind you about one of the tenets here at Georgetown, or at any university."

"I know, I know."

"There's really only one thing for you to do. And that's to stop seeing her immediately. Call it off, whatever it is, before it's too late and it brings you and her great harm."

"What you say is right, of course. But there's a problem, a big problem."

"And that is?"

"I'm immensely attracted to the girl. I think I'm in love."

THREE

Catherine Caldwell and Cynthia Stewart were best friends. They also were roommates, sharing an apartment in Arlington, not far from the Pentagon. Located in Fairlington Village, a red brick complex built originally to house wartime workers, the apartment was spacious, nicely landscaped, with ample parking. Georgetown University was an easy fifteen-minute drive away.

The two girls had met in their sophomore year, in an English class. At first not paying much attention to each other, they soon discovered they had much in common. Both were good students. Both had played field hockey in high school. Both had birthdays in April. Both had been accepted at Vassar but chose Georgetown. More importantly, each of them had lost her father. Cynthia's dad, a doctor in Boston, had died the year she started college. At the time Cynthia was eighteen, he was forty-six. Her sense of loss, the gap in her life Morton Stewart's death had created, was an emotional reality Catherine well understood.

The roommates also differed. Catherine felt out of place in a kitchen. Cynthia liked to work with food and in time became an accomplished cook. Catherine enjoyed musicals and popular tunes. Cynthia preferred jazz and the classics. Catherine favored clothes that were striking and somewhat offbeat. Cynthia dressed conservatively.

Her uniform of the day was a blouse, skirt, and sweater. She always looked nice, but it was her redheaded roommate who drew the stares.

Nonetheless, in the fall of 1950 it was Cynthia who had a boyfriend, not Catherine. His name was Dan Brown and he was a senior at Villanova. Cynthia assumed he would ask her to marry him upon graduation. More traditional than Catherine and hoping to have a family of her own, she intended to say yes.

Being college students, the furnishings in their apartment were modest. Bookshelves were wooden planks resting on cinderblocks. A Philco victrola sat upon a small table that, along with several lamps, had been purchased at a yard sale. The couch, a dark gray corduroy, came from the McCreedy basement. A green wing chair, torn in two places, once had belonged to Cynthia's aunt.

Each girl had a bedroom upstairs. Cynthia's room was decorated in pale hues, mostly yellow and blue. The colors were soft in tone, the look tasteful. The room itself was tidy. Each morning the bed was made and each evening clothes and shoes were put away. Catherine liked more vivid colors. Her room was painted in purple and black. Her clothes seemed to reside on her bed and on the floor. Once a week Catherine would put them away, only to have them shortly reappear.

Only in the kitchen did differences cause friction. Cynthia kept the kitchen spotless. Catherine tended to leave things out and about. Because Cynthia did most of the cooking, the kitchen was her domain and at her request Catherine tried hard to put food and plates where they belonged. Cynthia appreciated the effort and the friction gave way to occasional reminders.

Though busy with schoolwork, the two females found time each day to converse, either at breakfast or at night before going to bed. They enjoyed the other's company and, as good friends do, they confided in one another. And when one of them needed to talk, the other would listen.

One time when Dan was being difficult, Catherine spent fifty minutes on the corduroy couch paying close attention to what Cynthia was saying.

"I love him to death, I really do, but sometimes he drives me to distraction."

"What has he done?"

"It's what he's not done."

"What do you mean?"

"Well, his fraternity at Villanova is having their winter carnival next month and he's not asked me to it."

"Is he taking someone else?"

"I don't think so. I'm sure of it. He just hasn't told me about it. He'll wait 'til the last minute and then drop it on me."

"And you would like him to do what?"

"I want him to ask me ahead of time, so I can plan to go up there without being rushed at the last minute."

"Do you want to go?"

"You know the answer to that. I most certainly do. And I'm pretty sure I will be going. I went last year."

"And that's when a certain something happened in the backseat of a convertible."

Cynthia sighed. "Indeed it did. And I'm glad it did. He's really a wonderful guy."

"With whom you're in love."

"Yes, with whom I'm in love."

"So the problem is?"

"I just want to be asked in advance. I want not to be taken for granted."

"That's pretty reasonable. There are two things you could do."

Cynthia's response was to ask what they were, but she did so with a facial expression, not her voice.

"You know the date of the carnival, right? So you could tell him that on that date you're going home to Boston to see your mother. Then have him ask you to change your plans so you can go up to Philadelphia. Make him ask you several times and then only at the end, when he's pleading with you, give in and say you'll come to the winter carnival. Make him sweat a bit, have him contemplate your absence that weekend, let him think about the backseat of his Mercury without you on it."

Imagining her boyfriend's pained expression, Cynthia was smiling as Catherine expanded on the scheme. Ensconced in the green chair, she then asked Catherine what the second course of action was.

"Oh, that's a bit more direct."

"And it is?"

"Just talk to him about it. Next time you see him or talk to him on the phone tell him directly what's bothering you. Or maybe write him a letter. Tell him that respect for you requires him to act as a gentleman and that gentlemen don't take ladies for granted."

"Which, of course, they occasionally do."

"True, but it's not nice, and guys sometimes need to be reminded on how to behave."

"Like Jack Stevens."

"Exactly."

Jack Stevens had been Catherine's boyfriend. He was a basketball player at Drexel whom she had met on a blind date sophomore year. Jack was tall and handsome, a fine athlete, though not the world's best student. At first Catherine found him quite appealing. He was friendly and outgoing, an engaging conversationalist who approached life with an infectious enthusiasm. He thought Catherine was "a great looking gal, with brains to boot." Jack spent considerable energy pursuing this young girl from Montana, a state he insisted on calling, incorrectly, the Blue Sky State. His effort eventually paid off, for one night in Philadelphia, after a game with Temple in which he scored twenty-two points, he scored again, achieving his goal of bedding Catherine Caldwell. She found the experience not without pleasure, later remarking to Cynthia that beds were more comfortable than the backseat of automobiles.

Thereafter, their relationship slowly went downhill. Jack started to believe Catherine would be available to journey up to Philadelphia whenever he wished. He seemed not to realize that on occasion she needed to spend weekends studying, an activity he studiously avoided.

More importantly, he assumed that whenever she came to the City of Brotherly Love she would be seeking love of another sort. Catherine was no prude. But she believed romance should involve more than sex. So when Jack twice refused to spend Sunday afternoon at the Museum of Fine Art, Catherine ended the relationship.

Both girls often talked about their fathers. They missed having a father to whom they could turn for advice. And they missed the advice a father would provide. Without a male parent, each girl experienced a gap in her life. They told each other that they'd had something precious taken from them. Their lives, they both realized, were and would always be incomplete. This sense of loss was felt most actively in June on Father's Day. Others would send a card or ring their fathers up. Catherine and Cynthia could do neither.

Both having attended a parent's funeral, the two roommates were not unfamiliar with the rituals of death. Each had endured hospital vigils, visits to funeral parlors, and receipt of casseroles and sympathy cards. These they recognized as part and parcel of dealing with a death in the family. Yet one aspect of this "most unfortunate business," as one uncle described it, neither girl liked nor accepted. This was the tradition of open caskets. Cynthia thought it horrible. Catherine considered it ghoulish. They believed human dignity required a body in repose to be seen by immediate family only. Being still young, the girls did not understand the value of others having visual contact with the deceased, the sight certifying that an individual is indeed gone from this Earth.

On more than one occasion Catherine talked to her roommate about whether there was life after death. This time the girls were in their living room, having returned from a late night movie.

"The Church says there is," said Cynthia.

"Do you believe them?"

"I do, I think I do. I mean, I really want to."

"I feel the same way," said Catherine who continued to speak. "I want to believe, and I've been taught to believe, and I do, I think. There has to be some meaning to our time on Earth."

"I'm listening." As Cynthia spoke she knew Catherine was, in effect, thinking out loud.

"Well, if there is no life after death, if all there is is what he have now, what we see, then isn't it a bit pointless? It wouldn't matter how we live. If evil goes unpunished, if good is not rewarded, then maybe it doesn't matter how we live."

"But it does matter. I believe there is a God and that someday, on Judgment Day, we will be held accountable for how we lived our lives."

"I agree with that. God is sorta testing us. He's given us the tools to live a good life, or one not so good. Free will, I think the Jesuits call it. And it's up to us."

"But there's something I don't understand."

"I know what you're going to say," responded Catherine.

"If God is good, and I believe He is, why is there so much evil in the world?"

"You know my answer to that."

"Go ahead, I need to hear it again and again."

"There's evil in the world because mankind lets it happen. Look at the Nazis. What they did was despicable, truly awful. But God didn't make that happen. Men and women did. I really believe life is a test, the ultimate test. And how we do, how we live the life God has given us, will determine our fate once our time here has ended."

"You mean heaven or hell?"

"Yes, actually I do. I don't know what heaven is like. I can't even imagine it, but I believe it exists and that each of us—our soul if not our body—has a chance to enter it."

"And hell?"

"Hell is the opposite. I don't know if it's a place or a state of mind, but I believe it's where cruelty and injustice find their reward. I don't know much about it except it's not a place I wish to be."

"So it comes down to how we live?"

"I think so. One believes in God and His Church, but relies upon one's self to lead a decent life. And, if one does, there's some sort of eternal happiness."

"I hope you're right."

"Me too."

Not all conversations between the roommates were weighty. Because the girls liked motion pictures and went to see them often, they frequently discussed movies and movie stars. They were doing so again one night after seeing Spencer Tracy and Elizabeth Taylor in *Father of the Bride*.

"So what, this week, is your favorite movie?" queried Catherine, who knew that Cynthia changed her favorite on a regular basis.

Taking no offense at how the question was phrased, Cynthia responded cheerfully. "Well, this week, it's *How Green Was My Valley*."

"Do you remember what it was last week?"

"I do. It was *Little Women* with Elizabeth Taylor and June Allyson. They're both awfully good movies."

"Indeed they are." Catherine's favorite film was *Gone with the Wind*. She liked the story, loved the music, and considered Rhett Butler as portrayed by Clark Gable to be the perfect hero. And, she would say to herself, as Fletcher Christian, Mr. Gable was again one extremely attractive fellow.

Regarding actresses, Cynthia was a fan of Bette Davis and Maureen O'Hara. Catherine's favorites were Katherine Hepburn and Rita Hayworth, though she acknowledged that the two were different in appearance and talent.

"Yes, I know, they're not very much alike. Katherine Hepburn is sassy, smart, and just terrific. But Rita Hayworth is much better than she's given credit for. She actually can act. She's a terrific dancer; just watch her with Fred Astaire in that movie I can never remember the name of. And she looks great. And besides," here Catherine took out her comb, "I think her hair is just wonderful."

Catherine's encounter with McGrath did not remain a secret from Cynthia. Catherine first told her roommate about it the next day, at breakfast. Cynthia was supportive, intrigued, and alarmed, all at the same time. She wanted to know what he was like, what they talked about, what Catherine thought about this man and what she expected to take place over the next several weeks. Over a bowl of Cheerios and bananas, Catherine responded. She recounted their conversation in full and told Cynthia she found McGrath most compelling.

"Even though you've just met him?"

"Even though. There's something about him. I can't properly define it, but I feel it, and I really, really like it."

"I think they call it chemistry."

"Perhaps. All know is that he's the most interesting and exciting man I've ever met."

"Isn't this all rather sudden?"

"Yes, but so what. I know what I feel and, besides, I find myself thinking about him all the time."

"Sounds like Cupid has struck a mighty blow."

"Straight into my heart. That's why I went into Max's. It's like I had no choice. I had to."

"Well, I'm glad you did. At least I think I'm glad you did. Are you in love?"

"I guess. I'm not sure. All I know is that something has happened, something special, and that I'm on a course that will make me very happy or full of despair."

"I hope it's the former."

"Me too."

"So what happens now? A relationship with your professor is not something Georgetown will approve of."

"I know."

"But if this is the man of your dreams . . ."

"It's crazy, but I think he is."

"Life is full of surprises, isn't it?"

"Yes, as we both know."

"The nice thing is that not all of them are bad."

"For sure."

"Well, I can think of only two things to tell you."

"And they are?"

"First of all, be careful."

"And the second?"

"Go for it. Follow your heart and see what happens."

"That's exactly what I intend to do."

FOUR

With baseball season over, McGrath's interest in athletics turned to football and basketball. He particularly enjoyed the former and, as a youngster, he often had watched the New York Giants play other professional teams. But his stay in England and his time at South Bend eroded his attachment to the teams of the Empire State except, of course, for the Yankees, to whom he remained loyal his entire life.

Now, wondering whether he might find the Washington Redskins a team to root for, McGrath purchased two tickets for their November 12th game against the Philadelphia Eagles. The tickets cost $3.95 apiece. McGrath thought that pricey, but as they were second row, upper deck on the forty-yard line just above the Redskins' bench, he considered them a good value.

Two tickets meant he needed to ask someone to accompany him to the game. He first asked Roger O'Boyle. The Jesuit said he'd love to go, but was committed that Sunday to a day-long retreat. Briefly, McGrath then pondered whether to ask Catherine, realizing almost immediately that might not be wise, nor her first choice on how best to spend a Sunday afternoon.

Whom to invite to the game? The answer came two days before the contest from an unexpected quarter. On Friday McGrath received a telephone call from his father, who said he would be in D.C. on

Monday to meet the Comptroller of the Treasury and wondered whether his son might be free for dinner that night. McGrath responded that he most certainly would be, but suggested that his dad instead come down on Sunday and go to the game with him. John McGrath thought the suggestion a good one. He readily agreed and said he would catch an early morning train from Penn Station.

McGrath met his father at Union Station one hour before kickoff. Their greeting was affectionate and the two men were comfortable with one another as the taxi took them to the Mayflower Hotel where the elder McGrath checked in. Another cab soon delivered them to Griffith Stadium where the Redskins played. Father and son arrived ten minutes before kickoff, in time for a quick lunch that consisted of two hotdogs each, embellished with mustard and sauerkraut. As they ate, the Redskins Marching Band performed a rousing rendition of the team's fight song, which it had played at every home game since 1937, when the team had moved to D.C. from Boston.

For the Redskins, the game did not go well. They lost to the Eagles 33-0. The score was indicative of the season, for in 1950 the team went three and nine. More successful than the play on the field was the reaction by fans not in the stadium. Thousands watched at home as the Redskins became the first team in professional football to televise its games.

Despite the outcome, McGrath enjoyed the game. It and dinner provided time to talk with his dad, something he appreciated but of late had little opportunity to do. The two men were at Blackie's, a steakhouse on M Street a few blocks east of Georgetown.

"I'm thinking of buying a new car," McGrath said to his father.

"That's probably a good idea. What kind are you thinking about?"

"Well, I'm not sure. Maybe a Chevrolet or a Pontiac."

"What about a Chrysler?" John McGrath always drove Chryslers and they were always black.

"They're nice of course, but I think they're out of my price range."

"They are nice, son, and you ought to have a solid, well-built car. I ride the subway everyday but a man needs a car, a good car, to get around."

"I don't disagree. Washington doesn't have a subway and while bus transportation in the city is pretty good, a car makes life a lot easier."

"It does indeed. But I think you ought to at least consider a Chrysler. They're fine automobiles. They last a good while."

Inwardly, McGrath smiled at this last remark. His father bought a new Chrysler every other year.

"I'm sure they do, but it's a grownup's car and I'd like something a little sportier and certainly one that's not too expensive."

"I can help you out with that."

"Thanks Dad, but no. I need to do this on my own. I have a savings account with money in it from the air corps and I've been keeping it for when I need a new car."

"Why don't you let me—"

"No Dad, really." McGrath was speaking more forcefully now. "I can do this on my own and should."

"Fair enough." The elder man was proud of his son for refusing his offer, but said nothing to that effect.

"Besides, as an assistant professor of history at Georgetown University, I'm making a lot of money." Now McGrath was smiling, for both men knew university salaries, particularly at Catholic schools, were far from generous.

"Tell me again what Georgetown is paying you."

"The princely sum of $2,600 a year, or $216 a month."

"That's before taxes?"

"Oh yes. I get to contribute some of it to Uncle Sam."

"I'm sure you do. Don't we all."

"Death and taxes, Dad. That's what you've always said. They're the two things in life we can absolutely count on."

"Indeed. I don't mind so much paying taxes when I'm alive. The money goes for useful things, for the most part at least. What I do mind is having to pay taxes after I'm gone."

"What do you mean?"

"Estate taxes, my boy. You get to pay Uncle Sam part of your wealth once you're dead. A lawyer adds up your assets and a portion of them, not too large, but still, a percentage, gets transferred to the government."

"Wow. I hadn't realized that, or at least thought about it."

"No reason to, at least not when you're young."

"Although, now that I do think about it, I suppose there's a logic to it."

"Which would be?"

In responding, McGrath sounded like the college history teacher he was.

"Well, this country's traditions are about the individual and the entrepreneur. Everybody in America has a chance to make it on his own and is expected to. Money and success come from hard work and individual initiative, not from family and accidents of birth. In America you're supposed to create wealth, earn it, not inherit it. So the laws are made to help you do that. They discourage an aristocracy."

"Perhaps. I wonder if Mr. Rockefeller understands that."

"I said discourage, not prohibit. In any case I think I'll take the money I've put away and spend it now. My heirs, whoever they may be, will have to do without. And besides, there's one immediate consideration I have to deal with."

"And that would be?"

"I actually need a new car."

Three days later McGrath bought a DeSoto Custom convertible. He had looked at Chevrolets but couldn't obtain one at a price he considered fair. The DeSoto was listed at $2,578 but, as it was one of the last 1950 models in the showroom, McGrath got the car for four hundred dollars less. The DeSoto had a 112 bhp engine and a fluid drive semi-automatic transmission. Top speed was ninety mph. The car was painted creamy white and had a black top. It was one of 133,854 DeSotos sold in 1950. McGrath liked the car and hoped his dad would approve. After all, DeSoto was a brand of the Chrysler Corporation.

"I ran into Jimmy Rodgers' dad last week." John was speaking.

"Oh, how is he?"

"He's good. Like everyone, he's getting older. He asked to be remembered to you."

"I still can't believe what happened to Jimmy. At times it seems like it was yesterday and other times it seems like it was another life, which it sorta was."

"A sad, sad story."

Jimmy Rodgers and McGrath were the same age and grew up together. They were the best of friends, popular at school, both good students. McGrath was a fine athlete, Rodgers an outstanding one, especially in track and field. Then polio struck. Jimmy could no longer walk, much less run and jump. Confined to crutches, his personality changed. Once cheerful and outgoing, he became angry, morose, and withdrawn. Even so, McGrath spent much of his time with him, forgoing the tennis team, to provide after-school companionship.

Then one day McGrath came by the Rodgers house to see his friend. Jimmy was not where he usually could be found, a comfortable chair in the breakfast nook. Nor was he anywhere downstairs. McGrath called out but heard no response. He went upstairs and found Jimmy in his bedroom, dead. His friend had killed himself with his father's pistol. The scene was gruesome, incomprehensible. McGrath was in shock for days, unable to process what had happened. Sadly, cruelly, the image of Jimmy that McGrath carried the rest of his life was not the wise-cracking, ever-smiling young athlete he had been, but that of the shattered young man who was lost to him forever.

When Jimmy Rodgers was buried, McGrath had begun to learn one of life's harsh realities: that life is unfair, that death arrives on its own schedule and no one else's. McGrath was an eighteen year old in pain, grieving for his friend. In the months following, as the pain became less immediate, McGrath developed a hardness, a shield to protect him from the anguish of death. This would serve him well in England, if less well outside of the cockpit. He would treat the loss of fellow pilots in a matter of fact fashion. Some thought him callous. Others said his attitude was essential to the function of command. In fact, he was just hardened to death, reacting in the manner he thought best. He did not mean he felt no loss. He did. It meant simply he strove to carry on, treating death as an unhappy but inevitable fact of life.

That night, after his father had retired to the Mayflower and he had returned to Decatur Place, McGrath recalled the good times he had had with Jimmy Rodgers. In turn, this led McGrath to reflect upon his own good fortune. It was, he realized, ample. He enjoyed good health. He had survived the war. He liked his job. He had met a young woman he intended to know better. For McGrath, the roll of the dice that is life had come up seven. That evening, alone in the living room of his apartment, McGrath was aware he led a life many would envy.

Part of his good fortune was his parents, particularly his father. McGrath was old enough to understand the key role John McGrath had played in shaping his life. Where he was situated and how he looked at the world were not simply the result of his own efforts. No, sometimes subtly, sometimes not, the older McGrath had exerted a defining influence on his son's character and journey. It was an influence, the son understood, all to the good.

But McGrath also realized something else about his father. His dad was getting old. There comes a moment in time when children see parents differently. True, the lens has changed but so too have the objects in view. In appearance and behavior, mother and father no longer seem the same. Physical changes take place. Mental agility slows down. Energy is less. Attitudes change as well. In the case of John McGrath the aging process was apparent, though this sixty-six year old man was still alert and in good health.

McGrath knew that someday he too would grow old. He wondered what it would be like. Would he still like airplanes and be able to fly? Would he still delight in books and find comfort in the world of ideas? Would he continue to be a fan of baseball and take notice of an attractive female? Would his health allow him freedom of movement and of choice? Would he remain a person comfortable with himself?

To these questions, McGrath had no answers. But he found the asking to be of interest and, continuing on, raised additional questions. Eventually, these went beyond the subject of getting old. McGrath wondered about death. How and where would he die? And when? What, if anything, happens afterward? Is life on Earth all there is? Does one die and simply lose consciousness for eternity? Is there an existence beyond what we know of here on Earth? Was Marx correct when he described religion as opiate for the masses? Or was Roger O'Boyle right, in his faith of a forgiving God and a life hereafter?

A sincere curiosity drove McGrath to ponder such questions. However, when he decided to go to bed he was not seeking answers. He was contemplating why the questions so intrigued him.

The next day questions of a different sort were asked. Three students were awaiting McGrath upon commencement of his office hours. Two were female. The other was Daniel Powell, a history major who was first in line.

"What can I do for you today, Mr. Powell?"

"I'm here, Professor, for some advice." Powell was speaking as he eased into a chair in response to McGrath's direction.

"Well, that I can give you, though since it's free I'm not sure how much it's worth."

Powell, a serious young man, ignored McGrath's attempt at light-heartedness, an attempt McGrath silently acknowledged to himself as feeble. Daniel Powell had come to McGrath for advice about graduate school and spoke directly to the point.

"I think I want to get a Ph.D., but my father thinks I should go to law school."

"Either step makes sense."

"True, but law school just doesn't appeal to me."

"Then probably you shouldn't go. Why does your father think you should?"

"Because he says it's great preparation for a variety of things."

"He's right, Daniel." McGrath was thinking of all the sound advice he had received from his dad and was reluctant to oppose whatever a father suggested to a son. "The skills you learn in law school are transferable to many careers."

"I accept that, but I think studying torts, contracts, and civil procedure sounds boring."

McGrath agreed but did not say so. "There are other things to study
in the law. Tax policy for one. That's actually pretty interesting. What's
important is deciding what you want to do with your life."

"I want to get a Ph.D., I think."

"You think, or you're sure?"

"Well, I'm pretty sure. Yes," here Powell paused, "that's what I want
to do."

"Then that's probably what you should do. But with one caveat."

"What's that, sir?"

"That you think not just of getting a doctorate but of what you
want to do with it. It's not the degree that counts; it's what you want to
do with it. One way of thinking about it is to ask yourself what you
want to be doing when you're forty. How does a Ph.D. fit into that?
What does the degree mean in terms of options you'd like to have in
the future? I think, Daniel, you should be thinking long term, not just
next year or three years down the road."

"Well, Professor McGrath, I've been trying to do that."

"Good. Think hard about it and you'll probably come up with the
answer. But remember one other thing, Daniel."

"Sir?"

"It is important, I think, to go to graduate school. I believe you go
to college to get an education. To learn some skills and broaden your
outlook. You go to graduate school to learn a trade."

This last remark caused McGrath to smile, for in 1942 John
McGrath had said the exact same words to him. Like father, like son.

The next student to enter McGrath's office was not seeking advice;
Leah Towers had come to complain. In a paper produced for *America in
the Twentieth Century*, she had received a B. Miss Towers believed the
paper deserved an A.

McGrath disagreed. He pointed out to the disgruntled student that
the paper, a twelve-page essay on architecture, while discussing Frank

Lloyd Wright at length, had made no mention of Louis Sullivan. Moreover, he expressed disappointment in the quality of the writing.

"I believe, Miss Towers, you're capable of writing much better than this. This reads like a first draft."

"Well, there wasn't time to do it over."

"Of course there was. Everybody has the same amount of time and you, for whatever reason, chose to do something else."

McGrath continued. "And there are simply too many mistakes in the paper. Basic ones. Words were misspelled, punctuation was erratic, and your conclusion was actually a summary. Really, college students can do better than this."

Leah Towers was now looking glum. She realized McGrath was not going to change the grade and that her paper was not what it ought to have been. Her teacher decided to alter course, and speaking less severely, offer some advice.

"Here are three things you can do to improve your writing. The first is to make sure the paper is properly proofread. The best way to do that is to have someone else read it. If that's not possible, try reading it out loud. You'll be surprised at what you'll find."

The expression on Tower's face signaled she had never tried either of these approaches.

"The next thing you can do is to vary the length of your sentences. Paragraph after paragraph of long sentences is tedious and boring to read. Remember you're writing in English, not German. Try using short sentences once in a while. It reads better and can be an effective way to make your point."

"And the third suggestion?"

McGrath was wondering what to say next. The possibilities were many, but he recalled the advice he had received from Professor Earle at Notre Dame when he was in a situation not unlike that of Leah Towers.

"Well, try not to start every sentence with the subject of the sentence. It sounds repetitive. Vary how sentences begin. Dependent clauses can be very useful. So too can questions. But with questions, one thing is real important."

"What's that?"

"If you ask a question in an essay, you better be sure to answer it."

When Towers walked out of McGrath's office she passed a young coed sitting in a chair awaiting her turn to see McGrath. This young woman, a student like Leah Towers, was dressed in a pink sweater and gray skirt. Her blond hair was curt short but worn with style. Neither thin nor heavy, she presented an image of an attractive female comfortable with an understated appearance. As university students often do, she was reading a book. A casual observer would have assumed the book related to one of the courses she was taking. Not so. Rather, it was a cookbook of New England recipes.

"Come in, Miss Stewart," said McGrath, who was standing in the doorway of his office.

"Thank you, Professor." As she spoke, Cynthia walked past McGrath and sat down in the chair previously occupied by Powell and Towers.

"What can I do for you?" McGrath's voice had a helpful tone.

Cynthia proceeded to talk about a variety of subjects. She asked McGrath's opinion about graduate school, inquired whether study abroad was valuable, discussed her course load, and commented upon student life at Georgetown. She even brought into the conversation her future plans, including the subject of marriage. Cynthia raised these topics intelligently and McGrath responded in kind. He believed that part of his job was to listen to students and offer guidance when asked. But when, after twenty minutes, Cynthia Stewart left his office, he was uncertain why she had come.

Cynthia had a particular motive. She wanted to see and hear McGrath up close. Her best friend was becoming involved with this man and Cynthia intended to determine whether it was wise for Catherine to do so. Cynthia concluded it was, despite the inherent danger. To her McGrath seemed smart but not arrogantly so, serious but not without a sense of humor, and—here Cynthia found herself envious of her roommate—handsome though not in a typical way. Only later, upon further thought, did she realize what about McGrath she found most appealing: he appeared at ease with himself, fully relaxed, yet capable of achieving whatever he set his mind to.

The next day, a Wednesday, McGrath found himself far from his university office. He was on an early morning plane to Boston, for a job interview at Harvard. The plane was a Capital Airlines DC–3, the C–47 military version of which he had ridden often while in the air corps. The job was an entry-level position in the undergraduate college. Roger O'Boyle had encouraged McGrath to apply for the job.

"It's Harvard, for heaven's sake."

"True, but the chances of me getting the job are not very good."

"So what. You're more than qualified, you'd do a good job, and the whole thing, the interview and all that, would be good experience."

On the plane to Boston, McGrath realized O'Boyle was correct on all counts, particularly the last. The experience of going through the application process would be beneficial. As he was unlikely to remain at Georgetown forever, finding another job someday would become necessary.

McGrath knew what he wanted to do with his life. He wished to teach history at the college level. Along the way he hoped to publish a few books. He also wished to continue to fly. Aviation had been a major part of McGrath's life and he expected it to continue to be so.

Sitting at the window seat on the DC–3, McGrath put down the book he was reading and wondered about his future. *How long am I going to stay at Georgetown? Where am I going to go next? Am I always going to have a job? Where's all this going to end up?* McGrath viewed life as an interesting journey. So far his life had been one. He saw no reason why that would change.

Despite an interview that went well, McGrath did not get the job. Except to Roger O'Boyle, he managed to hide his disappointment.

Flying home, McGrath slept as the DC–3 droned south. As the plane flew south down the Potomac on its approach to National Airport, he awoke as it banked left over Georgetown. He heard the thump as the wheels locked in place, and as the DC–3 touched down, McGrath realized he was glad to be home. It meant he would soon see the young woman who might well be a part of his future.

FIVE

Garfinckel's was located at 14th and F Streets NW, not far from the Treasury Department. The eight-story, Art Deco building was a Washington institution, a department store that catered to the wealthy while serving the middle class. Throughout the metropolitan area, from Arlington, Chevy Chase, and Foxhall Road, the women of Washington would journey downtown to shop, selecting items for themselves, for relatives and friends. To sustain this sometimes strenuous activity, the store's fifth floor restaurant, the Greenbrier, coincidentally of the same name as a famous resort in White Sulphur Springs, offered lunch 'til two P.M. Here, among pale blue tablecloths and fine cutlery, shoppers could relax and dine, sometimes alone, sometimes with company.

Catherine Caldwell and her aunt had just arrived at the Greenbrier. It was 12:45, and they had spent more than two hours on several floors seeking dresses for a fancy dinner party Laura was hosting in ten days. While looking they each had made other purchases. Catherine had found a charcoal gray wool cape, lined in red satin, that had a hood and would keep her warm once winter arrived. The cape was a bit formal and decidedly romantic, two reasons she had made the purchase. Her aunt, older and more practical, had bought a burgundy two-piece suit. Designed by Patricia Parker, the suit was stylish yet conservative. Laura thought it would serve her well at the military functions she was required to attend.

"May I take your order?" A Greenbrier waitress was speaking.

"Yes, thank you. I'll have the chicken salad and, to start, a cup of tomato soup."

"Hum," muttered Catherine, "that sounds good. I'll have the same with a cup of tea."

"Make that two teas, and thank you," said Laura.

"Certainly ladies, I'll bring the soup right away. And the salads will be coming up in a jiff."

"Aren't we eating sensibly," declared Catherine. "The paté and cheese plate was tempting but chicken salad and soup will keep my waistline thin."

"My dear, at your age waistlines stay slim no matter what you eat."

"I wish that were true. I'm hoping to stay trim all my life, as you have."

"Thank you. That's sweet of you to say. A woman can never be too rich or too thin."

"Someone said that, someone famous, yes?"

"It was the Duchess of Windsor, Wallis Simpson."

"The lady from Baltimore, the woman the King of England abdicated for. Imagine giving up a throne to marry the woman you love. How romantic."

"I guess so. Though in this instance I'm not so sure. The woman is no role model. She's divorced and a scheming, horrid person actually."

"Really?"

"I'm afraid so. She connived her way into royal company, making friends with all the right people. Then she went after the king, and got him. It's scandalous. All she does now is socialize, one party after the other. They live in Paris. I'm told she's a cold, greedy person who cares for no one but herself."

"And what of the king, now the duke?"

"I'm afraid he's not much better. A weak man, given a life of privilege, he gave nothing back. The man devoted his life to clothes and parties. And when his country needed him, he turned his back on them. There's nothing about the man I admire."

"Even his decision to step aside, to give up something special for the woman he loved?"

"What he gave up, Catherine, was his duty."

"I'm not so sure. I mean rightly or wrongly, he loved this woman. And he was willing to sacrifice everything for her. Surely, that's not wrong."

Laura McCreedy had not wished to talk about the Duke and Duchess of Windsor. She wanted to hear about Georgetown and how her niece's studies were progressing. As co-trustee with Riggs Bank of funds left to Catherine by her father and mother, Laura felt obliged to oversee the young woman's schooling. But her interest went beyond a fiduciary responsibility. She not only loved her niece, she also wanted her to succeed, to have a fulfilling career. Pivotal to success, Laura believed, was a good education.

Such an education would help Catherine overcome the barriers all women faced when considering their future. In medicine, in business, in science and the law, women confronted discriminatory obstacles that denied them both access and advancement. Laura herself had experienced this. Hoping to be a doctor, she was turned down by medical schools despite having ample qualifications. Instead she became a nurse. The older woman sought for the younger an opportunity to pursue a profession without regard to gender. The place to start, she reasoned, was college. That meant Catherine needed to do well at Georgetown.

Of course education alone would not suffice. Laura understood what many in 1950 assumed, that a woman would have to work harder than a man simply to achieve equal consideration. More than once she had told Catherine, "Remember, Ginger Rogers did everything Fred Astaire did, but she did it backwards and in high heels." Laura herself was never one to shun work. She was not certain Catherine was equally diligent.

"Enough of Mrs. Simpson and her royal husband. Tell me about Georgetown. You're now a senior and soon will be finished. How time flies. Is it going well? Are you enjoying yourself? Is it challenging enough?"

Catherine smiled. She knew of her aunt's interest in education and appreciated Laura's interest in her studies.

"Let's see, where to begin? Yes, I'm still enjoying it. Classes are interesting, at least most of the time. The work is hard but not too hard, and I do study more than you think I do. I'm learning and I find it's nice to be able to concentrate on four subjects I like."

"And these would be?" Catherine's aunt knew the four courses her niece was taking, but wished to hear more about them.

"There's my *English Literature in the Nineteenth Century*, course, *Italian*, a history of Russia that's very good and not very difficult. And another history course, *America Enters the Twentieth Century.*"

And which is the hardest?"

"Italian." And for the next ten minutes, Catherine explained why. The conversation then turned to Russia and Catherine related to her aunt the events surrounding the 1917 revolution. Laura McCreedy listened politely. Less interested in Lenin's rise to power, she found more rewarding Catherine's grasp of the subject and her interest in it. When Catherine began to talk about Stalin, however, Laura decided it was time to switch topics. So she asked Catherine about life on campus. Catherine responded that on the whole Georgetown was a friendly place, that athletics seemed to be important to the university, and that the library seemed far too small for the number of students enrolled. Laura then asked whether co-educational schools fostered intellectual pursuits among women or whether an all-girls college might be more conducive to studies. In response, Catherine fibbed. She said she thought the learning environment in co-ed institutions was as strong as that in a school where males were absent. Laura was more honest. She said she thought girls-only schools were more academic because there were fewer distractions. Yet both women agreed that having men around made college a lot more interesting.

"Speaking of men, there's only one that you seem to mention."

"Oh?"

"Yes, you seem, my dear, to speak often of your history professor, the one in your American history class."

"Professor McGrath?"

"That's the one. You have lunch with him, I gather, or so you've said."

"Yes, I do." Catherine's demeanor registered neither surprise nor guilt, and purposely so.

"He must be a very interesting fellow."

Catherine responded cautiously. "He is, he's a fine teacher."

What Laura McCreedy next said took Catherine completely by surprise.

"I'm sure he is. Your uncle and I would like to meet him. Why don't you invite him to the dinner party we're having?"

"Really? Do you mean it?"

"We do. Nothing wrong with having your history professor come to dinner, is there?"

Once again, Catherine spoke less than the whole truth. "Nothing that I know of."

McGrath learned of the invitation the next day. He and Catherine were at Max's having lunch. Both had come to the delicatessen with a question for the other. Both were anxious, believing that the answer, and perhaps the question itself, would signal a change in the relationship neither now considered totally innocent. McGrath and his student knew they were about to break the rules. They understood the risks. Each could feel the heat of the fire they were playing with.

McGrath began the conversation. "I have a question for you."

"Oh." Catherine was surprised. No small talk had occurred, no prelude, no opening remarks about schoolwork or the university. McGrath usually did so, in part Catherine believed, out of nervousness. He did not appear nervous today. Recovering, she replied in kind, "And I have one for you."

"You should go first then."

"No, I'd prefer that you do."

McGrath did not wish to argue. "Okay, here goes."

But he did not speak immediately. His mind returned to what O'Boyle had said and to what he knew was right. He should stop seeing the girl. He should tell her what they were doing, and what they were about to do, was wrong, harmful to them both. No one would condone their behavior. They would be alone, and most likely outcast. All this McGrath realized. He knew what he should say. He had practiced the words many times over. But he wanted not to say them. Within McGrath propriety and romance were locked in battle, and romance would win. But not immediately.

"You and I have been seeing each other for some time now, here at Max's. And that's okay because I'm your teacher, you're my student, and we've just been having lunch. It's all been on the up and up, or at least it appears that way. But I think it's time we stop."

Catherine's face showed the surprise and disappointment she felt. McGrath continued.

"You know, Catherine, what we're doing is wrong. Professors are not supposed to go out with their students. And since I want to, and since it's wrong, I think we should stop, before things really get out of hand."

"You want to?" Catherine's voice and expression reflected relief and pleasure.

"Yes, I do, but that's not the point."

Catherine Caldwell had not been as troubled as her professor. She believed she had found the man of her dreams and he, unknowingly, had won her heart. Her aunt once had said that when she first met Lieutenant McCreedy she knew he was the man for her. "Call it chemistry, or fate, or even love, but right away I knew your Uncle Mike was the only man I'd ever need or want." Now Catherine felt what Laura McCreedy had experienced thirty years ago. McGrath was the man for her. She knew she had to speak up or have him leave her life. The necessary words had not been practiced, for Catherine had assumed they would not be needed until much later. After all, other than at Max's they had not yet dated. But her instincts and desires now told her to speak up. Sooner than expected, the future had arrived.

"Of course it's wrong if you accept their rules. But I don't, and I don't care what they think. I care how I feel, and I know that whatever it is—and I believe it's true love, or something very close—it's good and right, and needs to continue and grow."

She then took hold of McGrath's hand and softened her voice.

"And besides, it's already out of control. Nothing really has happened, but already it's far beyond just lunch here at this corner deli. You know that; I've seen it in your eyes."

Hearing these words, seeing her defiance, McGrath gave way. His hold upon the proper course of action, already tenuous, collapsed. Captivated by the spirit of this young woman, beholden to his own desires, McGrath took hold of Catherine's hand.

"Yes, you're right. It is out of control, and is something dear and very sweet."

Unexpectedly, but without embarrassment, Catherine began to cry. They were tears of joy and hope. Gently wiping them away, she placed a kiss upon her hand and brought it to McGrath's cheek. Without words, she had told McGrath she loved him. To his credit, he understood.

Neither of them spoke. Aware of the moment, each decided to cherish what had occurred.

The silence continued, nourishing love as rain does a garden. Then Catherine, with a hint of mischief across her face, addressed the man to whom she now felt very close.

"Now, you said you had a question for me. What is it?"

"Ah yes, the question." McGrath's anxiety was gone. "I was wondering if you would have dinner with me?"

Catherine's response was not what McGrath expected. She started to laugh. Lovingly, her mouth broadened to a warm smile.

"Why are you laughing?"

"Because that's the question I was going to ask you."

McGrath looked puzzled.

"I was, I am, asking you to dinner. My aunt and uncle are having a dinner party a week from Saturday and I'm hoping you can come."

"Do they know you're asking me?"

"Yes, they've said they'd like to meet you."

"Really?"

"Well, my aunt did, and she's the one who suggested I invite you."

"And what do you think of the idea?"

"Me?" Catherine's expression had turned mischievous. "I think it's splendid."

McGrath's demeanor suddenly changed, as if considering consequences. "Catherine, these are dangerous waters we're entering. We must be careful."

Her response was immediate. "But we must proceed. I can't imagine not."

"Nor I."

"So here's your answer. Yes, I will."

"Then I," he said with a smile, "accept your invitation to dinner."

At that moment, Maxwell Hopkins appeared at their table, egg salad sandwich in hand as well as the bowl of chicken noodle soup Catherine had ordered. "Drinks will be here in a few minutes, folks."

As he returned to the kitchen, Max's emotions were mixed. He was pleased the Colonel had found a lady friend. She seemed quite nice, and certainly was a pretty young thing. But he realized she was a student, and that he knew signaled danger, like a pair of Messerschmitts coming out of the sun.

Purposely, the restaurant McGrath had chosen for their dinner rendezvous was far from Georgetown. He thought it prudent to dine where neither faculty colleagues nor college students were likely to gather. McGrath was determined to pursue this risky liaison but not do so recklessly. In this instance, caution meant dining in the Maryland countryside. The restaurant was called Normandie Farm. Located near a crossroad nine miles from the district line and even further from the university, it was a French country inn, famous for its popovers and rustic charm.

They met in the parking lot, as planned. When McGrath arrived in his new car, he spotted the blue Ford, easy to do so as the other cars were all black and less spiffy. Approaching the convertible, McGrath was to receive a shock. Catherine was standing by her car waiting for him, having just gotten out of the Ford. What he did not expect was how lovely, how utterly compelling she looked. He had seen her only in classroom clothes. What Catherine had on this evening was definitely not school wear. The college coed had become a tantalizing young woman. Her dress was black, cut low with a wide black satin stripe across the top. Around her neck she wore a simple strand of pearls that had belonged to her mother and teardrop pearl earrings, a sixteenth birthday present from her uncle. Black high-heeled shoes and her Garfinckel's cape completed the ensemble. Catherine Caldwell looked like what she was, a young, beautiful woman intent on capturing her beau's attention.

McGrath was speechless. Never before had he seen such an attractive female in person. His entire being, body and mind, was overcome with desire.

Recovering, he greeted her pleasantly. She replied in similar fashion. That's when desire struck again. McGrath took hold of Catherine, gently pulling her to him. Then he kissed her, half expecting her to pull back. She did not. She returned the kiss. As McGrath held her close to him, Catherine let her body melt onto his. The embrace was not brief. Neither wished to stop, so they continued.

Finally they separated. "Wow," was all that McGrath, in a soft voice, could utter.

At first Catherine said nothing. Then, having regained her composure, she stared straight into the eyes of the man she now realized she loved. "Do you always do that on a first date?"

"No ma'am, I never have. Do you think we could do it again?"

"Yes, we can, but not here and not now. You promised me dinner and here we are outside, in the middle of nowhere, next to what looks to be a nice restaurant." Catherine then kissed McGrath on the cheek. "So take me inside and feed me."

"Okay, but did I mention that you look lovely, absolutely fabulous?"

Pleased at the compliment, thrilled given her intent to dazzle,

Catherine responded with far less emotion than she felt. "I'm glad you approve."

"I do indeed, I do indeed."

Upon entering Normandie Farm, McGrath was aware that the men present in the restaurant all took note of Catherine as the maitre' d escorted them to a table for two. McGrath reacted to their envy with a sense of triumph. He was in the company of a beautiful woman and felt, as men often do in such circumstances, a sense of pride—masculine and victorious.

The table was off to a corner near one of two fireplaces, as McGrath had requested. Atop the fireplace mantles were copper pots. Nearby were three large wooden hutches displaying a variety of china plates. Iron ceiling lamps that hung from heavy wooden beams provided low lighting. Additional light came from candles inserted into wine bottles that sat upon checkerboard tablecloths. Overall the atmosphere was informal but warm and romantic. Whether it was French provincial, McGrath could not say. He had never been to France, though from the air he had seen the country often.

Dinner was a great success, both in terms of food and conversation. Catherine ordered leg of lamb, starting with onion soup that she pronounced excellent. McGrath began with a mushroom tart and, as a main course, had beef burgundy. Accompanied by roasted potatoes and a medley of green beans and carrots, both entrees were well prepared. For dessert McGrath took charge and ordered Crepes Suzette. Their taste was as good as their flamboyant preparation. Coffee and tea completed the meal, which at $24.25 McGrath considered expensive but well worth the money.

The two lovers, if people in love can be so described, conversed easily and intensely. They talked about growing up and getting old, about the world they knew and the one they wished to see, and about each other. Georgetown University and the Air National Guard were not topics of conversation. The more they spoke, the more connected they felt. Never had Catherine experienced such a union. Nor had McGrath.

"I suppose I shall have to rearrange the slices."

Catherine had no idea what McGrath meant by this remark.

"My life, dear lady, is like a pie. It can be divided into slices. And each slice represents an activity. But the size of the pie remains the same, just as there's only twenty-four hours in a day or seven days in a week. Some slices are big, such as my work at Georgetown; some are very small, like the time I have for my mother and father. And some are medium, like the dry cleaners."

"Dry cleaners? Part of your life is devoted to dry cleaning?"

McGrath was smiling when he responded. "Metaphorically speaking. Everybody has to spend time doing things to stay afloat, just to keep going so that real things can get done. Like going to the dry cleaners. And buying food, and paying bills, and getting your car repaired, or doing laundry or straightening up your apartment. That sort of thing."

"Like shopping." Catherine too was smiling.

"Yes, shopping is one of those activities. Though I don't do much of it myself. Do you?"

"According to the Constitution, I don't have to answer that."

"Fair enough, but you get the point."

"I do. But why mention it now?"

"Because now the pie has to be cut differently."

"How come?"

"Because, sweet girl, because of you."

"Oh, I see."

"Before, I didn't have a slice for you."

"And now you do?"

"Yes, unless this date of ours is a one-shot affair."

"I think not." With a twinkle in her eye, Catherine posed a question to McGrath, "How big is my slice?"

"That I can't tell you."

"And why not?" Catherine pretended to pout.

"Because the size has not yet been determined. And besides, for now, it should be a secret."

"I think it should be a big slice."

"Do you now?"

"I do, and my question to you, my dear man, is how big do you think it will be?"

"Can I take the Fifth?"

"No."

"You did."

"Doesn't matter. How big, Mister Professor Colonel McGrath, is my slice?"

"Pretty big."

"How big?"

"Oh, it's about the size of my dry cleaning."

The evening ended as it had begun, with kisses. They were at McGrath's apartment, the first floor of a townhouse on Decatur Place NW, near Sheridan Circle. Consisting of five rooms, one of which McGrath used as a study, the apartment was furnished eclectically. One room contained quality pieces given by McGrath's parents. Another had furniture purchased at Sears. The rest McGrath had secured by various means, including yard sales. No one would confuse the overall look with artistry or good design. But McGrath did not care. He found the space comfortable and functional, and had said to himself that once married he would leave home furnishings to his wife.

Catherine took little notice of the apartment's decor. She was otherwise occupied, softly caressing McGrath. He was at peace, holding the girl that had won his heart.

At 12:45 A.M., they parted. Catherine got into the Ford and headed back to her apartment, having first kissed McGrath passionately while standing on the sidewalk.

"I think I'm in love, Mr. McGrath."

"And you, dear lady, are now a part of my life," replied McGrath, who was wondering how this part would fit with the others.

McGrath had expected to see Catherine next in class. However, she did not appear, nor did she stop by Max's at lunch. After lingering at the delicatessen hoping Catherine would appear, McGrath hurried back to the university. He was late for the office hours that he held twice a week. Invariably, students wanted to see him. Some sought extensions on papers due. Others, like Leah Towers, wished to contest grades. Still others came for academic counseling. McGrath welcomed them all, especially youngsters who were new to the college and shy about raising subjects they considered difficult or controversial. Actually, there was one group of students McGrath disliked seeing. These were graduate students, some smoking pipes, so taken with academic life they would extend course work and dissertations, forgetting the objective was to complete their program.

Toward the end of office hours, when students with appointments had been seen, McGrath was sitting at his desk, appreciating a moment of quiet. There was a knock on the door, to which McGrath responded, "Come in."

It was Catherine. "Good afternoon, sir," she said formally.

Surprised by her presence and her tone, he was even more surprised by what happened next. Catherine first shut the door and locked it. She then proceeded to blow him a kiss. Catherine then sat down and fixed her eyes upon him.

"There will be more of those, and real ones, if you continue to see me."

Taken aback, McGrath said nothing.

After checking with a pocket mirror to see that her appearance was in order, Catherine walked to the office door and unlocked it, then opened it and spoke briefly to McGrath as she departed.

"I'll see you at Max's on Thursday. And by the way, I'm dropping your course."

SIX

Tuesday's lecture was not a success. McGrath spoke about the year 1900. The purpose was to place in context American power and potential at the turn of the century. In 1900, said McGrath, the world was a vibrant, busy place. The Boer War was underway in South Africa. Hawaii was organized as a U.S. territory. Count Zeppelin flew his first airship. The Boxer Rebellion began in China. Paul Villard discovered gamma rays. And excavation for the New York subway system began. The year also produced fine literature: Joseph Conrad wrote *Lord Jim*. Anton Chekhov penned *Uncle Vanya*. And George Bernard Shaw put forth *The Devil's Disciple*. Nor was the year 1900 devoted exclusively to weighty matters. A Mr. D. F. Davis presented a cup for victory in international tennis. Beatrice Potter wrote *The Tale of Peter Rabbit*. Charles Dana Gibson created images of young, beautiful women. And in Germany, the minister for war defended dueling as an antidote to manslaughter.

The aim of the lecture was to portray the world as it was in 1900. McGrath wanted to capture the mood of people and the direction of history. He hoped to present a unifying sense to the events of 1900, to portray the totality of civilization as it existed fifty years ago, so that his students might better understand America in 1900 grasping the changes in and similarities with the world of 1950. McGrath was aware he had chosen a daunting task. He thought thorough preparation, clear thinking, and lively presentation would carry the day. It did not. Midway through the talk, McGrath realized he had failed. The lecture was disjointed. Full of facts, covering a vast array of material, it lacked cohesion and conclusion. The colorful, integrated canvas he had hoped to paint did not emerge. The result was more a Jackson Pollack than a Rembrandt.

Sensing that all was not well, McGrath took appropriate action. He ended the lecture sooner than planned. Instead of ninety minutes he spoke for sixty-five. And abandoning his practice of taking questions when finished, he simply closed his notebook, wished his students a pleasant afternoon, and walked out of the classroom. In military terms, he lived to fight another day.

Walking over to Max's, McGrath chose not to think about the lecture. He was focused on the immediate future. McGrath expected to meet Catherine at the delicatessen and wanted to be on time. He knew their conversation would be pivotal. His life, he understood, was about to reach the proverbial fork in the road. So McGrath was not unhappy that the lecture had ended when it did. It gave him more time to wonder what he and this young woman were to do.

Arriving at the delicatessen, he ordered his egg salad sandwich and then, regarding Catherine, considered his options. There were two, he realized, and they were obvious. He could end the relationship or continue to see her. The first was the simplest, and the wisest. However, McGrath did not want to do this and knew he would not. A feeling, a need, compelled him to pursue Catherine Caldwell. He tried to define what he felt, to understand the force that was propelling him forward. Was it love? Was he merely lonely? Were carnal instincts overriding good judgment? Or was there an unspoken desire to have a companion share the everyday adventures of life? What McGrath did not realize was that it was all of these. Nor did he understand that such needs and the wish to understand them meant simply that he was human.

Accepting that Catherine was to be part of his life, McGrath proceeded to consider what part she would play. Clearly, she would be more than a girlfriend, with a slice of his life larger than that of dry cleaning. As he thought about Catherine Caldwell, McGrath realized once again how deeply he cared for this young woman. And how much he wanted her to be in his life. That's when, to his surprise, a solution presented itself. That the solution was bold, bordering on reckless, did not concern him. After all, once he had attacked sixteen Messerschmitts high above Berlin.

As promised, Catherine appeared at Max's. She went immediately to the table where McGrath sat and noticed approvingly that he rose as she approached.

"Hello, dear man, I'm here as I said I would be."

"I'm glad. We need to talk, I think."

"I'm not going back to your class," said Catherine bluntly, anticipating an argument with McGrath. "I've made up my mind."

"And I'm not going to ask you to."

Relieved to hear this, Catherine correctly interpreted McGrath's comment to mean he intended to continue to see her.

"But after today's class," said McGrath, "I'm not sure you're going to miss much."

McGrath went on to explain how the lecture on 1900 had not gone well. Catherine listened sympathetically. She then offered a few suggestions that McGrath considered sensible. However, neither wished to talk about school. They wanted to talk about each other and what they should do. So they did, for fifty minutes. At one point in the conversation Catherine said she would drop out of Georgetown if necessary to continue on with him. Surprised to hear this, McGrath nonetheless was pleased, for her statement confirmed that she felt for him as he felt for her.

"I don't want you to do that, Catherine."

"I will if I have to. There are other schools around here, and I'll go to one of them. I love you and all the rest is unimportant."

They continued talking and once again conversation seemed to bring them closer together. Sometimes men and women connect such that words and ideas run parallel with passion as an indication of love.

This occurred at Max's, between McGrath and his former student. Both were aware it was happening. Both treasured the experience.

Maxwell Hopkins also was aware something special was taking place. Purposefully he had left them alone, sensing McGrath and the young woman wished no interruptions. Only when Catherine gasped with surprise did Max look over at the Colonel and his lady friend. What he saw made him smile. Catherine, utterly happy, had tears in her eyes and was holding both of McGrath's hands. Hopkins then saw McGrath rise and walk over to Catherine, putting his hands gently around her cheeks. Kissing her forehead, he spoke words Max could not make out. These had great effect, for Catherine stood up and kissed McGrath, oblivious to others in the deli. Holding both of her hands, he replied in kind. Then they sat down and continued talking, their hands still together as if two people had become one.

They talked for another hour. Catherine kept her eyes upon McGrath. For the first time since entering Max's she paid attention to what he was wearing. Her companion was nicely attired in what he called his Georgetown uniform. This consisted of gray wool slacks and a navy blazer. McGrath owned two of the latter, both purchased at Brooks Brothers. One he wore and one he kept in reserve, rotating them every two weeks. This day his dress shirt was light blue and his tie yellow-and-blue striped. Black loafers and black socks completed the picture. The overall image was conservative yet attractive, which was the look McGrath was seeking. Not disinterested in clothes, his wardrobe was modest in size and scope. He owned two suits. The charcoal gray pinstripe was his favorite. The other, a dark brown Hickey-Freeman three piece his father had given him, seemed too stylish, too substantial for classroom duty. Of course, once summer arrived the suits and navy blazers went into storage, surrounded by mothballs. In late April McGrath would pull out his summer clothes. These consisted primarily of two sport jackets—one royal blue, one forest green—and a striped seersucker suit. Not having any dark summer clothes, McGrath hoped, from April through August, to avoid weddings and funerals. Shirts for the summer were the same as for winter. McGrath disliked short-sleeved dress shirts and was prepared to sweat rather than wear them.

Catherine was wearing an outfit she had bought at Garfinckels. It was a red and green tartan plaid skirt with a large silver clip on the side and a white, high-collared wool sweater. She wore no earrings but clipped to the sweater was a pin, a butterfly of sterling silver. The clothes were of high quality and not unattractive, but they were more utilitarian than fashionable. Later Catherine wished she had been wearing something more memorable.

Just when the topic arose of where the great event would take place, McGrath took notice of the time.

"Oh, my Lord, I'm late."

"You're not going to run off, are you? Not now?"

"I must, Catherine. I'm already late for a department meeting, after which I'm to meet and have dinner with Roger O'Boyle."

"You're having dinner with Professor O'Boyle tonight?" Catherine was incredulous.

"Of course I'm not." If nothing else, McGrath was flexible. "I'm having dinner with you."

"Sweet man," Catherine was smiling as she blew McGrath a kiss. "And I might even be convinced to cook it for you."

"Really?" McGrath was intrigued. He remembered that Catherine had said she did not like to cook. "And what do I have to do in order for that to happen?"

"Nothing much. Just give me a key to your apartment. We're going to eat in tonight."

Never had McGrath given a woman a key to his place, though two had given him theirs. Now was not the time to think of them, he reasoned. So quickly, and without hesitation, he reached into his pocket and slid the key across the table.

"2236 Decatur Place," he said.

"Yes," Catherine replied, "I know."

"Should I pick up some steaks on the way home?" As McGrath spoke these words he laughed to himself at how domestic they sounded.

"Not necessary, my dear. I'll go by the market once I leave here. Do you like lamb chops?"

"I do."

"Broccoli?"

"Yup."

"Good. Add some roasted potatoes and a salad and we have ourselves a meal."

"How about dessert? I could get some ice cream."

"That's sweet, but not necessary." Catherine's voice and pose then turned seductive. Whispering to McGrath, she said, "For you, dear man, I have something else in mind."

As usual, the departmental meeting was long and boring. Professor Grafton Donahue, chairman of the history department, ran the meeting. Both as a teacher and a chairman, Donahue was past his prime. Yet he was a kindly man who had served Georgetown well so few people complained. McGrath remained quiet at the meeting. As the junior member of the department he felt much like a child at a grownup's dinner party—best to be seen and not heard.

While long, McGrath's meeting with Roger O'Boyle was not boring. At first they talked about what the Jesuit had expected. This was the research each man was conducting. Advancement at Georgetown required producing scholarship, which meant teaching was secondary. Reluctantly, both men accepted "publish or perish" as reality in academic life. Because scholarly writings were solitary, difficult work, McGrath and O'Boyle served as critic and cheerleader for each other, helping with ideas, editing, and moral support. Both men believed their work benefited from such assistance. O'Boyle was preparing an essay on Karl Marx he intended to submit to the American Political Science Association. McGrath was writing a book on Theodore Roosevelt and the Russo-Japanese War of 1905. He hoped to have a reputable publisher accept the manuscript but, given the vagaries of publishing, he was not optimistic. More than once McGrath had told himself all he could do was submit a first-class piece of work.

After discussing the early writings of Marx the Jesuit noticed that

McGrath seemed distracted. His friend was not focusing on research—his own, or O'Boyle's. Finally, the priest asked McGrath if something was amiss.

"No, I'm fine. I just have some things on my mind."

"Want to share them with me?"

"Actually, I do."

"Good. That's what friends are for."

"I'm afraid, Roger, I'm not going to be able to have dinner tonight."

"Oh, that's too bad. I was looking forward to it."

"Me too."

O'Boyle sensed that canceling dinner was not the cause of his friend's distraction.

"Are you okay?" O'Boyle's voice reflected concern.

"Oh, I'm fine. Actually, I'm better than fine."

"Then what's up? Something's on your mind and it's not dinner or research."

"That's for sure." McGrath decided to go step by step. "I'm having dinner with Catherine Caldwell."

"Oh." Roger O'Boyle was surprised. But his feelings were not hurt, for he perceived there was a good reason for what McGrath was doing. So he remained quiet, bidding his friend to continue.

McGrath complied. "Of course, that would be a problem, except it's not."

"Because."

"Because, Roger, are you ready for this? Catherine Caldwell and I are getting married. I proposed three hours ago, and she said yes."

"Good heavens!" Roger O'Boyle was not ready for such news. His face registered complete surprise. But it did not reflect disapproval, for he felt none. His next reaction was two-fold. First he digested the news. Then he accepted it as good friends should, with joy and pleasure.

"Let me be the first to congratulate you."

"Thank you."

"And the first," said the Jesuit, "to offer my blessings."

"Thank you, my friend."

"As your friend and as a man of the cloth I wish you only good fortune and God's blessings."

"Which I—" McGrath then corrected himself, "Which *we* accept with thanks."

"Besides, you're too old and have seen too much for me or anyone else to lecture you. If you love this girl and she loves you, and you both seek a life within God's grace, then may your union be one of great happiness."

O'Boyle and his friend then talked at length about the news McGrath had disclosed. The Jesuit learned more about Catherine Caldwell and, in doing so, learned more about her fiancé. McGrath, it appeared, had been considering marrying this girl but a short time. Yet he had thought hard and deeply. His decision, O'Boyle concluded, was not without calculation. In dating and caring for a student, McGrath had a problem that he addressed and solved. For the first time O'Boyle saw in McGrath the decisiveness those in England had seen many times.

Marriages, O'Boyle reasoned, might be blessed in heaven, but they were not made there. So this day and others he would pray that McGrath and his bride, in addition to passion and love, would bring wisdom and character to theirs.

A faculty office at Georgetown University was not the only place where McGrath and marriage were discussed. The next day Catherine and her aunt were in the living room of Laura McCreedy's home on McComb Street NW. The topic was the forthcoming dinner party. First settled was the menu. With assistance from the premier caterer in town, Avignon Frere, Laura was serving Beef Wellington, two vegetables, and Potatoes Anna, a cake of potatoes thinly sliced and laced with butter. First course would be French onion soup. Dessert would be Cherries Jubilee. Laura thought the menu was perfect for the party she had planned. Including herself and her husband, there would be fourteen people—seven couples at two tables of seven.

Laura and the general would sit at different tables. Where to seat Catherine and McGrath was an issue. Catherine wanted to sit at the table with her aunt. Laura thought her husband would appreciate having his niece and their guest, Professor McGrath, with him.

"We are so looking forward to meeting this Professor McGrath of yours."

"I'm so glad he's coming. I can't wait for you to meet him."

Catherine then took hold of her aunt's hands. "Laura, dear Aunt Laura, something wonderful has happened. I'm so very happy."

Intuitively, Laura McCreedy knew what her niece was about to say.

"This dear man, my history professor, has asked me to marry him and I've said yes."

"Oh my dear, let me give you a hug." Laura began to cry, then reached out and embraced her niece.

The conversation that followed made no mention of the dinner party. Two women, one older than the other, were extremely happy. Laura McCreedy had many questions of her niece, who could answer but a few. When would the wedding take place? Catherine said in late June, which gave the women seven months to plan the event—sufficient, but not ample, time. Where would they honeymoon? Catherine replied that she hoped to convince McGrath to go to Italy. Questions left unanswered included where the wedding would take place and how many people would be invited.

"There is one thing I hope and pray will happen," said Catherine midway through the conversation.

"What's that, my dear?"

"I do want Uncle Mike to give me away."

Laura smiled. "I'm sure he will. I'm sure he'd be upset were it anyone else."

"Good, I'm glad. I love him, and you, so much."

"And we, dear girl, love you."

Only later did Catherine reflect that Laura McCreedy had expressed no opposition to the marriage. There had been no skepticism, no concern that McGrath might be too much older or not the proper choice. What Laura's niece did not know was that her aunt was recalling the time when a young junior army officer had proposed to her.

Laura remembered how happy she was and how disappointed to hear her mother voice doubt that Lieutenant McCreedy was suitable for marriage to her daughter. In 1922, Laura McCreedy vowed never to act that way. Twenty-eight years later, when the time came, she did not.

The only reservation Laura had concerned Catherine's education. When her niece said she and McGrath had every intention of Catherine remaining at Georgetown, Laura's concern evaporated.

"Well, my dear, how shall we tell your uncle this wonderful news? And when shall we meet this lucky fellow?"

"Actually, he's coming over tonight and plans to ask you and Uncle Mike for permission to marry me."

"The general will like that," said Laura, again embracing her niece. "And so will I."

Lt. General Michael McCreedy arrived home late that day. A meeting with the chief of staff had lasted longer than expected. The generals had discussed delays in production of F–84s and F–86s. These were slowing Vandenberg's efforts to rebuild the air force. When McCreedy walked through the door at McComb Street he was not in a pleasant mood. This changed upon seeing his wife, who had ready for him the scotch and soda he partook of each evening before dinner.

"Thank you, my dear."

"You're welcome, Michael," said Laura, who kissed him on the cheek.

At once the general knew something important was about either to happen or be said. Whenever Laura used his given name McCreedy paid close attention.

"Yes, my dear, what is it?"

"We're having company for dinner, despite the hour. Catherine and her professor friend are here, and they're joining us. And Professor McGrath has asked to see us alone."

Mike McCreedy had no idea why, nor any inkling of what was to follow.

Laura knew her husband tended to be obtuse about such things. So she placed her hands upon his shoulders and spoke firmly after again kissing him on the cheek.

"Michael, I want you to be nice. Remember when you did this." She then gazed directly into his eyes, and spoke again. "This is not some officer you're trying to intimidate. So be good."

"Aren't I always?"

"No, you're not. And one other thing."

"And what's that?"

"The answer is yes."

Two minutes later, after changing into civilian clothes, Mike McCreedy listened to McGrath ask for the hand of his niece in marriage. He acceded to the request, saying all the words Laura wished him to speak. Yet he was not enthusiastic. He thought Catherine too young, this man too old, and the idea of marriage too hasty. As for McGrath, he seemed nice enough. His war record was distinguished. But he had opted out of the service, preferring to be a university professor, living in a world where pay was low and ideas too liberal. His niece, Mike McCreedy believed, could do better.

That night after Laura had gone to bed McCreedy pondered what had taken place during the day, at the Pentagon and in his living room. Already he had devised a plan to force Republic and North American to speed production. Now an idea came to mind about McGrath. It was a long shot, but it might work. He would talk to Milo Hawkins in the morning.

The dinner party was a great success. This was due almost entirely to Laura McCreedy, who excelled as a hostess. The general's wife believed successful parties required several ingredients. The first was good food. With Avignon Frere as caterer, this was assured. The second was a pleasant setting. For this party Laura sat her guests on the porch where the two tables filled the room, creating an intimate environment. Located off the kitchen, the porch had been bricked in, so the guests remained warm as did their food. The third ingredient was liquor. Both the general and his wife and their guests enjoyed their cocktails. Hence the McCreedy's liquor cabinet was well stocked. Chivas Regal and Beefeaters were beverages of choice.

Another ingredient was capable service. More than once Laura had seen dinner parties ruined by incompetent staff. Laura, of course, did not serve the meal or drinks. As the wife of a senior air force officer, her job was to socialize. Moreover, she wanted to enjoy herself, which she usually did, especially in her own home where, by military standards, parties tended to be informal. To provide the necessary help she relied upon the caterer who supplied people as well as food. These individuals performed the hard work dinner parties required, except for tending bar, which, atypically, Mike McCreedy enjoyed and insisted upon doing.

However, most important to successful dinner parties were the guests. Laura McCreedy had a knack for selecting diverse, interesting people who enjoyed each other's company. Deftly mixing personal friends with colleagues of her husband, Laura produced parties people were reluctant to leave.

Guests this evening included Susan and Fred Wade. She was an old friend of Laura's from nursing school. They were seated at the table with the general, as were Catherine and McGrath. This table also included Stephen and Charlene Butler. He was a successful lawyer who lived on McComb Street. Rounding out the table were Vice Admiral Kirk Boggs and his wife Stephanie. The admiral was the navy's director of policy and plans. She was an interior decorator.

Prior to dinner being served Catherine was talking with Stephanie Boggs while McGrath was conversing with the admiral. Intrigued to learn that McGrath had flown fighters in Europe, Boggs, who had commanded an air wing in the Pacific, was asking McGrath his views about the future of naval aviation. The subject was timely, for in 1950 the navy and air force were at war with each other, competing for funds and control of aeronautical assets.

"Yes, I'd like to hear what the professor has to say," said General McCreedy, who with a drink in his hand for Kirk Boggs, had joined the small group.

"Well, Admiral," replied McGrath, who acknowledged his host with a nod, "I'm no military theorist, just an aging fighter pilot." These last three words surprised McGrath, who never had so described himself.

"My guess is that we need both, the carriers and the B–36s," McGrath continued.

Catherine's uncle frowned. The admiral turned to his friend. "See Mike, a man with perspective. Continue. my boy."

"Well, Admiral, it seems to me that carriers are truly useful. They're flexible, they're terrific symbols of national strength, and their planes can pound coastal targets. But they're tactical in nature. The country needs a strategic strike force and that force needs the B–36."

McGrath felt good about his answer. He had been diplomatic, saying something to which Catherine's uncle would resonate while placating the navy with kind words about its beloved carriers. Better still. McGrath liked his response because he believed it to be true. The navy's carriers were useful and the country needed them. But the nation could not do without the Strategic Air Command and its B–36s.

The conversation was about to get more lively when Catherine intervened.

"Excuse me gentlemen, I'm going to steal this man from you." She then gently pulled McGrath away, saying to all that she wished to have him meet an old nursing school friend of her aunt. Only later did he wonder whether she had done so deliberately to avoid his saying something that would inflame her uncle.

Catherine was wearing the fancy dress she had bought at Garfinckels expressly for this party. It was three-quarter length, long-sleeved, wine red, with a beaded top. She and Laura thought it extremely elegant. McGrath agreed though he preferred the black dress she had worn at Normandie Farm. Wisely, he had not said so.

Three days later, sitting in his office at Georgetown after meeting with several students, McGrath recalled both dresses. True, the red one was elegant, and in it Catherine looked most attractive, if older and more chic. But the black dress was sexier and McGrath, being a man, would opt for that look five days out of six.

Daydreaming about Catherine and her wardrobe, he was brought back to reality by a firm knock on the door, which was open. Standing in the doorway was an air force brigadier general. Instinctively, McGrath stood up and motioned for the officer to come in and sit down.

"Colonel McGrath, my name is Hawkins, Milo Hawkins. I work in OP&P and I'm here to make you an offer." The general was nothing if not blunt.

Surprised, McGrath was also perplexed. Why would an air force general come to see him? Generals had better things to do than call upon mid-ranking Guard officers. As to the offer, would not a letter have sufficed?

Instead of revealing to McGrath why he had come, Hawkins engaged in a monologue about the air force. He talked about Vandenberg and his goal of bringing the service back up to strength. He mentioned the B–36 and the vision Curtis LeMay had for SAC. He spoke of leadership and the need for the air force to have more career officers with combat experience. This last subject gave McGrath a hint at the reason why Hawkins had appeared at his door.

"We're calling up reserve and Guard officers to meet the requirements for qualified pilots."

McGrath stayed quiet, content to let the brigadier do the talking.

"I'm here to offer you a permanent commission in the air force, with the rank of full colonel and good prospects for a star."

Now McGrath did speak, though without visible emotion. He wanted Hawkins to discern neither desire nor disapproval. "And what do I have to do?"

"We want you back in the service. We're looking for someone to go to Korea for four months, fly combat in the F–86, and come back and tell us, off the record, what the score is. How good is the MiG? What are their tactics? What are we doing right? What are we doing wrong. How capable is the Sabre? We need an unfiltered report, from someone who knows. General McCreedy thinks you're the man for the job."

"I'm flattered." But again, and purposely so, McGrath gave no hint of his reaction.

"There's a real shooting war going on out there." Milo Hawkins then shook his head and continued speaking, "Granted, it's small time stuff. But we can use it to learn, to get ready for the big one."

SEVEN

McGrath had no intention of accepting Milo Hawkins' offer. McGrath liked the academic life. He enjoyed teaching. He felt intellectually challenged by students, and he found fulfillment in research. Why trade this for a career in the military where reflection was rare and discussion unwelcome? True, military life could be rewarding. Comrades were many. Pride and purpose were evident. Honor was valued. Moreover, medical care was provided and retirement pay was secure. And the air force possessed high performance aircraft, which McGrath enjoyed piloting. But he could still fly them and remain a university professor by staying in the Air National Guard. To him, at Georgetown, he had the best of both worlds.

However, McGrath had another, more compelling reason to turn down the general's offer. Truth be told, he felt no obligation to fight in Korea. He had fought once before, in the Big War. Eight years ago when his time to serve had come, McGrath had responded. Then, with the war won, he had moved on. Now he felt others should do their duty. He had done his.

Politely, McGrath told Milo Hawkins that he was not interested in going to Korea. He said that he was content where he was and that he had no desire to make the air force a career, despite the prospect of making general.

"Besides, General Hawkins, there are plenty of pilots with combat experience who could do this job. Why select me?"

"Because you're the one we want," replied Hawkins. "General McCreedy will be disappointed."

"I'm sorry to hear that. I have great respect for the general. He's a fine officer."

Milo Hawkins made no effort to persuade McGrath. Hawkins believed such offers were made just once. If they were rejected, so be it. Anyone unwilling to accept assignments from senior commanders were not, in Hawkins' mind, the kind of officer the air force needed. If a general wanted you to do something, you did it. That's how the air force conducted business. Milo Hawkins believed this to be an entirely proper and effective modus operandi.

Upon leaving McGrath's office General Hawkins left the Georgetown campus, driving across Key Bridge into Virginia, then south to the Pentagon and its very large parking lot. Ten minutes later he was reporting to General McCreedy that Lieutenant Colonel McGrath had declined the officer or, as Hawkins put it, "had chosen not to serve."

"I'm not surprised," said McCreedy. "I didn't think it would work."

"I've prepared a list of seven other candidates, sir. Any one of them would seem to fit the bill. They're all qualified pilots with combat experience."

"No, I wanted McGrath. Crazy idea actually. Put the list away, Milo. Maybe we'll haul it out down the road. But for now let's drop it."

Upon Milo Hawkins' departure from the university, McGrath remained in his office, reviewing what had just occurred: a general officer had offered him a promotion and a combat command. In times past he would have jumped at either. Now neither were of interest. He was a civilian. Military life was behind him. And he wished to focus on the present. His father once had told him that men often seek to relive successes they once enjoyed. John McGrath had gone on to say that an individual's energy was better employed targeting the future. McGrath had followed his father's advice. Rarely did he mention his aerial exploits.

As McGrath had no desire to repeat these exploits, he had no hesitation in declining General Hawkins' offer. Often McGrath would make decisions quickly. He considered this to be acting decisively. A brief assessment of the situation would be followed by an immediate decision. He took pride in this practice and held in low esteem those who avoided decisions or took forever to reach them. And once a decision had been made McGrath rarely engaged in second-guessing.

He was about to do just that. Once Hawkins left, McGrath was planning to review his notes for a course he would teach in the spring. Instead, and unexpectedly, he was pondering his decision to marry Catherine Caldwell.

She was, he realized, still young, a college student, someone who had yet to make her way in the world. Older than she, he already had embarked upon a career. He knew what he wanted. She did not. McGrath turned to one of his favorite books, the dictionary, and looked up the word "rash." Reading "tending to act too hastily or without due consideration," McGrath questioned whether this characterized his proposal of marriage. He recognized he had known Catherine but four months since the semester began in September. True, they had talked often, but the amount of time spent together had not been substantial. McGrath asked himself if he was acting wisely. Was he ready for marriage? Was Catherine? Was she the girl with whom he should spend a lifetime? For a moment McGrath concluded he was unsure of the answers. Marriage was forever, and not lightly entered. He knew he needed to be certain.

That's when the doubt disappeared. McGrath wanted Catherine to be his wife. He wanted her in his life. Wisely, McGrath decided that love was not the product of analysis. Rather love was a feeling, an unexplained desire to which he should give in. So he did. Rightly or wrongly, he told himself he loved Catherine Caldwell. Dispel doubt, dispense with second thoughts. He would marry this girl and, if they did not live happily ever after, they would do well together and find in each other ample amounts of companionship and love.

Satisfied that marriage to Catherine was the proper course, McGrath turned to the subject he had planned to consider. This was the course for next semester, which began in mid-January, now less than three weeks away. The course was entitled *New Perspectives on the American Revolution*. This title drew the inevitable query, first from Roger O'Boyle.

"So what exactly are the new perspectives?"

"Do you want my public answer, or the truth?"

"I'd prefer the latter," replied the Jesuit, who was smiling.

"I haven't any idea." McGrath spoke in deadpan fashion.

"So why the title?" O'Boyle now was laughing.

"To jazz it up, to give it a contemporary flair."

"I'd call that a bit unnecessary. The American Revolution is pretty jazzy by itself."

"I'd call it marketing. You and I know the revolution is pretty darn interesting. But your average Georgetown University student doesn't."

"True enough."

"And it's working. Twenty-eight students have signed up."

"I'm impressed."

"Actually, I do have a plan to make the course a little different."

McGrath explained that each lecture—there would be thirteen—would focus upon an individual whose life story would lead to an explanation of a key feature of the revolution. McGrath would begin with Edmund Burke. The Englishman's life would shed light on and lead to a discussion of the Enlightenment, the set of ideas that provided the revolution's philosophical underpinnings. Josiah Wedgewood's career would characterize the rise of industry and the middle class that began late in the eighteenth century. Lord Jeffrey Amherst's story would set the stage for 1776 by focusing on the wars with France that established Britain's control of the American continent.

"And what of the revolution itself?"

"I'm glad you asked. The life of John Adams provides the American perspective. For the British perspective I'm looking at either Charles Townsend or Lord North; I haven't decided which."

"And what about the actual war, the battles?"

"For that I'm considering Gentleman Johnny Burgoyne, whose defeat at Saratoga convinced the French to intervene. And for the rebels, Colonel William Smallwood."

"Who?"

"William Smallwood. He commanded the Maryland regiment that was part of the Continental army. It fought hard and well throughout the war."

"I'm sure it did. But what about Washington?"

"Oh, there's enough out there about George. I thought Smallwood or maybe Nathaniel Greene would make it more interesting."

"That's it!"

"What?"

"That's it. That's the new perspective. A course about the American Revolution that pays scant attention to George Washington."

"Well, I was planning to mention him."

"That's good. I'm sure Martha will be glad." O'Boyle then turned professional. "How do you plan to conclude this course? Who's the last individual and what does he represent?"

"I'm going to end with James Madison and the Constitutional Convention. They're just as much a part of the story as Burgoyne and Saratoga."

"And a very good place to stop."

"So what do you think?"

"Truthfully," now O'Boyle spoke as friend and colleague, "I think it sounds terrific. I wish you luck, which you will not need. There are going to be twenty-eight students in this college who will learn something next semester. So I say three cheers for you."

The National Bank of Washington stood prominently at the corner of M Street NW and Wisconsin Avenue in the heart of Georgetown. Conservatively styled, the bank was several stories high, unlike many of its neighbors. The resulting impression was of strength and durability, appropriate for a financial institution. To this bank McGrath walked following his conversation with O'Boyle. Through the university's main gates, down cobblestoned O Street, across 34th Street, then right on Wisconsin past Billy Martin's Tavern where he and Roger often dined. The walk took less than fifteen minutes. Given the cold December day, McGrath welcomed the warmth inside the bank, where he withdrew fifty-five dollars, his self-imposed allowance for the week. This would cover food, both groceries and eating out, and sundry bills for which he needed cash, such as dry cleaning and gasoline for the DeSoto.

Despite the cold, he decided to take a walk before returning to the university. He crossed Wisconsin Avenue and turned left, intending to meander up to Q Street before heading back to campus, essentially completing a large square. Halfway up Wisconsin was a movie theater. McGrath saw what was playing and chuckled. The film was *Twelve O'Clock High*, with Gregory Peck. It told the story of a brigadier general in World War II who takes over a failing B–17 group and whips it into shape, at great cost to himself. McGrath wanted to see the movie but decided to wait: he had had enough of brigadier generals for a while.

Walking beyond the theater, thinking about both Gregory Peck and Milo Hawkins, McGrath passed a small jewelry store. Something in the window caught his attention, triggering an immediate reaction. He realized he had not given Catherine an engagement ring. McGrath was embarrassed that he had forgotten. He wondered whether Catherine had noticed. Probably. How sweet of her not to say anything. McGrath looked at his watch. He needed to be back at Georgetown in twenty minutes. This meant there was plenty of time to buy the ring. He would then surprise his bride-to-be at dinner. They were dining this evening at Decatur Place. The purpose was to discuss plans for the wedding, though McGrath assumed he would have little to contribute. Catherine and her aunt were in charge. He felt like he needed simply to show up. But it was dear of the girl to pretend he had a vote. The ring would not change that, but likely would add sparkle to the evening.

Pleased with himself, McGrath went into the shop. Never having purchased fine jewelry, he felt out of place. Nevertheless, he persevered. He had noticed two rings in the window that seemed suitable and expected to buy one of them, assuming the price was reasonable. McGrath thought he would spend no more than ten minutes in the store.

However, McGrath had not reckoned with Daniel Gottheim, the owner of the shop. Gottheim was from Czechoslovakia. He had spent forty-four years in the jewelry business and considered the purchase of a precious stone akin to drinking fine wine. It was not to be rushed. Subtleties of color and cut, heritage and shape, were to be examined and appreciated.

From the window display Gottheim took the two rings McGrath had identified. He explained the quality of a diamond—for these were diamond rings—was based on color, clarity, cutting proportions, and carat. This last criterion, McGrath learned, was a measure of weight, not to be confused with size. Diamonds, Gottheim explained, were select-ed for wedding and engagement rings because they were considered indestructible, as true love is supposed to be. Such rings were worn on the third finger of the left hand where a vein ran directly to the heart. This analogy Gottheim did not have to explain, though he did tell McGrath that the ring as a symbol of eternal love had begun with the ancient Egyptians, who considered the circle a reminder that love has no beginning and no end.

McGrath found what Gottheim had to say genuinely interesting. But he wished to buy a ring and return to campus. So he interrupted a discourse by Gottheim about how, in the eighteenth century, the dia-mond engagement ring had become de rigueur, and said to the jewel-er that it was time to make a purchase.

Of the two rings, one was truly stunning. The diamond sat in an open mount supported by six prongs, a setting invented by Tiffany that allowed the fullest amount of light to enter the stone. Gottheim said this ring was of the finest quality. McGrath expected the price to be high, and it was. The ring cost $2,750. This was far beyond what McGrath could afford. So he settled for the other one. Next to the first ring, it looked skimpy. But by itself the diamond shone, enhanced in appearance by the simplicity of cut and fullness of color. McGrath liked the ring. He thought it pretty and hoped Catherine would be pleased.

She was. In fact she was thrilled, though not at first. McGrath had been late, thus spoiling Catherine's surprise, which was to have dinner on the table when he arrived. Dinner was not a gourmet meal, but Catherine had labored diligently to prepare something she hoped McGrath would enjoy. Dinner consisted of baked chicken with rice, along with green beans and a walnut apple salad. The recipes had come from the Fanny Farmer cookbook that Catherine had found in McGrath's kitchen. Catherine had followed instructions precisely and had produced a commendable meal, but not one that improved while in the oven awaiting McGrath. When finally they ate, McGrath, having apologized for being late, wisely praised the food.

Catherine had set the table, including two candles she relit when dinner was served, having done so initially when McGrath was due to appear. She also had put on some music, selecting records of Jo Stafford and Frank Sinatra that McGrath had in his collection. The mood thus was romantic, even more so given what Catherine was wearing. She had on a green silk dress that, in fit and style, hugged her slim figure. Her red hair was pulled back, held with two combs that, he later learned, had belonged to her mother. Small emerald earrings sparkled in the candlelight. Once Catherine took off her apron, the image was of a beautiful young woman intent on pleasing her man.

McGrath noticed, and liked what he saw. But while he complimented how she looked he again apologized for being late. Catherine appreciated both comments. When she realized the meal itself was not ruined, she relaxed and began to enjoy herself, listening to the sweet sounds coming back from McGrath's record player. That's when he took out the ring, placing the small felt box Gottheim had given him on a clean plate near where Catherine, who was clearing the table, was sitting. Upon her return she immediately knew what the box contained. Her excitement was evident as she opened it. Upon seeing the ring

Catherine beamed, telling McGrath several times that the ring was "lovely, absolutely perfect."

Before Catherine could put the ring on her finger, McGrath stood up and came to her side. She was staring at the stone, overcome with such emotion that the diamond remained in the box, far from its intended home. McGrath took hold of the ring, kissed Catherine on the forehead, and slipped the ring upon the appropriate finger of her left hand. He told her he loved her and would do so "'til the end of time." Her response was a wave of feelings she never before had experienced. Overwhelmed, she felt triumphant, complete as a woman. Officially, and willingly, she now belonged to McGrath. She was happier than she ever had expected to be.

After dinner they made love. For her part, Catherine was wildly passionate. Her actions were uninhibited, her body given up entirely to physical pleasure. In the bedroom at Decatur Place she became an erotic fantasy for McGrath, who responded completely to her needs and his own. Yet throughout the evening, despite moments of delicious ecstasy, McGrath remained self aware, conscious of a new responsibility. This lovely creature no longer was just a female to pursue. She was, and would become, his partner in life. McGrath knew he would continue to bed her. But he also knew that he would need to comfort her, to guide her in life, to listen and react, to encourage her to flourish as an individual. Never had McGrath envisioned such duties. Now that he did, he thought at first he would find them overpowering, but he did not. Glancing across the bed at Catherine, who lay naked except for a diamond ring, McGrath welcomed the job of taking care of this young girl, a woman really who had become part of his existence.

Well before midnight, Catherine asked McGrath a question he had not expected. McGrath thought she would enquire about the honeymoon. Specifically, he had anticipated a question about New York. They were considering a trip to Italy in June, once the semester had ended. But for April, McGrath had suggested a two-day visit to Manhattan. Catherine had agreed, but still unsettled were travel plans, hotel arrangements, and what Broadway show to see. However, instead of a trip in the future to New York, Catherine spoke to McGrath's past in England.

"I feel I know you pretty well, at least parts of you. But there's a gap missing and I want you to fill it in for me."

"What do you mean?"

"I mean about the war."

"What do you want to know? There's really not much to say. And most of it I suspect you already know. I was in the Army Air Corps, served in England, and flew a fighter plane."

"But I don't know and I want to." Catherine's next words were an entreaty. "I need to know about all of it."

"It was years ago, and doesn't matter now."

"Yes it does."

"Why?"

"Because it was an important part of your life. It took up several years and your life is something I need to know about. I've never asked before, so please tell me."

At first McGrath pondered the request, then acceded to it. Lying in bed he found it difficult to resist whatever Catherine wanted. Equally compelling, he realized she was justified in wanting to know of his role in the great conflict. He had spent four years in the service of his country and, though he wished them not to be the highlight of his life, he could not deny their importance. So he spoke at length.

"I graduated from college in 1942 and right away went into the air corps. I had talked to an army recruiter earlier and he told me to finish college and come back to him when I did. He was an older guy and was looking out for me. So in mid-June of '42 I came back, enlisted, and was sent down to Randolph Field in Texas for primary and basic flight training, where I did pretty well. I wasn't first in my class, but I wasn't last either.

"August 1, 1942 was a big day in my life. I soloed for the first time. The plane was a PT–13 biplane with open, tandem cockpits. My instructor, Lieutenant Tauber, hopped out of the plane after we had done some landings and said to take her up. So I did. What a wonderful feeling, a truly great thrill. The sense of control, the beauty of what you see, well, it was just a terrific experience, one I'll never forget. And the good news is that I nailed a perfect three-point landing, which made me feel good, as I'm sure it did Tauber.

"After primary we moved to basic. We learned how to fly on instruments, did a lot of cross-country navigation, learned radio procedures, did more acrobatics and generally became decent pilots. This was challenging, and not everyone passed the test. One of my buddies, Peter Nummy, flunked out and became a B–17 bombardier. He was killed on a raid just before the war ended.

"By now we're at Kelley Field, still in Texas, and the army assigns you to fighters, bombers, or transports. I picked bombers 'cause I thought the multi-engine experience might be useful later on. So the army, in its wisdom, assigns me to fighters.

"At Kelley we started to fly high performance aircraft, at least in comparison to what we had been flying. We also started to learn tactics and something about gunnery. The daily routine became more serious and there were constant reminders we were in the military. Some fellas accepted that, even liked it. Others rebelled. I tried to ignore it and concentrate on the job, which was to learn how to fly and fight.

"We graduated, got our wings, and were commissioned in the United States Army. I was assigned to the 44th Fighter Squadron, flying P–39s down at Eglin in Florida. This really was a form of advanced training and when we finished we were supposed to be combat ready, which of course we weren't.

"I then took a boat ride to England, aboard the *Queen Mary* no less, and true to form it was raining when we arrived. Then a train ride to a place called Turner Hall, where we exchanged the P–39s for the P–47 Thunderbolt. And a good thing we did. The Airacobra wasn't up to the job and would have gotten us all killed.

"The Thunderbolt was a terrific aircraft. Rugged, with eight guns, it could hammer an opponent. True, it climbed like a dog but it outdove everything in the sky and, if you knew what you were doing, would always bring you home safe and sound.

"Only problem was range. Like the Spitfire it had short legs, even with auxiliary fuel tanks, which we'd dump once the enemy was sighted. The continent of Europe is still littered with aluminum fuel tanks made in the U.S.A.

"By this time it's late 1943, and I'm getting comfortable with what I'm supposed to be doing. I've flown a bunch of missions, shot at a few Germans, and have been promoted. But the air war is not going particularly well.

"The British are bombing at night, and we're doing it during the day. The theory was that our B–17s and B–24s would conduct daylight precision bombing and hit targets of true military value rather than trying to wipe out cities, which is what RAF Bomber Command was attempting to do. The problem was that our bombers couldn't survive raids into Germany without fighter escort, and the P–47 couldn't fly that far. The Luftwaffe was still strong, and without fighters to fend off the Jerries, the bombers were getting hammered.

"Enter the Mustang. Early in 1944 we get a new airplane, the P–51 Mustang, powered by the Merlin engine developed by Rolls Royce but built under license here by Packard. Well, the Mustang turns out to be the airplane we need. It's fast, maneuverable, a delight to fly, and from England it can fly to Berlin and back. Herman Goering said that when he saw Mustangs over Berlin he knew the game was up.

"The powers that be then decided I should leave the 44th and take command of the 27th Fighter Squadron, which I do in February 1944. It's based at Falmer, which is a real nice, pre-war RAF station. On the tarmac when I arrive are sixteen brand new 51s, with blue spinners and blue tails. What a sight! More aircraft arrived in the next two days and after a few test hops we're ready to go. Our first mission was escorting a bunch of B–24s to Wilhelmshaven. We lost one Mustang but shot down two Messerschmitts and damaged two. It was a heck of a scrap but the boys did well. It sort of set the tone for the rest of the war. We'd lose a plane or two. The Luftwaffe would lose a lot more. By early 1945 the Germans were basically finished, at least in the air. In May when the Krauts finally surrendered, the 27th had done well. We flew 302 missions and destroyed 209 enemy aircraft. That's in the air. We knocked out another 67 on the ground. All in all, a pretty good record. We didn't get a lot of medals, but we did our job.

"And then we came home. Actually, we stayed in England for another three months. We gave Falmer back to the RAF and another squadron took our Mustangs over to Germany. A train ride to Liverpool, and to complete the circle, another ride on the *Queen Mary*, this time going west. Into New York harbor, past the Statue of Liberty, what a welcome sight! And onto U.S. soil on August 31st. The Army Air Corps was getting smaller so they were happy to let me leave, which I did. I spent two months at home with my parents, and then, with the G.I. Bill in my pocket, headed out to South Bend. Came to Georgetown three years later, a freshly minted Ph.D. And the rest you know."

Catherine had listened carefully. She found what McGrath had to say interesting but incomplete. He had given her a chronology, which she appreciated. But she wanted more. Catherine wanted to hear about personal things. Who were his friends? What were his feelings? What was his day-to-day life like? Did he meet any girls? Was England what he expected? Facing danger, how did he cope?

Catherine decided to address this last issue first.

"Were you afraid? People were getting killed, people you knew. And the Germans were shooting at you. That must be awful."

"Everyone was afraid, at least I think they were. But you learned to control your fear. You had a job to do and you did it. That's what all the training was about. Once in the cockpit you were too busy to worry about fear. That came earlier, or in my case, later. I would have the shakes after a mission. When I was alone, once the adrenaline had stopped."

"What would you do?"

"I'd just lay down in bed and feel the fear, like something physical. But it wouldn't last."

"Why not?"

"I wouldn't let it. I had too much to do. And I figured I've always been lucky and that my luck would hold."

"Were you afraid over Berlin?"

"What?" McGrath was curious as to why Catherine had mentioned the German capital.

"Berlin. I'm told you once took on half the German air force by yourself over Berlin."

"And who told you that?"

Catherine smiled and kissed McGrath. "You forget, my uncle is an air force general and I happen to know a former technical sergeant who now runs a deli and is a big fan of yours."

"Unlike your uncle."

"No, Uncle Mike is fine. He's come around. He now thinks you're more than suitable. And my Aunt Laura thinks you're wonderful."

"I really like her."

"Me too. But enough about my family. Did you really attack the Germans?"

McGrath recalled the event and told Catherine the story, recounting that on March 4, 1944 the Eighth Air Force struck Berlin. Jimmy Doolittle, its commander, sent 730 B–17s and B–24s deep into Germany. Losses were heavy; 69 bombers—690 men—did not return. But the mission demonstrated the long reach of American air power, and its strength.

McGrath's squadron flew cover over the Third Division's B–17s. Intercepted over Dummer Lake, several B–17s were destroyed despite the efforts of the 27th Fighter Squadron. The sky was filled with parachutes and burning aircraft. McGrath had destroyed one Me–109, knocking it down after a long chase that brought him to the suburbs of Berlin at two hundred feet. With his wingman nowhere in sight, McGrath climbed for altitude, aiming for a group of aircraft to the northwest, thinking they were B–17s. They were Messerschmitts.

"So I could run and probably get shot down. Or I could attack and keep 'em busy. So I waded right in. I shot at anything I could and they got in each other's way. Things started to get dicey and I figured I needed to leave, which turned out to be not so easy. But one of the Krauts made a mistake. I got some hits on him and dove, throttle rammed forward. I was really moving and glad to leave Germany behind."

"That was very brave of you."

"No, not really."

"That's not what Max Hopkins thinks, or my uncle. They think you're a true American hero."

"There were many heroes that day, Catherine, but I wasn't one of them. I was just doing what I was paid to do."

"Well, I think they're right. And I'll tell you something else I'm sure of."

"Which is?"

Catherine took hold of McGrath and kissed him. "You're my hero, and I love you very much."

EIGHT

New Year's Day was not a holiday McGrath favored. The day off was nice but unnecessary, while the prior evening's celebration struck him as artificial. Many times he had attended New Year's Eve parties where people stayed up too late and drank too much. He preferred Christmas, although he liked Thanksgiving best.

He enjoyed Thanksgiving because it was uniquely American. Moreover, he found appealing the concept of setting aside a day to appreciate his country's good fortune. On this particular Thursday in November McGrath again realized that he personally had much to be thankful for. He had survived the war. He had his health, he had an interesting job, and he had parents who had taught him right from wrong. And now he had "a woman friend," as he had described Catherine to John and Eleanor McGrath. All in all, McGrath felt God had been good to him, and He had.

Thanksgiving 1950 had been spent with Catherine at the McCreedy home. Located at 3562 McComb Street, NW, the residence of General and Mrs. McCreedy was large and attractive, if in need of a paint job. Its steeply pitched roof, asymmetrical facade, bay windows, and wraparound porch marked the house in the Queen Anne style of Victorian architecture. Mike McCreedy had purchased the house in 1933. It turned out to be a wise investment, both financially and domestically. Regarding the latter Laura loved the house. Over time she had made it a warm and truly comfortable home.

Laura McCreedy was responsible for McGrath spending the holiday with Catherine and her family. Midway through November the aunt suggested to the niece that she invite her "beau" to Thanksgiving. Catherine did so and to her surprise, McGrath accepted.

"I thought you'd be spending Thanksgiving at home with your parents."

"Usually I do."

"Won't your parents miss you?"

"Yes, I'm sure they will. It's the first Thanksgiving, except for the war, when I won't be there."

"Are you sure you want to, you won't mind?" Catherine was hoping for the answer she received.

"I'm sure. There's give and take involved here. And it's my turn now. Yours will come."

Catherine understood McGrath's message. "Mine will be in December, late December?"

"Correct, my love."

"I've never spent Christmas in New York."

"You'll have a good time, I promise."

"As you will on Thanksgiving."

He did. Laura McCreedy prepared a wonderful meal and the general was on his best behavior. Served late in the afternoon, dinner was sumptuous yet traditional: roast turkey, cranberry sauce, stuffing, sweet potatoes, corn, and pumpkin pie. McGrath enjoyed the food but found odd Laura's second vegetable. Brussels sprouts were not something he liked. The McCreedys loved them, as did Catherine. McGrath never had Brussels sprouts on Thanksgiving and hoped he never would again. There were seven on his plate. He ate three immediately and moved those remaining around his dish, hoping to give the appearance that he had eaten many more. It didn't work. General McCreedy noticed and was about to make an amusing remark but withheld comment upon seeing his niece silently plead for restraint.

Instead, Mike McCreedy asked his guest about the war in Korea.

"Tell me, my boy, do you think the war will be over by Christmas?"

"General MacArthur thinks so, General."

"True enough. Never liked the man, a truly pompous fellow. But what do you think?"

"I think we should be worried about the Chinese."

"Hmm." The general's reaction, in voice and demeanor, suggested he agreed. But he wished to test McGrath. "And why is that?"

"Well, if I were the Chinese and I saw an American army approaching my borders, led by a general whose words conveyed contempt and hostility, I'd be very nervous, and do something about it."

"And what would you do?"

"I'm not sure."

"Come now, son, you're a historian, comfortable with strategy and the scope of events." Politely, McCreedy pressed forward. "So what would you do?"

"Okay. I'd send a message to the Americans, secretly of course, telling them to back off. Or face the consequences."

"Hmm." Again, McCreedy was conveying his agreement. "And what would they be?"

"Sir?"

"The consequences. What would they be, were we to continue to advance?"

"General, the Chinese have one very large army. I don't know if it's any good, but I suspect they're not afraid to use it."

"I suspect you're right, young man. I think they would. So what does Mr. Truman do then, if the Chinese attack?"

"We can take 'em on, General McCreedy. We beat the Japanese. I assume we can defeat the Chinese."

"Yes, we can, but at great cost."

McGrath then decided to shift the discussion. As a teacher he knew the best way to do that was to ask a question.

"And President Truman, has he done the right thing?"

Laura McCreedy glanced at her husband. Her message was unmistakable. She was silently telling him to avoid intemperate remarks.

"Well, as my wife will tell you, I'm not a fan of the little man, nor of his cronies. He's let the armed forces run down. He's soft on the Red threat here at home. He's created problems by forcing us to have Negroes side by side with us—it's the right decision but the wrong time. He's given in to the unions and ignored big business at a time when it's big business that will get us out of the economic mess we're in. So no, I'm no fan of Harry S. Truman. I suppose you are."

McGrath ignored this last remark. "But he's fought the Reds. In Greece, in Europe, and now in Korea."

"True enough, but he's simply not presidential material. Anybody can see that."

"Perhaps not, General McCreedy, but he is the president."

"God help us, he is indeed. Whatever was Roosevelt thinking? I worry what Truman will do next, here at home and in Korea, especially if the Chinese move south. I've fought in two world wars. I'm not anxious to fight a third." Here McCreedy paused, becoming the warrior he was. "Unless I have to."

No such discussion took place at Christmas dinner. Neither President Truman nor the war in Korea was mentioned. Instead, family matters were discussed. Eleanor McGrath was particularly interested in the wedding. Not having a daughter, she was eager to hear what Catherine and her aunt were planning. Of great interest to McGrath's mother was the wedding dress.

At first Catherine had chosen something unorthodox. Seen at Garfinckel's, the dress, by Christian Dior, was a chiffon mermaid with a cowl-draped empire bodice, a sequined bust line, and flounced cuffs. Available in ivory or white, the dress was dazzling. Catherine thought it elegant yet romantic, which it was. Laura McCreedy did not disagree, but convinced her niece that the dress was more suited for a fancy charity ball than a wedding. Reluctantly, Catherine agreed. She then selected a one-piece corset princess-line dress, white with lace and a cathedral train. Worn with long gloves and a lace choker it was lovely, if less sensual. Laura described the dress as "absolutely perfect" while Catherine, slightly less enthusiastic, called it "absolutely lovely." It was, she believed, a near perfect balance of the traditional and avant-garde, of glamour and propriety. That the dress cost $275 made Catherine believe it was also a balance of fiscal extravagance and restraint.

Other aspects of the wedding were brought to the attention of the groom's parents. The marriage would take place at Holy Trinity Church in downtown Washington. The Rev. Roger Francis O'Boyle, S.J. would officiate. Maid of honor would be Cynthia Stewart. Best man was to be McGrath's younger brother, Timothy, who was in law school at Fordham. The wedding reception was planned for the Chevy Chase Club on Connecticut Avenue, just north of the District/Maryland line. The rehearsal dinner, to be paid for by John McGrath, would be at the Shoreham Hotel.

Catherine and her aunt wanted to have a wedding with many guests. McGrath preferred a smaller affair. Thus a large wedding was decided upon. Invitations for 240 people were ordered from the printer. What McGrath did not realize was that weddings, despite the focus upon bride and groom, were also events for parents—in this case aunt and uncle—who wished to share their happiness with relatives and friends.

While Eleanor McGrath and her future daughter-in-law were discussing the wedding dress, John McGrath and his son were in the family Chrysler heading to the hardware store. Their purpose was to buy a much-needed stepladder in order to patch a crack in the dining room ceiling. But their conversation had little to do with home repair.

"You know, son, I'm very proud of you."

In reply McGrath said nothing. He sensed that his father had more to say.

"And it's not just what you did during the war, splendid as that was. No, it's about what you're doing now, being a teacher."

"I thought you wanted me to go to law school or become a banker like you are."

"I did. But I guess Tim will be the lawyer in the family."

"Is he doing well? At law school, I mean."

"Apparently so. He's made law review so he'll find a good job once he graduates."

"Good for him. He's a great kid."

"He is indeed. But I'm a bit worried."

"About what?"

"Not about Tim. About you."

"Me?"

"Yes, you."

"About Catherine, about our getting married?"

"No, she's fine. A nice girl—young, but a very nice girl. And quite pretty, I might add. Reminds me of a young Rita Hayworth. I wish you only happiness."

"Then what?"

"I worry about your income. University types don't make much money."

"Enough to get by."

"That's my point. It's enough to get by, but not enough to enjoy or pay for the finer things in life."

"Such as?"

"Such as a nice house, like the one your mother and I live in. Nice vacations once in a while. And eventually a good education for your kids."

"I'll do all right."

"I know you think that. It's just that I'm concerned. The problem is that kids today make career decisions early on, when money doesn't matter. But careers determine income and later on, when money does matter, when you need it, not just for yourself but for your wife and children, you find yourself in a job that doesn't pay enough. You can't afford the things you need. Money looks different at the age of forty-five than when you're twenty-five.

"But at the same time, I'm proud of you. I truly am. My son went out and got a Ph.D. and now teaches at Georgetown. Those are real accomplishments."

"I'm doing what I like, Dad. And I think I'm pretty good at it."

"So you're happy?"

"Yes, I think so."

"So I shouldn't be worried?"

"Not really."

What McGrath did not realize was that his father would worry nonetheless. Parents worry. They worry about their children's health, about their happiness, about their life. And they worry regardless of their child's age. When the youngster becomes an adult, they worry about the kid having a good job, about the child's finances, and importantly, about the son or daughter finding a spouse, a partner with whom to share life's journey. Parents worry because of love. They wish only the best for their children. John McGrath loved his son. So he worried.

And I think I'm pretty good at it. That's what his son had just said. The elder McGrath had little doubt that it was true. The boy had been successful at everything he attempted. In athletics, particularly tennis, his son excelled. Academically strong, he was outgoing and personable and, by the looks of Catherine Caldwell, successful with the opposite sex. And then there was England. The air force did not turn over command of P–51 squadrons to non-achievers. Yes, his son was blessed with success, abundantly so.

So the father worried anew. John McGrath thought such success led to great difficulty once failure appeared. He worried that his son might not be able to handle lack of success. Failure, the father believed, was an inevitable component of life. Some folks experienced more than others but no one was immune. However, failure had its beneficial attributes. It made success more appreciated. It was humbling. It led, or should lead, to reexamination and further effort. John McGrath had witnessed many successful people cope poorly once their success vanished. How would his own son handle failure?

He had another concern as well, one he expressed only to Eleanor. Son Tim was intelligent and hardworking like his brother. But Tim possessed a dash of humility that his brother did not. John McGrath detected in his older child a self-confidence that at times crossed over into arrogance. Sometimes this was reflected in a simple remark, other times in a tone of voice or in expectations. The arrogance troubled John McGrath. He found it unattractive and believed it hindered careers and relationships. Eleanor thought it a natural extension of the constant success her elder son had enjoyed. She didn't like it either, but told her husband that both boys were honest and exercised good judgment, qualities that would temper any negative traits they possessed.

Once the errand to the hardware store was completed McGrath returned home. After lunch, he and Catherine changed clothes, for they were to spend an evening in Manhattan. McGrath would wear his charcoal gray pinstriped suit he had brought with him from Washington. Catherine wore a new silver sheath, a dress with long sleeves and a calf-length skirt. Wistfully Eleanor gazed at the young girl and wondered what it would have been like to have had daughters instead of sons. Taking note of Catherine's youthful figure and attractive dress she thought her son's fiancée looked dramatically beautiful. Her husband thought so too, thinking the boy would be much envied when escorting such a pretty thing into the restaurant and theater.

McGrath was taking Catherine for a late dinner at the Edwardian Room in the Plaza Hotel. This was to be preceded by a Broadway show. McGrath had no difficulty in acquiring tickets. The problem had been what show to choose.

In late December 1950, Carol Channing was appearing in *Gentlemen Prefer Blondes*. Ethel Merman was on stage in *Call Me Madam*. Rex Harrison was in *Bell, Book, and Candle*. Louis Calhoun was performing *King Lear* while Mary Martin was "washing that man right out of her hair," in *South Pacific*. McGrath decided he and Catherine would see something else. He bought tickets for *Kiss Me Kate* with Anne Jeffreys. McGrath loved the music of Cole Porter and hoped Catherine would as well.

She did. The music was lively and melodious while the lyrics—also by Cole Porter—were catchy and clever. Catherine had never seen a Broadway show on Broadway so attending a live performance at the Shubert Theater on West 44th Street was a thrill. Having seen several shows in New York, McGrath was less easy to impress. Nonetheless, he thoroughly enjoyed the Tony Award-winning musical. He thought Anne Jeffreys was truly talented, if under appreciated. She sang well, looked great, and acted with grace and style. McGrath figured, fame wise, she was outgunned by Channing, Merman, and Martin. As to *Kiss Me Kate,* McGrath marveled how the *Taming of the Shrew* could be the basis for a musical play within a play.

Catherine also found dinner to be a wonderful experience. The Edwardian Room was on the first floor of the hotel, in the corner facing 5th Avenue and 59th Street. The room was neither large nor small. With a tall vaulted ceiling, a formal dining decor in pinks and ivory, and lighting that was dim but sufficient to read the menu, the room conveyed the impression of an English men's club at the turn of the century. Service at the Edwardian Room was excellent. The food was quite good. Catherine had grilled butterflied lamb. McGrath had Lobster Newburg. Both dishes were served with salad and broccoli, the lamb with scalloped potatoes. For dessert McGrath ordered a chocolate soufflé they both found delicious.

During the meal McGrath learned a culinary footnote to his main course. The waiter explained that Lobster Newburg originally was called Lobster Wenber, Mr. Wenber being a favored patron of Delmonico's, where the dish first was served. However, Wenber and Delmonico had a falling out and the name was changed. The waiter, one Joseph Monroney, did not know who Mr. Newburg was or even if there were such a gentleman. Jokingly, McGrath suggested the name might be in honor of the town along the Hudson. A native New Yorker, Monroney did not appreciate the humor. He pointed out that the town of Newburgh was spelled differently than the dish.

Midway through dinner snow began to fall. From inside the Edwardian Room McGrath and Catherine could see the flakes drift downward, glistening from the light of the street lamps. As the snow continued traffic declined and the city lost its characteristic energy, absorbing the snow and becoming a silent beauty, urban in location but quiet like a field in Vermont. A sense of romance pervaded the dining room, aided by the candle and three roses that rested upon their table. Both Catherine and McGrath felt its presence. They welcomed the dreamy, sweet mood it produced.

With dinner over Catherine expected they would head back to Port Washington. They did, but not before McGrath took her on a hansom cab ride. Kept warm by her wool cape and a blanket spread across them both, Catherine snuggled up against McGrath singing softly, "So in Love with You Am I," as the driver steered the carriage through Central Park. Twenty minutes later they emerged from the park at 79th Street to amble down 5th Avenue, soon reaching the Plaza and the end to a memorable ride.

With the snow accumulating, the drive home took longer than usual. It was 1:30 A.M. when McGrath pulled the Chrysler into the driveway. The house was dark, save for a few lights. Once inside they tiptoed upstairs, with McGrath thinking the wooden staircase creaked more than usual. At the top of the stairs McGrath went left to Tim's room. Catherine turned right toward the guest room, which once had been McGrath's. They parted awkwardly, each wishing the sleeping arrangements were different. Eleanor had told her husband, "There will be no monkey business in my house, at least not until the wedding," a decision McGrath and his bride-to-be had to respect. As McGrath fell asleep he mused that while thirty years of age and a combat veteran of the Eighth Air Force, in Port Washington he was still a kid who had to follow house rules laid down by his mother.

In 1950, New Year's Eve fell on a Sunday. Back in Washington McGrath and Catherine were present at a party given by the McCreedys in their home on McComb Street. McGrath had tried to beg off, but Catherine had insisted they attend.

"We must go."

"Yes, I know. I just don't want to. New Year's Eve parties are not my idea of fun."

"It would be rude of us, of you, not to be there. My aunt would be hurt and she wouldn't understand why you didn't come."

"You're right, of course."

Catherine looked at McGrath seductively and blew him a kiss. "Just think of it as part of the give and take."

To McGrath's surprise the party turned out to be pleasant. Many of the guests were military officers and their wives, the former being colleagues of Mike McCreedy at the Pentagon. Senior among them was Hoyt Vandenberg. McGrath avoided him and Milo Hawkins, spending most of the time chatting with civilian friends of Aunt Laura and the general. But Catherine's uncle wanted McGrath to meet Vandenberg, so when bringing a scotch and soda to the air force chief of staff, he corralled McGrath and introduced him to Vandenberg. Pleasantries were exchanged, including congratulations to McGrath on his upcoming marriage. Vandenberg had been well briefed. He knew the story behind each of the guests.

"I gather you're now teaching at Georgetown."

"Yes, sir." Though Vandenberg was in civilian clothes McGrath could imagine the man's blue uniform, each shoulder glistening with four stars. Instinctively, McGrath fell into a subordinate role, and disliked himself for doing so.

They talked about the university and the importance of teaching, about academic standards and the need to mobilize America's brainpower not just in the war against communism but also to keep the country economically prosperous. Vandenberg was a Cold War warrior but he saw beyond that. He felt America's advantage lay upon the twin foundations of freedom and technology. Regarding the latter, he saw education as the key.

"We need smart people, and we need good schools to push them and teach them how to think. We need scientists and linguists," here Vandenberg paused, "and historians and people who can write proper English."

McGrath thought he sounded more like a liberal arts college president than commander of the United States Air Force.

"And we need good people and smart people in the military. And our own schools not just to train them but to educate them. My hope is that one day soon, senior air force officers like myself won't be graduates of West Point. We'll have our own academy, just for the air force. We'll take youngsters from every state of the Union and turn them into officers capable of taking the service into the future."

Mike McCreedy's face broke out into a smile. It appeared, after all, that the chief had read his memorandum.

The next day McGrath arose early despite having stayed late at the McCreedys'. After a breakfast of cornflakes and orange juice he sat down to read the *Washington Post.* The headlines reported a major new Chinese offensive in Korea. The paper also gave coverage to a speech by Secretary of State Dean Acheson warning potential aggressors of America's ability to retaliate as well as Senator Kenneth Wherry's demand that Acheson be replaced given what the senator called "the failure of American diplomacy." On a less combative note the front page reported on the 1950 census. This decennial project estimated the population of the United States to be 152,340,000.

McGrath finished reading the newspaper by 10:15. He planned to work on a new course he'd been contemplating and then attend a basketball game at Georgetown, after which he and Roger O'Boyle were to have dinner.

The basketball game pitted Fordham against LaSalle and was part of an East Coast Catholic College Holiday Basketball tournament. The game was a semi-final contest, Fordham having beaten Villanova and LaSalle knocking off favored St. John's. The winner of the game would meet Boston College in the finals.

The course was an elective he planned to propose to Grafton Donahue for the academic year 1952-53. Entitled *From Dreadnought to Vanguard,* the course would follow the rise and fall of the modern battleship, HMS *Vanguard* being the last such warship to be commissioned. By focusing on the big gun ships McGrath would cover both international relations and military strategy. He would be able to review the origins of the First World War and the arms limitation efforts of the 1920s and '30s. He also would discuss Jutland and Pearl Harbor, battles of historic importance in which battleships played featured roles. The concept was to employ the warship as an avenue for the study of history in the first half of the twentieth century. McGrath thought the course might appeal to students, particularly males. Whether it would appeal to the chairman of the history department, he was less certain. But McGrath knew what other members of the department did not: that Donahue had served in the Coast Guard during World War I and therefore might find the proposed course of interest.

McGrath was reading about the Washington Naval Conference of 1921 when the phone rang. Telephone calls to Decatur Place were unusual so McGrath wondered who it could be. He was surprised to hear the voice of Michael McCreedy.

"You'd better get over here," said the general. "There's been an accident."

McGrath was alarmed as much by the tone of his voice as by the message. "What's happened?"

"Catherine was crossing Wisconsin Avenue and has been hurt badly. Some stupid drunk, left over from New Year's Eve. You'd better come over. Laura's gone to the hospital. I'll wait for you, and we'll go over together."

"I'll be right there."

McGrath drove fast. Around Sheridan Circle, up Massachusetts Avenue, right at the Naval Observatory onto 34th Street. Up the hill, past the red brick schoolhouse, then down, then left at McComb. When he arrived at 3562, General McCreedy was waiting on the sidewalk. Without comment or chitchat they rushed to the hospital.

At Georgetown they went immediately to the emergency room. There they witnessed a scene McGrath never forgot. A doctor had his arm sympathetically around Laura McCreedy's shoulder. She was sobbing. Michael McCreedy went over to his wife who, upon seeing her husband, shrieked in despair, jarring the quiet waiting room that was empty save for a little boy and his mother. The general tightly held onto Laura, who continued to cry.

McGrath just stood there. For an instant he felt intrusive, not part of the private grief the McCreedys were sharing. Then reality came into play. The woman he loved, the girl he was to marry, lay dead in a nearby room. To his surprise he felt no pain, no need to show emotion. He had an unusually strong awareness of his surroundings. He saw and sensed everything in the room, every detail vividly etched in his consciousness. Then the compulsion to see Catherine, to be with her, hit home. He walked past Laura and Mike McCreedy, through swinging doors into the emergency room. Never having been in such a place, he looked about, implanting the image in his memory. A nurse he ignored politely asked him to leave. She then spoke again, by which time McGrath had found Catherine's body. Wisely, the nurse said nothing. Kindly, she closed the curtain in the emergency room stall, enabling McGrath to be alone with the individual who was to have helped define his future.

He looked at her face. It both resembled Catherine and appeared to be someone else. The outline was hers. The color and expression were not. In repose Catherine looked at peace, for McGrath did not see the rest of her body. This lay beneath a gray hospital sheet and would have reminded him of the gruesome remains he saw at Randolph Field when a fellow student pilot cartwheeled upon landing and died horribly, crushed by the wreckage of a once graceful flying machine.

McGrath stayed alone with Catherine for several minutes, then was joined by Laura and the general. The three who were living then spoke of the one who was not. Their voices were hushed; their comments intended to comfort each other. They remained bedside for what they thought a few minutes but was in fact twenty, grappling with the reality of the unexpected, undeserved death. When the nurse reappeared she was accompanied by the priest on duty. He offered condolences. She guided them back into the waiting room. Hospital staff, having certified death, then removed Catherine from the emergency room, carting her body downstairs to the mortuary.

Instead of a wedding at Holy Trinity Church, McGrath attended a funeral mass that was held three days after Catherine's death. Roger O'Boyle conducted a service rich in emotion and tradition. To everyone but McGrath what took place in the church was a moving experience, expressing faith in God and love for the deceased. McGrath found the service hollow. He observed the ritual, recited the prayers, and listened to the music. It all rang false.

Walking out into the sunshine at the conclusion of the mass, McGrath was angry. The service had provided neither solace nor answers. In no mood to talk, he spoke only briefly with O'Boyle, avoided Maxwell Hopkins, and cut short a conversation with the McCreedy's. As soon as he could McGrath left the church, and together with his parents, drove in procession with others to the cemetery.

McGrath had dealt with death before. Many times in England he had seen pilots die. Several of them he had known, a few rather well. Their deaths, he believed, had purpose. They had died for a noble cause. Moreover, they were soldiers at war and he expected that not all would return home alive. While he regretted the loss of comrades, once gone, he carried on with his life and his job as though they had not existed.

Catherine's death was different. She was not at war with anyone. She was just a young woman in college, living a life, which, if not dedicated to a great cause, harmed no one and brought pleasure to friends and family. McGrath believed Catherine deserved to live, not die. He could find no purpose in her death, no meaning or lesson. She had been cheated of life, dying before her time. Now, to many Catherine would be forever young. To some this would be bittersweet. McGrath considered it obscene.

NINE

For several weeks after the funeral McGrath diligently met his university obligations. He attended departmental meetings, held office hours, and taught classes, including *New Perspectives on the American Revolution*. Away from Georgetown he continued with the routines of life. McGrath paid bills, shopped for food, had laundry done, and, as before, ate three meals a day. In addition, he paid calls upon the McCreedys, who welcomed him as family. The three dined together at least once a week, usually at the Chevy Chase Club.

McGrath planned to continue life as if nothing unusual had occurred. He had done so once before, during the war, and now expected to do so again. In pursuit of normality McGrath was almost obsessive. "Life goes on," he said, "and one must do whatever one does."

The plan failed. McGrath was unable to put Catherine out of his mind. She was with him everywhere, at all times. He sensed her presence and felt her absence. He spent much time at Decatur Place alone, thinking of her, missing her. More than once, tears would stream down upon his cheeks. Moreover, his anger at her death did not recede. Indeed, it intensified. The effect was to make McGrath bitter. In turn this made him less agreeable as a person, less effective as a teacher. McGrath thought the world had gone to hell, a place he believed it deserved to be.

The problem was that McGrath did not know how to grieve. He did not understand that the death of a loved one is painful, and often unfair. He did not realize that time is required to soften the loss, and that, while life goes on, it is different than before. Nor did McGrath know that the true antidote to death is living. Once a loved one is gone a period of mourning is necessary. Yet to be effective, mourning ultimately must involve reaching out to others, affirming the connection of one human being to another. Honoring the deceased requires more than grief and solitude. It requires a reaffirmation of life.

Come spring McGrath was in need of change. He acknowledged this to Roger O'Boyle, who was concerned for his friend.

"I'm worried about you," said the Jesuit. He and McGrath were alone, following a meeting of the committee on foreign language requirements.

"Oh, I'm alright. I'm coping."

"So you say."

"I just still don't understand it. She didn't just die; she was killed. Why did this happen?"

"I don't know the answer to that." O'Boyle knew that faith in God and in His love were not subjects to which McGrath, given his state of mind, would respond. So he kept them as thoughts, not releasing them as words. "I do know simply that it happened."

"And that I have to accept it?"

"I'm afraid so. Not because it's fair, or just. Simply because it is."

"But it makes me so angry. Nothing in life seems right. It's all simply out of alignment."

"That's because you've suffered a great loss and don't know how to accept it."

"I won't accept it. I'll deal with it, but I won't accept it."

"The question, my friend, is how best to deal with it."

"Your advice would be to accept God's help and understanding." McGrath spoke softly, not wishing to sound sarcastic and thus offend the Jesuit.

"True enough. That's not such a bad approach. It has worked well for many people, for many years."

"And for me?"

"It would work, I suspect, if you wished it to work."

"And if I didn't?"

"Then you must find an alternative."

"I think I have."

"Oh? What is it?"

"I can't say just yet. It's something I've been thinking about. I'll let you know when, and if, it happens . . . which may be quite soon."

"Whatever it is, I wish you well." Then, as a man of the cloth, O'Boyle addressed his friend. "And may God be with you and guide you along the way."

The next morning McGrath felt he did not need God's assistance in finding his destination. He knew where the Pentagon was and how to get there. He arrived early in order to secure a parking space. This also left time for a donut and cup of coffee, which he enjoyed in a cafeteria bustling with men in uniform. He wondered what their lives were like. And he wondered if any of them were curious as to who he was and why he was there.

Upstairs, above the cafeteria, Lt. General Michael McCreedy had left the office of the air force chief of staff, where he and Hoyt Vandenberg had reviewed contingency plans for Korea, in case the Chinese overran U.N. positions. Though that seemed unlikely now that Ridgeway had revived the army, plans had to be in place should the spring offensive of the People's Liberation Army succeed.

Turning the corner into the corridor where the Policy and Plans Office was located McCreedy found Milo Hawkins waiting for him.

"He's arrived, sir. I showed him into your office, as you requested."

"Good. I assume he arrived on time. My meeting with General Vandenberg ran late."

"Yes, sir. He showed up early, four minutes early to be exact. And declined an offer of coffee. Seems he had some downstairs."

"His orders are ready to go?"

"Yes, sir. As you instructed. Are you sure that's why he's here?"

"I'm sure. And more importantly so is my wife, though she thinks we should turn him down."

Despite its importance, the office of the air force Director of Policy and Plans was not large. McCreedy had a desk, chair and credenza; a small conference table with six chairs; a bookshelf nearby next to which stood a coat rack and an old-fashioned wing chair where the general would read when staying late. Behind the desk, to the sides of the credenza, were two flags. One was the Stars and Stripes. The other was the flag of the United States Air Force. Within the office three airplane models occupied visible positions. Two, on the credenza, were of first line airplanes—the B–36 and F–84. These reflected the strategic and tactical nature of the plans McCreedy helped to devise. The third was of a SPAD XIII, a French-built fighter of the First World War. McCreedy had flown the aircraft in combat, destroying three German Fokkers, just before the armistice of 1918. The SPAD wore the markings of the 22nd Aero Squadron of which Mike McCreedy, then twenty years of age, was the youngest member.

"Good morning, General," said McGrath as Catherine's uncle entered his office.

"Sit down, son," replied McCreedy, motioning McGrath to the conference table.

Despite the general's personal reference McGrath wished not to appear to be taking advantage of his special relationship with the senior officer, although he knew that was exactly what he was doing. So he kept his words and demeanor business-like which, given that he was a lieutenant colonel and McCreedy a lieutenant general, was wise.

"I'm here, sir, to make a request."

"Go ahead. I think I know what you're going to ask."

McGrath ignored the remark and proceeded. "I'd like to go back on active duty and if that job General Hawkins once mentioned to me is still available, well, I'm ready to volunteer and would like to have it."

Here McCreedy paused and examined the man before him. McGrath seemed like an ideal choice for the job. He was a seasoned airman with combat experience, still young enough to fly high perfor-mance aircraft, yet old enough to be given a sensitive task. The job would be to command a special unit of F–86s and, in four months, come back with an assessment—outside the chain of command—of air force equipment and tactics. Moreover, by giving the job to an air guard officer, McCreedy would have a retort to those National Guard pretend generals when they complained that he was ignoring them.

McCreedy also understood that McGrath needed a change of venue, something that would force him to concentrate on the task at hand, without any reminders of Catherine. Korea would do that. Up by the Yalu the pilot who did not concentrate was the pilot who failed to return.

The only obstacle Mike McCreedy had faced in giving this assign-ment to McGrath was his wife. Laura understood the young man's need for change. But she told her husband a posting to Europe or California would accomplish the same thing. She wished to have McGrath not placed in harm's way. The general's answer was that the air force, while full of pilots, did not have the number it needed of men qualified in jets. Plus, as he pointed out to her, the task required a leader, someone will-ing and able not just to fly, but to fight. McGrath, he told his wife, was the right man for the job. He had made the decision and she simply would have to accept it. Being a near perfect service wife, Laura did so.

"Your request, Colonel, is approved. General Hawkins has cut your orders."

Hearing these words, McGrath knew his life was to be irrevocably changed. Momentarily he wondered whether he was making a wise decision. Then he thought of Catherine, of the hospital, and of the five days that followed the accident and he knew that he had chosen well.

"Thank you, General. I do have one related request, sir."

"And that is?" McCreedy started to frown.

"I'd appreciate, and I'm sure Georgetown would as well, having two weeks to wrap up my affairs at the university. We're near the end of the semester and I owe it to the school to finish the job I signed on for."

The frown receded. "Your orders require you to report to Far East

Air Forces Headquarters, Tokyo, by June 2nd. That gives you three weeks plus time in transit. I assume that's sufficient?"

"Yes, sir. That's more than fair, and thank you."

For the next twenty minutes McCreedy and McGrath discussed the new assignment. The general emphasized that "Washington," by which he meant himself and Vandenberg, wanted to have honest, unadulterated feedback on the air war in Korea. McCreedy wanted to know how well or how poorly U.S. aircraft performed. In particular the general wished to learn all there was to know about how the F–86 stacked up against the MiG–15. McCreedy explained that McGrath would command a detachment of Sabres, six aircraft in all, assigned to the 4th Fighter Interceptor Wing then in Korea. The only F–86 equipped unit in the Far East, the 4th had the responsibility to clear the skies of MiGs so that U.N. planes could operate without interference. Detachment Q, the unit's formal name, would be a separate organization, much like a fighter squadron, but be detailed to the 4th and operate under its control.

Upon conclusion of the discussion, McGrath started to leave the general's office, but not before again thanking McCreedy for the assignment.

The general responded with a simple remark. "You're the right man for the job, Colonel."

"Thank you, sir."

As McGrath was walking toward the door, McCreedy spoke again, this time sounding more like a parent than an air force general. "Take care of yourself, son. Laura and I want you back here in four months."

"I will do my best, sir."

When McGrath had gone, Milo Hawkins entered the room.

"General, I have the list you wanted."

"Hmm." McCreedy's mind was elsewhere. He was reflecting on the nature of modern warfare. Old men like himself sent young men like McGrath to fight and die. However necessary, it seemed unfair. Then he concluded it had always been that way and probably always would.

"Yes, Milo." McCreedy now focused on the brigadier.

"The list, General, the one you wanted, of the reserve and guard officers we intend to call up. I have the complete roster. There are 235 pilots on the list. The orders will be sent out in four days. They're being prepared now."

Hawkins handed the list to McCreedy and left the office. The Director of Policy and Plans then retired to his wing chair and examined the names. On page eight he found the name he was looking for. Taking out his fountain pen, Mike McCreedy drew a line through the name of the man he had just ordered sent to Korea.

From the Pentagon, McGrath drove across Memorial Bridge, then up Rock Creek Parkway to Massachusetts Avenue, turning east toward Sheridan Circle. From the parking lot to Decatur Place took less than twenty minutes, a benefit of not driving in rush hour traffic. Once home McGrath called his father and told him of his decision to go on active duty. John McGrath said nothing, expecting to hear more. The son then explained the assignment to Korea, not mentioning however the requirement to report back to Washington. For the father the news was not happy. He did not want to see his son in another shooting war. Sensing that revealing his thoughts would serve no useful purpose, he spoke generally about the war, expressing the hope that it would remain a limited conflict. The conversation ended on a different note. The elder McGrath told his son to stay safe and to remember that back in Port Washington there was a family of three that loved him dearly.

Roger O'Boyle's reaction surprised McGrath. The Jesuit stated that communism was an evil force in the world that needed to be expunged from every country on Earth. O'Boyle continued on, speaking forcefully. He said that America had a mission to confront immoral ideologies wherever they existed. Korea was the chosen battlefield, so the U.S. was obligated to fight. While he would be sad to see McGrath leave Georgetown, O'Boyle would not object to having his friend join the crusade against the Hammer and Sickle. Yet his parting words, expressed ten days later, were more personal.

"Take care, my friend. Write to me, and don't be reluctant to ask for God's help."

"I will do the first two, Roger. Perhaps you might do the third."

"I will, indeed, each day you're gone," replied the Jesuit. O'Boyle fulfilled his pledge. Each night, before retiring for the evening, he appealed to God to keep his friend safe.

Getting ready to leave was more time consuming than McGrath had expected. He had to put his furniture in storage. He had to pack his books and ship them to Long Island where they would be safe. He had to arrange for most of his clothes to be stored once they no longer were needed. He had to arrange for his car to be stored, and sublet his townhouse. All the while he had to teach his classes and carry out the day-to-day tasks necessary to keep one's life afloat.

Thus the two weeks he had obtained to put his affairs in order were busy. When the time came to leave, McGrath was tired, though pleased that he had accomplished what needed to be done. He had allowed seven days to get to Tokyo. When the first of those days arrived McGrath was at National Airport about to board a Military Air Transport Service C–54 Skymaster. With him, to say goodbye, was Laura McCreedy.

When boarding began McGrath leaned over and sweetly kissed her on the cheek. With tears in her eyes she held on to him and spoke words he never forgot.

"You're family now. So be good, be safe and remember that Mike and I love you."

She then kissed him, as a mother would a son, and waved as he boarded the aircraft.

The plane flew to Detroit. The stopover lasted several hours, after which another C–54 took McGrath and an assortment of military personnel to San Francisco. This second flight was uneventful but long. McGrath slept most of the way, although he did finish reading *Scaramouche*, a favorite novel by Rafael Sabatini. For the trip to Tokyo McGrath had brought along four books. Two were academic in nature. Two were by Sabatini. When not in the cockpit, McGrath thought airplane rides boring. They were good, he had concluded, for just two activities: reading and sleeping. Given the time it would take to reach Tokyo, McGrath figured he'd do a lot of both.

By sea the voyage to Tokyo from San Francisco took thirteen days. By air the time was measured in hours. Chugging along, the sound mind-numbing, the propeller-driven aircraft took McGrath first to Hawaii, then on to Midway. From this tiny island, after a day's delay to fix a faulty hydraulic line, the MATS C–54 carried one admiral and twenty-six air force officers, one of whom was McGrath, to Japan. They arrived at Haneda, outside of Yokohama, in pouring rain. Including layovers, the entire trip had taken forty-one hours.

McGrath was exhausted. Yet he was not sleepy. So, luggage in hand, he climbed into a taxi for the ride into Tokyo. The taxi was old yet spotless, as was the driver who chatted constantly along the way. McGrath understood little of what the man was saying. If the driver could not communicate, he certainly could navigate. Less than thirty-five minutes later McGrath was dropped off precisely at his destination. This was a small hotel three blocks away from the headquarters of Far East Air Forces.

The hotel was far nicer than McGrath had expected. His room, on the third floor, while small, was clean and comfortable, as were the bath facilities. After checking in, a young woman showed him his room. Her name was Miko and several times in broken English she said he should call upon her if in need of anything. McGrath estimated Miko to be in her mid-twenties. He noticed she was quite lovely, slender and delicate as many Japanese women were.

Still not ready for bed, McGrath decided to tour Tokyo. With Miko's help he secured a cab whose driver understood he was to drive around so McGrath could see the sights. The city was bustling, full of people who did not look like they had been defeated but five years ago. Damage to buildings was evident yet seemed not to deter men, women, and children from moving rapidly about the city. The driver showed McGrath the emperor's island-like residence, which he called "Number One House." Several restaurants and hotels also were pointed out. These too were described as "Number One," leaving McGrath to ponder the true meaning of the phrase.

Suddenly McGrath realized he needed to sleep. Forty-one hours crossing the Pacific caught up with him. He told the driver to return to the hotel. Once there he hurried upstairs, said hello to Miko, and entered his room. Clothes still on, he lay down on the bed and promptly fell asleep.

Ten hours later he awoke. He did not notice that he was wearing only his underwear. He did notice that his clothes, including those he had not unpacked, had been washed or dry cleaned. They were now neatly arranged, either folded on the table or hung in an open closet.

McGrath looked at his watch. It was ten o'clock, with daylight shining through the window. He got up and dressed, putting on one of his better uniforms.

Deciding to pursue business, McGrath walked the three blocks to the headquarters of the Far East Air Forces. This was a large masonry four-story building formerly belonging to a Japanese aircraft company no longer in business. Once inside McGrath was surprised by the lack of activity. Typewriters, telephones, and teleprinters were all in use. Yet the sounds were muffled and the pace of work seemed oddly slow.

When McGrath inquired as to where exactly he should report, a lieutenant politely told him the office was on the second floor, Room 234B. McGrath thanked him and walked up the stairway, easily finding the room.

With a knock on the door McGrath entered 234B. No one was there, although from the furniture he could tell the room housed two officers. A door led into another room, which McGrath saw labeled as 234.

"Hello, anyone home?"

"I'm coming, sir," responded a tan, overweight, disheveled major who emerged from the other room.

"Your name and rank?" inquired McGrath.

"Ferguson, sir. Roger B., major, United States Air Force."

"Then perhaps you should look and act like one."

"Yes, sir."

In one concise sentence McGrath explained why he was there, choosing not to show Ferguson his orders.

"Yes, sir. You and several other officers are expected, sir, but I'm sorry to have to tell you your paperwork isn't ready."

"Then go find it and get it ready."

"I can't do that, sir." Ferguson was sounding more like an air force officer, but not a happy one.

"And why, major," McGrath emphasized the man's rank, "is that?"

"Because Colonel Small is in charge of those incoming personnel, sir."

"So go find the colonel."

"I can't do that, sir. The colonel is out of the office today and only he has the keys to those files, which in any case are empty."

"As I said, so find the colonel."

"I can't do that, sir."

"I'm getting tired of hearing that, Major." McGrath was irritated and it showed in both his voice and body language.

"Yes, sir. I understand. But it's Saturday morning and Colonel Small plays golf every Saturday morning. I have orders not to disturb him, sir, and he'd kill me if I did. May I suggest you come back on Monday? I'm sure Colonel Small will see you then and we'll have the paperwork ready."

"How long have you been in grade, Major?"

"Seven years. Three more and I'll have my twenty."

McGrath wondered how the air force would survive, let alone prosper, with officers such as Ferguson and Small. Good men were needed to man the service's support units. Where were these men to be found? Not all the jobs in the air force were glamorous, yet they nonetheless had to be filled with capable people. Contemplating the difficulty of recruiting these men, McGrath let his irritation recede, but not disappear.

"Tell your colonel that I'll be back on Monday and that I'm looking forward to meeting him."

"Yes, sir, I will."

"And Ferguson."

"Sir?"

"If you wish to retire as a major have the paperwork ready."

TEN

When McGrath left FEAF Headquarters he took a taxi to the University Club, a hangout frequented by U.S. military officers in Tokyo. The club had a garden terrace on the roof. There, an individual might have a drink and a nice meal while listening to big band music. The terrace offered a panoramic view of the city, which from above looked truly serene, masking the commotion below.

Despite arriving early for lunch McGrath found the terrace full, save for one small table he promptly requisitioned. Ordering a Coca-Cola "with ice" from a formally attired waiter, McGrath looked about the large open-aired room. The place was packed. Officers from the army and navy were present as well as from the air force. McGrath saw several generals and more than one admiral. One of the generals was Otto P. Weyland, the new commander of the Far East Air Force. McGrath mused that one well-placed bomb might destroy the entire command structure in Tokyo. Then, smiling to himself, he wondered if any of the waiters had had the same thought.

About to order his meal, McGrath noticed a naval lieutenant scanning the room, looking for a place to sit. No tables were available and the lieutenant seemed resigned to wait. McGrath caught the officer's attention and waved him over.

"Come join me, Lieutenant, eating alone's no fun."

"Thank you, Colonel, that's most kind of you. Sure I'm not intruding?"

"I'm sure. Sit down and relax."

The navy man did so, joining McGrath for lunch. His name was Harry Brubaker and he was a twenty-nine year old lawyer from Denver. Like McGrath he was a flyer, wearing the naval aviator's wings of gold. He flew twin-engine McDonnell Banshees and had seen much combat in Korea, ending one mission in the very cold Sea of Japan. However, unlike McGrath, Harry Brubaker was not pleased to be back in uniform. With a wife and children back home he thought other, younger men should be doing the fighting. He simply wanted to practice law and get on with his life.

"Seems Uncle Sam had other ideas," said McGrath.

"Apparently so. I must tell you this war seems hardly worth the effort. We don't appear willing to do what it takes to win."

"But we can't afford to lose."

"You're right of course. I just think the whole thing stinks."

"It does Harry, but we're here, and you know what follows."

"And we need to get the job done."

"And so we will. And sometime soon I hope. You'll get back to Denver and Korea will be nothing but a lousy memory."

Harry Brubaker would not return home. Six weeks after his lunch with McGrath his Banshee was hit after an air strike against bridges in North Korea. Brubaker attempted to coax his plane to the sea, but the jet was losing fuel and could not climb. Within sight of the water, Brubaker had to put the Banshee down in a field. The aircraft hit the ground hard yet slid to a stop in one piece, allowing Harry to get out safely and find cover in a ditch. Overhead Banshees and later Corsairs held the enemy at bay. When they departed Brubaker was alone, until a navy helicopter arrived. This the North Koreans riddled with bullets, killing the gunner. Its pilot joined Brubaker in the ditch. Together they shot a few of the enemy. But the gunfight was one-sided. Two Americans faced over forty North Koreans. The helicopter pilot died first, while throwing a grenade back at the advancing soldiers. Hoping to find an escape path Brubaker ran down the ditch, staying low beneath the line of fire. Then, by instinct, he stopped and stood up. Turning, he fired his gun, hitting two of his pursuers. But seconds later soldiers he had not seen took aim and fired. Their aim was true. Harry Brubaker died instantaneously, falling face down in the ditch, far from the family in Denver he never would see again.

During the latter part of his conversation with Brubaker, McGrath had seen a young woman sitting nearby. She was quite pretty, with short blonde hair and a pleasing face not unlike Betty Grable's. Dressed conservatively, she had a light blue cashmere sweater draped over a simple yellow dress. McGrath guessed she was in her late twenties.

After Brubaker left McGrath lingered, enjoying a cup of coffee and wondering what he might do in the afternoon and evening. The idea of doing nothing appealed to him, as did the idea of exploring Tokyo and its environs. He decided he would do whatever he felt like doing when the time came to decide. In the meantime he would relax, drink his coffee, and take in the sights at the roof terrace.

The plan was unfolding nicely when a young army captain approached the girl. Despite her objections he insisted on sitting down. Clearly the man had had too much to drink. He also was speaking loudly, embarrassing the young woman. The soldier continued with his boorish behavior, suggesting several times that she accompany him to his hotel. She urged the officer to keep his voice down. She told him she had no intention, then or ever, of going anywhere with him again.

The situation was not getting better when McGrath decided to intervene. He stood up and walked over to the captain. Tapping him on the shoulder, he spoke firmly when the officer turned around.

"Okay Captain, that's enough. It's time for you to leave."

"This is between me and her, not you."

"Not you, *sir*," said McGrath, who then spoke bluntly. "Captain, you're already in trouble. The only question now is whether you wish to get into more."

This time the soldier kept his mouth shut. He realized he would lose any argument he might have with an air force lieutenant colonel. McGrath continued.

"You now have a choice, Captain. You can walk out of here on your own never to return. I repeat: *never to return*. Or I can escort you downstairs and hand you over to the MPs. It's your call. Just make it right now."

Begrudgingly, the soldier made his decision. "I'll go, Colonel." He straightened his tie and jacket, ran his hand through his hair, and started to leave. Then he turned to the girl and in a low but audible voice said one word.

"Bitch."

McGrath heard it, and didn't like it.

"That's an ugly word, my friend, one we don't use with ladies."

McGrath took hold of the man's shoulder and forced him to apologize. He then escorted the soldier off the terrace. They took an elevator downstairs and entered the lobby, McGrath now twisting the man's arm, causing considerable pain.

"Keep your mouth shut or I'll make it hurt more."

The military police were never far from the University Club. When they arrived McGrath handed the officer over to them. He told the MP in charge, a sergeant, a big man who looked like he played tackle for the Chicago Bears, to throw the man in jail and have him pay for his behavior.

"Not to worry, Colonel. I'll make sure justice is done."

"I'm sure you will, Sergeant. He's all yours."

Having disposed of the captain McGrath considered leaving the club. The afternoon beckoned and he had decided to explore the Tokyo PX, the place where military personnel could purchase practically anything. Then McGrath realized two reasons compelled him to remain. The first was his tab for lunch, which he had not paid. The second was the girl. It would be rude not to see her, if only to ensure she now was okay.

So McGrath returned to the rooftop terrace. Once there he walked to where the girl was sitting. She rose, and thanked him several times.

He acknowledged her remarks but downplayed what he had done. McGrath then started to leave. But the girl objected and invited him to stay.

A voice inside McGrath's head advised him not to accept.

"Well, that's nice of you, but unnecessary."

"I'd like you to join me."

"Are you sure? You really don't have to do this. I'm fine in just going about my business."

"Please stay."

McGrath went back to his table and paid his bill. He again thought about leaving despite what the girl had said. But when he looked toward her she smiled, and with her foot, gently slid the empty chair away from the table. Accepting this silent invitation McGrath walked over and sat down.

Her name was Martha Dawson. She was a schoolteacher in Tokyo, employed by the Department of Defense, which operated schools in Japan for children of U.S. military personnel. A graduate of Pennsylvania State University, she taught third grade. Her goal, she explained to McGrath, was to put aside sufficient money to support aging parents in Scranton.

"That must be difficult to do," said McGrath aware that teacher salaries were not high.

"It is, but I'm saving bit by bit. Every dollar will help."

"Are your parents in good shape?"

"My mom is. My father is not. He's now sixty-nine and is tired all the time. I think his body's just worn out from work."

"What did he do?"

"He was a plumber and worked all his life, until two years ago. He started working at fifteen."

The conversation continued, but turned from the subject of parents to that of the plumber's daughter. McGrath learned that Martha was the first of her family to attend college, that her childhood had not been one of ease and comfort, and that she hoped eventually to enter graduate school. McGrath also learned that in 1947 Martha Dawson had been Penn State's homecoming queen.

This last piece of personal history made McGrath realize that the girl across from him was indeed attractive. Her face, round rather than angular, was pleasing. Her hair, though blonde, had more than a hint of strawberry. The girl's mouth was wide—perhaps too wide—but when she smiled her entire face radiated a girl-next-door beauty. McGrath noticed too that beneath the yellow dress and blue sweater she had compelling curves. Yet something about the girl made McGrath ignore her physical charms. At first he could not identify what it was. Then it struck him. The young woman downplayed her appearance. She wore little make-up, no earrings, and plain clothes. It's as if, thought McGrath, Martha Dawson wished men not to notice how pretty she was. But McGrath did notice. This girl was easy on the eye. She also was pleasant to talk with. McGrath realized she was the first female since Catherine to hold his attention. For a moment he wondered if he were being disloyal to his fiancée's memory. He concluded he was not. Catherine's memory was safe, and untouchable. Besides, McGrath said to himself, life is for the living. Catherine was dead, and Martha Dawson was very much alive.

Their conversation continued for another hour. McGrath was at ease, and in response to Martha's questions, told her about himself. He hurried through the chronology, saying little about England, concentrating on his time at Notre Dame and at Georgetown, and his new career in the air force. She seemed puzzled by his leaving teaching. So he told the whole truth and narrated the story of his romance with Catherine Caldwell.

McGrath expected Martha to draw back upon hearing about Catherine. To his surprise she did not. Quite the contrary. The tale seemed to strengthen her interest to continue the conversation.

At 2:30 Martha looked at her watch and said she had to leave. McGrath realized he would like to see her again. He sensed that she would not be opposed to the idea.

"I know this is a bit sudden but if you're not busy, perhaps we might have dinner tonight."

Martha smiled and took hold of his hand, their first physical contact. "I'd like that, but I'm busy."

"Oh, that's too bad. At least for me."

"For me too, but I'm free tomorrow afternoon. We could meet for lunch."

"I could do that." Here McGrath paused before adding words to complete his thought, "And would like to."

"Good. Then it's a date?"

"Yes, indeed. Where should we meet? You know Tokyo much better than I do?"

"Well, tomorrow is Sunday so our choices are limited. I'll tell you what, meet me in the lobby downstairs and by then I'll have found a place."

"You've got yourself a deal. What time is good for you?"

"Twelve-thirty would be good."

"Twelve-thirty it is."

Martha rose, and started to leave. As she departed Martha spoke words McGrath found welcome.

"I'm looking forward to it."

Hardly a cynic McGrath nonetheless wondered whether she had uttered this sentiment as a matter of politeness. He would have been pleased to know that she had meant what she said.

When McGrath left the University Club he headed to the Tokyo Post Exchange. This was a five story building in the heart of the city. It contained just about anything a serviceman or his wife could wish to purchase. From food to clothes, from tools to housewares, the PX had it, and at a price military personnel could afford.

McGrath looked for and found a pair of flight boots of higher quality than normally issued. He stocked up on toiletries and, on a whim, bought a pair of lined gloves he would wear come winter.

Saturday night McGrath stayed in his hotel room. He decided a night on the town was not an activity he needed. Instead, after a modest dinner at the small restaurant next to this hotel, he returned to his room and read a book he had purchased at the PX. The book was a novel, *The Cruel Sea* by Nicholas Monsarrat. It told the story of the Battle of the Atlantic as seen by the captain and first lieutenant aboard a Royal Navy corvette.

The next day, he met Martha Dawson as planned, in the lobby of the University Club. He was ten minutes early; she was ten minutes late. He wore one of his better uniforms. She wore a simple skirt and blouse. He expected they would spend two hours together. She had planned for the entire afternoon.

They had lunch in a tiny restaurant not far from Douglas MacArthur's headquarters. Tutored by Martha, McGrath ate food he had never seen before, much less eaten. He found most of it agreeable, though he concluded that raw fish would never replace rare steak as an American favorite. While dining he employed chopsticks though with varying degrees of success. He noticed, however, that Martha used them skillfully, the result of constant use over a lengthy period of time.

After lunch, when McGrath thought Martha would have to leave, she surprised him by saying she wished to show him something special. He had no idea what it might be.

They went to a Shinto shrine. McGrath found it only mildly interesting. Yet that was not what Martha wanted him to see. Taking his hand, placing herself close to him, she guided McGrath down a narrow path among a grove of tall trees. They soon arrived at her objective. It was a rock garden, a sea of white pebbles, with several rocks of different colors artfully placed about. Stone benches occupied the garden's perimeter.

Never had McGrath seen such a display. It was as lovely as it was simple. It conveyed such serenity that at first he and Martha, sitting on one of the benches, spoke not at all. They simply took in its silent beauty. McGrath found it difficult to believe that such a quiet, peaceful oasis could exist in the middle of Tokyo.

They remained at the garden for two hours. While they conversed they held hands. As they stood up to leave McGrath impulsively but gently took hold of Martha and kissed her. She responded, though with some reluctance. He then moved away and was about to apologize when she brought her hand to his mouth, preventing him from speaking. She then spoke softly.

"No words, not now."

Martha moved close to McGrath, sliding her body into his. As she did so, she kissed him. He felt her body against his. Her mouth was inviting and the kiss long and hard. When the embrace ended McGrath needed to catch his breath. Martha stepped back, regained her composure, and told McGrath she did not do that with and for anyone. He then responded with a twinkle in his eye.

"Then aren't I a lucky fellow?"

Martha was laughing when she responded. "Yes, I think you are."

When the time came for them to separate McGrath asked a simple question.

"How do I reach you?"

Martha took out a piece of paper and handed it to him. "Here is my telephone number. You can call me. The best time is late afternoon, after school."

She then had questions for McGrath.

"When might I see you next? Where are they about to send you?"

"I suspect I'll soon be in Korea. That's why I'm here. But I need to check out in the 86 and put my group together. So I'd bet I'll be somewhere around here for a week or so."

"And you'll call me?" Martha spoke these words with less than full confidence.

McGrath noticed this, and was surprised. He spoke to reassure her.

"I will, Martha, I promise."

The next morning McGrath marched into Room 234B of Far East Air Forces Headquarters at precisely the time the administrative offices opened for business. To his surprise Major Ferguson was there, smartly dressed.

"Good morning, Colonel. Here are your orders." Ferguson handed McGrath a sealed envelope. "You'll find everything in order, sir."

"Thank you, Major."

McGrath considered complimenting Ferguson for having the orders ready and for looking like a proper air force officer. At first he decided against it. Ferguson merely was doing his duty, doing what he was paid to do. Then McGrath changed his mind. He remembered that everyone, from students to soldiers, appreciated something nice said about them. Moreover, and perhaps more importantly, a compliment could lead to improved performance. McGrath knew that to be true in a classroom. He suspected the same would apply to Room 234B.

"I appreciate your efforts, Major. Well done."

"Thank you, sir." Ferguson, who had received few compliments in his career, long remembered this one. He then again spoke to McGrath, though in a more business-like tone.

"Sir, before you leave, there's a Lieutenant Perkins downstairs who says it's urgent that you see him."

"Urgent?"

"That's what he said, sir."

"Fine, I'll go see this lieutenant."

McGrath soon found Perkins, who turned out to be the polite officer who had directed McGrath to Room 234B when he first arrived at FEAF Headquarters.

"Yes, sir. Good morning, Colonel," said Perkins.

"What can I do for you, Lieutenant?"

"I'm glad I caught you, Colonel, before you left. General Weyland wants to see you, sir. Today, this morning."

"Weyland wants to see me?"

"Yes, sir."

"Got a clue as to why?"

"I sure don't, Colonel."

"When am I to report?"

"At ten hundred hours, sir."

"Fine, I'll be there."

McGrath was about to ask a question when Perkins provided the answer.

"It's on the third floor, sir. Room 318. You can't miss it."

"I'm sure of that. Thanks, Lieutenant."

"My pleasure, sir. One more thing, Colonel. There's a cafeteria downstairs, with magazines and newspapers. It's a nice place to kill some time. You've got a while before the general is ready to see you."

"Sounds good. Thanks again."

McGrath walked down to the cafeteria and had breakfast. He paid no attention to the newspapers and magazines, however. For, from his briefcase, he took out his copy of *The Cruel Sea,* which he read 'til it was time to go upstairs.

"What the hell is going on, Colonel?" The commanding general of U.S. air power in the Far East was not happy. He continued to address McGrath.

"I wasn't born yesterday. We're short of fighters and then you show up and get six brand new Sabre jets and eight pilots along with a support team in something called Detachment Q, whatever that means. And I haven't been told beans."

Standing in front of Otto Weyland, McGrath was most definitely not at ease.

"General, I've been ordered to take Detachment Q to Korea."

"I know that. What I don't know is why."

"To help out the Fourth Interceptor Wing."

"Don't play games with me, Colonel. There's something else going on here."

"Sir?"

"Wait a minute. I know what it is. Who sent you out here, Colonel?"

"General McCreedy, sir."

Upon hearing McGrath's response Weyland's expression changed, from one of anger and annoyance to one of revelation and amusement.

"Mike McCreedy. Smartest general officer in the air force. So you're one of Michael's boys. Now I understand. You can go, Colonel."

"Sir?"

"You're dismissed. Only one thing, Colonel."

"Sir?"

"When you report back to General McCreedy, to tell him privately what you think is going on in Korea, why don't you first drop by my office and have a chat with me?"

"Sir?"

"Come now, Colonel. As I said before, I wasn't born yesterday. I've known Mike McCreedy a very long time, and know most of his tricks. So come by my office. I'll inform the general you'll be talking with me first. And Colonel, don't sugarcoat what you have to say. I want to hear it exactly how you'll be telling it to General McCreedy."

"Very good, sir."

"There's one other thing, Colonel."

"Sir?"

"When you're in Korea," Weyland now spoke like the warrior he was, "go get some MiGs."

"I'll do my best, General. I'll do my very best."

ELEVEN

From Tokyo to Johnson Air Base took two hours by train. During the trip McGrath divided the time equally between work and play. The latter consisted of reading *The Cruel Sea*. The former was spent thinking about the immediate tasks ahead. These were three in number. The first was to get checked out in the F–86. The second was to form the pilots assigned to Detachment Q into a cohesive unit. The third was to ensure that the support people were ready to carry out their jobs.

McGrath knew the first task would be the least difficult. Upon arriving at the base, once settled in, he decided it would be his first priority. How could he lead Detachment Q sitting on the ground?

An instructor pilot, Major Fred Cox was given the assignment of transitioning McGrath to the F–86. Cox began by having McGrath sit in the plane's cockpit and memorize the location of all that he could see and touch. Concurrently, Cox explained operating procedures and aircraft capabilities. These McGrath had to know completely. After two days of instruction Cox gave his student a written examination and an oral quiz, tests that were preceded by having McGrath, blindfolded in the cockpit, identify instruments and switches.

McGrath did well in these initial steps so Cox allowed his student to proceed to the next level, actual training flights. These took place over a period of six days, two of which were spent on the ground waiting for rain to stop. The first flight was to familiarize McGrath with the area surrounding Johnson. In fact the mission took Cox and his pupil well beyond the air base. They flew down and back to Yokohama, the city McGrath recalled was the sole port in Japan visited by the Great White Fleet. From eight thousand feet McGrath could see numerous ships in the harbor. One was an Essex-class aircraft carrier. He mused that this single ship was far more potent than Teddy Roosevelt's entire collection of battleships.

The four days of flying included navigational exercises, instrument flying, and aerobatics. It also included more advanced activities such as formation flying, air defense intercepts, and gunnery practice. The last two flights were mock dogfights with Major Cox. The instructor won the first one. In the second McGrath was the victor.

Upon conclusion of the practice air battles Cox told McGrath he was qualified on the F–86.

"You're ready to go, Colonel. I'll write up my report and all that, but as far as I'm concerned, you're checked out."

"Thanks, Major. I appreciate what you've done. You're a fine instructor."

"Appreciate that, Colonel, but I'd rather not be."

At first McGrath was surprised by what Cox had said. Then he realized that he wanted to fight, not instruct. Cox must be a tiger, a true fighter pilot. The major continued speaking.

"I've got a request to make of you, Colonel."

"I think I know what's coming."

"I'm sure you do. Over in Korea there's some fighting going on, up by the Yalu River. But I'm here when I ought to be there. Hell, Colonel, this training stuff is okay. It's necessary and important and I understand that. But I've done my share. Now it's time to get me some MiGs. Got any room for me in your group?"

"Not at the moment, Major. But I'll tell you this. If something comes up and I need a pilot, I'm gonna come looking for you."

"I'll be there, Colonel, and ready to go."

Shortly before this conversation McGrath had met the other pilots assigned to Detachment Q. They were far from the usual cast of characters. Two were exchange pilots: one from the Marine Corps, the other from Britain's Royal Air Force. Two were combat veterans of World War II both of whom had flown P–38s in the Pacific. Each had shot down two Japanese aircraft. One of the new pilots was just out of flight school. McGrath thought he looked no more than nineteen, though in fact Lieutenant Peter Heller was twenty-four. Another pilot was an older fellow, with gray hair. His name was Roberts and, while proficient on the F–86, he seemed lacking in the confidence fighter pilots must have to succeed. The final pilot assigned to the group was someone McGrath knew. Major Charles Hickock had flown P–51s in England, though not in McGrath's squadron. He had done well, downing twelve German planes. Hickock likely would get a few MiGs, McGrath reasoned, unless he first got himself killed. Charlie Hickock took unnecessary risks. He was lucky to still be alive.

For two weeks, the eight pilots of Detachment Q flew hard and often. McGrath emphasized teamwork and basic flying skills. Their success in Korea would depend on both.

Success also required that the detachment's support team be capable and hardworking. To see that they were McGrath had found a ground executive officer who was perfect for the job. Major Edward Brumbaugh had administrative talents few men in the air force possessed. He was career military and devoted to the idea that his group of airmen were to serve and support those who flew and fought. Brumbaugh had many characteristics that enabled him to succeed in the air force. But he had one trait that amused those who knew him. Edward did not like to fly.

"Oh no, Colonel, I can't stand it."

"Then why did you pick the air force?"

"Good question, Colonel. I don't really have a good answer for you. I've never liked flying. I'd much rather go by train or car."

"That will be difficult given that in three days we're going to Korea."

"Yes, sir, I realize that."

"Well just be sure you and your men are ready to go. There will be four C–47s taking you to K–13."

K–13 was the designation of the airfield at Suwon, thirty miles south of Seoul. In June 1951, F–86s in Korea flew out of K–13. A numerical identification was given to all U.N. air bases on the peninsula as Americans had difficulty pronouncing Korean names.

"We'll be ready, Colonel."

"I'm sure you will. And there is good news, Edward." McGrath had begun calling Brumbaugh by his given name. It was a mark of respect and friendship, but occurred only when they were alone.

"What would that be, Colonel?" For Brumbaugh, McGrath's first name always was "Colonel."

"The flight to Korea."

"Yes?"

"It's very short. The plane will go up, level off, and then go down."

"I'd still rather go by boat, sir."

"Yes, I know. But Edward, it is the United States *Air* Force."

Two days before their scheduled departure for Korea, Major Brumbaugh brought news to McGrath he knew the colonel would not like.

"Sir, I had occasion to talk ten minutes ago with the folks at base HQ who told me we won't be leaving on Tuesday as planned. Seems the transport aircraft we were going to use have been assigned elsewhere; they wouldn't say for what. We're here at Johnson for another week it seems."

McGrath was walking toward the officer's club when Brumbaugh spoke. They had passed the Japanese Baka Bomb on display near the club. The bomb was a Japanese suicide weapon—a small, piloted rocket plane designed to crash into its target. McGrath had been thinking about the kamikaze when the ground exec had found him.

"Is this official or just a rumor?"

"The former, sir. You'll get the word after lunch, back in your office."

"After lunch I'm taking an 86 up for a test hop. Then I'll go and hear the bad news. Why don't you try to find out exactly when we will get out of here?"

"I have, Colonel. Colonel Blanton—he's deputy of base operations—says we'll be on our way one week from tomorrow. We leave Johnny on Tuesday, July 31. Colonel Blanton says he's lined up four other C–47s to transport our men and material."

"You'll be ready to go?"

"Colonel, I'm ready to go now."

"Well done, Edward. I'm confident you are. It's like we're in the army."

"Sir?"

"Hurry up and wait. That's what we're doing."

"Sir, can I ask you a question? About our pilots?"

McGrath considered the request. It was somewhat unusual. Curious, he responded in the positive.

"Fire away. We're alone."

"Well Colonel, our little group is about to go to Korea and fight. Detachment Q is going off to war. Well, some of us were wondering, how will we do? Are we ready?"

"What you mean is, are the pilots up to it?"

"Yes, sir, that's what I mean, if you don't mind me asking."

"I don't mind, Edward, as long as you ask as you have, alone and in private."

"Well, then, sir, are we? Are we ready?"

"Yes, Major, we are. The pilots are good. We should do fine. I'm not worried."

That was only half true. McGrath was not worried per se. The eight pilots seemed to be capable flyers. The airplane was superb. The support team, led by Brumbaugh, appeared outstanding. Detachment Q, its leader believed, was well prepared. Yet McGrath knew that the true test would come only in combat. Only above the Yalu would he learn if the pilots were up to their job. The training at Johnson had been solid, but even the best training in the world did not assure success. Aerial combat demanded more than expert aeronautical skills. It required what fighter pilots call situational awareness, the ability to think and act spatially, to conduct a three dimensional duel, with real guns and real bullets. Yet this too was no guarantee of success. For the Sabre pilots needed, above all, to be warriors. They needed to have desire, the desire to seek out and destroy the enemy.

McGrath understood all this. He knew too that soon he would know who among them were hunters.

After lunch McGrath went to the flight line where the six Sabres of Detachment Q were parked. They were F–86As, the first combat capable version of the aircraft. North American would build 554 of the A models, each costing $178,408. Other models would follow, incorporating improvements large and small. Eventually 8,823 Sabres would be built and flown by numerous American allies, including Canada, West Germany, Japan, and Australia.

The F–86 was 37 feet, 6 inches long. At takeoff it weighed 14,108 lbs. The plane was fast though not supersonic. Maximum speed at thirty-five thousand feet was 601 mph. Service ceiling was slightly above forty thousand feet. Its combat radius was limited, approximately 330 miles. The A was powered by a single General Electric aerial-flow J–47 turbojet, which gave off a long plume of black smoke, making identification easy for both friend and foe.

The F–86 was the first American fighter plane to have sweptback wings. The two wings, 37 feet from tip to tip, were set at an angle of thirty-five degrees to the fuselage. Engineers had found that swept wings reduced drag at high speed while increasing lift. However, sweeping the wings caused instability at low speeds. North American solved this problem by employing movable edges at the front of the wing, called slats. Later models of the Sabre did away with the slats, which were a hindrance in high-speed turns, substituting a larger wing set at a thirty-seven degree angle.

Unlike many aircraft of the time, the F–86 was designed with maintenance in mind. For example, the left side of the fuselage had twenty-seven access panels for inspection. The right had twenty-three. Given that field conditions in Korea were primitive, and temperatures were either quite cold or uncomfortably hot, mechanics appreciated the convenience. Major F–86 repair work was done in Japan, initially at Johnson, with Sabres being ferried back and forth as necessary.

For most of 1951 Johnson also was home to one of the 4th Fighter Interceptor Wing's three squadrons. This provided air defense for the island of Japan. At least four F–86s were always on alert, given the potential for the North Koreans or their Chinese or Russian mentors to widen the war by striking their old nemesis. Eventually, this squadron would be deployed to Korea, with other Sabre units assuming its defensive role.

Johnson was in effect a small city where several thousand men lived and worked. Simple but sturdy wooden buildings covered the landscape as did curbed roads, Quonset huts, and canvas tents. Formerly home to Mitsubishi Zeros as Irumagawa Field, Johnson was now a major installation of Far East Air Forces. Concrete runways, ample taxiways and ramps, and large heated hangars gave the F–86 force a most capable home.

The six Sabres were parked off by themselves, away from other aircraft. Each carried the war paint of the 4th Fighter Interceptor Wing. These were black and white stripes near the center of the fuselage, slanting forward, with similar stripes out by the wing tips. The stripes were to aid in identification during combat, important given the similarity of the swept wing MiG–15 with the F–86. B–29 gunners were known to shoot at any airplane with swept wings while in air-to-air engagements, friendly pilots sometimes mistaking the Sabre for its Russian-built counterpart. Several months into 1952, the black and white stripes were replaced by yellow bands edged in black. The change was mandated by Far East Air Forces. By this time a second F–86 wing had entered the fray. It adopted the yellow markings. FEAF wanted to have its Sabre force conform to one design and considered the new color to be more effective. But throughout 1951 and a few months beyond, 4th FIW Sabres flew to the Yalu carrying their distinctive black and white stripes.

Detachment Q's six aircraft also had special markings. Soon after arriving at Johnson McGrath had ordered the Sabre's rudder and nose cone be painted navy blue. He believed the units' espirit de corps would be enhanced with aircraft markings unique to Detachment Q. His own flight helmet was painted the same color, as were the names of the crew chiefs of each plane, carried on the right side of the fuselage just aft of the gun ports. Crew chiefs were critical to the group's success and the chiefs were pleased to have their names featured on their aircraft. McGrath knew that the crew chiefs considered the plane to be on loan to the pilots, ownership residing with the man who kept the craft flyable.

McGrath's own name appeared on the aircraft he usually flew. His rank and name were detailed in white Gothic lettering on a field of navy blue that covered the bottom of the canopy on the left side of the aircraft. His Sabre carried no nickname, unlike many F–86s in Korea. Often pilots would adorn their planes with an assortment of colorful images. The highest scoring American ace of the war, for example, Captain Joseph McConnell, named his F–86 "Beauteous Butch" after his wife. Perhaps the best known Sabre marking belonged to the craft assigned to Lieutenant James Thompson. His F–86 carried a large, fire-breathing green dragon artistically painted below the cockpit.

McGrath had considered naming his aircraft "Catherine." The name would be spelled out in red letters set against a black silhouette of the Georgetown University campus. He had found an airman talented with the paintbrush to draw the image. The airman produced two designs, one of them particularly attractive. However, hours before the plane was to be painted, McGrath changed his mind. Catherine, he felt, had nothing to do with the war in Korea. Nor, for that matter, did the university. Moreover, she was gone and McGrath decided to preserve her memory inside his heart rather than on his airplane.

Of course the six F–86s carried the national insignia found on all American military aircraft. This was a white star in a circle of dark blue flanked by white bars in the middle of which ran a red stripe. The insignia was placed on the side of the fuselage, near the center, just forward of the tail. It was also found on top of the left wing and beneath the right one. Other air forces had their own national marking. The Royal Canadian Air Force's featured a red maple leaf within a white circle surrounded by a ring of blue. The air force of the Soviet Union, whose pilots fought in Korea in MiGs carrying the insignia of North Korea, had a simple red star as its national insignia. North Korea's was similar to Russia's. It was predominantly a red star on a field of white, encircled by a red stripe that itself was surrounded by a circle of blue.

McGrath's flight that afternoon was a test hop, to verify that the Sabre's cockpit heating and canopy pressurization systems were in working order. The day before, on an early morning training flight, the two systems malfunctioned, necessitating a premature return to Johnson. Both systems utilized compressed heated air from the engine. The air was routed to various places throughout the aircraft. Temperature was regulated by an electronic control box that proportioned the amount of hot and cold air furnished to the cockpit. A small refrigeration unit provided cooler air while a four-kilowatt electric heater reheated the air when required. Cockpit air pressure was maintained usually at 2.75 p.s.i. by a regulator mounted at the rear of the sliding canopy. Engine rpm was necessary to maintain both systems, with rpms needing to increase as the aircraft gained altitude.

The test flight went well. McGrath lifted off smoothly, retracted flaps and landing gear, set the trim, and began a gentle climb. The goal was forty-two thousand feet, about as high as the F–86A could go. With the throttle set at ninety-six percent rpm, McGrath's plane took slightly over thirteen minutes to reach the ceiling, losing approximately fifty knots of airspeed for every ten thousand feet of altitude.

During the flight both systems appeared to function properly. However McGrath noticed that when the canopy began to frost up, the aircraft's defroster struggled to clear the glass. Upon landing McGrath reported the situation to the plane's crew chief who, shrugging his shoulders apologetically, told his pilot that all F–86s suffered the same malady. McGrath knew that. He knew too, that his crew chief, Sergeant

Norman Ricks, would do whatever could be done to alleviate the problem.

McGrath's next flight occurred the following morning. He and Lieutenant Heller took two Sabres up to thirty-eight thousand feet, an altitude where F–86s and MiGs often met. McGrath then had Heller place his Sabre about four hundred feet behind his own. The Detachment Q leader then did a series of turns, rolls, and dives. The objective was to have Heller stay right behind him, which the lieutenant did. The two planes then reversed positions with McGrath's Sabre trailing Heller's by two hundred feet. The youngster's task was to shake McGrath off his tail. It was "anything goes" flying. Heller threw his Sabre around the sky: sharp rolls, high G turns, split Ss, counter reversals. Heller flew hard, demonstrating to McGrath that he could handle an F–86.

So could McGrath. Later, at the officer's club, Heller told the other pilots of the detachment that he simply could not lose their colonel.

"I'm telling you, fellas, this guy can drive an airplane. I tried to shake him and, let me tell you, I tried real hard. Every time I glanced back, there he was. It was like having an 86 decal stuck on my rearview mirror. All I ever saw was his big blue nose cone."

"Gentlemen," said Flying Officer Robin Urqhart, the exchange pilot from the RAF, "it would appear we have ourselves a winner."

"Let's hope so," chipped in Charlie Hickock. "McGrath was the real thing in England, and I suppose he will be in Korea."

"Life in Detachment Q," continued Urqhart, "is about to become somewhat sporty."

Weather curtailed flight operations for the next three days. The sky became a constant gray. Clouds were low and full of moisture. The resulting rain drenched most of western Japan. Several planes coming into Tokyo were diverted north. Flight schedules, both civil and military, were disrupted. Johnson Air Base was shut down. Its runways looked like long, rectangular lakes. Even some automobiles were immobile. Pilots got bored. Crew chiefs had time to spare. No one was in a good mood except the officer in charge of the PX, where sales of rain-coats and umbrellas soared.

Unexpectedly, McGrath was summoned to Tokyo. A brigadier general at FEAF wanted to see him. McGrath did not mind. Given the rain he was not going to fly. And Tokyo meant an opportunity to see Martha Dawson.

The general was named Smith. He wanted McGrath to pay a call upon Air Vice Marshal Peter Kent who was the senior RAF officer in Japan. Kent wanted to have McGrath come by because His Majesty's government was contributing to Detachment Q, in the person of Flying Officer Urquhart. McGrath did what Smith wanted. Kent, a former Spitfire pilot, turned out to be extremely pleasant. The two pilots talked for thirty-five minutes, mostly about the Luftwaffe. When he left Peter Kent's rather large office McGrath was not sure why the meeting had occurred. Nothing of consequence had transpired. He later concluded that, as protocol was important to the Brits, simply meeting with the air vice marshall satisfied diplomatic niceties.

Before leaving for Tokyo, McGrath had telephoned Martha. To his surprise he reached her. The schoolteacher was at home in the late afternoon, as she had said she would be. Martha seemed pleased to hear his voice and said she was delighted to learn he was coming into Tokyo.

"That means you'll come and take me out."

"I was certainly hoping to."

"I'd be hurt if you came and didn't see me."

"Well, hopefully that's not going to happen. I have to meet a general early Friday afternoon. Why don't we go out Friday night? I'll take you out to dinner, and wine and dine you."

Martha's response to this invitation was an awkward silence. When she did speak, her tone was apologetic.

"I can't Friday. I'm sorry. But I do wish to see you. Honest, I do."

McGrath hid both his surprise and disappointment. Deciding that were she free on Saturday only for lunch he would decline, despite wanting to see her, McGrath now spoke in a confident, commanding voice.

"Well, then, it shall have to be Saturday night."

The way in which Martha responded told McGrath she truly wished to see him.

"Oh good. I was hoping you'd say that. Saturday it is. And I'll have a surprise for you."

"What's that?"

"If I tell you it won't be a surprise." Martha then paused. "Let's see, you'll never find my place, even taxi drivers have trouble with it. Let's meet in the lobby of the University Club. Can you be there at seven o'clock?"

"I can, and will."

"Good. I'll be there at seven."

"As will I. Are you sure you don't want to tell me the surprise?"

"I'm sure." Martha's tone of voice then changed. She sounded more mature and more feminine. "Trust me, my boy, you're going to like it."

McGrath had decided against staying at the small hotel three blocks from FEAF headquarters. He told himself he wanted a nicer place, a larger more modern hotel.

Late Friday afternoon he went to the Tokyo PX. While there he ran into Lieutenant Perkins who seemed pleased to see him and wished him success in Korea. When Perkins departed McGrath continued to search for what he hoped to purchase. He was looking for baseball caps, blue ones. McGrath had decided Detachment Q personnel would wear them as marks of identification. He hoped they would contribute to the unit's morale. The hope was not farfetched, nor was the purchase. Throughout the war in Korea, air force units adopted such caps. Squadrons had their own colors, with emblems or insignia stitched on the hat. McGrath wanted navy blue, with the letters DQ in white. Royal blue and white were the colors of the Brooklyn Dodgers. McGrath wanted his team to have hats similar to those worn by the Yankees. The caps, he thought, would be both handsome and distinctive, much like those worn by DiMaggio and Berra.

McGrath found navy blue hats and ordered four dozen, in assorted sizes. Lettering the caps would take ten days, by which time McGrath would be in Korea. The clerk assured him that the hats, when ready, would be mailed to him. McGrath was less certain. The potential for foul-up seemed large. Yet he had little choice but to accept the clerk's word. Upon leaving the PX, McGrath wondered if he ever would see the forty-eight baseball hats he had just paid for.

Back at the hotel McGrath did something he rarely did. He took a nap. When he woke it was time for dinner. Originally, he had planned to dine at the University Club. But he decided to forego the club and eat where he was staying. The hotel, the Akura Palace, had two dining rooms, one Japanese and one Western. McGrath chose the latter and had a pleasant if undistinguished meal.

Before dinner McGrath had decided he was in need of female companionship. His body signaled to him that it required the touch, taste, and smell of a woman. In twenty-four hours he was to see Martha, but McGrath was impatient. He wanted a woman and he didn't want to wait.

How to find the kind of woman he wanted? Never had McGrath been with a lady of the evening. He had not needed to. Women—more often they were girls—had been available when he sought their company. Even in England females were there, if an effort was made to find them. Focused on commanding a fighter squadron in 1944 and '45, he had no interest in women. Now he felt differently. Was he just older, more cynical, or less committed to his job? He didn't know. He just wanted the company of a female, and was addressing the question of how to obtain it.

McGrath knew he did not want a common streetwalker. So he needed to contact someone who might procure the kind of classy woman he was seeking, or might know an individual who could.

That someone, McGrath soon realized, was located quite close by, indeed at his own hotel. The doorman of the Akura Palace had to be a person of many talents given the size and success of the hotel. So with a five-dollar bill in hand McGrath approached him and explained what he was looking for. The doorman, a heavyset fellow whose name was Yoshio and who six years before had been a chief petty officer in the

Imperial Japanese Navy, smiled and said simply that a woman of beauty would come to McGrath's hotel room at ten o'clock this evening. She would need, he explained, fifty dollars. For his part he would need nothing, although he gladly accepted what McGrath placed in his hand.

After dinner McGrath retired to his room. With an hour to spend before the woman was to arrive, McGrath took a shower and put on a fresh uniform. He did not shave, as his unshakable routine was to put blade to cheek only in the morning. He decided to pass the remaining time by reading. Having finished *The Cruel Sea* he began a novel he had read before. This was *Master-at-Arms* by Rafael Sabatini, the author of *Scaramouche*. McGrath had purchased the book in Washington before leaving for Tokyo.

Able to concentrate on the task at hand, McGrath had made headway into *Master-at-Arms* when he heard a knock on the door. Surprised, he looked at his watch. Time had gone by quickly. It was four minutes past ten o'clock.

He put down the book, turned off the bright light he was using to read, went to the door, and opened it.

Standing in front of him was a woman dressed all in black. The doorman was correct. She was beautiful, extremely so. She wore a sleeveless, high-neck silk dress. Tight fitting, it had a slit along the side that revealed a shapely leg sheathed in black stockings. High-heeled shoes and a chic hat from which netting flowed completed the ensemble. These too were black. The look was elegant yet sexy. It permitted dinner at a fashionable restaurant in New York or a night alone in a Tokyo hotel room. McGrath liked what he saw. The woman conveyed an image of erotic romance. This caused excitement to ripple through his body.

There was but one problem. The woman was Martha Dawson.

TWELVE

"Oh my God, it's you." Martha spoke first. Her voice conveyed more than surprise. There was anger as well, which showed on her face. What did not show, in either words or her expression, was the regret and shame she felt, the former more than the latter.

McGrath reacted differently. Completely surprised, he said nothing. He just stood at the doorway, his eyes taking in a woman whose appearance he found compelling, his mind recalling a pretty girl he'd sat next to at a rock garden.

Finally, he spoke. "I can't believe it's you."

"And I can't believe you couldn't wait 'til tomorrow." Martha's anger now was revealed in words. "Men are all alike."

"I hardly think this is the time for blame. I haven't done a thing."

"Nor, my friend, have I."

"Well, what are we to do?"

"That's up to you. What do you want? Or, rather, whom do you want, the schoolteacher, or the woman before you?"

McGrath was thinking he wanted both. Wisely, he did not say so. But before he answered, Martha spoke again.

"Be sure you're certain. It's an important decision." Her words continued but were not spoken out loud. *At least for me, if not you.*

"I can't believe this."

"That's not an answer."

"Okay, the truth is that right now you're a woman any man in his right mind would want."

"Then you can have me, *for the night.*" Martha emphasized her last three words.

McGrath paused, knowing that if he made love to her now he'd never see her again.

"So tonight it is." Martha spoke dispassionately. Disappointed, she nonetheless had decided that, if necessary, she would perform this evening and earn her fifty dollars. But she was sick inside. Here was a man who had potential, a possible partner for the future, and all he wanted was a romp in the sack.

She was wrong.

"No. If I have to choose and I know I do, I'll take the schoolteacher."

McGrath had reasoned that with the schoolteacher he eventually would get the other, but that if he chose the lady in black the schoolteacher was gone. In truth, he was more than fond of the girl he had met at the University Club and did not want to give her up.

Martha's reaction was a sigh, and a smile.

"Are you sure?"

"Yes, I'm sure."

"So what happens now?"

"I really don't know."

"Well, you could invite me in."

McGrath did so, and Martha entered the room, deliberately sitting in a large upholstered chair that was not near the bed. McGrath sat where he had been reading.

Martha said nothing, forcing McGrath to speak first.

"Well, this is most awkward, so let me say that you know what I was looking for so tell me why it is that you have this other life. I realize it's none of my business but if I'm to go out with this schoolteacher, which I think I'd still like to do, I'd like to know how and why you're doing what you're doing."

"You sound like you're trying not to be judgmental, but not succeeding."

"I'm trying to understand. Allow me at least to be surprised."

"If you allow me the same. Look, I'm just leading two separate lives, just like you."

"What do you mean?"

"I have two lives—one in the daytime and one at night. And I keep them separate, as though they're two different people."

"Which they're not."

"True, but in my head they are"

"But you said I did the same. I hardly think so."

"You do. You just don't realize it."

"How so?"

"You're a pilot in the air force and a college professor, at least you were. But you're also a cold-blooded killer. That's what fighter pilots do. They kill people. They take out the guy who's flying the other plane. And you separate that from your normal way of life. On the ground you're one person, in the air you're somebody else. You have two different personalities, two different lives."

"But—"

"I'm not finished. I have two different lives as well. But mine are split between day and night. And, like you, I get paid for both."

"What do you mean?"

"You get flight pay and combat pay. Yes?"

"I do."

"So there you are. You get paid extra to kill people. I get paid to sleep with them. What's the difference?"

"There's lots of difference."

"Perhaps some, but not at the core. Society approves of one and not the other. But society is so full of hypocrisy that it barely has the right to judge people and their behavior."

McGrath wanted to speak but Martha would not let him.

"What I do doesn't hurt anybody. What you do does."

"What I do, I do for my country to defend its freedom."

"I could be cynical and say three cheers for you, but I won't. I'll only repeat that your job is to kill people and in mine, my evening job, no one gets hurt."

"But how can you do it?"

"I do it because I have to." Martha did not verbalize the *you idiot* she was thinking. "Schoolteachers don't make a lot of money. Not here or in the States. I have parents to take care of, bills to pay, and someday I'd like to go to grad school."

"I still can't believe all this."

"You have to. Men separate their lives into components, divide their activities, isolate one part from the other, and are proud to do so. But let a woman do so, and men get hot and bothered."

"It's not the same."

"It is. It's just that you don't approve of what I do at night."

"That's true. I don't."

"But you have no problem in doing it, or accepting it. You'll pay for sex but not approve of the woman who does what you want. That, my friend, is a double standard if there ever was one."

McGrath paused, pondering their conversation. He had not found it awkward. He realized, however, that he had been challenged intellectually and while he was sure he was right he was not sure he had won the debate.

"Perhaps I have been hypocritical. But I still don't like it."

"I'm not overly fond of it either though it is what it is, nothing less, nothing more. And I'm putting together a piggy bank that will allow me to do what I have to do now and want to do in the future."

"So what do we do now?"

"That depends on you. What do you want?"

McGrath realized he was at a crossroads. Martha Dawson was full of risk, of that he was sure. Yet beyond her physical appeal—and that was substantial—there was a pleasing disposition, a brain that functioned, and admirable ambition, which is why, McGrath reasoned, he had been interested in the first place. Moreover, the girl simply intrigued him. He found himself wanting her and wanting to be with her, despite her evening occupation. Of course that would have to end, he told himself, adding that she no doubt would expect fidelity from him as well.

"So what will it be?" she queried for a second time, aware that McGrath appeared lost in thought.

"I want the schoolteacher."

"You can have the schoolteacher if you really want her."

"I'm pretty sure I do."

"But you're not certain."

"How can I be? In one sense I've just sort of met you. But what I've seen is pretty nifty."

"That's a sweet remark, you know." Martha was smiling.

"Well, it's meant to be. And it has the added advantage of being true."

"Is there a 'but' to all of this?"

"Of course there is, and you know what it is. I'd like to pursue the girl I met at the University Club, and get to know her better."

"And I the pilot," Martha continued, a mischievous twinkle in her eyes complementing the smile, "even though he does what he does."

"Don't start. I'm trying to work this out in my head so we can have a happy ending."

"I'm sorry, go on." The twinkle disappeared, though the smile remained.

"That's all, really. I like this schoolteacher I met and would like to see her again, and then again some more."

"And the but?"

"The but is obvious. I'm not sure I can handle having a girlfriend sleep around at night, especially for money."

"So I'm your girlfriend?"

Again McGrath took the plunge. "I'd certainly like you to be."

In response the lady in black spoke as the schoolteacher she was.

"I'd like that too."

"But there's a condition."

"Which is that I have to give up my evening work."

"That's right."

"Well then I have a decision to make."

"You do indeed."

"And I suppose you want that decision to be made right now."

"I do. Look, I've made my decision. Now it's your turn. Despite everything, I'd like to see you again. I'd like to get to know you better and spend time with you, the schoolteacher. I can't promise anything except I'll try my best to be a really good boyfriend. God, that sounds so moronic. Let me try this another way. I'll do my best—my very best—to treat you right and we'll let what happens happen. We're not kids anymore and this may not work. But I think it might and I think we ought to try."

McGrath stood up and walked over to Martha, being careful not to touch her.

"Now, schoolteacher, it's your turn."

Martha wanted to say she would quit her job. She wanted to be decisive, to have no hesitation in telling McGrath that henceforth, her nighttimes would belong to him alone. He seemed, she realized, sincerely interested in her and certainly was a man most women would consider a catch. He obviously was smart. He had rank and stature in the air force. And unlike most pilots, his ego seemed in check. Yet committing to him was risky. There were no guarantees they would do well. And if, initially successful, might they not fail once the glow wore off? Moreover, by instinct and her night work, Martha knew men and she did not altogether trust them.

But embracing McGrath involved an additional risk. Money, Martha long ago had learned, may not make the world go 'round, but it did pay the bills. She derived significant income from her night work and did not relish living off a schoolteacher's salary. Nor did she wish to be dependent upon another person, for dollars or for happiness.

And yet, Martha Dawson long had known that the time would come when her double life would have to end. She had accepted this as fact, and more than once had said to herself that she would be relieved when that day came. But Martha had not expected it so soon.

And she had not expected it to occur because an attractive man had entered her life.

"I'm waiting."

"Yes, I know."

"I'd feel a lot better if you didn't seem to be deliberating, to be weighing the factors pro and con."

Martha repeated herself. "Yes, I know." Then she spoke what she was thinking. "It's not that simple."

"Yes it is. It's about you and I having something special, together. At least I think we do."

When Martha remained silent, McGrath continued.

"I thought you wanted this. You just said you'd like to be my girl-friend."

"I would."

"But?"

"But I'm not certain. Not about the girlfriend part. I like that, I really do. But all this is happening so quickly. It's so unexpected."

"True, but it's something we should cherish, and wrap our arms around, not run away from."

"That's easy for you to say."

"No, Martha, it's not. And given what I've told you, you should know that."

"Yes, I'm sorry. You're right. Look, I'd like to be your girl. In one way I already am. But all this is so sudden."

"Life's that way. It tends not to be convenient."

Martha's courage was about to fail, and she knew it.

"I can't. I think I could fall in love with you, but I just can't. I'm not ready for this."

"You mean something real." McGrath spoke with a hint of harsh-ness in his voice.

"Don't be mad, please."

"Mad? That's only part of it. I'm disappointed. I'm disappointed in you. The moment of truth has arrived and your courage has disap-peared."

"It's not that simple."

"Martha, my dear, it is exactly that simple. When opportunity comes along you grab it. When a challenge is in front of you, you meet it head on."

"And I suppose you've done just that."

Before answering McGrath thought not just of Catherine, but also of the P–51 Mustang and the skies above Germany.

"Yes I've had my share, maybe even more than my share."

McGrath now realized he was about to lose this girl. The schoolteacher was turning him down. He was as surprised as he was hurt. And he was angry as well. But, remaining calm, he addressed Martha in a soft and surprisingly gentle voice.

"I believe I love you, Martha Dawson, or will. You're my favorite schoolteacher, to be sure."

He hoped these words and their tone would sway Martha and he half-expected her to reply with a similar declaration.

She did not. Instead of speaking she rose and walked over to McGrath. There she kissed him, on the lips, holding his head in her hands. Though the kiss was not passionate it was done with feeling and was meant to convey far more than just affection.

"This is all too sudden. I've got to go. If I stay here any longer I'll start to cry."

Martha moved to the door. Then she turned and faced the man who had discovered her secret, thereby upsetting the established stability of her life.

"Goodbye, my dear. You are truly wonderful and I am, in so many ways, a terrible fool."

With that she left, closing the door behind her.

Still surprised, McGrath remained in his chair, disbelieving what he had just seen and heard. Despite feelings on her part he correctly interpreted as deep and genuine, she had walked out on him. He had told her he could love her, and to his astonishment, she had responded by leaving. For the first time in his life McGrath seemed to have lost a battle he thought he would win.

The feelings he had of intense failure did not remain front and center for long. McGrath repressed them, deciding he simply would end this particular chapter of his life. By willpower alone he would remove Martha Dawson from his consciousness. He would, he told himself, put her in his past.

It didn't work. He tried reading *Master-at-Arms* and found Sabatini's words less than compelling. After a futile forty minutes he put the book down. He then went for a walk. This too provided no relief. He spent the entire time recounting conversations he and the girl had shared. He also drew pictures in his mind of how she looked, marveling at the contrast between the plain but pretty schoolteacher he first had met at the University Club and the woman in black who radiated sensuality. Upon returning to his room McGrath chose to do nothing save climbing into bed. Recalling Scarlet O'Hara's dictum that "tomorrow is another day" he went to sleep hopeful that the frustration and loss he felt would be gone once the new day arrived.

McGrath slept well, and long. He awoke at 8:30 and went through his morning ritual, which ended with breakfast. This he ate at the hotel's Western restaurant, which prepared eggs and toast much like Howard Johnson's did back home. During the meal the events of the previous night were not absent. But they were not dominant. Instead of Martha Dawson he focused on Detachment Q and the job that lay ahead.

Breakfast was leisurely so it was ten o'clock by the time McGrath returned upstairs to his room. He had to plan his day, and evening too, as the date with Martha obviously was canceled. However he soon realized that without the schoolteacher there was no reason to remain in Tokyo. Though he toyed with the idea of spending the day seeing the sights he decided to return to Johnson. There was, after all, a war to fight.

McGrath found a train schedule and chose an early afternoon departure. Once packed, he had time to spare before checking out of the Akura Palace. So, ever comfortable with a book, McGrath picked up *Master-at-Arms.*

Sword in hand, Quentin De Morlaix had gone back to his former estate of Chavaray when time accelerated. McGrath, returning from the eighteenth century, heard a knock on his door. A glance at his watch told him it was time to leave, which meant the bellboy had come for his luggage.

"Come in," said McGrath who put down the book but remained seated.

The door did not open so McGrath repeated what he had said. The response was a second knock on the door similar to the first. Mildly annoyed, and wondering whether Japanese bellboys were deaf or simply too polite to enter a guest's room, he walked to the door and opened it himself.

No bellboy was in sight. In front of him stood Martha Dawson.

"I was afraid you wouldn't be here," she said, with a hint of desperation in her voice.

McGrath was both surprised and speechless. He simply looked at her. She was wearing a pink dress that favored both her skin tone and figure. The look was decidedly not that of the schoolteacher, though compared to the evening before her appearance was quite modest.

Not knowing why she was there, he tried to conceal his pleasure in seeing her. In this he failed. Upon seeing his reaction she in turn broke into a smile. When she spoke the words come out with confidence and joy.

"I'm so glad you're still here. I needed to see you."

"Why don't you come in?"

"First I need to tell you something, and hear your reply. Then I'll come in if you want me to."

"I want you—"

"Hush. And hear me out. Last night I did something I now regret. And that was to walk away from a man I think I'm in love with and who I hope loves me."

"He does. At least he's pretty sure he does."

"Good, but I'm not finished. I'm no saint and have done some things most people don't approve of. Some folks would think I'm used goods and have nothing to do with me, at least in daylight. If I heard you right, you're willing and able to overlook my less than virtuous past and take me on as your girlfriend provided I give it up and devote my working hours to the children at school."

"That's what I said."

"And do you still mean it? Despite all that I've been?"

"I do. I once met this schoolteacher and really, really liked her."

"But she was more than a schoolteacher."

"So I learned last night. But why don't we, both of us, put the past behind us and focus on the future? A new beginning, so to speak. No promises, but I suspect we might make a go of it."

"Oh God, I do love you." Martha moved toward McGrath and kissed him.

Recovering, McGrath started to smile. "That was very nice. Since you're now my girlfriend—we need to find another word—would you like to come in now?"

That day McGrath did not take the train to Johnson Air Base. He and Martha spent the day together. They played tourist, though the sights they saw were secondary. Their focus was on each other. Conversation came easy and their bond grew strong as they talked and talked. Martha's evening occupation was not ignored, though the words employed tended to be more refined than raw. She pledged to stop and McGrath accepted her at her word. He spoke of Catherine and here the words were sweet and reverent, as befitting the dead. He pledged to hold dear her memory and Martha told him never to stop doing so.

Late in the afternoon they were having tea at a small shop near the Diet called August Moon. McGrath had a question for Martha.

"So what would you like to do next?"

"Next? Oh, I have a date tonight. A guy I know, an ex-college professor, told me he was taking me out to dinner. It was set up a few days ago."

"Oh really? Nice fellow?"

"Actually, he is. I'm quite taken with him."

"Lucky boy. Here's another question for you."

"I'm ready."

"You once mentioned you had a surprise for me, remember?"

"I do indeed."

"And?"

"And tonight, after dinner, I'm going to give it to you."

"Will I like it?"

Martha responded with a gesture that caught McGrath by surprise but captured his attention. Seductively, she ran her hand lightly across her body, then turned it face up toward him and blew a kiss across it.

"I suspect you will."

THIRTEEN

McGrath put his Sabre down upon Suwon's concrete runway at 125 mph. The landing was perfect. The main wheels touched down smoothly and as speed decreased McGrath brought the nosewheel gently down. The aircraft then rolled along the runway, slowing rapidly. Turning right at the end of the runway onto a temporary, pierced steel planking taxiway, McGrath steered his blue-nosed F–86 to a parking area, guided by an air force Jeep that had a large FOLLOW ME sign on its back seat.

Shutting down the engine, canopy already open, McGrath welcomed himself to Korea. Looking about he saw the rest of Detachment Q's aircraft do what his had just done—land and taxi to a predetermined dispersal area. Very soon the six Sabres were in line abreast, engines quiet.

Deplaning, McGrath was met by three men. The first was his crew chief, to whom he reported that the F–86 seemed in proper working order. The second was Edward Brumbaugh, who told McGrath that the detachment's support personnel and equipment had arrived safely and intact. The men, he said, were busy settling in.

"Not exactly Johnson, is it, Edward?"

"No sir, it's not."

They both spoke the truth. Suwon was, by air force standards, a primitive affair. There were no aircraft hangars. Maintenance was done in the open air. With only one runway, operations were limited and needed to be conducted with considerable care. The control tower was a temporary wooden structure not particularly large and reached by two ladders masquerading as stairs. The garage for five trucks and crash crews was a row of empty fuel drums with camouflage netting for a roof. M16 halftracks, each with four .50 caliber machine guns, were spotted about, providing a limited defense against air attack. Pierced steel planking, a World War II invention, was everywhere the aircraft were. The PSP kept the planes from sinking into the mud whenever it rained, which in Korea it did frequently. However, the planking when wet was slippery and hard on tires, which added to the woes of crew chiefs who often could not secure the parts they needed to keep their charges ready to fly.

Yet the most striking feature of Suwon was the tents. When Detachment Q arrived, the airfield, save for the runway and surrounding PSP, was a sea of tents. Olive brown in color, they were made of canvas and accommodated up to twelve individuals. Men lived in tents, ate in tents, worked in tents, and, to a limited degree, played in tents. To some, life in the tents reminded them of Boy Scout camp, though in the scouts the comforts of home were not far away.

The third person greeting McGrath was also a lieutenant colonel. His name was Preston and he was the commander of the 4th Fighter Interceptor Group. The group was the sharp edge of the 4th Fighter Interceptor Wing, which included two other groups: the 4th Maintenance and Supply Group and the 4th Air Base Group. Commanding the wing, which comprised 1,325 men, was Colonel Herman Schmid.

Ben Preston was not an officer McGrath knew. But the group commander welcomed McGrath warmly. He was pleased to have six additional Sabres at his disposal and he was bothered not at all by the unusual arrangement accorded Detachment Q. Excluding the six aircraft McGrath had just flown in, Preston had thirty-eight Sabres with which to battle the MiGs. These F–86s were assigned to two fighter squadrons, the 334th and 335th. The group's third unit, the 336th Fighter Interceptor Squadron, was in Japan, performing air defense duties. Preston had his hands full. Two hundred miles away, parked safely in Manchuria just north of the Yalu, were four hundred MiGs.

"I'm going to treat your little group as a separate unit," said Preston, "much like a squadron, though smaller."

"That's fine, Colonel, however you want to do it. We're here to help."

"Call me Ben. I've heard good things about you and we can use all the help we can get."

"Tell me about the MiG–15."

"I'll tell you what I know, which isn't much, but first let's have you pay a call upon Colonel Schmid."

"Good idea, since I'm to report to him first thing. What's he like? I don't know him at all."

"He's fine. He's a damn good administrator and he's not one of those staff weenies who won't climb into a cockpit."

"Sounds okay."

"He is. Last week he knocked a piece off a MiG."

The two men walked to the tent serving as Colonel Schmid's office. The tent was larger than most. Inside was an array of desks, file cabinets, telephones, and typewriters. Also inside were seven men— three officers and four enlisted personnel. They were quite busy, seemingly concerned with all sorts of documents and piles of mail. The air force may have fought with aircraft, but it floated on paper.

The atmosphere in the tent was more formal than McGrath expected, but this changed once he and Preston met with Schmid. The wing commander was friendly. He welcomed McGrath to "beautiful downtown Suwon" and asked if Detachment Q were operationally ready. Preston replied first, saying that he and McGrath were to have an orientation flight that afternoon. All pilots in Korea, regardless of rank, undertook such flights prior to their first combat mission. Schmid directed that these be conducted rapidly because, he said, intelligence had indicated that the MiGs were about to come out in force.

175

"We're short of 86s and we need your aircraft," he was addressing McGrath, "but make sure you're ready. The MiGs are plenty in number and some of them know exactly what they're doing."

There were, at Suwon, several places to eat. Called "messes" and set up in tents, they were run by the 4th Food Service Squadron, a unit of the 4th Air Base Group. Kindly stated, the food provided was more nutritious than tasty. It was fuel for the body, and if *Life* magazine did not like the cuisine, which it didn't, at least 1,325 men did not go hungry.

To one of these messes McGrath and Preston repaired following the meeting with Herman Schmid. They intended to have an early lunch, after which the latter would take the former on his orientation flight. A tour, Preston explained, "of not terribly scenic northwestern Korea, featuring such points of interest as Pyonyang and the Chongchon River."

Once inside the mess, McGrath and the group commander went through a cafeteria line. Grabbing grilled cheese sandwiches and a salad that looked like it had been made months ago, the two pilots sat down at one of the tables.

Of the four military services, the air force was the most informal. And given that Suwon was conducting military operations, this informality was reinforced, especially at the messes. Hence, other officers were not reluctant to join McGrath and Preston at their table. One who did was Major Peter Parker, the senior intelligence officer of the 4th Fighter Interceptor Group. He too had chosen grilled cheese sandwiches and was about to start eating when McGrath asked Preston a question, an inquiry that made Parker put down the sandwich and await the answer.

"So, what do we know about the MiGs?"

"The answer, unfortunately, is not a whole hell of a lot." The group commander spoke in a matter-of-fact tone. "We do know that the MiG–15 is a damn good airplane. It's fast, well armed, and has a much higher ceiling than the 86."

"So they have the advantage of height."

"Indeed they do."

McGrath's next remark reflected a widespread belief. "I was led to believe that Russian aircraft weren't all that good. They beat the Germans with an army, not an air force. What happened?"

"I'll let our intel officer answer that," said Preston.

"Colonel," Parker was looking at McGrath when he replied, "I think three things happened. The first is that the Reds got hold of some German aviation people at the end of the war—the guys responsible for the Nazi jets—and encouraged them to work for them, probably at the point of a gun. Second, the stupid British actually sold the Soviets some Rolls Royce jet engines, which had to be one of the craziest things to have happened in the last fifty years. And finally, the Russian airplane industry is not that bad. Maybe not as good as ours but capable of producing pretty decent flying machines."

"Which the MiG most certainly is," added Preston.

"We don't know a lot about the MiG," continued Parker. "We do know its cannons pack a punch and that the aircraft can accelerate real quick."

"Sounds like a first-rate interceptor." McGrath was looking at the intelligence officer.

"It is. And I think it was designed as such. Stalin and his buddies took a look at our B–36s and decided they needed a weapon capable of stopping an aerial armada heading toward Moscow."

Everything that Major Parker had said to McGrath and Preston was true. The MiG–15 was a fine aircraft. In many ways similar to the Sabre, with its sweptback wings and tricycle landing gear, the Russian craft could outclimb and out-accelerate its American rival. Its three cannons were more lethal than the F–86's six machine guns and, unbeknownst to Parker and his colleagues, the MiG could absorb considerable punishment.

Yet the aircraft was far from perfect.

The cannons of the MiG, two NS 23 mm guns on the port side of the nose and one NS 37 mm gun on the starboard, had relatively low rates of fire. More significantly, the aircraft itself was unstable at top speed. Combined with an inferior gunsight and limited range, these kept the MiG from dominating the Korean sky.

Moreover, the Sabre was not without strengths of its own. The F–86 could out-dive the MiG. At low or medium altitude it could out-maneuver its opponent. With greater range, more armor, and a pressurization system superior to that of the MiG, the advantage at times lay with the Sabre. But where the American plane clearly excelled was in its gunsight. Manufactured by Sperry, the A–1CM radar-controlled device made the F–86 a killer of MiGs. The Sabre pilot "dialed in" the wingspan of the target. In the case of the MiG this was thirty-three feet. Closing in on the enemy, a yellow light would come on in the cockpit once radar lock was established. The pilot would then place the "pipper," an aiming dot that was reflected onto a reflector glass aft of the windshield, on the target and fire. If the Sabre pilot could attain a firing position, if the pipper was on the MiG, his guns would strike home.

McGrath had additional questions for Preston and Parker.

"What about the pilots? Are they any good?"

By the way Preston looked at the intelligence chief, Parker understood he was to respond.

"Well, theoretically the pilots are North Koreans and Red Chinese. And they're not up to our standards. We do real well against them."

"Is there a 'but' to this?"

"Indeed there is, Colonel. The 'but' is that there are Russian pilots flying the MiGs."

"Russians?"

"Yes, Russians. Despite this being a U.N. effort, and with Russia, or rather the Soviet Union, being a member of the United Nations, there are Russian pilots flying the MiGs, at least some of them. Of course this is top secret and we're not supposed to broadcast the fact. But there's no doubt there are Russians in the cockpit."

Parker then answered a question that McGrath was thinking but had not yet verbalized.

"They're not bad, the Russians. Oh, some are, but the average pilot is pretty decent, though we can handle them. The problem is the honchos."

"Honchos?"

"They're the real good Red pilots. They're probably World War II veterans or instructors, or both. They know how to fly. They know how to fight. And they can be real dangerous."

"Just ask my predecessor," said Ben Preston.

Parker explained that Lt. Colonel Glenn Eagleston, a World War II ace who previously had commanded the 4th Fighter Interceptor Group, had a celebrated encounter with one of the honchos. The MiG pilot was very good at his job and severely damaged Eagleston's F–86. There were cannon strikes all over the aircraft, which had to make a wheels-up landing at Suwon, skidding off the end of the runway. The Sabre was a complete write-off. Its pilot was fortunate to survive.

Russian pilots in Korea belonged to several Soviet air divisions that were rotated into Manchuria throughout the three-year conflict. Lest their identity be revealed, in case they were shot down, the pilots were forbidden to fly south of Pyonyang or out over the Yellow Sea. And while they flew their own aircraft, their MiGs carried North Korean makings. At first their roles were to defend Manchuria in the event of a U.S. attack and to teach North Korean and communist Chinese pilots how to fly the MiG. Soon, in a bid for air superiority, the Russians became more aggressive. They attempted to block American bombing of targets in North Korea. Despite downing large numbers of aircraft—alone the Fourth Fighter Interceptor Group had thirty-two pilots killed in action—the MiGs were unable to gain control of the sky. However, they did disrupt numerous missions of the F–84s. More importantly, the Russian pilots gained combat experience. This, their generals considered essential if a wider war with the West were to break out.

The briefing for McGrath's orientation flight was a casual affair. Colonel Preston said simply, "Stick with me." He added that they'd make ever-widening circuits around Suwon and then head northwest, on a course of 330 degrees, climbing to a cruising altitude of twenty-eight thousand feet. Earlier Preston had queried intelligence and weather officers. The latter told him skies would be clear; the former said sixteen F–84s would be returning home after striking two truck convoys east of Pyonyang.

A Jeep took McGrath out to his F–86. Once there, Sergeant Ricks informed him that the aircraft was ready to go.

"She's in good shape, Colonel."

"I'm sure she is."

"Don't break my bird, sir."

"I won't, Norman."

McGrath then conducted the usual preflight inspection pilots performed prior to climbing into the cockpit. Starting at the front of the aircraft he circled the Sabre, stopping at five locations. He made sure that the nose gear ground safety lock was removed, that the pitot tube cover was off, that the leading edge slats were moveable, that the tail pipe was clear. All this, and more, Norman Ricks already had verified. But in a ritual as old as aviation, McGrath as pilot double-checked to make sure all was in order.

Using the port ammunition compartment access door as a first step McGrath climbed into the cockpit, first making sure that the canopy ejection ground safety pin had been removed. Before starting the engine an F–86 pilot had an extensive checklist to review. Over forty items needed to be examined. These included the emergency fuel switch, the wing flap lever, speed brakes, and oxygen regulator. Methodically, McGrath went through the list, confirming all was as it should be.

Meanwhile Ricks had ensured that the immediate area fore and aft of the F–86 was clear of personnel. Suction at the intake duct of the Sabre's J–47 engine was sufficient to draw a person into the nose, causing injury or death. Behind the aircraft the danger arose from the high temperature and velocity of exhaust shooting out of the tailpipe. With the J–47 at military thrust, the temperature at twenty-five feet from the Sabre reached 350 degrees Fahrenheit, while the exhaust velocity peaked at 460 mph.

Ricks already had moved the C-6 auxiliary power unit cart into position. Painted yellow, this small, rather clumsy machine was employed to power up the F–86. Inside was an air-cooled, light aircraft engine coupled to a generator. Ricks took the cables from the APU and plugged them into the side of McGrath's Sabre, in an outlet on the fuselage that was covered by the 4th's black and white combat stripes.

Of course the crew chief alone could not service the F–86. Responsible for McGrath's plane, Ricks could and did draw upon others to maintain the Sabre. These included radar and radio technicians, armorers, engine specialists, and men to provide the jet fuel. In total, to keep an F–86 operational in a combat zone, eighteen people were required. This included the pilot and a cook, the latter necessary to feed himself and the other seventeen.

With the throttle at off and the engine master switch on, McGrath held the starter switch momentarily at the start position. Within two seconds the J–47 ignited. McGrath moved the throttle slightly forward, carefully watching exhaust temperatures. Hot starts, in which the exhaust temperatures exceeded GE guidelines, resulted in expensive and time-consuming engine overhauls.

Norman Ricks disconnected the APU cart and removed the wheel chocks. McGrath checked his instruments and released the parking brake. He then advanced the throttle to sixty percent rpm, and quickly pulled it back. This got the aircraft moving. He steered the Sabre using the nose wheel, depressing a switch on the stick while employing the rudder pedals. The F–86 had excellent ground handling characteristics, and McGrath had no difficulty in maneuvering the plane onto the taxiway. As he did so Sergeant Ricks threw him a smart salute, which he returned.

McGrath taxied to the end of the runway, arriving there in conjunction with Preston. The two pilots then performed their preflight checks, of both the aircraft and its engine.

McGrath closed his canopy, double-checked flaps and trim, and advanced the throttle first to eighty percent rpm, then full open, allowing the rpm to stabilize at one hundred percent. Brakes were on and the aircraft shook, anxious to sprint like a Kentucky thoroughbred in the gate.

In the cockpit, ready to fly, McGrath's mind suddenly wandered. This was not intentional and lasted but momentarily. He thought of Catherine and how special she had been. He thought of Notre Dame and of his satisfaction at earning a Ph.D. He recalled that day in April, six years before, when he returned from his final mission over Germany. His entire life did not come into view, just these three events.

Later, in his tent, he would attempt to understand the significance of these thoughts. Why had they arisen? Why these three? Why then? McGrath would conclude that, taken together, they were an affirmation of life, a natural reaction to the veil of death that shrouded Korea. They also were a warning. They signaled that life must be appreciated and celebrated, for its nemesis was close at hand. Not given to ponder grand questions of the human condition, McGrath nevertheless reached a conclusion not all great minds achieved. Namely, that death ultimately arrives but does not triumph if life has been well lived.

His life, McGrath concluded, had been. So he did not worry about dying. In truth, despite the dangers he would face in Korea, despite the obvious fact that not all Sabre pilots would survive, McGrath never once conceded to the possibility of being killed. He had faith in his ability and faith in his aircraft. More importantly, McGrath just did not believe he would perish. He might be wounded but he would not die. Others might, others would. But not he. There was no Russian cannon shell with his name on it, or so he believed.

And if he were not soon to die, he had no reason to be afraid. Fear gripped many pilots in Korea. Some succumbed to it. Most contained it. Bravery is not the absence of fear. It is victory over it. McGrath did not consider himself brave. He considered himself different. McGrath believed he would survive in Korea simply because he knew he would.

As the control tower flashed a green light, McGrath's radio came to life.

"Red One, you're cleared for takeoff."

Red One was Preston's call sign. Flying the commander's wing, McGrath was Red Two.

Preston's Sabre accelerated quickly, as did Red Two's. At fifty-eight mph the rudder controls became effective. At 120 mph McGrath moved the stick back slightly and the nosewheel lifted off. Seconds later, with the plane's speed still increasing, the two main wheels left the ground and McGrath's F–86 was airborne. He and Preston continued to fly straight, remaining over the runway. Before its end wheels had come up as had the flaps.

As the two F–86s made their first circuit around Suwon, McGrath got a pilot's view of the airfield. There was nothing special about it. One concrete runway, Sabres parked closely together, and more tents than McGrath had ever seen. Most noticeable was the construction work underway. At air force direction, nine hundred Korean laborers were building a new runway. The Koreans did not complain. The meager pay they received provided for food and shelter. From above, dust created by their efforts covered much of the landscape west of the field. At three thousand feet McGrath looked down to the east. Vegetation was minimal. There was more brown than green. No lakes or streams were apparent. Everywhere, scars of war—burnt tanks, shell craters, and buildings in ruins—were visible. If Korea had beautiful vistas, and it did, Suwon was not one of them.

Six minutes later, after completing the third circuit, Preston broke off the commentary he'd been providing. His tone of voice changed as he spoke to McGrath.

"Red Two, let's head north."

McGrath was flying to the right and slightly behind Preston's Sabre, separated by ninety feet. The two aircraft began a climbing turn. At 28,000 feet they leveled off, setting their speed at 510 mph. Ahead of them, not far, was Pyonyang. Approaching the city, they skirted its eastern perimeter, bypassing antiaircraft guns that nevertheless fired at the two F–86s. The shots were wildly inaccurate and the Sabres continued north, unperturbed.

With the Chongchon River in sight they turned due west and flew to the coast. As they did, the F–84s passed below. The Thunderjets flew in pairs of two. One aircraft was spitting a thin line of black smoke; another was losing altitude. As other Sabres were covering the withdrawal of the F–84s, Preston and McGrath made no effort to escort the fighter-bombers. Heading south the two F–86s overflew Peng Yeng Do, an island just below the easternmost point of the Korean peninsula. For the 4th Fighter Interceptor Group the island's significance lay in its wide, five thousand feet long beach, upon which Sabres in trouble could and did land.

From this sandy safe haven Preston and McGrath headed directly back to Suwon, landing there exactly forty-seven minutes after they had departed. Taxiing to dispersal, McGrath felt particularly good. The orientation flight had gone well. He now had a sense of the territory. He was comfortable in the F–86, and settled in at Suwon. As McGrath signed Air Force Form One, which pilots filled out upon completing a flight to indicate problems with the aircraft, he realized he was eager to take Detachment Q up north.

That night in his tent, after contemplating what had occurred just before takeoff, he picked up *Master-at-Arms*, hoping to finish the book. He had enjoyed the work so far and had obtained a copy of *Mistress Wilding*, one of Sabatini's lesser-known novels. This he planned to read next. Someday, he mused, he would return to serious, academic works. For now, given the intensity and stress of his current occupation, he would relax with authors such as Rafael Sabatini and C. S. Forester, whose *Hornblower* novels he greatly admired.

The tent assigned to McGrath was in no way fancy. It contained four government issued beds, three wooden, fold-up chairs, and ten empty ammunition crates that served both as tables, walls and dressers. Each bunk had a cheap, metal night lamp, the kind with a flexible base. On one crate, resting upon another, a large *National Geographic* map of Korea was posted. On others there were pictures of females, the wives of McGrath's two tentmates. In the middle of the tent, which had a wooden floor, was a heater—unnecessary now, but useful once winter came. There were no fans. Air conditioning was nonexistent, save for raising the flaps of the tent, which frequently would bring in dust as well as fresh air. The only amenity in the tent was a coffeemaker that had been permanently borrowed from a storeroom at Johnson Air Base, along with enough cans of ground coffee to last three men well into 1953. Officers called their canvas dwelling their "hooch." McGrath did not care for the term, but employed it, as it was part of a pilot's everyday vocabulary.

The two men with whom McGrath shared his tent were absent when McGrath, having finished his book, flicked off his lamp. One of the men, Peter Parker, was in a nearby tent, winning at poker. The other, Larry Duff, was working late. Duff was a North American Aviation technical representative. A civilian, he monitored the performance of the F–86, advising both air force personnel at Suwon and company colleagues at the plant in California. Each of the contractors that manufactured major components of the Sabre had liaison employees at air force installations operating the F–86. In Korea these "tech reps" provided yeoman service, rarely receiving the credit they deserved.

Alone in the darkened tent McGrath's mind wandered, as it had at the end of the runway. This time he was thinking of a more recent positive event. He thought about Martha Dawson and the Saturday they had shared in Tokyo.

She had held McGrath to his promise of a dinner date. Meeting at the University Club, they dined at a restaurant Martha selected. It was Indochinese, a kind McGrath had never patronized. The food was excellent, delicate, and tasty. McGrath greatly enjoyed it, but had difficulty keeping his eyes off Martha.

She wore a black dress, not unlike the previous night's apparel. This one, however, had no slit along the side. It did have a beaded top with long sleeves and a high neckline. Martha wore shoes that were red, as were her gloves. Her hair was pulled to one side causing ruby earrings to be visible.

McGrath thought she looked fabulous.

"You're staring again."

"Sorry. You look terrific; it's hard not to."

"I like the commitment, but I need you to talk to me too."

"Will do."

McGrath did converse. He and Martha talked throughout dinner, both individuals realizing that they enjoyed a chemistry only a man and woman in love can achieve. As the meal came to a close McGrath had a question for the schoolteacher.

"About that surprise you mentioned, when do I get it?"

The answer came in a soft voice, but without hesitation.

"Tonight, dear man, tonight."

Never before had McGrath found a woman so erotically pleasurable. It was, for him, and unbeknownst to McGrath, for Martha as well, a night like no other.

In the tent at Suwon McGrath recalled that night and their time together, recounting in detail what they had done and what they had said. Then he did something he needed to do. He put Martha Dawson out of his mind, parking her memory where she could be retrieved when circumstances allowed. He was about to take Detachment Q into battle. There could be no distractions.

Thus McGrath fell asleep as a warrior, not as a man in love. In the excitement surrounding his arrival at Suwon and of thinking about Martha Dawson he had forgotten a significant event. Tomorrow was his birthday. McGrath would be thirty-one years old.

FOURTEEN

Orientation was over. Each pilot of Detachment Q had flown north at least twice. McGrath had four such flights to his credit, two up to the Yalu. On these he flew as Preston's wingman. No MiGs had come up to play although McGrath had seen the airfield at Antung, just across the river, where the enemy based its planes.

"They're sitting ducks, Red Leader," McGrath had radioed to Preston as the two Sabres began a patrol along the Yalu's southern shoreline.

"Indeed they are, Red Two. Shame we can't pay them a visit."

MiG bases such as Antung were off limits to U.S. aircraft. The airfields were located in Manchuria, a province of China with whom the United Nations was not at war. So the F–86s were not permitted to cross the river. North of the Yalu, the MiGs were safe. Without risk of attack they could take off and land, practice, and be repaired. Manchuria was a sanctuary for the MiGs, much to the frustration of the Sabres, who enjoyed no such safe haven.

Detachment Q's first combat mission took place on Sunday, August 12. The task was relatively simple. The six F–86s were to cover the withdrawal of the main Sabre force upon completion of its patrol along the Yalu. Loitering just north of Pyonyang, the six aircraft were to ensure no MiGs pounced the returning Sabres, who by then would be low on fuel.

Detachment Q easily performed its mission, as no MiGs appeared. Once the main force had passed to the south McGrath decided to take his group north. He calculated that fuel loads were sufficient for seven minutes at the river. And seven minutes in a combat situation was no quick visit.

At thirty-eight thousand feet McGrath could see far below and ahead. North Korea was mostly mountains, a drab monotonous brown that lacked scenic beauty. Nor was the Yalu in any way spectacular. North Korea's longest river, it flowed west 490 miles into the Yellow Sea. It too was visually dull, mostly gray, sometimes brown, rarely blue. Referring to North Korea the country, McGrath concluded it was simply a piece of real estate without charm. Though not, he realized, without significance, as there were two million men contesting its ownership.

As the six aircraft approached the Yalu McGrath's radio came alive.

"Blue Leader, this is Blue Five. My oil pressure's looking low. I'm heading home." Blue Five was Major Willard Roberts.

"Roger, Blue Five." McGrath then spoke to Robert's wingman. "Six, go with him."

The rule in Korea was never to fly alone. The pilot who did so was inviting trouble. Aircraft usually flew in flights of four, occasionally in pairs. In 1951 when the 4th Fighter Interceptor Wing went into combat, sixteen Sabres—four groups of four—took part. But whenever an F–86 needed to return another Sabre was detached to serve as escort. To survive in combat four eyes were required, not two.

"Roger that, Blue Leader. This is Blue Six, turning south. Good hunting."

As the two Sabres peeled away from the formation McGrath spoke to the other pilots, conveying a message he realized was unnecessary.

"Keep a sharp eye out, gentlemen. We're now playing for keeps."

The pilots did so, scanning the sky for signs of the enemy's presence. Sometimes this was a glint of sunlight reflecting off the MiG's aluminum skin. Other times contrails revealed the MiG's presence. Still other times sharp-eyed Sabre pilots simply saw the aircraft in the distance, its large tail fin and horizontal stabilizer high up the tail making identification more certain.

On this mission, however, no MiGs were seen. As McGrath was about to order one more patrol along the Yalu, Heller and Urqhart transmitted the code word "Bingo." This meant their fuel supply was low. Internally the F–86 carried 455 gallons of jet fuel. Two external tanks under the wings each contained an additional 120 gallons. Pilots usually called "Bingo" at 250 gallons, an amount sufficient to return home, with enough fuel for several orbits of the field should that be necessary. Yet, occasionally, Sabre pilots eager for a MiG remained on station when fuel got low, heading home only when absolutely necessary. More than once fuel tanks were dry when their aircraft came to a stop.

Upon hearing Heller and Urqhart, McGrath played it safe. He turned his F–86 toward Suwon, as did the others. Thirty-five minutes later the four Sabres were in the landing pattern. McGrath landed first, and taxied to the parking area, guided to the stop position by Norman Ricks.

The crew chief was disappointed. By the absence of residue at the gun panels he could tell the weapons had not been fired. Prior to a mission a light coat of grease was applied to the panels. This would absorb the residue of smoke were the guns fired and made cleaning the panels much easier. No patches of black on the panels meant the guns had remained silent.

"Welcome back, Colonel," said Ricks, hiding his feelings. "Any problems with the aircraft?"

"None at all, Norman. She worked fine." As he spoke McGrath was signing the air force form the crew chief had handed him.

Unlike Sergeant Ricks, McGrath was not disappointed with the mission. Detachment Q had accomplished its task. It had covered the withdrawal of the F–86s. Moreover, it had patrolled the Yalu, gaining what McGrath hoped would be valuable experience. True, no MiGs had been sighted. But McGrath reasoned that in due time that would be rectified.

Yet seven days later, during which four missions were flown, McGrath's group had yet to engage the enemy, or even see the Russian-built planes. The reason was simple, at least to McGrath. Preston had continued to assign the detachment to cover the withdrawal of his Sabres.

Irritated, McGrath decided to raise the subject with the 4th Fighter Group commander. He was going to speak bluntly, telling Preston he and his unit had come to Korea to shoot MiGs, not baby-sit Sabres.

McGrath found the colonel in the operations room, which in Suwon of course was a tent. McGrath was about to speak when Preston held up his hand, informally signaling silence.

"I've been expecting you and can tell what you're about to say. Relax, you're going north tomorrow. I needed to be sure your group was ready. It's no game up there."

"We're ready, Colonel."

"Good. We're putting up everything we've got. With your six we'll have thirty-two Sabres in the air."

"Sounds like a fight is brewing."

"I sure hope so. That's why we're here."

The Sabres were to form a first line of defense for an attack on rail lines used by the North Koreans to support Chinese troops at the front. Forty-six F–84s were to strike three rail junctions northeast of Pyonyang. The F–86s were to draw off the MiGs as they came south to attack the Thunderjets. In theory the plan was sound.

Briefings for the mission began early the next day. First to speak was the wing's commander. Colonel Schmid outlined the day's overall strategy, emphasizing the deployment of the F–84s and commenting that Far Eastern Air Forces, in the person of General Otto P. Weyland, was taking a particular interest in this mission. An army colonel then reviewed the situation on the ground, noting the importance of depriving the Chinese of their supplies, especially ammunition. Peter Parker followed, providing an intelligence overview. This consisted of remarks about the disposition of MiGs, greater detail about the location of known and likely antiaircraft sites, and general comments about evasion and escape "should anyone present find himself on enemy terra firma." In this case, said Parker, best bet was to head west to the sea where navy rescue helicopters were on duty. Despite what the major said, the pilots in the ops room knew chances of retrieval were slim were they to come down in North Korea.

After Parker, Lt. Colonel Merrill Edwards addressed the group. He was the 4th Fighter Interceptor Wing's senior meteorological officer. Of a reserved manner, Edwards was a superb weatherman. But even he had difficulty in making accurate predictions. In Korea weather patterns came down from the north. Thus, forecasters in the south were at a disadvantage. Nevertheless, Edwards gave his assessment, which in this event, turned out to be remarkably accurate. It was to be, said the colonel, a fine day for flying—clear and bright.

Colonel Preston spoke next. As Tiger Leader, he would be commanding the Sabre force. He discussed tactics and assigned duties to each flight of F–86s. He reviewed start-engine times, radio frequencies, rendezvous locations, and withdrawal routes. Preston's tone of voice reflected his determination to succeed. He eschewed theatrics and spoke matter-of-factly. But there was no confusion regarding message. There was a job to be done, said Preston, and he expected it to be done well.

After the briefing McGrath met with the pilots of Detachment Q. He discussed the plan in general, and in detail went over their particular role. They would be in the vanguard of the Sabres. Their F–86s would be off to the left on the trip north, then be the second group to proceed up the Yalu.

"Sounds good to me," said Charlie Hickok. "I'm hoping to meet up with some MiGs."

"Charlie," said McGrath, "you're about to get your wish."

The pilots soon donned their flight gear and by Jeep or truck made their way to the aircraft. Like the others, McGrath wore a flight suit, jacket, and life preserver with a parachute strapped on his back. To prevent blackouts during violent aircraft maneuvers, jet pilots in Korea also wore a G-suit that prevented blood from pooling below the waist. In addition they carried maps, a compass, first aid kit, knife, and a .45 caliber pistol. Many took with them additional gear, such as extra clothing, food rations, and weapons in case they found themselves in unfriendly territory. McGrath did not do that. Not expecting to be shot down, he was content simply to take along an extra pair of socks. And he alone had the fine flight boots purchased in Tokyo.

Whenever a maximum effort was underway—and thirty-two Sabres certainly qualified as such—the taxiways at Suwon were packed with airmen and officers who were rewarded with an extraordinary sight.

Aircraft, two abreast, lined the end of the runway, spilling onto the taxiway. Manmade birds of prey, graceful in appearance, lethal in purpose, the Sabres shook in anticipation. The noise was deafening. As they took off in pairs, black smoke, exhaust from the J–47 engines, filled the air. Every five seconds two F–86s gathered speed and lifted off. Peter Parker, who had seen such takeoffs more than once, marveled at the sight. A rare mixture of delicate beauty and raw power, he imagined a Wagnerian overture accompanying the spectacle.

McGrath and his wingman, Lieutenant Heller, were the third pair in line. McGrath advanced the throttle and his aircraft accelerated down the runway. Heller's craft was not far behind. Taking off they felt the turbulence of Preston's four craft ahead of them. Once airborne McGrath and Heller reduced power to enable the other Sabres of Detachment Q to catch up. Climbing at 360 mph, McGrath moved the rudder pedals, causing his plane to fishtail. This was the signal for the others to take up a combat formation, which they did.

McGrath was calm, with no sense of fear. He was about to do what he had come to Korea to accomplish. Acutely attuned to sight, sound, touch, and smell, he felt completely alive. Focused on the job ahead, he did not recall that only in the skies above Germany had he felt this way.

Passing over the Taedong River, McGrath switched on his gun sight and test fired his guns. As he did so the aircraft shuddered in recoil.

Testing the guns was standard practice when heading north. Thirty-one other pilots soon did the same. Notice had been served to the pilots at Antung. The Sabres were coming to do battle.

"Tiger Leader, Dentist Charlie here. Looks like we have a bandit train crossing over the Yalu. Thirty plus, high up. And a second train is leaving the station."

"Roger that," answered Preston.

"Dentist Charlie" was the code phrase for a U.S. radar site on Cho-Do Island, thirty-five miles off the western coast of North Korea. It monitored air space near the mouth of the Yalu, providing information to the Sabres on the whereabouts of MiGs. "Bandit train" meant a large formation of enemy aircraft. The "station" was Antung.

In addition to radar the island was home to a squadron of Gruman SA–16 Albatross amphibians, which conducted search and rescue missions for pilots in the water. Thus, for the F–86s, Cho-Do was extremely valuable.

McGrath heard the transmission to Preston, whose flight he could see off to the right, slightly ahead.

Preston then communicated to the entire Sabre force. "MiGs are up today. Let's go get 'em."

The F–86s veered inland, thirty-two pilots looking upward, searching the sky.

"Blue Leader, MiG formation in sight, two-o'clock high. Jesus, there's a whole bunch of them." The pilot speaking was Lieutenant Peter Heller.

McGrath replied, "I got 'em, Blue Two. Stay calm."

McGrath informed Preston of the sighting, then turned his formation toward the MiGs. Detachment Q moved closer to Preston's main force. All the Sabres were building up speed, which, given the disadvantage of height, was critical to success, and to survival.

"Blue Flight, drop tanks, now." As McGrath spoke he pushed the jettison button, thus releasing the tanks. His Sabre lurched as the two tanks flew off, tumbling over and over with spilled fuel vaporizing into twisted shards of white smoke. The tanks hindered maneuverability and always were dropped prior to aerial combat. So often did this occur that severe shortages in tanks resulted.

"Blue Leader, this is Blue Five. One of my tanks is stuck."

"Blue Five, head to the coast and try to shake it off. Blue Six, go with him."

Willard Roberts did as ordered. However, the tank remained affixed to his aircraft. So he and Blue Six flew back to Suwon, the rule being to avoid engagement with MiGs when a tank could not be detached.

McGrath led his four-ship formation in the direction of the enemy.

"Here they come." It was Lieutenant Heller once again. "Now they're off to our right."

"Blue Flight," McGrath was speaking to his group. "Turn into them, NOW."

McGrath's tactic worked, avoiding the MiGs attack, although several of the enemy fired.

MiGs and Sabres then mixed it up. Turning, rolling, diving, climbing as each tried to gain competitive advantage.

McGrath latched onto one and was about to fire when Heller screamed, "BREAK LEFT!" which McGrath promptly did. The MiG that overshot him flew by so closely that he could see its red nose and identification number.

McGrath soon found another MiG and this time was able to shoot. Though his bullets struck home, no fire or smoke resulted. His burst of fire lasted two seconds and was all the shooting he was able to do. The MiG turned left and began to climb. Anticipating a climbing turn to the right, he had positioned his aircraft accordingly, and was left with open sky and no enemy aircraft.

Lieutenant Heller had better luck. When a second MiG attacked McGrath from the side he turned into the enemy plane. The MiG flew past both Sabres and skidded off to the left. Heller reversed course, rolled his Sabre over McGrath's, and from the rear drew a bead on the MiG. Three seconds later .50 caliber shells struck the wing root of the MiG. A second blast also struck home, walking down the fuselage to the tail. Heller was about to trigger a third shot when the MiG's canopy flew off, followed seconds later by the pilot. Unwisely, the fellow immediately opened his parachute. At forty-one thousand feet, where the air is thin, he had little chance of survival, and was dead well before he hit the ground. His aircraft began to fall awkwardly. When its wing fell off the sleek fighter became but metallic wreckage, no longer capable of flight.

Heller's gun camera recorded the entire episode. It resulted in his being awarded a confirmed kill. The film was quite spectacular. Ten days later it was released by Far Eastern Air Forces public relations staff to promote the air force and its activities in Korea. In movie theaters across the country Americans saw Heller's victory in newsreels shown prior to the main attraction.

Throughout the battle McGrath had fought hard and well. Frustrated at the lack of personal success, he was pleased with the performance of Detachment Q, at least with the four that engaged the enemy. Not only Heller but Charlie Hickok had downed a MiG. Two kills for the group was outstanding. It sent a message to Schmid, Preston, and company that McGrath's group knew its business.

Moreover, the overall mission seemed successful. Preston's Sabres had downed two MiGs and damaged several, losing only one F–86, whose pilot was rescued by one of the Albatrosses. In Tokyo, describing the engagement as a "potent display of American air power," Far Eastern Air Forces proclaimed a great victory.

Peter Parker wasn't so sure. He and McGrath were in their tent, having had dinner together after agreeing not to see the movie being shown at Suwon's movie house, a tent that enlisted men sarcastically called "the Rialto."

"Come on, Peter, we knocked down four of them, with only one 86 lost. Four to one—in my book that's called winning."

"True, but that's only part of the story."

"What do you mean?"

"Well, remember the purpose of the Sabre's mission was to protect the F–84s as they beat up the Red's railroad system."

"Right, the straight wings were to hit three rail junctions and our job was to block the MiGs from getting at them, which we did."

"Only partly."

"What do you mean? We broke up that bandit train and sent the MiGs still flying back to China."

"True, but you'll recall there was a second train which, unlike the first, crossed the river unopposed and met up with the 84s."

Hearing this, McGrath realized he was not going to like what Porter said next.

"Well, this second group of MiGs, about forty in number, crossed the Yalu at fifty-one thousand feet, flew south and hit the Thunderjets. Now remember there were forty-six good guys. Sixteen of them were acting as escorts. Their job was to cover the others, to break up any attack MiGs might make."

"And . . ."

"The escorts did their best. They even got one of the MiGs, a minor miracle of and by itself. But one of the escort jets went down and two other 84s fell to the MiGs."

"Oh God!"

"There's more. At one of the rail junctions, the MiGs forced the Thunderjets to drop their bombs early, so twenty five-hundred-pound general purpose bombs—two apiece from each jet—landed on some dumb rice paddy in the middle of nowhere. The second group of 84s, again ten aircraft, got to their target, but these were the guys hard hit by the MiGs. They didn't do too well, though apparently a few bombs were dropped where they were supposed to."

"And the third group of Thunderjets?"

"These guys did real well, fortunately. All ten aircraft found the target, and with the MiGs busy elsewhere, they were able to do their job. Apparently, they really plastered the place. They got seven locomotives, a whole bunch of buildings, even a small bridge."

"So we hit the Reds pretty hard, at least in one place."

"Indeed we did. The rail junction at Ho-Ran—that's the one we got—is a complete mess."

"But overall . . ."

"Overall I'd call it a draw. We knocked down four MiGs, lost one Sabre, and three Thunderjets. Both sides flew planes home filled with holes. On the ground one railroad junction was untouched, one damaged slightly, and one blown to kingdom come. Like I said, I'd call it a draw."

"That's not very satisfying."

"No, it's not."

"The answer is pretty simple."

"And that would be?"

"Get more 86s. The problem is not that we're not good enough, we are. The problem is that we don't have enough Sabres. The MiGs just outnumber us, by a lot."

"You're right, of course. You'll not be pleased to hear that my sources tell me Weyland has asked for more and has been turned down."

"Oh swell. Of course there's another way to solve the problem."

"I don't think I want to hear what I think you're about to say."

"Come on, you know it would work. Let's take a bunch of 86s and pay a visit to Antung. Hit their airfields hard and a whole lot less MiGs would be crossing the Yalu."

"That's true, but then we'd be risking World War III. This is a new kind of war, a limited conflict. Truman's right. We're going to meet the Red challenge here in Korea but not provoke a wider war."

"I understand, and geo-politically I guess it makes sense."

"It does."

"Unless of course," McGrath was looking straight at the intelligence officer, "you happen to be flying an F–84."

In the next three days Detachment Q was scheduled to fly three missions, all to the Yalu, all to cover interdiction strikes by F–84s. On one of the days rain blanketed Suwon, so the Sabres took to the skies only twice.

Both missions were eventful. On the first, MiGs were sighted and a dogfight ensued. Contrails revealed the presence of the enemy, who made the mistake of not attacking in numbers. Instead, pairs of MiGs sequentially dove upon the Sabres. The F–86s turned into the attackers and then, gaining speed, pursued the MiGs. The enemy seemed lacking in combat experience. The results were predictable. Two MiGs were shot down, one by Charlie Hickok. Five were damaged. No Sabres were lost.

On the second mission the MiGs stayed home. The F–86s landed with gun panels unsullied and wing tanks attached. What made the mission eventful was that they landed not at Suwon, but at Kimpo, an airfield farther north. This gave the Sabres an additional five minutes at the Yalu.

Kimpo, K–14 in the United Nations' numbering system, was Seoul's municipal airport, eighteen miles northwest of the city. The runway was longer and wider than at Suwon and, while PSP was widely employed, the airfield possessed concrete taxiways and parking areas. Yet everywhere at Kimpo the destructiveness of war was evident. The main hangar was a burned-out shell. The terminal building was pockmarked with bullets, in no way usable. At the main gate, wrecked T–34 tanks had been bulldozed aside. The ground itself was pot-holed from artillery fire. Roads were destroyed, buildings demolished. At Kimpo and environs the image was of a battlefield far from recovery. But K–14, by F–86, was but a thirty-minute flight to where the MiGs were based. For the 4th Fighter Interceptor Wing it would be home for the rest of the war.

Also at Kimpo was the 67th Tactical Reconnaissance Group flying F–51 Mustangs, twin-engine Douglas B–26s, and Lockheed F–80 Shooting Stars, all configured as reconnaissance aircraft, which meant cameras were substituted for guns. Reconnaissance was a critical activity for the air force in Korea, constituting thirteen percent of all combat sorties flown. Everyday "reccy" aircraft would scour the landscapes of North Korea. They were either identifying new targets or assessing damage to targets already struck. Unarmed and without great speed, the reconnaissance planes required fighter escort when venturing north. This was provided by the F–86s.

Two days after arriving at Kimpo, Detachment Q was tasked to escort an RF–80 on a mission to Taefen. The Shooting Star was to photograph the entrance and exit of a railroad tunnel used by the North Koreans to hide locomotives during daylight. Upon examining the pictures, F–84 Thunderjets were to bomb both ends, hoping to seal off the tunnel and thereby deprive Kim Il Sung of several train engines.

All six Sabres of the detachment were to participate in the mission. McGrath had selected the pilots who would fly when one of them confronted the detachment's commander two hours before takeoff.

"What can I do for you, Major?" McGrath was in a good mood, looking forward to the flight.

"May I speak with you alone, sir?"

"Sure, Roberts. Let's go for a walk."

Willard Roberts and McGrath headed away from the detachment's operations room. Ambling toward the radar shop, the major soon stopped. Addressing McGrath, he spoke in a calm, cold voice, showing no emotion.

"I can't do this anymore."

"What? What do you mean?"

"I mean I can't do this anymore. I can't fly anymore, at least not here in Korea. I don't have what it takes. Maybe I'm too old. Besides, I've done my share, in the Big War. I want out."

At first, McGrath did not know how to respond. Though he was not surprised, having noticed Roberts' less than stellar performance.

"How old are you, Major?"

"I'm thirty-five, sir."

"This could wreck your career."

"I know that, Colonel. So be it. I just don't want to do it anymore. I can't. My nerves are shot. I just need out."

McGrath knew that Roberts had a respectable record in the air force. He had flown combat in World War II, shooting down an Me–109 in North Africa. Then he had been an instructor pilot, later becoming the executive officer of a P–38 squadron in the Canal Zone.

McGrath had a choice. He could raise hell and have Roberts court-martialed. Or he could have the man quietly reassigned to a desk job. The latter would avoid embarrassment to him and the air force. More important, it would retain in the service a man who, in the right position, might still contribute. McGrath chose this second option, hoping he did not do so because it was easier. The man, he concluded, was not a coward. He simply had reached the point of no return. And, once he had been a decent fighter pilot. That alone, perhaps, entitled him to a break.

That night McGrath summoned Major Brumbaugh to his tent. Neither Duff nor Parker were there, so when the ground executive officer appeared, the two men were alone.

"Edward, I want you to make two personnel assignments happen, and happen quickly. Do whatever it takes. But do it quietly and quickly."

"Yes, sir."

"First, I want Major Roberts transferred out of the detachment and into an administrative post, preferably back at Johnson."

"Consider it done. And the second, sir?"

"There's a Major Cox at Johnson—Fred Cox. He's an instructor pilot, a good stick and rudder man. He wants to come to Korea and fight. Let's give him his wish. I want him assigned to our little group."

Six days later Major Willard Roberts became chief assistant to the Deputy for Facilities and Management at Johnson Air Force Base. When this occurred, Fred Cox already had joined Detachment Q.

FIFTEEN

Despite Robert's withdrawal, Detachment Q flew the reconnaissance mission. McGrath assigned one of the other pilots to take the major's place. The RF–80 took off first and was cruising at fourteen thousand feet when joined by the Sabres. McGrath placed his aircraft and Heller's well above the Shooting Star, with two Sabres to each side and two in front. No MiGs were sighted and, while light flak greeted the planes at Taefen, the RF–80 safely carried out its task photographing the tunnel's entrance and exit.

Upon their return to Kimpo, the F–86s, in echelon formation with McGrath in the lead, flew down the runway at low level but high speed. As they reached its end McGrath banked to the left and climbed. The others followed in four-second intervals. With speed brakes now open the aircraft slowed. On the downwind leg McGrath lowered both flaps and landing gear. Entering the turn onto final approach, his craft moving at 184 mph, he aligned the Sabre with the runway, continuing to bleed off speed. Touching down at 156 mph, he brought the nosewheel down quickly, then applied brakes intermittently while returning the throttle to idle. The aircraft rolled to the runway's end and stopped. McGrath then raised the wing flaps, closed the speed brakes, and engaged nose wheel steering, which, with a slight burst of power, enabled him to taxi to dispersal where, as always, Sergeant Ricks was waiting.

The next mission was not so easy. Returning to the Taefen tunnel, this time escorting twelve F–84s, the detachment's jets engaged ten MiGs just prior to the Thunderjet attack. Alerted by the radar on Cho-Do, McGrath positioned his Sabres to intercept the enemy.

"There they are, Blue Leader, twelve o'clock high." Once again Lieutenant Heller had been first in sighting the MiGs. Blue Leader was McGrath.

"I see 'em, Blue Two."

McGrath now spoke to all his pilots.

"Blue Flight, let's go, on my call . . . NOW!"

Upon McGrath's command the six Sabres spread out and climbed toward the MiGs. At long range they all opened fire, blanketing the enemy formation. The goal was not so much to destroy aircraft as to disrupt the MiG attack. The tactic worked. The ten MiGs flew off in different directions, forestalling a concerted assault upon the Thunderjets.

The Sabres then dove in pursuit of the enemy. Their radios came alive with voices both calm and excited.

"Stay with me, Blue Four."

"Jesus, that was close."

"Watch your airspeed, Blue Three."

"Come to me, baby."

"I've got my pipper right on the bastard."

"Anybody seen the straight wings?"

"He's over to your left, two thousand feet."

"Your six o'clock is clear."

"He's coming down, break now."

"Scratch one MiG."

This last transmission was from Lieutenant Colonel Hickok. Flying as Blue Five, Hickok had spotted a MiG several thousand feet below turning to the west. Immediately he pounced, leaving his wingman far behind. The veteran came down steeply, then pulled up as the MiG straightened out. Hickok was traveling so fast he risked overshooting his target despite the MiG's speed. So he deployed the Sabre's speed brakes, panels of the fuselage that moved outward. This slowed his aircraft, allowing Hickok to position his plane behind the MiG, though not directly so. Off center there was more target area than if the F–86s were aligned precisely in line with the MiG. Hickok had attained the ideal firing position and did not waste the opportunity. As he pulled the trigger, his six machine guns spit forth their deadly fire. The bullets struck home. The MiG was hit in the rear of the fuselage, with such impact that its engine exploded. The entire aircraft then broke apart, enveloped in an ever-enlarging sphere of black smoke and red flame.

McGrath was not as fortunate.

He too had spotted a MiG below.

"Blue Two, there's a MiG at ten o'clock low."

"I see 'em, Blue Leader."

"Let's get 'em."

"I'm with you, leader."

The two Sabres dove toward the enemy. The MiG continued on its way, seemingly unaware of the F–86s. With Heller covering him McGrath closed quickly. He was about to fire when the enemy aircraft pulled sharply to the left and began to climb. McGrath curved to the left, attempting a deflection shot. It's didn't work. At jet speed the most assured way of hitting the enemy was from behind—the six o'clock position. Shooting from the side, determining how far ahead of the MiG to aim, was difficult, even with a radar-controlled gun sight. McGrath fired a two second burst, but was wide of the mark. He too pulled back on the control stick and had his aircraft gain altitude. But, with its greater acceleration, the MiG outdistanced McGrath's F–86.

Disappointed, McGrath leveled off at twenty-seven thousand feet and, with Heller, looked about for MiGs. None were present. Nor were the Sabres. He soon realized they were east of the tunnel and thus unable to offer further protection to the F–84s.

The Republic jets were doing fine without him. Two F–84s strafed the area around the entrance to the tunnel, eliminating several antiaircraft guns. Four Thunderjets followed, dropping bombs, which, as hoped, sealed the entrance. A similar approach dealt with the exit.

The mission was a complete success. The tunnel was made inoperable. No trains could come or go. Five steam engines, and their crew, were locked inside. All the men perished for lack of oxygen. The engines were not recovered for five weeks (after which a second strike of F–84s closed off the tunnel once again). No Thunderjets were lost nor were any Sabres shot down. Three MiGs were damaged and one, the MiG Hickok got, destroyed.

Preston was delighted, and impressed.

"Good show, McGrath. That was a textbook operation."

"Thank you, Colonel." McGrath appreciated the compliment. As he continued to speak, he was saying to himself, "All in a day's work."

On the next seven missions, which took place over a period of nine days, Detachment Q met up with MiGs four times. Each of these were on patrols along the Yalu, the purpose again being to intercept the enemy aircraft before they could fly south. When the MiGs did appear, the combat was fierce.

And successful. McGrath's group downed two enemy planes and damaged several. No Sabres were lost, although on one occasion Squadron Leader Urqhart's F–86 had a large hole in its wing courtesy of a 37 mm cannon shell. Major Cox destroyed one of the MiGs. Charlie Hickok downed the other.

"You've got a real tiger in your outfit, Colonel." Preston was speaking to McGrath in the officer's club, whose interior was more elaborate than its canvas exterior suggested.

"Sir?"

"Hickok. He's not been here two months and already has four kills to his credit. He's gonna make ace and be one of our stars."

McGrath did not reply. Charlie Hickok was a good pilot, and aggressive. No doubt he would become an ace, the informal title given a pilot who downs five enemy aircraft. But the Detachment Q leader worried about his comrade. To McGrath, Hickok seemed MiG-mad, so set upon getting kills that he took foolish risks. There was, McGrath knew, a fine line between fighting hard and fighting recklessly. Colonel Hickok, in McGrath's view, had crossed over.

Later, McGrath wondered if Preston's intent was to send him a message, one that expressed disappointment that he, McGrath, had not gotten any MiGs. Leadership was leadership by example. Preston had destroyed a MiG and damaged three. Perhaps he expected flight leaders under his command to do the same. Did the 4th Fighter Interceptor Group commander think Detachment Q's boss was not up to the job?

McGrath need not have been concerned. Ben Preston considered McGrath a fine leader. He was glad to have him at Kimpo and assumed that in due time he would get a MiG or two. Moreover, Detachment Q's performance had been outstanding. Its six aircraft had made the 4th a more potent weapon.

Hickok did not share Preston's view.

In conversation with Urqhart he more than once expressed his own opinion. This time the two pilots were walking to the mess.

"Look, McGrath's not a bad pilot. Actually, he's quite good. But we're here to kill MiGs and he hasn't got any."

"So what are you saying . . ."

"I'm saying perhaps he's not up to it anymore. He's had his chances and he hasn't done it."

"I'd be careful about what you're saying."

"I'm just saying what I believe."

"Well, old boy, I believe you're dead wrong. Colonel McGrath is doing just fine. I might add he's a rather splendid fellow."

"I'm not saying he's not a good guy, a fine officer and all that. He is. I'm just suggesting that he's not up to commanding our little group, at least in this war. To succeed we have to get the MiGs and, as the record shows, he's not doing that."

"But the detachment is."

"True," Hickok now stared at Urqhart, "but by whom?"

As this conversation was taking place McGrath was in his tent, opening a large package that had been delivered from the mailroom by Edward Brumbaugh.

"What is it?" asked Peter Parker.

"I haven't a clue."

"Well, it's too early for Christmas and whatever it is, it doesn't weigh much, for Major Brumbaugh carried it in here with one hand."

As he began to open the package McGrath thought it might be a gift from Martha. What could she possibly be sending him in a box so large yet so light? The thought crossed his mind that it might be pajamas, though he immediately dismissed the idea as unlikely and a bit odd. Then, seeing a return label, he realized what the box contained.

"I know what it is," he said. He took one of the items from the now open package and gave it to Parker.

"Baseball caps?"

"Indeed. There are forty-eight caps in here. All blue, all with the letters DQ on them. Pretty neat, huh?"

"A high honor."

"Actually," said the detachment's group's commander, "it is."

McGrath soon had the ground exec distribute the baseball caps to all members of the detachment. The hats were a big hit. Worn by enlisted men and officers, they appeared wherever the men of Detachment Q lived and worked—from the mess hall, to the repair shops, to the flight line.

Robin Urqhart secretly treasured his hat, keeping it long after he left Korea. But the RAF officer enjoyed teasing his fellow pilots about their blue headgear.

"It's such an American thing."

"Well, yes," replied Peter Heller. "We are, after all, Americans and baseball is an American game."

"Quite. But you chaps seem to wear them everywhere, whenever there is sun."

"Of which, I might say, London seems to have very little."

"I beg your pardon."

"Sunshine," said Peter Parker, who had entered the conversation. "I'm told it rarely appears in London, or in England for that matter."

"What's this? Did someone mention one of my favorite cities?" McGrath now joined in.

"Yes, sir," the intelligence officer was speaking. "I was saying to our English friend here that the sun, which once never set on the British Empire, now rarely shows itself in London."

"Sad but true," said McGrath, looking at Urqhart.

"Perhaps so, old boy, but remember rain makes the grass grow and accounts for one of England's national treasures."

"Which would be?"

"Gardens, of course. What's prettier than an English garden?"

"He's got a point there," commented Parker.

"Let me paint you a picture." Urqhart was now in fine form. "Imagine a small English village, say south of London, in Sussex. They'll be an old stone church, no doubt built in the twelfth century, cottages and shops on High Street, a town hall, a memorial to the soldiers of the Great War, and lest we forget, at least three different pubs. But everywhere you look, next to buildings, in window boxes, and on the common grounds, there will be flowers, all lovingly cared for and looking splendid."

Urqhart went on for some time. Clearly, the man loved his country and its gardens. What he did not love was the British Labour Party and its head, a man who happened to be the prime minister of the United Kingdom.

"Atlee? Don't get me started."

"He's not really that bad, is he?" Smiling at McGrath, Parker, the intelligence officer, spoke which a mischievous grin.

"He's a bloody idiot."

"That's a bit harsh, don't you think?"

"I certainly do not. He's a damned Socialist." For Urqhart the term was anathema.

"So?"

"So? He's going to nationalize everything and destroy what made England great. You just can't give everyone what they want; they have to earn it, or at least pay for it. Some people are just lazy. The government should ignore them, and encourage the folks who work hard, the people with energy and vision. Mark my word, that man and his comrades are going to be the ruin of England."

Then, with the disdain that only a Brit can muster, Urqhart issued his verbal coup d'grace.

"With Atlee at the helm, our sceptered isle will become no better than France."

The very thought made Urqhart cringe. Yet he continued, aiming his words at the Americans.

"And, my friends, remember what Clem has done to you."

McGrath and Parker knew to what Urqhart was referring. Heller did not.

"He's the man who sold Rolls Royce jet engines, the pride of British industry, to the Soviet Union. And what did they do with them? They copied them and very sensibly put them in the airplane we see whenever we visit the Yalu."

"I suppose he's got a point there," said Peter Parker.

"Bloody hell, I most certainly do."

From Clement Atlee to Winston Churchill was not a large jump, one that the squadron leader soon made. Proud of the British Lion, Urqhart called Churchill England's greatest prime minister. He recited the man's tenure in British politics and spoke of his eloquence and determination, two qualities he said made their mark in history when England stood alone.

"So, of all the prime ministers, he was the best?" queried Lieutenant Heller.

"Indeed."

"More so than Gladstone, than Disraeli?" For the moment McGrath reverted to a college professor.

"Absolutely. They were great men, and great ministers. But the England of their day did not face the dangers we faced in 1940."

"That's true, I suppose."

"So you see, Winston Churchill is without peer."

"Yes, I'll have to agree, and I suspect history will as well. Times of great danger require a nation to produce great men. And England, when threatened by Hitler, rose to the challenge and produced a man equal to the task. Remarkable, really, when you think about it. His finest hour, and England's," remarked McGrath.

The man they next spoke of was neither British nor a minister of state.

Major Parker, wishing to hear no more of Atlee or Churchill, turned the conversation to a member of the clergy, more specifically to a cardinal of the Roman Catholic Church.

"He's coming here, to Korea?" asked an incredulous McGrath.

"Yes, Stephen Cardinal Fermoyle, Archbishop of Cincinnati, is coming. Not just to Korea, but here, to Kimpo."

"Good Lord! A cardinal of the Catholic church, here."

"Yes indeed, in two days. He comes in the morning and leaves the next day. He'll say mass at least four times and dine with the men and with us. Colonel Schmidt says Far Eastern Air Forces has told him to treat the man with fanfare and respect. This is no ordinary guest. We're going to roll out the red carpet."

"I bet we are."

McGrath knew that the Church was strongly anti-communist. So, he, reasoned, having one of its leaders come to where the forces of good were in battle against an atheistic ideology made sense.

"He'll come and pray with us and for us," said Parker.

"Can't hurt, I suppose. What do we know of His Eminence?"

"Well I hear he's a pretty good guy. Not at all pompous. He's from Boston, spent time at the Vatican, and was a parish priest in New England. He's supposed to be extremely bright but doesn't come across that way. Like I said, he's supposed to be an okay fellow. But you and I will probably find out."

McGrath looked puzzled. "How come?"

"Because he and his entourage are sleeping in the tent right next to ours."

McGrath soon forgot about the cardinal's pending visit. The air war was in full swing, and Detachment Q had a part to play.

Three missions were flown during the next forty-eight hours. On one of them McGrath volunteered to serve as mobile control. This was an experienced pilot sitting in a radio-equipped truck at the end of the runway. In effect an auxiliary control tower, the mobile control's purpose was to monitor aircraft departures and arrivals. Regarding the former, the controller checked for fluid leaks and proper configuration on the F–86s. For the latter, he advised pilots returning with a problem and warned those making an unsafe approach. Sabre pilots appreciated having one of their own at the end of the runway.

McGrath's tour in the truck lasted a full day. He watched over two reconnaissance missions by F–80s and one fighter sweep of the Sabres. Each went off without a hitch, although watching close up sixteen F–86s prepare for take-off made a lasting impression. Their sheer beauty—graceful machines even on the ground—combined with their deadly purpose, augmented by the shriek of J–47 engines, conveyed a compelling image of American air power.

The only tense moment for McGrath came when a C–47 Skytrain came in for a landing. The plane, the military version of the ubiquitous DC–3 airliner, was on final late in the afternoon. So too were a pair of F–86s completing a flight from Cho-Do Island. One of the Sabres was in trouble.

"Kimpo, I'm ten miles out, at seven thousand feet, flamed out."

This last remark meant the aircraft's engine had died. The plane was gliding home.

"Roger, we're landing to the south," said McGrath, who then advised the main tower, "Hold the C–47, we've got an 86 coming in, engine off."

The tower did not respond. So McGrath spoke again. Still no response. By now he could see the C–47. The F–86 he could not see, but knew it soon would be in sight. If the C–47 did not abort its landing, the odds were good that the Sabre, unable to swerve, would run into it on the runway before the C–47 turned onto the taxiway.

"Tower, get that 47 out of the way!"

Again, nothing from the control tower.

"Hello Six, there's a 47 ahead of you."

"Roger . . . oh swell."

Still not hearing a word from the tower, McGrath grabbed a flare gun and fired a red flare at the transport aircraft. He then sent a second flare skyward. Realizing all was not well, the C–47 acted swiftly. Gunning his engines, its pilot pulled the plane up and to the left. Six seconds later the silent Sabre touched down, moving fast at 149 mph. When the second F–86 had landed the C–47 came round and, now in contact with the control tower, landed safely.

"Close," McGrath said later, "only counts in horseshoes."

No repercussions from the incident occurred other than Colonel Schmidt chewing out the officer in charge of the control tower. Of course a full colonel irately conversing with a major is not, for the junior officer, a pleasant experience. The major, a man by the name of Franks, made sure nothing similar ever happened again, which is exactly the goal Herman Schmidt had in mind.

The C–47 pilot took it all in stride. He was an experienced aircraft driver who had been in numerous sticky situations. He and his squadron often flew at night, occasionally unloading propaganda leaflets on North Korean soldiers, frequently dropping flares to aid night-bombing B–26s. His most unusual mission, however, had taken place earlier in the year. He and five others took their C–47s up to Pyonyang one evening and dumped eight tons of roofing nails along main roads south of the city. To ensure accurate placement, the planes released their hardware forty feet off the ground. As intended, the nails punctured the tires of North Korean trucks. Immobile, twenty-eight vehicles were later destroyed by fighter-bombers.

The commander of the C–47 was told he would receive the Distinguished Flying Cross for the mission. He did not, profanely having told a senior air cargo command officer what he could do with the medal, suggesting that he and his crew each receive a case of beer. As the beverage was not forthcoming the pilot later picked up numerous cases of Blatz at Johnson, distributing them freely to his squadron mates upon returning to Korea.

The two missions McGrath flew prior to the cardinal's visit were both to the Yalu. Each time sixteen Sabres flew up the coast to the mouth of the river. Once there they went upriver, flying racetrack patterns, making broad sweeping ninety degree turns. The F–86s were looking for MiGs. Both times they found them.

On the first mission, twenty-eight MiGs crossed the Yalu several thousand feet above the Sabres. In flights of four, one after the other, the MiGs attacked. The F–86s turned into them and survived the attack. What followed was an aerial rugby match. Aircraft were turning, rolling, diving, and shooting. In the melee, which took place at altitudes as high as forty-one thousand feet and as low as fourteen thousand feet, sixteen Sabres expended 4,088 rounds of .50 caliber shells. Despite the gunnery no MiGs were downed, though several landed full of holes. All sixteen F–86s returned safely.

The second mission was more successful. This time twenty MiGs crossed the river, so the sides essentially were even. Again the Russian-built planes came screaming down from above, cannons blazing. And again the Sabres turned into the attackers, spoiling their aim. MiG and Sabre then paired off against each other. The fighting was intense. Individual duels took place south of the river, over the river and, on two occasions, north of the river. Having crossed the Yalu in hot pursuit, two F–86 pilots destroyed three enemy aircraft. One other was downed in North Korea. No Sabres were lost, though three came back to Kimpo with damage.

Detachment Q did well in the battle. Major Chris Graham, the Marine Corps exchange pilot, accounted for the MiG lost in Korean airspace. Charlie Hickok got one of the three destroyed in Manchuria. This brought his score to the magical number five. McGrath did not down a MiG. His score remained at zero.

The incursions north of the Yalu were not reported to Far Eastern Air Forces. Schmidt and Preston said nothing, at least officially. Privately, they expressed displeasure. Fortunately for the pilots, gun camera footage from the offending F–86s did not reveal the Sabres' locations.

McGrath did speak to Hickok. He told him "orders were orders" and that he did not want Detachment aircraft north of the river. Showing neither regret nor disrespect, Hickok replied that he had not realized where he was at the time of the shooting. This was untrue, as both men realized. But McGrath did not challenge the man. He simply repeated his directive: Detachment Q Sabres were to stay south of the Yalu River. Hickok acknowledged the order, saluted, and walked away. McGrath knew what Hickok knew, that he again would cross the river should an opportunity arise to down a MiG.

The question McGrath later asked himself is whether he would have been tougher on Hickok if he himself had a MiG to his credit.

In celebration of their day's work, the 4th Fighter Interceptor Group threw themselves a party. The absence of women was made up for by the abundance of alcohol. Jack Daniels, Johnnie Walker Red, and Blatz flowed liberally. Several pilots needed assistance to reach their tents once the party had ended. McGrath did not. He was completely sober, having had all of three Cokes the entire evening. The advantage, other than sobriety, was that he won six games of ping-pong, reaping five dollars per game from opponents who should have known better.

Entering his tent once the celebration was over, he noticed someone sitting on the bunk next to his, one that normally was unoccupied. He was about to question the man when the fellow rose and greeted him warmly.

McGrath recognized the voice before he saw the man's face.

It was Roger O'Boyle.

SIXTEEN

At age fifty-two Stephen Fermoyle was still a handsome man. With wavy black hair, a solid physique, and above average height he looked much like he did at Boston College, where he played football and baseball. Then, girls found him attractive, as women still did. Yet Fermoyle had forsaken feminine companionship, devoting his body and soul to the Church. Through faith in God and trust in Catholic doctrine he had found an inner peace. His intellectual powers, evident at college and in seminary, were challenged as never before now that the pope had made this son of Boston a prince of the Catholic Church. Yet, for all his accomplishments, Stephen Fermoyle remained a man modest in demeanor, friendly to all he met and served.

He also remained a fan of the Boston Red Sox. Born not far from Fenway, the cardinal had been a Sox fan since the day his father first took him to see a major league game. Watching the Red Sox beat the Philadelphia Athletics 6–2, Fermoyle was intrigued by the excitement and strategy of the game. And now that the team had baseball's best hitter, the cardinal was hoping the Red Sox would soon win the pennant.

"It's true, Your Eminence," McGrath was speaking to the cardinal on the day Fermoyle was to leave Kimpo. "Ted Williams may be the best hitter in the game."

"Please, call me Father Fermoyle."

"Yes, Your Eminence, I mean Father. But baseball is a team sport and the Yankees, well, they're just better than the Red Sox."

"Sadly, I have to agree with you."

"With Allie Reynolds, Vic Rashi, and Eddie Lopat, the Yankees have three terrific pitchers, maybe the best in all of baseball."

"And good pitching beats good hitting."

"That's what the experts say. And besides, the Yankees have the best center fielder in the game."

"That would be Mr. DiMaggio."

"Yes, sir," McGrath was speaking most respectfully, as though addressing a four star general, "Jolting Joe himself."

"Well, you know, Colonel, the Red Sox have a DiMaggio on their team as well."

"They do?" Peter Parker, who was sitting next to McGrath, looked surprised.

"Yes, it's true. Dom DiMaggio—Dominic. He's on the Red Sox."

McGrath was correct. Joe DiMaggio's younger brother Dominic played eleven seasons with the Red Sox and did quite well. Baseball must have run in the DiMaggio blood for an older brother, Vincent, played ten years in the National League. All three were center fielders.

"Joe DiMaggio is going to retire soon, is he not?" Cardinal Fermoyle was speaking to McGrath.

"Yes, Your Eminence. Sadly, he's not the player he once was."

"Age does that. But perhaps now the Red Sox will be able to make a run for the pennant. Without Joe DiMaggio the Yankees at last might be beatable."

"Perhaps, Father, but I would not want you or any of your close friends to bet on it."

"And why not, my son?"

"Well, for two reasons. One, because the Yankees always seem to win regardless of the situation. And two, because the kid who's going to replace Number Five is supposed to be one heck of a ballplayer."

"And who would that be?"

216

"He's got a funny name, and he's just a youngster straight out of Oklahoma. But Casey says he's got a huge amount of raw talent."

Cardinal Fermoyle let out a sigh, then spoke with a twinkle in his eye.

"Maybe we could have him come to the Red Sox, make up for trading Babe Ruth to the Yankees."

"No, Father, I think he's going to stay in New York. His name is Mickey Mantle."

This discussion about DiMaggio was the second conversation McGrath had shared with Cardinal Fermoyle. The first had taken place earlier, at breakfast in the mess tent. Fermoyle had finished saying an early mass, which McGrath, against his wishes but at the urging of his Jesuit friend, had attended.

The mass took place outside on a flatbed truck the air force had rigged as an altar. The weather cooperated. There was no rain, little wind, and a rising sun that dissipated the morning chill which had greeted the inhabitants of Kimpo. Resplendent in the red robes of his high office, Fermoyle performed the ancient rite with Roger O'Boyle serving as an altar boy.

For several reasons McGrath found the service unsatisfying. To begin with, the setting seemed odd. From where he stood McGrath could see four F–86s being prepared for combat. And the planes that were not on the ground, whether taking off or landing, made noises that interfered with the mass. Not that McGrath or most of the others understood what was being said. Fermoyle spoke in Latin, a language— save for the cardinal and the Jesuit—no one there understood. More importantly, McGrath's objection to the role of priests resurfaced. Why, he pondered, if God loved each and every person, were priests necessary to act as intermediaries between God and His creations? After all, were not priests mere men, often ordinary in intellect and shielded from life's realities? And why would salvation be achieved only under auspices of the Church? Back home McGrath never had found convincing answers to these questions. He would not find them in Korea either, despite the presence of Stephen, Cardinal Fermoyle.

Yet McGrath found his sermon most interesting. As good sermons must be, the cardinal's was meaningful to those he addressed. The subject was evil, its nature, and how it appears in everyone's life, regardless of personal circumstances. Evil, said Fermoyle, was not an abstraction. It was morally wrong behavior, whether by an individual or a group. Certain actions and the belief systems upon which they rested were simply not acceptable. They were offenses against mankind and the will of God. They could not be absolved by social theories or situational ethics. Inherently destructive, these offenses were exposed by the ageless teachings of the Church, which could differentiate between right and wrong, between good and evil. Tested by time, reinforced by society's sense of self-preservation, these teachings provided a framework of values around which to organize human existence. Adherence to them enabled men and women to live righteous lives, ones not just favored by society, but more importantly, blessed by God and His church.

Evil, continued Cardinal Fermoyle, was to be found at home and abroad. Here in Korea evil was close by. It took the form of communism, an ideology that had foresworn God, suppressing both democracy and the Church. Such evil, said His Eminence, must be dealt with. It must be vanquished. Its troops, be they North Korean or Chinese, must be defeated in battle. Stephen Fermoyle blessed the men he addressed. He called them crusaders, soldiers of God confronting evil on the battlefields of Korea.

Listening to the cardinal, McGrath realized how effective good oratory can be. The men Fermoyle addressed responded to his message. They had been told, not by a general or a politician, but by a man of God, that they were waging the good fight. Their service in Korea was time well spent. The risks they took would make the world a safer, better place.

Part of Fermoyle's success lay in how he delivered his sermon. Despite his strident message, the cardinal did not speak in harsh tones. Rather his words flowed in a gentle, soft voice whose sound itself gave reassurance. Rarely did he resort to dramatic flourishes. Instead, intellectual rigor, everyday examples, humor, and references to air force life all were employed to explain and reinforce his message. And by appearing not to take advantage of his rank and prestige, Stephen Fermoyle enhanced the impact of his words, as well as his moral authority.

Neither evil nor the communist threat were mentioned when McGrath had breakfast with the cardinal after mass. Roger O'Boyle had arranged for McGrath to sit on one side of Fermoyle. Colonel Schmidt sat on the other. Sitting across from them were Colonel Preston and Major Parker. The breakfast served was typical military fare. Creamed chipped beef and pancakes were the featured items. As always, coffee, toast, and canned orange juice were available as well. McGrath chose the pancakes. Cardinal Fermoyle selected the creamed beef.

Parker, Preston, and Schmidt had started eating when their guest who, with McGrath, had just sat down, spoke words that unintentionally embarrassed the three officers.

"Gentlemen, before we break bread, let us give thanks."

The three military men stopped and appeared not to know what to do. McGrath came to their rescue by saying, "Yes, indeed, Your Eminence," as he bowed his head. The three did likewise, as did O'Boyle, who seemed amused by the incident.

"Bless us, oh Lord, for these, thy gifts, which we are about to receive from thy bounty, through Christ our Lord, amen."

"Amen," said the others including Schmidt, Preston, and Parker.

During the meal the cardinal turned toward McGrath and spoke to him directly.

"You and Father O'Boyle are old friends, he tells me."

"Yes, Your Eminence."

"I do wish you'd call me Father Fermoyle."

"I'll try, Your Eminence."

Both men then laughed at McGrath's response.

"Yes, Father, we were colleagues at Georgetown and have become good friends."

"He told me of your loss, and I am deeply sorry. I have said a prayer for her soul, my son."

"Thank you, Father, that's most kind."

McGrath surprised himself, believing that this prayer would be helpful to Catherine wherever she was, if in fact she or her soul were anywhere. But then, characteristically, he wondered whether a prayer from a cardinal carried more weight than that of a parish priest.

At the cardinal's request McGrath told Fermoyle of his student days at Amherst and Notre Dame, of his teaching experiences at Georgetown, of his courtship of Catherine, and of his decision to rejoin the air force.

"And now you're here, flying jet fighters."

"Yes, Father, it's now what I do and who I am."

"These are two different things, I think."

"Sir?"

"In my experience with people in high positions or men with dangerous professions, they come to believe that what they do defines who they are."

"Yes, I suppose that's right."

"But that's not the case. An individual is someone special, God's unique creation. What a person does is simply their occupation. Their identity comes from their humanity, from being a person. As does their value. They're defined by who they are, not what they do. Meaning and dignity are found in all men, regardless of how they earn a living."

"I hear what you're saying, Father, but I'm not sure I can agree with you."

"You don't have to, my son. But let's look at you. Before, you were a teacher of students; now you're a commander of men at war. You're a pilot, someone who flies a high performance aircraft, and so Colonel Preston tells me, a success at what you do. But it's not who you are."

"Perhaps, but many men, at least the ones I know, get so caught up with what they do that what matters most is their job. They, in effect, become what they do. It gives their life meaning and purpose."

"That's true. It happens, and often in our society. Yet one's job is not of prime importance."

"How we live our lives is?"

"I believe that's right. The measure of a man is how he spends the time God has granted him. God judges us by how we live, not what we do. In God's eyes we are all equal."

"But not here on Earth."

"No, despite what Jefferson said. Nor, I suppose has it ever been true. But life here on Earth is secondary. Of prime importance is the everlasting."

To Stephen Fermoyle, "everlasting" was a noun, not an adjective.

"Which my Jesuit friend told me is reached by faith."

"Faith and God's forgiveness, I suspect is what Father O'Boyle said or meant to say."

"As I recall, he mentioned both."

"And he's told me that you have come to doubt the reality of faith."

McGrath looked startled. The cardinal's remark struck home with the force of a battleship's broadside.

"To that, Your Eminence, I must confess."

"I will pray for you, my son, and I have but one request to make of you."

"Yes, Your Eminence?"

"I'm not here this morning to bring you back under God's wing, though I believe He would protect you and bring you peace."

"And your request?" McGrath's curiosity was aroused. He was truly interested in what Cardinal Fermoyle would ask of him, and wondered whether he would agree, or be able to agree. He also was worried that he might have to say no.

McGrath need not have been concerned. Stephen, Cardinal Fermoyle's, request was a simple one.

"When you're finished here, when your tour of duty ends, come visit me in Cincinnati. Before your next assignment, spend a few days with me, as my guest."

McGrath could see no reason why he could not do that. And the manner in which Fermoyle spoke made clear it was an invitation kindly issued, not an imperial summons.

"Come to Cincinnati, and let us talk of God and men, and life on Earth, and what lies beyond."

McGrath found himself responding with total sincerity.

"I would like that, Your Eminence, and I will do so. I promise."

"I'm glad you will come, my son. But you will have to make me another promise."

McGrath looked puzzled, a reaction to which the cardinal responded with a grin and words he had spoken before.

"It's simple, really. I would like you to call me Father Fermoyle. Will you promise to do that?"

"Yes, Father, I will. I will indeed."

Roger O'Boyle was pleased to learn that Cardinal Fermoyle had invited McGrath to Cincinnati.

"That means he's fond of you, and intrigued. I've heard he takes an interest in certain people and wishes to get to know them better, and sometimes guide them along the way. Sorta like a parish priest might."

"Or a father."

"Yes, that too. The folks he gets to know become like family to him. It's a way for him to get away from bishops and mayors and corporate execs and deal with what he calls 'the real folks.' If it works—and I can't imagine it won't—you'll have an acquaintance, a friend really, for life."

"Sounds rather nice. I suppose in my case there's a bit of missionary work going on as well."

"Could be. I suspect he might try to bring you back to the Church."

"No doubt you had something to do with this."

"Me? I'll say simply that I did what I thought was best."

"I bet you did. Now, to change the subject, tell me again how you got hooked up with the cardinal and came to Korea. You told me the night you arrived but it was late, I was tired, and I'm not sure I heard the whole story."

O'Boyle complied with McGrath's request, this time relating a more embellished version. He explained that when Cardinal Fermoyle was invited to Korea by the Secretary of Defense he looked about for three young priests to accompany him. He would benefit from their assistance and they would gain exposure to a world they otherwise would not see. The cardinal was an old friend of the Right Reverend William Hanlan, the president of Georgetown University, whom he telephoned to ask for possible candidates. Hanlan recommended O'Boyle. Fermoyle then interviewed the Jesuit.

"The interview went splendidly. We talked for two hours," said O'Boyle, who provided details galore about what was said.

"But what about your classes?"

"Father Hanlan said he would take care of them."

"How convenient."

"Yup. So here I am, at an airfield in the middle of Korea. Let me tell you, it's one long trip from D.C."

"That I know, but how glad I am you made it."

With this remark the two men embraced, as they had done the night McGrath found O'Boyle in his tent. While doing so, McGrath reflected how different he and his friend were. O'Boyle was a man of God, devoted to reason and the pursuit of truth. He, McGrath, was a man of war intent upon aerial destruction. Once, at Georgetown, they had been similar in purpose and profession. For the teacher turned fighter pilot that now seemed long ago.

Cardinal Fermoyle and his aides left Kimpo on a Thursday morning. That afternoon the flatbed truck again was used for a special event, though one quite unlike that employed by the archbishop of Cincinnati. The event was an awards ceremony. Periodically, medals and commendations were given to the air force personnel at Kimpo for outstanding performances. These occasions produced considerable cynicism among both the officers and enlisted men. They reasoned that half of the individuals receiving medals did not deserve them while many who did were ignored. At the same time, the ceremonies reignited a sense of pride among those at the airfield. The occasions were formal military events, though uniforms were of the everyday variety and the music came from a record player. Flags, parade ranks, salutes, and speeches were integral to the events. The result was a reaffirmation of purpose. All involved felt a sense of accomplishment. They were proud to be part of the 4th Fighter Interceptor Wing, which they rightly considered to be an elite organization.

At this awards ceremony several pilots received the Distinguished Flying Cross, a medal given to those who completed their tour of duty, having flown one hundred missions. DFCs were also given for the destruction of an enemy aircraft. Air medals were handed out to those who completed twenty-five trips. For truly exceptional performances the air force awarded the Silver Star. These were given to pilots attaining the title of ace. Downing five enemy aircraft was an exceptional performance. The thirty-nine men who did so in Korea certainly earned the honor.

The first pilot to become an ace in Korea was Captain James Jabara. He shot down numbers five and six on May 20, 1951, becoming the first jet ace in history. When not flying, Jabara usually had a cigar in his mouth. Later he was named Cigar Smoker of the Year and awarded five hundred cigars. This, no doubt, he appreciated at least as much as the medal.

Charlie Hickok did not smoke cigars. He preferred Johnnie Walker. Having accomplished in September what Jabara did in May, Detachment Q's first ace was entitled to the Silver Star. This he received at the afternoon ceremony. The medal was bestowed on him by FEAF's General Smith, who had flown in for the occasion. Smith, the officer who had summoned McGrath to Tokyo prior to the deployment of the detachment to Korea, also awarded a Silver Star to Lieutenant William Garnett who, though not an ace, destroyed three MiGs, saved the life of a fellow pilot, and sank a North Korean patrol boat north of Pen Yeng Do—all in the course of twelve minutes. It was, said Smith, an "exceptional performance."

Hickok accepted the medal from the general, saluted, and returned to the ranks. Afterward, the first person to congratulate him was Squadron Leader Urqhart.

"Good show, old boy."

"Thank you, my limey friend. As you Brits would say, it was a piece of cake."

"Quite. I hope now though, Charles, you'll be a bit more careful. You're in the air force history books so there's no reason to take unnecessary risks. I'd like to see you alive at the end of the conflict."

"Don't worry about me. I intend to live to a ripe old age. I also intend to get me more MiGs. Jabara may have been the first jet ace. I plan to be the first double jet ace. Ten MiGs. Five more to go."

"I hope you get them," said McGrath, who had joined the conversation. "Congratulations, Hickok, it's an award richly deserved."

"Thank you, sir, nice of you to say so."

Once the ceremony was over the men at Kimpo went back to work. Sixteen Sabres were scheduled to patrol the Yalu late that afternoon. Detachment Q was to provide four of them.

McGrath's two remaining F–86s were AOCP—aircraft out of commission—due to lack of parts. One needed a hard-to-find vacuum tube for its radio. The other required a cylinder sleeve for one of the air brakes. Throughout 1951 and early 1952 spare parts for the Sabre fleet were in high demand but low supply. While McGrath was in Korea, about half of the F–86s were grounded due to a scarcity of parts. The problem was twofold: first, the Sabre was new to the air force inventory. Thus, a sufficient number of parts simply had not yet been manufactured. And second, the F–86s in Korea, despite their combat operations, did not receive priority attention. Air defense of the continental United States was considered more important.

The Yalu River was approximately 230 miles from Kimpo. The Sabres were to launch at 4:15 P.M., 1615 military time. That meant the force would reach the river about 4:40, leaving just enough daylight for both the patrol and the flight home.

Sergeant Ricks had McGrath's F–86 ready to go well before start engines. Preflighting the aircraft, the crew chief had removed the camouflage netting placed over the plane as well as the screen protecting the open intake of the J–47 engine. He also checked the Sabre's fuel, oil, and oxygen tanks. He made sure the armorer had certified the guns were in working order and that a technician had double-checked the aircraft's radio. To Ricks it was imperative that his charge be in tiptop condition, which it was when McGrath arrived at the flight line.

Hopping off the Jeep, McGrath, who was anxious to leave, made eye contact with Ricks, whose silent response indicated the Sabre was ready. McGrath did a quick walk around the aircraft.

"I see she still has wings, Sergeant."

"Yes, sir, and I believe they will stay on."

"Good. We're gonna find some MiGs today, Norman, I can feel it in my bones."

"I hope you do, sir. Bring my plane back in one piece, Colonel."

"I will, Norman. I will."

McGrath climbed aboard and, once in the cockpit, went through the preflight drill as Ricks adjusted the harness straps, resulting in the pilot being strapped tightly to the aircraft seat. As McGrath started the engine Ricks removed the ejection seat safety pins. Four minutes later McGrath had steered his aircraft to the end of the runway, past several severely damaged Sabres now serving as decoys should enemy aircraft strike Kimpo. He also passed three U.S. Army halftracks mounting quad .50 caliber machine guns. These constituted a major part of Kimpo's antiaircraft arsenal.

McGrath paid no attention to either the decoys or the halftracks. He was focused on the mission. As he advanced the throttle he and his aircraft felt as one. McGrath believed that on this mission he at last would get a MiG.

His F–86 was the ninth Sabre to become airborne. As usual, Lieutenant Heller was on his wing and the tenth aircraft to lift off. Hickok and Urqhart, the two F–86s next in line, completed the detachment's flight.

Twenty minutes later the sixteen aircraft were at the mouth of the river. Turning northeast, they proceeded up the Yalu. Radio silence had been maintained until Preston, in command of the Sabre force, spoke the words all the pilots were eager to hear.

"MiGs at eleven o'clock. Stay sharp, everyone. Let's get 'em."

The Sabres did not wait to be attacked. At full power they climbed toward the enemy. The results were disappointing. The MiGs ignored the F–86s. Piloted by North Korean student aviators, the Russian-built craft stayed above the Sabres, out of reach. They swept once across the Yalu, turned north, and flew home to Antung.

"Seems they're not coming out to play."

"Chickenshits," said Hickok.

Preston kept the Sabres above the south bank of the river. Several patrols up and down the Yalu took place but no further sightings of the enemy occurred. Everyone was disappointed. Back at Kimpo, Hickok was the most outspoken.

"Damn cowards," remarked Detachment Q's only ace.

McGrath was more philosophical, at least outwardly.

"Calm down, Charlie. We're here for a while and I suspect we'll see the MiGs more often than not."

That night, as he retired to bed, McGrath was much less calm. He was upset with himself that after two months in Korea, he had yet to down a MiG. Others had, why had he not? For the first time, McGrath wondered whether he still had what it takes. And when sleep came, it was in no way restful.

SEVENTEEN

McGrath's next flight was not north to the Yalu but east to Japan. A C–47 took him and Urqhart to Johnson Air Base where they were to pick up two new F–86s. These they would ferry to Kimpo, thereby augmenting the Sabre fleet at K–14.

Colonel Preston had insisted McGrath make the trip. Every six or seven weeks fighter pilots in Korea received several days of leave. These were spent in Japan rather than in Korea. During the war American pilots stayed on base. Little fraternization with Koreans took place. Rest and relaxation occurred off the peninsula. Preston thought McGrath needed a rest. So he ordered McGrath to Japan. Detachment Q's leader protested.

"Relax, Colonel," said the group commander. "Get a few days of rest and then come back with the 86s. And don't worry. The MiGs will still be here."

"Colonel, I really think I should stay. I'm here to fight and—"

"McGrath," Preston was speaking without harshness, "do as you're ordered. I promise you the war will still be on when you get back."

Upon deplaning at Johnson, McGrath and Urqhart discovered that the two Sabres were not ready. Both their radios were in need of repair. The necessary parts were in Japan but not at Johnson. The officer in charge of maintenance said he needed four days to track down the parts, have them delivered to Johnson, install them in the Sabres, and flight test them. McGrath and Urqhart had no choice but to wait.

Urqhart left Johnson almost immediately. Officially, he went to Tokyo to call upon Air Vice Marshall Kent. In fact, he went for "I and I"—intoxication and intercourse. After briefing the RAF's senior officer in Japan, Urqhart easily found an attractive woman who, for a reasonable sum, spent the next three days with him, much of it in bed. When he returned to Johnson the squadron leader declared he was well rested and extremely fond of Hiro, "at least I think that's what the ol' girl's name was."

McGrath expected to see Martha and, once in Japan, was looking forward to her company. She had written him twice a week. Her letters, McGrath soon realized, were of two kinds. In one she recounted her activities, describing the happenings at school. In the other she expressed love for McGrath and spoke, with surprising specificity, of romance and passion. McGrath, of course, preferred the latter. Though he responded to both types his letters were brief and far fewer in number. However, he did tell the woman he loved her, though intentionally making no mention of a future beyond Japan.

Once, when about to write Martha, McGrath, in rummaging about for a fountain pen, found a small wooden jewelry box he had not opened since leaving Washington. Immediately, he knew what the box contained. Hesitantly, he opened it. Inside was the sterling silver butterfly pin Catherine had worn the day he proposed. Laura McCreedy had given him the pin three days after the funeral.

Seeing the pin brought great sadness to McGrath. Suddenly, he realized that he and Catherine never had written letters to one another. Never would there be correspondence to reread or come upon in a drawer or attic. McGrath had but three photographs of Catherine, plus memories and this pin. It seemed so little. That day, after returning the pin to its box, he decided to write Martha another time.

At Johnson, McGrath initially spent time with F–86 pilots who had drawn air defense duties. He then met with two FEAF intelligence officers who were eager to interview a pilot with experience in combating MiGs. Not until late afternoon was McGrath free to call Martha. Which he did.

There was no answer. Mildly annoyed, he waited thirty minutes and called again. Still no answer. McGrath imagined several reasons why she was out, one of which he found disturbing. Thirty minutes later he tried again. This time Martha Dawson was home.

"Hello."

"Hi, it's me."

Martha was delighted to hear McGrath's voice. "Oh, how are you and where are you?"

"I'm at Johnson."

"Oh goodie. When do I get to see you?"

"Tonight, I hope. I can be in Tokyo in two hours."

There was silence at Martha's end of the phone. Then she spoke.

"I can't tonight."

This time the silence occurred at the other end. Realizing that McGrath was awaiting an explanation, Martha continued.

"I can't, dear man, not tonight. And it's not what you think. I don't do that anymore. There's a teachers' meeting at school, with the principal and vice principal, and everybody has to be there. I have to show up; I really do."

"Well, that stinks. Can't you tell them something's come up and you'll meet with them another time?"

"Not if I want to keep my job. I really have to be there."

"Well, phooey."

Martha laughed. "I've never heard you say that."

"True enough. I save it for special occasions."

"I love you, McGrath. So when do I get to see you? How long are you here for?"

"I've got three days, and no official business. I'm on leave."

"Wonderful. Tomorrow's Friday and I will take the day off. We can spend the day together and then there's the weekend."

"I'm at your service, for three days at least, and truth be told, I'm anxious to see you."

"And I you. I'm going to be extra nice to you."

McGrath enjoyed hearing these words. "So where and when?"

"Why don't we begin tomorrow with lunch? If I'm going to spend three days with you I need time to get ready."

"Martha, just throw some things in a suitcase and let's get going."

"Dear man, you obviously don't understand women. I need time to get things together—my clothes, my hair, my nails."

McGrath just sighed, glad he was not female.

"Okay, lunch it is. Where?"

"Where we always meet, of course."

"In the lobby of the University Club?"

"Yes, my sweet. I'll be there at eleven."

"With your bags packed."

"Yes, and ready to smother you with kisses."

"Eleven then. I'll see you there."

"Haven't you forgotten to tell me something?"

McGrath had no idea what she was talking about.

"Huh?"

"That you love me."

"Eleven o'clock, Martha, and yes, I think you're a swell gal."

"McGrath!"

"Fact is, lady, I rather do love you, very much."

"Better, much better. Eleven o'clock. I'll see you then. And I'm so very, very glad you called."

The next day McGrath was in the lobby of the University Club precisely at eleven o'clock. Earlier he had reserved a suite at the Akura Palace Hotel, registering as "Lieutenant Colonel and Mrs. McGrath." The rooms were expensive—thirty-three dollars a night. But in size, decor, amenities, and service they seemed good value. McGrath wanted he and Martha to be comfortable, and in this particular set of rooms—the hotel called them the Matthew Perry Suite—they would be comfortable in the extreme. McGrath believed that occasionally a person needed to go first class. Life had its expensive pleasures and he wanted to experience at least some of them. The Commodore's suite at the Akura Palace enabled him to do so.

By 11:35 Martha had not arrived. McGrath became concerned,

wondering if something terrible had happened. Given how poorly automobiles were driven in Tokyo, his concern was legitimate. McGrath recalled that once before a traffic accident brought tragedy to his life. Would one do so again? He thought not. God, or mere coincidence, would not be that cruel. Still, Martha was late, now very late, and he was worried.

When she walked into the club's lobby she was most apologetic. Martha explained she had gotten a late start and had difficulty getting a cab. McGrath was just glad to see her, relieved there had been no accident. He put his arms around Martha and hugged her. Sensing his concern, she was surprised but pleased. In her experience men were annoyed by tardiness. McGrath's reaction reinforced her belief that he indeed was special.

Once upstairs in the dining room McGrath let his eyes take in the woman across the table. She appeared as neither a prim schoolteacher nor a lady for hire. Martha looked like an attractive housewife, well dressed and comfortable in both manner and appearance. She wore a fashionable, charcoal gray skirt and a burgundy silk blouse, set off by a wide gray belt. Earrings that were conservative in style and a pewter pin completed the ensemble. McGrath liked what he saw. But he marveled at how this young woman could create such disparate images. To McGrath, Martha Dawson seemed capable of being different women. He found this fascinating, even exciting. And he wondered whether other women could do the same.

Early in their conversation Martha made a comment McGrath did not comprehend.

"You haven't said anything and I'm surprised, and a little hurt. Though you've told me you like how I look."

"I do, I think you look terrific."

"I'm glad. But don't you notice something different?"

McGrath's blank expression provided an answer, though not the one Martha was hoping to receive.

"My hair, silly. I'm wearing it differently."

"Oh right, gosh, it looks nice."

Martha just shook her head and sighed.

"Not what I was hoping for."

"It does look great, honest. It's longer and wavier, and you've combed it differently."

"Better. I thought men liked long hair on a woman."

"We do. And on you it looks terrific. Kinda sexy, I think."

"Well, I like it and I've gotten a number of compliments. I did it for you, you know."

"Well it does look nice. Very nice. And I might say you look just wonderful. I think you're one beautiful lady."

They stayed at the University Club for three hours, during which not one moment of embarrassing silence occurred. Conversation was easy and enjoyable. The only awkward time for McGrath came when he noticed a young pretty woman with red hair at a table nearby. Other men in the room thought she looked like Rita Hayworth. McGrath was reminded of someone else. At the time Martha had excused herself and gone to the lady's room. Alone, McGrath stared at the woman, who brought back a discrete memory of Catherine at Decatur Place. Then purposely he closed the vault. When Martha returned neither redhead occupied his attention. In both heart and head he focused on the attractive blonde with whom he was spending the weekend.

When Martha asked what their plans were for the weekend McGrath was prepared. He said they would have a fancy dinner that night in Tokyo, drive out of the city Saturday morning to Tsuchiura where they would have lunch at an old and famous inn known for its beauty and food. Then back to Tokyo, dinner somewhere and then, on Sunday, explore Tokyo as tourists. Martha said it sounded wonderful. She asked McGrath when "this weekend of ours" was to end. He replied that he needed to report back to Johnson early Monday morning and told Martha he thought he would catch a late train Sunday night. Sensibly, Martha said they should enjoy the time they had together and not worry about when they would have to part.

There was one question Martha had that McGrath could not answer. She wanted to know when the war was going to end. McGrath simply did not know. As a pilot in Korea he was isolated. He flew F–86s and that's all he did. He had little sense of the overall picture and was not privy to strategy and policies. He was, and felt like, a small piece of a large puzzle. Not that he minded. McGrath liked what he was doing. Not with anyone would he trade places. So he told Martha the truth. He said that he had no idea when the war would end, adding that individually his role was of little importance.

Martha disagreed. She told McGrath that what he did was essential and that "it was the most heroic thing anyone in Korea could do."

"Not really, Martha."

"I think so, and so do the newspapers."

"Which tells you how little they know. The air war gets lots of attention in the press but there's other stuff going on that's just as important."

"Such as?"

"Well, there are fighter-bombers flying everyday, F–84s, and they're taking great risks. The B–26s, World War II planes, are flying at night and hitting the enemy. Navy planes are striking at North Korea and doing a heck of a job. You won't catch me flying off the deck of some boat. And then there's the poor guys on the ground, doing a dangerous, dirty job, and doing it well."

"All that's no doubt true. But what you do is very important."

"Yes it is, but no more so than what the others are doing."

"But why then, do newspapers give what you do so much attention?"

"Good question. I think it's because they see us as gunfighters—knights of the air, if you will—fighting high above the dirt and mud, where the killing is impersonal and it's easy to keep score."

"What do you mean?"

"Well, they'll report that we went up north and knocked down two MiGs and lost none, or that we damaged several and had only one of ours hit. It's easy for them to see who won, like in a baseball game. And since by and large we do well the press can understand it and write it up. The ground war isn't that easy. The guys are slugging it out but there's not any big change in territory. A hill here, a hill there. All you can write about is that a bunch of guys got killed. By comparison the war with the MiGs is easier to keep track of, and it's a lot jazzier."

"The newspapers do seem to make it glamorous. When that pilot became an ace there was a lot of coverage, even here in Japan."

"True, but that probably was newsworthy. First jet ace in history. That's a big deal."

"He shot down five enemy planes?"

"Six, actually. And since then there's been a few other guys who've reached the magic number."

Innocently, Martha asked two questions, the answers to which she assumed were yes.

"Have you shot down five planes? Are you an ace?"

McGrath paused before speaking. He thought of the eleven German aircraft he had downed years before. He remembered each kill as though it had occurred yesterday. He could recall where, when, and how each combat took place. Then he saw the MiGs that had gotten away.

"No, I'm afraid not. I've shot at them a few times but haven't been able to bring one down."

In no way disappointed by McGrath's response, Martha's concern was personal.

"Oh well, I'm sure you will. Mostly though I want you to stay safe and come home in one piece."

After lunch the two of them walked back to the Akura Palace Hotel. The early October weather was ideal—not cold, yet far from warm. Summer appeared to have departed yet winter had not yet arrived. People in Tokyo were wearing coats and hats but not gloves or scarves. As they walked Martha Dawson held onto McGrath's arm. He in turn kept her close.

Once at the hotel they retired to the Matthew Perry suite. Martha was impressed by the rooms. She never had been in such luxurious quarters. McGrath, who had, admitted to himself that they were extremely nice.

"They'll do," he said to Martha.

"Silly man." She wandered about the suite, excited like a child, examining the furnishings. In one corner she came across a small icebox.

"Oh look, isn't this wonderful? It's full of juice and soft drinks, and there's some liquor too, and plenty of ice."

"Would you like a drink?"

"No, thank you. It's a bit early."

"Well, if not a drink, here's something you can have."

McGrath came up to Martha and placed his hands upon her waist and shoulder, gently pulling her to him. He then kissed her, with feeling. She did not object and returned the kiss, then nicely backed away from the embrace.

"It's too early for that too."

So they talked and spent the next hour in further conversation. At 4:30 Martha told McGrath she needed to get ready. Their dinner reservation was for seven o'clock and she intended to look her very best. As she went off to the bedroom and its adjoining bath McGrath picked up the book he was reading and moved to a more comfortable chair.

Ten minutes later Martha came out from the bedroom intending to surprise McGrath. Wearing but a towel and with her hair not yet washed but pulled up, she planned on giving McGrath a preview of the pleasures he had in store later that night.

Quietly—she was tiptoeing—Martha came up to the chair. However, the surprise was hers, not his. She found McGrath to be fast asleep, with the book laying awkwardly on the floor. Martha smiled, and ever so softly caressed his face with her hand. Passion, she concluded, would have to wait.

Dinner took place at a restaurant not far from the hotel. Called, in English, the Paper Moon, the restaurant was decorated with exquisite examples of origami. It served traditional Japanese food, which Martha wanted McGrath to sample. She had selected the restaurant thinking it would broaden his culinary horizons. It did

Their first course was miso-shiru with wakame and tofu. This was a flavorful broth with dried sea vegetables and bean curd. Martha explained that tofu was extremely healthy, being rich in vitamins and easy to digest. She had made an effort to learn about the food of Japan and was convinced it could be both tasty and nutritious if prepared properly. The next course was kamaboko, steamed fish cakes that were popular throughout the island. Those served to Martha and McGrath were made with green onions and beaten eggs. The next item, comprising the main meal, was lemon and steamed chicken rolls accompanied by rice with chestnuts. Dessert was a simple plate of melons and strawberries, artfully arranged.

Throughout dinner Martha drank saki, the most popular of Japanese alcoholic beverages. Clear and colorless, Martha's saki was served hot, as preferred by the Japanese. McGrath did not know what to drink. There was no Coca-Cola and he cared not at all for beer, of which several brands, none American, were available. So he drank tea, to which he added lemon and sugar.

Truth be told, McGrath enjoyed the food at the Paper Moon more than he had expected. Yet he was not won over to Japanese cuisine. Nothing, he concluded, beat a good steak, string beans, and a baked potato.

Far more pleasing to McGrath than the food was the dress Martha was wearing. It was a dark red sheath with long sleeves and a high neck that revealed, in outline form, the woman's compelling features. The dress was silk and oriental in style. On Martha it looked stunning. McGrath was smitten. His eyes focused on the dress and not on the girl who was wearing it.

"I take it you approve of what I have on."

"I certainly do. You look lovely in it." In fact, McGrath thought she looked seductive and sexy but deliberately chose a more gentle description.

"I'm glad, but remember we have the whole night to do what I think you're thinking about, so for now pay attention to me. In other words, talk to me and make me feel special."

With three simple words, McGrath complied.

"I love you."

So immediate and definitive, the words caught Martha by surprise, then made her glow in delight.

"That, dear man, is a very good start."

"I do, I really do. I'm not sure how this can happen so fast, in such a short time. And special? Oh, yes, you are one truly special person."

McGrath did not understand why he felt so strongly about this woman. So soon after Catherine, he wondered whether he might be on the rebound. Or just lonely. Or simply in need of a female companion to bed and be with. Whatever the reason McGrath looked at Martha Dawson and saw a woman he cared for deeply. For now, and maybe for later as well, he believed that would suffice.

Tears now appeared on Martha's face. She reached across the table, took hold of McGrath's hands, and spoke to him as if in prayer.

"And I love you with all my heart."

Dinner was a great success. McGrath and his lady stayed at the Paper Moon well past ten o'clock. Walking back to the hotel, each believed that life was about to start over, to begin again.

As they entered the Akura Palace, McGrath noticed that Yoshio, who was holding the door open, winked as he walked by. Only later did McGrath realize why.

Once up in the suite McGrath took off his jacket and went over to the refrigerator. Opening it, he took out a Coke and a bottle of Beefeaters, the latter for Martha who, before disappearing into the bathroom, said she would like a gin and tonic. McGrath made the drink, though without a lime, and with Coke in hand went over to the chair where earlier he had fallen asleep. This time, when Martha appeared, he was wide awake, and full of anticipation.

Martha did not disappoint. Her red silk dress now hung carefully in the bathroom. She wore instead a long diaphanous black robe that billowed about her body. Beneath the robe McGrath could see a black nightgown. This too was long, with a halter top that showed off her bosom to great advantage. Black slippers and a ribbon in her hair, also black, completed the late evening's attire.

McGrath was about to speak when Martha put her index finger to her lip, signaling silence.

"Not now, my love. Words can come later."

When the words came it was morning. McGrath awoke and was alone in bed. Yet he could sense her presence. The bed's aroma was that of the woman whose passion had been genuine, whose body had been warm and willing. Now she was gone, or so it seemed.

McGrath got up, washed, and put on a pair of shorts. He then walked into the next room, where, to his pleasant surprise, Martha was sitting at a table, pouring tea.

"He awakes. I thought you might sleep forever. Good morning, my dear."

With these last words, Martha sweetly kissed McGrath on the cheek, as someone might a spouse of twenty years.

"I've ordered you tea, toast, juice, and scrambled eggs—an American breakfast. It's under the lid, ready for you."

Surveying the scene, Martha dressed and cheerful, breakfast served, and the day belonging only to them, McGrath said to himself that life, at least for the moment, seemed almost perfect.

After breakfast they took a walk, for exercise and to do some sight-seeing. One store they passed was a jewelry store whose location McGrath noted. Another was a camera store where he purchased a 35 mm camera for Martha. For himself McGrath bought a pair of used, German-made binoculars. He intended to use them along the Yalu.

With the walk completed they then secured an automobile, employing the services of Yoshio who, McGrath concluded, was a man of many talents. Martha had talents as well, one of them previously unknown to McGrath, for bargaining with the doorman, she got him to reduce the price of the car. The vehicle was a prewar Nissan, black in color and neither fast nor comfortable. But it did run and, with directions from Yoshio, carried McGrath and Martha Dawson safely to Tsuchiura.

There they found the inn, arriving in time for lunch. Overlooking the sea, the inn offered a splendid view along with fine food and expert service. It was the perfect spot for a private getaway.

McGrath and his lady sat out on a terrace. They dined comfortably and happily until an older man and young woman sat down at a nearby table. The woman was European and quite attractive. The man was well dressed, looking more like a diplomat than the business executive he was. She took no notice of McGrath and Martha. He, however, did, and stared directly at McGrath's companion.

She soon became uncomfortable and spoke to McGrath, interrupting a comment he was making about Japanese food.

"We have to go."

"What?"

"Please, we have to go. Now."

"But it's lovely here and we're having a nice time."

"Yes, I know, but . . ."

Then Martha's reasoning struck home. McGrath realized that she had been with this guy. He'd been a client in her evening job.

So they left, driving back to Tokyo in silence. At the hotel the conversation that needed to occur took place. Martha pointed out that this sort of embarrassing encounter might well happen again and more than once. McGrath replied that if it did, he didn't care and that they would simply have to endure such encounters whenever and wherever they occurred. To this Martha responded with a hug and told McGrath he was wonderful. Taking hold of her as a father might a daughter, McGrath said that they could not change the past, only shape the future. Moreover, people could think whatever they wished but that he and she should focus on one another. Martha then hugged McGrath more closely.

When Martha rose to take a bath and get ready for dinner McGrath told her he was going for a short walk, which he did. Where he walked was to the jewelry store. Once inside he selected a small diamond set upon a simple gold band. Unlike the purchase from Daniel Gottheim in Georgetown, this transaction took less than five minutes.

That night they dined in the hotel and went to bed early. Unlike the previous night, Martha wore nothing seductive. This night she resembled the college student she had been. In the dining room she had on a simple yellow dress and sweater. In the bedroom she wore an over-sized Penn State t-shirt.

Disappointed, McGrath wisely said nothing.

The next morning they made love in a fashion more raw than sweet. If romance thereby suffered, it recovered during the day as Martha and McGrath enjoyed their Sunday together. Throughout the afternoon and early evening they explored the city and its shops, usually holding hands. Unlike the morning, there was an air of innocence to their union.

When the time came for McGrath to depart, Martha accompanied him to the train station. On the platform, just before boarding the train, McGrath remarked that the scene reminded him of a World War II movie: boy going off to war, girl at the station about to cry. Martha told him to be serious.

"Okay, I will be. Martha Dawson, I love you, and to prove it, I have something for you."

From his pocket he took out a small jewelry box and gave it to her. He then stepped onto the train, which began to move, and blew her a kiss.

Both curious and excited, Martha opened the box. What she saw inside made her heart skip. Sliding the ring onto her finger brought about a unique and wonderful sensation. She now belonged to someone. No longer alone, she had found a man. She felt proud that she could say to herself and to others that he was a good man and that she truly loved him.

Walking down the platform toward the station's exit, a different feeling arose, one not so enjoyable. Martha realized that McGrath might not survive; he might not come back. His was a dangerous profession and Korea was a dangerous place. So she began to worry and silently to pray.

EIGHTEEN

The return flight to Kimpo was uneventful. McGrath and Urqhart left Johnson at mid-morning and by lunchtime had Mount Useless in view. This was a name air force pilots gave to a rugged peak near the airfield in Korea that served as a beacon for the Sabre pilots. Upon landing the two steered their new aircraft past several badly damaged F–86s that, stripped of all useful equipment, were placed to the side of the runway. As McGrath climbed down from the cockpit he looked to his left as two Sabres took off, engines at full power, on their way to escort an RF–80.

Once on the ground McGrath and Urqhart were given a ride to the shack where pilots stored their flight equipment. Items such as parachutes, helmets, oxygen masks, and the like were kept under lock and key, accessible only to pilots. The sergeant in charge of the shack told McGrath that Colonel Preston wished to see him immediately upon his return. Unconcerned, McGrath nevertheless hurried over to group operations where Preston, were he not flying or sleeping, usually could be found.

Upon McGrath entering the tent Preston looked up, stopped what he was doing, and spoke to the Detachment Q leader.

"Glad you're back, McGrath. Let's go for a short walk."

"Yes, sir."

Once outside the tent, in October weather best described as chilly but not cold, the 4th Fighter commander spoke again.

"Hickok's dead. So is Lieutenant Heller. They were low on fuel up north but went chasing some MiGs across the river. Two of your boys saw what was going on and went after them. It wasn't pretty."

"Jesus!"

"Once across the river they were jumped by about ten MiGs. Might have been a trap. Hickok's plane just exploded, though not before he got one. Heller got one too. Then his plane was hit, the damn wing was on fire, and the aircraft rolled over and dove straight into a mountain. There were no parachutes, from either plane."

"And the other two?"

"Cox and your marine pilot, they got back okay."

"So the air force loses two good pilots."

"That's right. We're telling Far Eastern Air Forces they went down south of the river."

"Good." McGrath paused and changed his tone of voice. "Damn Hickok."

"Yeah, I know. He was MiG mad. He crossed that fine line."

"I don't mind Hickok getting himself killed. I half expected it. Charlie knew what he was doing. I mind him getting Heller killed. The kid was a good pilot and a fine officer, and now he's neither."

"And now you have two letters to write."

"No, just one. Hickok was divorced. He once told me his ex would send the letter back unopened. But Heller's a different matter. He had gotten married just out of flight school. I saw her picture once. Pretty girl. Though she looked awfully young."

"Just like Heller. Well, I'm sure you'll write her a nice letter."

"I'll give it my best shot."

"Good, and I'll make sure he gets his DFC."

"It still stinks, you know."

"It does that, Colonel, it does indeed."

Preston started to walk back to the tent, then turned and faced McGrath.

"I almost forgot. There is some good news. Word came down yesterday. Here, these are for you."

McGrath opened the small box Preston had handed him.

"Well, I'll be damned."

"Congratulations, Colonel, you've earned them."

Inside the box were two small silver eagle pins, signifying the rank of full colonel. General McCreedy had kept his promise.

"Put them on and wear them proud." Preston was smiling as he spoke.

He then shook McGrath's hand and continued.

"It's far from perfect but this is one fine air force we're part of and occasionally they do things right. Again, congratulations."

"Thank you, sir."

Preston continued to smile, and tapped the eagles on his shoulder.

"And welcome to the club."

The next time Preston spoke to McGrath they were at forty-one thousand feet, approaching MiG Alley. The term was used to describe a northwest corner of the Korean peninsula, an area between the Chongchon and Yalu rivers bounded on the west by the Korean Bay and on the east by a line running roughly between the Sui-Ho Reservoir on the border with Manchuria and the city of Huichon. As the name implies, MiG Alley was the place where the enemy aircraft operated. Rarely would they fly further south. Never would they operate over water. If the 4th Fighter Interceptor Group wished to engage the MiGs—and it did—they could be found in MiG Alley.

"This is Tiger Leader. Full power, gang. Drop tanks—now!"

At Preston's command thirty-two external fuel tanks blew off the Sabres and tumbled to the ground. The F–86s increased speed to 570 mph and spread out slightly. Their pilots scanned the skies, looking up and down, left, forward, and right, then forward, left, down, and up. In constant motion, they were looking for signs of the silvery birds with red stars.

Major Fred Cox, flying as Blue Three in McGrath's flight, saw them first.

"Tiger Leader, this is Blue Three. MiGs at eleven o'clock. I count ten plus."

"Roger, Blue Three. I have 'em. Tiger Flight, let's go get 'em."

Sixteen F–86s sped toward the enemy, spoiling for a fight.

They found one, and the resulting battle became legendary in the annals of the United States Air Force. Of course, there were more than ten MiGs. Intelligence reports later put the number at twenty-six. The Sabre pilots were not surprised They were used to being outnumbered.

The MiGs had the advantage of altitude, which they forfeited in a poorly orchestrated attack. Preston's planes reacted well, taking the fight directly to the enemy. Individual dogfights ensued, at altitudes high and low. Eight F–86s targeted MiGs. The other Sabres flew as wingmen, protecting their leaders, who thus could concentrate on downing their prey. Wingmen rarely destroyed MiGs. But they enabled other Sabres to do so. More than one F–86 ace lived to fly another day because the guy on their wing kept a watchful eye.

Fred Cox's wingman stuck with him throughout truly violent maneuvers of combat.

"Look now, Blue Four." Cox was telling his wingman to focus on the MiG the major was shooting at.

Cox put his pipper on the MiG and squeezed the trigger. Bursts of flame flashed alongside the Sabre as the six machine guns responded to Cox's touch. Each Browning M3 .50 caliber gun had three ammunition canisters holding three hundred rounds. However, to avoid jamming, the containers usually had 275 shells. This gave the Sabre pilot sixteen seconds of gunfire. Cox needed only five, in two separate bursts.

He hit his target in the rear of the fuselage. At the altitude both planes were flying, the air was too thin to support fire. So the MiG simply was peppered with holes. Often this was insufficient to bring the craft down. Many a MiG returned to Antung full of holes.

Not this one. Cox's guns struck not only the fuselage but also the engine it encased. The RD–45 was riddled by Cox's fire. The Rolls Royce-copied engine did not explode. It just stopped working. Once the MiG pilot looked at his engine instruments he knew the aircraft was lost. He thus released his canopy, which flew off immediately. He then attempted to ride the stricken machine to a lower altitude, hoping to parachute to safety.

Cox had other ideas. Chivalry be damned, thought the major, this is war and one less MiG pilot would make MiG Alley safer for the Sabres. So Cox followed the MiG down, and at thirty-one thousand feet, opened fire again. This time the bullets smashed into the now open cockpit. The MiG pilot was ripped apart. Pieces of flesh and bone spattered throughout the interior. Where once a human being had existed there now was nothing left either in form or function. Cox had achieved what he wanted. MiG Alley now was a less dangerous place.

Three weeks later, in an apartment outside Moscow, Nadia Lepikov received a letter saying that her husband, Lt. Colonel Fydor Lepikov, commander of the Soviet air force's 299th Fighter Regiment, had been killed in a training accident.

Lepikov was not the only Soviet fighter to die that day. Lieutenant Boris Shatski also perished. Shatski too flew with the 299th Regiment and, like Lepikov, was downed by an F–86. However, whereas the regiment's commander was killed at thirty-one thousand feet, Boris Shatski died at three hundred feet, after a low-level chase through the mountains.

Shatski was a fine pilot. He had graduated second in his class at flight school and, after just five weeks at Antung, had two F–84s to his credit. His comrades expected him to have a long and glorious career.

After the initial attack Shatski had flown downward to pick up speed, expecting to regain altitude once clear of the Sabres. But an F–86 caused his plan to change. The Sabre dove after him and for the next four minutes clung to his tail. Shatski flew like a madman, turning left and right, all the time losing altitude. Once on the deck the Soviet lieutenant piloted his MiG through several mountain passes. He flew expertly and assumed he soon would shake the Sabre. He did not. The F–86 followed him wherever he went, attempting to achieve a firing position. Over a small stream, in a flat valley three miles long that ended at the Yalu, the Sabre pilot was able to line up behind the MiG. Already the American had armed his guns. The circuit breaker had been punched; all the switches had been flipped. When he pressed the trigger the six machine guns responded. A three-second burst created a recoil that momentarily caused the Sabre to lose speed. But that mattered not at all. The .50 caliber shells invaded the tailpipe of the MiG. The result was a catastrophic explosion that sent pieces of the MiG in all directions. Shatski remained in the cockpit, unable to control what no longer was a flying machine. The wreckage cascaded into the stream, creating a watery tomb for the Soviet airman.

Triumphant, McGrath kept his Sabre low over the stream. At the Yalu he circled back, taking one quick look where the remains of the MiG had hit the water. There was not much to see, and no sign of the pilot. McGrath assumed he had not survived.

McGrath felt not a touch of remorse. To the contrary, he felt exhilarated. Victory was always sweet, and in the deadly game of MiG versus Sabre, he had won. Returning to Kimpo, McGrath was looking forward to his next encounter with MiGs.

Once on the ground McGrath learned of the day's accomplishments. Peter Parker gave him the news at the post-flight briefing. Sixteen Sabres had engaged twenty-six MiGs. The F–86s had knocked down seven enemy aircraft. Not one Sabre was lost, though one slightly damaged F–86 put down safely at Peng Yeng Do. A force of MiGs had been met and decisively defeated.

After each mission Sabre pilots were entitled to two ounces of whiskey. A few pilots imbibed. Many did not, instead building up the amount of free whiskey they could have when the occasion warranted a party. This battle with the MiGs was such an occasion. The party that night at Kimpo was almost as legendary as the fight with the MiGs had been.

McGrath attended the party and enjoyed himself immensely. He gave away his allotment of whisky, thereby further endearing himself to the officers of the 4th Fighter Interceptor Group. He drank his usual Coca-Cola and remained sober. But sobriety did not diminish his sense of fulfillment. At last, he had gotten a MiG and it felt very good indeed.

The party lasted well past midnight. Among the last to leave were several Australian pilots. They belonged to Number 77 Squadron, Royal Australian Air Force.

Based at Kimpo alongside the Sabres, the Australians flew the Gloster Meteor F. Mk8, a twin engine, straight wing aircraft that was developed at the end of the Second World War. In combat with the MiGs the Meteor fared poorly. Number 77 Squadron thus was reassigned to ground attack duties, which it performed admirably.

The Australians spent much of the night attempting to explain the game of cricket to their American hosts. In turn the Sabre pilots laid out the rules of baseball. Explanations were fuzzy as both tutors and students were tipsy. Only McGrath, the sober one, was able to explain clearly and fully America's national pastime. He was encouraged to do so having heard via the Armed Forces Radio Service that in game four of the World Series the Yankees had defeated the New York Giants 6-2, with Allie Reynolds the winning pitcher. The Yankees went on to win the series, becoming the 1951 World Champions. For a short time McGrath celebrated by wearing a Yankee cap his father had sent him.

Despite hangovers the pilots of the 4th Fighter Interceptor Group were up early the next day. With breakfast and briefings completed, they were in the cockpit by 8:45. Thirty-five minutes later the Sabres were at thirty-eight thousand feet over Sinuiju, turning northeast for a run up the Yalu. Given the previous day's success they expected the MiGs would appear, eager for a fight. However, the enemy stayed home. None of their planes left the runway at Antung.

McGrath did not fly on that mission. Cox, Urqhart, Graham, and one of the P–38 pilots represented Detachment Q. McGrath tended to administrative duties, ably staffed by Major Brumbaugh.

He did fly the next day. And with the binoculars purchased in Tokyo, McGrath took a close look at the MiG base where, once again, the MiGs chose to remain. Clearly, they did not expect to be attacked. They were lined up in three rows on a flight line that paralleled a secondary runway. In addition, about forty aircraft were parked in fields to the eastern side of the base. McGrath did not carefully count the MiGs he saw. Rather he simply estimated their number. Later he told Major Parker that at least 180 aircraft were at Antung.

"And they're just sitting there," queried the intelligence officer, "out in the open?"

"Yup. Lined up nice and pretty."

"Obviously, they feel we won't attack."

"That's for sure. They sure make a tempting target though."

"I'm sure they do. I hope you're not planning to do anything stupid."

"Me? Heck no. I have no intention of starting World War III."

"Good. I'm sure General Ridgeway would be relieved to hear it."

"Not to mention President Truman."

"Him too."

McGrath knew that an attack upon Antung was forbidden. But he, like the other F–86 pilots, was frustrated by the unwillingness of the MiGs to come up and fight. So, secretly, he hatched a plan. Code-named "Maple Tree," it involved only one other pilot, Squadron Leader Urqhart, who thought it a splendid idea.

The opportunity to execute the plan did not present itself until the next week. The Sabres were on patrol at the Yalu, about to return to Kimpo. The MiGs had remained at their base and the skies were free of clouds. McGrath could see Antung clearly.

When twelve of the F–86s had turned south for Kimpo, McGrath's flight of four was alone, flying southwest toward the mouth of the Yalu. Antung was on their right some twenty miles away. McGrath told two of the Sabres to head home, leaving him and Urqhart, to whom he now spoke.

"Blue Two, Maple Tree."

"Roger, Blue One."

Both pilots turned off their IFF beacons. This was a device, Identification Friend or Foe, that enabled air force radar to track the aircraft. With the beacons off the two F–86s were not identifiable to the Dentist on Cho-Do Island.

McGrath banked right, as did Urqhart, who remained on his wing.

Losing altitude, both aircraft increased speed. As planned, Urqhart tucked his Sabre close in to McGrath's. They now were traveling 605 mph, coming closer and closer to the ground. McGrath turned again, aligning their flight path with that of the runway on which the MiGs were parked.

At one mile McGrath brought his and Urqhart's planes down to two hundred feet. They both could see the MiGs, yet neither pilot had their finger on the trigger. As the Sabres approached the field all hell broke loose at Antung. Ground personnel dove for cover. Three trucks collided with one another. A tanker lorry drove into the MiG it was supposed to fuel. One MiG on a taxiway steered off into a ditch. Another MiG, aborting a takeoff, ran off the end of the runway. Fire engines came streaming out in anticipation of action. The commanding general screamed at his subordinates. For several seconds the Chinese air force base at Antung was in complete disarray.

McGrath and Urqhart maintained their high speed as they buzzed the field. Urqhart saw the trucks collide. McGrath watched the MiG go into the ditch. Each pilot looked up as they passed an apparently empty control tower whose staff had flung themselves onto the floor.

Down the length of the runway, past the control tower, and between two hangars the Sabres roared over Antung. Once beyond the field they separated. Then each did a victory roll in sight of the still stunned men of the Red air forces.

Gaining altitude, they reformed and turned south. Over the bay, still climbing, they switched their IFF back on. McGrath then called Urqhart.

"Blue Two, let's head home."

"Roger, Blue One. Good show, good show indeed."

Upon returning to Kimpo, McGrath and Urqhart attended a post-flight briefing where Parker and his staff attempted to glean information useful to the conduct of the war. Intelligence officers wanted to know everything about the mission. How many MiGs had been sighted? How many engaged? Were they aggressive? What tactics did they employ? How were the MiGs painted? Was there antiaircraft fire? If so, where and how effective? Were the enemy aircraft MiGs or were other types observed? How did the Sabres do? Did any F–86s go down? If so, where and why? Were any MiGs destroyed?

This last question often resulted in considerable discussion. Pilots in combat often believed they had shot down an enemy plane that in fact had only been damaged. To achieve credit for a kill, Far Eastern Air Forces required proof of destruction. This could be realized through camera film, a fellow pilot witnessing the action, or through the sighting of wreckage. In McGrath's case the motion picture camera in the lower portion of his Sabre's inlet duct recorded the earlier demise of Boris Shatski and his MiG. No doubt existed that McGrath had gotten his kill.

After the interrogation McGrath retired to his tent. He lay down upon his cot and dealt with the fear that inevitably followed a mission. For several minutes his body shook. Then, unexpectedly, it stopped whereupon the encounter occurred in his head. He reacted intellectually, acknowledging the reality of what he had just done. He understood that in aerial combat he could be killed, that his life could expire, his existence cease. Dueling with MiGs was not a game. It was an activity where men died. McGrath knew this, and accepted it. He did not believe he would die, but in his tent, alone and honest with himself, he realized that he might. For McGrath this possibility defined his fear. It was not a comforting thought. He wanted to live.

Next to his cot was a small table. This was simply a flat piece of plywood resting on two ammunition crates. Upon the table were four letters addressed to McGrath. They had been delivered to the tent while McGrath was flying, by instruction of Major Brumbaugh. McGrath had noticed them when lying down upon his cot, choosing to open them only when his personal routine of confronting fear was over. He now sat up and took them in hand.

Three of the letters were postmarked in the United States. One came from Japan. This letter, he knew from her handwriting and return address, was from Martha. This he put aside, looking forward to reading it. A case of saving the best for last.

Of the others one was from his father. The other two he did not recognize. The handwriting was unfamiliar as were the return addresses. One of them revealed a penmanship that was highly stylized and decidedly feminine. As McGrath took hold of this letter the address in the upper left corner of the envelope registered. It was 3562 McComb Street NW, Washington, D.C.—the home of General and Mrs. Michael McCreedy. The letter was from Laura McCreedy. With pleasant anticipation McGrath opened the envelope. The letter was not long, but in content and tone it was caring and sweet. Laura wrote that she and the general had McGrath in their prayers, that they wished him to consider them family, and that upon his return to the States they hoped and expected he would come stay with them for an extended visit. Folding the letter and placing it back in the envelope, McGrath felt a rush of loving remembrance. He looked at the picture of Catherine he still kept on the table. How pretty she looked and how young. God, what a wonderful girl. And how sad that she now seemed to be a part of a life that existed long, long ago.

The next letter he opened was postmarked Cincinnati. McGrath was puzzled. He knew no one in the Ohio city and saw no reason why anyone there would write him. This time the anticipation he felt in opening the envelope was one of curiosity.

In seeing who had written the letter—actually, it was more of a note—McGrath reacted with surprise and pleasure. On beautifully engraved stationery, the note was from Stephen Cardinal Fermoyle. Its content was brief yet gracious. The cardinal wrote that he had enjoyed meeting McGrath during his visit to Kimpo. He expressed the hope that McGrath was well and then repeated his invitation to have McGrath visit him in Cincinnati once he returned from Korea. Rereading the note McGrath discerned the hint of command hidden within the invitation. After all, Fermoyle was a prince of the Catholic Church and could not entirely shed his authoritative tone. Nevertheless, the invitation was sincere and McGrath expected he would accept and visit Cincinnati once back in the States. As he put the note back into its envelope McGrath smiled to himself at how the cardinal had ended the note, signing it simply, "Father Fermoyle."

McGrath's father wrote to his son once every two weeks. Typically, he reported on the activities of Tim and his legal prospects. He also wrote about what McGrath's mother was doing and how she seemed to enjoy her life, now made new by the departure of her two sons. He commented not at all about his work at Bankers Trust in New York, where he served as senior vice president in charge of private banking. However, he did speak of his passion for sailing, informing his elder son of the latest machinations of the Port Washington Yacht Club, where he kept his pride and joy, a twenty-eight foot sloop he had named *Reward*.

In this letter the pattern was repeated. John McGrath wrote that Tim was doing well at law school and leaning toward becoming a tax attorney. His mother was busy, doing volunteer work at the hospital and taking up the game of golf. The elder McGrath approved of these activities, expressing pride in both his wife and younger son. He also approved of what McGrath was doing and told him so in the letter. The United States, he wrote, was a great nation with an obligation to uphold democratic values. If this required a resort to arms, so be it.

But in this letter to his air force son, John McGrath went beyond the usual. He focused on a subject about which he felt strongly. The subject struck at the core of human existence. He believed, and so wrote his son, that the goal of a man's life ought to be to make the world a slightly better place. What mattered was neither wealth nor social status, satisfying though these might be. What mattered was the contribution a man made to those around him. Helping others, contributing to society whether by measures small or large, were essential to a life well lived. The focus of one's time on Earth, once essentials were taken care of, should not be self-directed. Building a better community, assisting those in need, were critical. McGrath's father felt he had done so at the bank and in his private affairs. He was proud of Eleanor for her work at the hospital. He expected his two boys, as they journeyed through life, to find their avenues of service.

Having digested his father's views, with which he agreed, McGrath turned to the letter he had saved for last. The envelope from Martha was thicker than usual. It contained a cardboard stiffener, which McGrath correctly guessed was employed to protect enclosed photographs. Upon opening the envelope McGrath discovered three pictures, two of them in color. These two had been taken with the 35 mm camera he had purchased for Martha in Tokyo.

The first photograph showed McGrath and Martha in Tokyo. Taken on the Sunday he had headed back to Johnson, they were standing together beside a red taxicab, Martha slightly in front of McGrath. Both of them were smiling, and with McGrath's arm around Martha, they looked like a married couple on vacation. The cab driver had taken the photograph, which was extremely colorful. McGrath had on his blue air force uniform. Martha was wearing a yellow dress. And in the background were several trees, all varying shades of green. Fortunately the driver, who earlier had driven tanks for the Imperial Japanese Army, had composed the picture nicely, so it was, as Martha described in the letter, "a very nice photograph, one to hold on to."

McGrath had taken the second photograph at Tsuchiura. In this picture Martha was standing alone on the terrace where they had eaten lunch. Her pose was casual yet feminine, much like that of a fashion model. Her smile was subdued, her hair not perfect, her clothing conservative. Behind her was the water, which nicely set off the image of a lovely young woman whose attraction lay in her spirit as well as in her appearance.

McGrath did not know who had taken the third photograph. It was unlike any photograph he had ever received, and he liked it very much. The picture was in black and white. It showed a young woman posing in a darkened room. She was sitting sideways in a wing chair, both legs over one of the cushioned arms. Her short hair was brushed to one side; her head was toward the camera. She was dressed simply, wearing only a man's shirt, nothing else. The shirt was unbuttoned, save near the waist, which created a slit that widened as it opened toward the neck.

Martha had bought the shirt expressly for the photograph, which had been taken by a professional Japanese photographer whose shop was near her apartment. In a session that had lasted well over an hour, he had taken several pictures. Both model and photographer thought this the best of the lot. The image created was similar to a pinup of World War II. While seductive, it also was tasteful. Attached to the photograph was a note Martha had penned to McGrath.

I hope you like this. Despite what you might think I've never done anything like this. If you show it to anyone, I will kill you, McGrath.

XX/OO
Martha

McGrath stared at the picture, recalling several erotic moments with this young woman. Just thinking about them fueled a desire for repeat performances. Yet he realized such thoughts were not productive, given where he was and what he was doing. And because she was hundreds of miles away in Tokyo similar encounters in the near future were unlikely. So he put aside such thoughts and slipped the photograph beneath his socks in a crate next to his cot. There it would be out of public view as Martha wished. Having done so, McGrath immediately took the photograph out from the socks to look at it once again. He then saw something in the photograph he previously had not noticed. Martha was wearing the ring he had given her at the train station.

Seeing the ring sharply altered McGrath's train of thought. She was not just his girlfriend. She was his fiancée. He was engaged to a schoolteacher from Penn State, a woman with a past, who appeared to love him very much.

McGrath pondered the situation. Was he ready for this? Did he really want to marry Martha Dawson? Was she the right woman? Would it not be better to wait, and take things more slowly?

Without hesitation, he answered these questions. McGrath decided she was the woman he wanted. What he did not realize, because he could not understand the yearnings that accounted for his desires, was that he needed not only the physical pleasures of a female, but the comforting companionship of a wife.

McGrath put the black and white picture back among his socks, along with the photographs of him and Martha by the taxi. The other picture, the one of Martha at Tsuchiura, he placed on the side of his shaving mirror. Next to it was a photograph of Catherine. Thus, each day McGrath confronted his past and his future.

NINETEEN

Major Philip Vinet, USAF, was the commander of the 9th Fighter Bomber Squadron, which, based at Taegu, flew Republic F–84s. Vinet was an excellent pilot, having downed seven German aircraft in the Big War. Equally impressive was his record in Korea. During the entire three-year conflict Thunderjets accounted for only eight MiGs. Vinet had gotten two of them.

Aircraft of the 9th FBS were decorated with red and white chevrons on both the tail and wingtip fuel tanks. The engine air intakes of the Thunderjets were painted red. These were partially overlaid with a black circle within which was the white helmet of a medieval knight. The effect was distinctive and attractive.

The markings were quite visible to McGrath, who found Vinet's squadron exactly where it was supposed to be. Thirty miles northwest of Pyonyang at twenty-two thousand feet, Vinet's F–84s were on track to hit enemy supply dumps. Passing by the Thunderjets were the Sabres of the 4th Fighter Interceptor Group. They were to provide a forward protective screen that would block MiG attacks upon the fighter-bombers. McGrath was in command of the F–86s. Colonel Preston had declared McGrath qualified to lead the group into battle.

Upon sighting the F–84s, McGrath radioed Vinet that he was taking the escort fighters to a higher altitude, at the same time telling his pilots to increase speed. As the Thunderjet commander acknowledged the message the Sabres climbed away. Their objective was to be slightly below the altitude where contrails formed. That way any MiGs above them would be easily visible.

When just south of the Yalu the Sabres were at forty-one thousand feet. At that altitude turns were gentle, for with a hard break the F–86 would fall out of the sky with the pilot possibly losing control of the aircraft.

MiGs soon were sighted. Two waves approached from the north. With contrails billowing behind what looked like silver arrowheads, they created an unforgettably beautiful image. McGrath and Cox saw them at the same time.

"Bandits, eleven o'clock. Two trains," radioed Cox.

"I've got 'em," replied McGrath.

Upon reaching the river one of the MiG groups reversed course. On a training flight, it was under orders to avoid combat. The other wave proceeded across the border. The Sabres expected an attack. But the MiGs stayed at altitude, ignoring McGrath's formation. Looking for easier prey, they continued to fly south.

McGrath then employed an unusual tactic. He turned the F–86s away from the river, keeping them under, but in sight of, the MiGs. McGrath was not going to allow the enemy to proceed alone. If they were to attack the F–84s they first would have to tangle with the Sabres.

With the benefit of ground control radar in Manchuria manned by Russian specialists the MiGs found Vinet's Thunderjets. From forty-three thousand feet the MiGs headed downward, targeting the fighter-bombers. But McGrath's tactics spoiled their fun. As did Vinet's. The Thunderjets turned sharply away while the Sabres pursued the MiGs as they attacked.

One of the enemy pounced on Vinet's F–84, which spoiled its aim by slinking left and right. The MiG was persistent. It kept after the Thunderjet, which continued a series of sharp turns. More than once cannon fire sped past the red and white wingtips—close but not on target.

After a series of harsh maneuvers that stressed each aircraft greatly, the two planes were at six thousand feet. They were heading west. Vinet's plan was to reach the sea, where the MiG most likely would break off the action.

Fourteen miles from the water, the formation of two aircraft became three. McGrath put his Sabre directly astern of the MiG, whose pilot was concentrating solely on the plane ahead. That was a mistake. McGrath squeezed the trigger. And his Sabre's six guns erupted. Fifty caliber bullets were less destructive than cannon shells but in this instance they were more than sufficient. They struck the MiG in the left wing, then moved to the fuselage, crossed over the cockpit, then impacted upon the right wing. The MiG's engine was left intact and continued to propel the craft forward. But its pilot was dead and its aerodynamics destroyed. The MiG tumbled and broke apart well before its multiple pieces struck the ground.

Vinet saw what happened and pulled up. McGrath came alongside and escorted the Thunderjet back to the supply dump. This was ablaze. The F–84s had pummeled their target prior to the MiG attack. As the Thunderjets withdrew McGrath took the Sabres back north. No one had called out Bingo. There was still time to hunt MiGs.

Reaching the river, McGrath's wingman reported his plane's tailpipe temperature was exceeding redline. McGrath's response was to order Cox's wingman to escort him home. As these two aircraft departed the former instructor slid his Sabre into McGrath's wing. Then two other F–86s turned south. That left twelve Sabres on patrol. Soon, all were running low on fuel. By then they had reached the Yalu. Flying downriver, the Sabre pilots hoped the MiGs would appear.

They did not. At the mouth of the Yalu, wide and full of silt, the Sabres turned left, their J–47 engines trailing an area of black exhaust along the sea. McGrath took the force home. In twenty minutes they reached Kimpo. In groups of four the Sabres raced down the runway, then broke off in pairs, circled round, and touched down upon the concrete runway, their tires noisily protesting the hard surface.

As the Sabres taxied to their dispersal points, crew chiefs approvingly noticed the black residue around the gun ports. Sergeant Ricks was particularly pleased, even more so when told that McGrath had downed a MiG. He assumed that the DQ commander was on his way to becoming an ace.

At the post-flight briefing Major Parker analyzed the pilot's reports and later reviewed the film. He concluded that the Sabres had destroyed three MiGs—one of them McGrath's—and damaged two. One Sabre had been shot up badly and would not fly again, though its pilot had brought the airplane home safely. From his counterpart at Taegu he learned that all the Thunderjets had returned. And the next day, from the pictures taken by an RF–80, he learned that the supply dump had been obliterated. The mission, Parker therefore concluded in his telex to FEAF headquarters, had been a complete success.

For McGrath the mission did not end with the briefing, nor with the conversation with himself in his tent. Two days after he destroyed the MiG, Edward Brumbaugh brought him a package that had been delivered by Jeep from Taegu. McGrath opened the package and found himself holding a bottle of Johnnie Walker Black. More satisfying to McGrath was the accompanying note.

Colonel—

Thanks for getting that MiG off my tail. Us straight wing boys appreciate the fine work you and the 86s are doing.

Regards,

Philip Vinet
Major, USAF

McGrath's two kills, the first against Shatski and the second over Vinet's attacker, had required considerable skill. The third did not. The earlier victories had pitted McGrath against experienced pilots. The next came at the expense of a pilot not yet prepared for combat. This unfortunate man was not Russian, but Chinese. A lieutenant in the People's

Volunteer Army Air Force, he had but twenty hours of flight in a MiG–15.

By October 1951, communist China's air force, the PVAAF, was still a new and untried organization. Dependent upon the Soviet Union for material and expertise, the Chinese air force struggled. Though large in size, it was short in capability. Its pilots were not yet ready for combat operations nor were they able to carry out the PVAAF's primary mission, providing air support for the Red Army. This contributed significantly to the failure of China's spring offensive in 1951. Five months later, though much improved, Mao's air force still could not contend with American airpower.

Wang Sung was a young man from Shanghai. An army veteran, he had transferred to the air force upon its establishment in 1949. Not until April 1950 did he sit in a cockpit. Several months later he passed out of flight school and was assigned to a second tier unit, the Fifth Air Division, which kept watch over Taiwan. In September 1951 the division departed for Antung. There it transitioned to MiGs and commenced operations. Russian instructors led its combat formations. By late October the Soviet pilots were taking their pupils south of the Yalu.

October 21, 1951 was a Sunday. McGrath and fifteen others were on patrol, their Sabres at thirty-six thousand feet west of Pyonyang along the coast. Preston was in command. He took the flight to Sinanju, at the southern edge of MiG Alley. He then flew in a northeastern direction, up the Chongchon River. The sixteen F–86s he was leading were looking for MiGs.

They found them at an unlikely altitude. Twenty-four MiGs were at thirty-two thousand feet, among them the aircraft piloted by Wang Sung. Rarely did F–86s find MiGs below them. Preston took full advantage of the opportunity.

Upon the group commander's call the Sabres dove onto the enemy formation, hitting them from behind. Surprised, the Chinese pilots and their Russian instructor scattered. MiGs flew in every direction. The Sabres followed in pursuit.

McGrath saw one MiG make a turn to the left. Remaining at

thirty-two thousand feet, the MiG made little effort to escape. McGrath placed his Sabre three hundred feet behind Wang Sung's aircraft. Its pilot was terrified. By mistake he lowered his landing gear. This caused the MiG to slow. McGrath's Sabre came close to ramming the plane. Then the F–86 slowed also. McGrath put his gunsight's pipper right on the MiG. The circle of light targeted the aircraft's fuselage, which is where the bullets hit. Fire erupted along the side of Wang Sung's aircraft. Both it and he were doomed.

McGrath fired three times and three times streams of fire struck the MiG. The third burst shattered the cockpit. Wang Sung died instantly.

McGrath felt no elation at the kill. Pleased he had destroyed a MiG, he was saddened that someone so ill prepared for combat had been sacrificed. McGrath felt Wang Sung had been murdered. Not by him, but by the air force commander who had sent the young man south of the Yalu.

The 5th Air Division suffered heavy losses that day. Six of its pilots were killed. Seven others flew home in severely damaged aircraft. No Sabres were shot down. The Russian instructor was cashiered and while the division remained at Antung for another two months, it rarely achieved success. On December 30, 1951 the air division was withdrawn from Manchuria, its legacy one of disappointment and defeat.

However, defeat was not limited to the MiGs of the PVAAF. FEAF Bomber Command also suffered setbacks. Employing B–29s, the command had been flying combat missions over North Korea since the war had first begun in June 1950. Unlike the agrarian south the north had industrial targets ripe for attack from the air.

Boeing's B–29 had been the United States Air Force's most advanced heavy bomber of World War II. With a combat range of 1700 miles and capable of carrying ten tons of bombs, the B–29s had struck the Japanese home islands from bases in the Marianas. The "Superfortresses" wreaked havoc upon their enemy. On the night of March 9, 1945, for example, B–29s firebombed Tokyo, a raid in which over forty-five thousand people perished. On August 1, 1945, 741 B–29s hit targets all over Japan. And finally, in dramatic closure to a war that had enveloped the entire world, single B–29s dropped atomic ordnance upon Hiroshima and Nagasaki.

Five years later the B–29 had been redesignated a medium bomber. No longer was it the pride of the air force. The B–36 had taken its place as the air force's heavyweight. Their numbers had dwindled as well. The largest number of B–29s to fly in one mission during the war in Korea was sixty-three. Usually the number was far less. Yet they caused considerable damage. From bases in Japan and Okinawa B–29s flew almost every day. In three years of warfare they dropped 167,000 tons of bombs onto North Korea. Pyongyang in particular was devastated. Hardly a building in the capitol was left standing.

One target of great interest to FEAF in October 1951 was a group of airfields under construction near the Chongchon River, well into North Korea itself. Were these airfields to become operational, MiGs would extend their presence southward. American control of the skies would be threatened.

Once these airfields were spotted FEAF drafted plans for their destruction. The job was given to the B–29s. Each raid would consist of nine aircraft. F–84s would provide the bombers with close escort. Sabres would comprise a forward screening force. The missions were considered top priority.

The first attacks were at night. They met with poor results, so FEAF switched to more dangerous daylight raids. The first such attack took place on October 18, 1951. An airfield was hit and no B–29s were lost. The second raid struck Taechon, where the MiGs downed one of the bombers.

FEAF selected Namsi as the next target. Namsi was approximately sixty-five miles northwest of Pyonyang. Fifty-five Thunderjets were to escort nine B–29s to the target. Thirty-four F–86s were on station, ahead of the fortresses, at twenty-nine thousand feet. For FEAF at the time, this was a maximum effort. Ninety-eight aircraft were assigned to this one mission. The results were not good. A hundred MiGs dispersed the Sabres.

Fifty others attacked the bombers, one of which had aborted. Of the remaining eight three were shot down, two were so damaged they never flew again. The others limped home, all with wounded aboard. Outclassed, the F–84s had failed to protect their charges.

After further attacks the missions were called off. The airfields had been put out of commission, but at a cost too high for FEAF. Daylight B–29 raids into North Korea ceased. The bombers switched to night missions. The United States Air Force had suffered a serious setback. Rightly so, the MiG pilots celebrated their victory.

McGrath did not participate in the attack upon Namsi. Nor on the raid the next day. But he did fly on October 28, the last day the B–29s conducted an attack in daylight. Oddly, no MiGs appeared. Yet for McGrath the flight was memorable. Low on fuel over Pyonyang, he turned his engine off, thirty-seven thousand feet over the city. He then glided to Kimpo, descending at 240 mph, benefiting from a tailwind out of Manchuria. At six thousand feet, he was over the airfield. He restarted his engine and proceeded to land.

Such a procedure was not unusual. Sabre pilots low on fuel often would shut down their engine and glide home. Occasionally, without any fuel or unable to restart the J–47, they would dead-stick the landing, putting their aircraft down upon the runway with the engine off. Later in the war such descents were so frequent that F–86 pilots jokingly called their unit the 4th Gliding Group.

McGrath's next kill occurred early in November. The Sabres were at forty-eight thousand feet, east of Antung, well up the Yalu River. A bandit train crossed the border, flew south, then turned toward the F–86s. Preston called the break and the battle began.

McGrath turned into two MiGs that were coming down upon him. As they passed by, he swung his aircraft sharply. They circled about, hoping to line up astern of McGrath. He dove away and they followed. Intent upon McGrath's F–86, the MiG pilots failed to notice Cox and his wingman. These two Sabres opened fire. Missing their targets, they nonetheless caused the MiGs to break away. Cox and his escort went after one of them. McGrath pursued the other.

The chase lasted less than a minute. The MiG veered left, then right,

266

then right again and left. Each time McGrath kept his craft behind the MiG. Coming into a valley, the MiG pilot chose to climb. It was an unfortunate decision. The geometry favored the F–86. McGrath squeezed the trigger and his guns responded. Bullets struck the MiG's right wing. McGrath fired again and again bullets struck the wing. The results were conclusive. The right wing separated from the craft, which then began to tumble. All this was recorded by the Sabre's gun camera.

What took place next was not. The MiG's pilot released his canopy and ejected. Safely, it seemed, until McGrath saw him swinging beneath his parachute, about two thousand feet above the ground. Turning toward the enemy pilot, McGrath switched off his gun camera. At the same time he slowed his aircraft and lined up his new target. McGrath did not like what he was about to do. But, were the MiG pilot to live, he would fly again and perhaps kill an American or two. Or three or four. So with little remorse McGrath pulled the trigger. The results were predictable. The man's body exploded. Bones and blood erupted in all directions. Little was left once the parachute hit the ground. McGrath flew home in silence. He was not proud of what he had done.

Once back at Kimpo, McGrath discussed the incident with just one individual. He told Peter Parker what he had done. Though surprised, the intelligence officer nonetheless was comforting. He told McGrath that war was fundamentally inhumane. Moreover, he said, it's not about parades and parcels of land. It's about killing, and to win a war, men must kill.

"There's no way to gloss over it."

"I suppose you're right."

"I am. We sometimes try to hide it, to speak of it in other ways, but the raw truth is that the idea is to kill the other guy."

"Before he kills you."

"Exactly."

"But this poor guy was helpless, just swinging in his chute."

"Colonel, I won't tell you it was a kind and generous act, 'cause it wasn't. But I will say that it was necessary and the right thing to do."

"Because?"

"Because MiG pilots are more valuable to the Reds than MiGs. Because one less MiG driver means the enemy is weakened and because that pilot, had he lived, would have come back and killed some of our guys."

"Yes, that's true."

"And one other thing."

"What's that?"

"Had the situation been reversed and you were dangling in the parachute, what do you think the MiG pilot would have done?"

"That's what I figured. But somehow it still stinks."

"Perhaps. But all it really shows is that Sherman was right."

"Yes, war is indeed hell."

With four MiGs to his credit, Detachment Q personnel believed their leader would become an ace. Edward Brumbaugh thought the fifth kill would come soon. The ground exec wanted McGrath to be one of the few to down five or more enemy planes in two wars. That, he knew, would put McGrath into the air force history books. Only seven men achieved such distinction. McGrath, however, was not to be one of them.

During the next two weeks McGrath flew every day, save two. Each time he went up to the Yalu and engaged the MiGs. Several times he was able to bring his guns to bear. Though he damaged two MiGs, he was unable to record a victory. Disappointed though not discouraged McGrath figured that opportunities would arise in the near future or rather, pointedly, that he would create the opportunities required. He also was content to have happen whatever was going to happen, though more than once he hoped Norman Ricks would paint a fifth red star on the fuselage of his F–86.

In mid-November, sitting in a folding chair, Brumbaugh was listening to a rebroadcast on the Armed Forces Radio Service of the Marciano-Lewis fight in which the challenger, Rocky Marciano, knocked out Joe Lewis, the heavyweight champion. The announcer, Don Dunphy, was describing the pandemonium at ringside. Listening intently, Brumbaugh failed to notice that Colonel Preston entered the tent. When he did so he immediately stood up. He then turned the radio off and asked what he might do for the group commander. Preston replied that he'd like to see McGrath at once.

At first the DQ ground executive officer thought McGrath might be in trouble. Or, as he said to himself as he went to find McGrath, "In deep kimchi." Kimchi was the national dish of Korea. It was a highly spiced mixture of cabbage, peppers, radishes, and fish paste. In both taste and smell the Americans in Korea found it extremely distasteful. They equated it with human excrement.

Brumbaugh left the tent in search of McGrath. He found him near the radar shop and conveyed Preston's request. Two minutes later McGrath was in the operations center, also a tent, standing before the group commander.

"Do you know a brigadier by the name of Hawkins?" asked Preston. The question was put in a matter of fact way.

"Actually, I do. Is this Brigadier *Milo* Hawkins?" McGrath emphasized the given name.

"That's the one."

"I wonder what he's up to. If I may, Colonel, why do you ask?"

"Well, he's in Tokyo, at Far Eastern Headquarters, and wants to see you. Tomorrow."

"Tomorrow?"

"That's what the telex says. Came through an hour ago. There's a C–47 going to Johnson first thing tomorrow. I think you'd better be on it."

"Why don't I fly an 86 there?"

"Because, Colonel, I think your time here is over. Here's the telex." After handing the message to McGrath, Preston continued speaking.

"You'll see it says in Tokyo you'll receive a new set of orders. Your combat flying days appear to be over, I'm afraid."

"I'll be damned."

"We'll miss you, Colonel, and there's one thing you should know."

"Sir?"

"You did one fine job. Detachment Q, whatever its reason for being, was outstanding. Helped us a lot."

"I'm glad, sir."

Preston then shook hands with McGrath, a gesture of both thanks and respect. As he left the ops tent, McGrath told Preston he was proud to have served in the 4th Fighter Interceptor Group.

"Best outfit in the air force," replied its commander.

As McGrath walked toward his own tent, he was in shock. His time at Kimpo was over. Just like that. No more flights to MiG Alley. No more command of Detachment Q. A few words from Preston and his life changed completely. What once had been the focus of his existence now belonged to the past. Glancing at the landscape around him McGrath felt out of place, audience to a play he once had been in. It was not a feeling he enjoyed.

Only when the C–47 departed Kimpo did the sense of not belonging fade away, to be replaced by a new, equally disquieting feeling. McGrath realized he had not appreciated what he had experienced at Kimpo. Life at the airfield had provided comradery and purpose, and a coupling to a cause greater than self. Sitting near the front of the plane, his belongings stuffed in a large, air force–issued, olive duffel bag, he realized he would miss several people, men who had become friends, among them Brumbaugh and Parker, Cox and Urqhart. He also would miss the power he felt at the controls of a combat-ready F–86. As the C–47 churned its way to Johnson, McGrath was not quite ready to have the experiences of Detachment Q enter the picture screen of memory. He wanted to hold on to them, to relive them, to understand them better. But he could not, and he knew he could not, so he sat silently on the plane contemplating how life was full of unplanned events.

Once in Japan, McGrath took command of himself and set about his business. This was twofold. First, he wanted to contact Martha and arrange to see her. Second, he needed to report to Milo Hawkins. Surprisingly, the first task was the more easily accomplished. Martha readily agreed to see him that night, at seven o'clock. At the University Club, of course. She said she was glad he was in Tokyo. General

Hawkins was difficult to pin down. Finally, the air force captain handling his schedule confirmed a meeting at four o'clock. This gave McGrath time to check into the Akura Palace, which he did.

Walking into the four-story FEAF headquarters building ten minutes before his scheduled appointment, McGrath wondered what lay ahead. Would his orders send him back to the States? Would he remain in the F–86 community? Would he have a desk job? And, closer at hand, why was Hawkins here? Washington to Tokyo was a long trip, just to meet with a newly minted bird colonel.

Inside the masonry building Captain Perkins once again directed McGrath to where he needed to go.

"It's Room 318, Colonel. Two flights up."

"318? Are you sure?"

"Yes, sir. General Hawkins is there, along with General Weyland."

"Weyland! Good Lord."

"The general's on schedule so I'd get up there ASAP, sir."

"Right you are, Captain. Thanks. And congrats on the promotion."

"Thank you, Colonel."

At the appointed time McGrath was ushered into Weyland's office. This was spartan in appearance. The obligatory flags stood behind a plain wooden desk that was covered with folders. A conference table, also made of wood, and six chairs combined with a blackboard, a large map of the Far East, several bookshelves, and a black metallic safe completed the décor, which, kindly, could be described as functional. Weyland was a workhorse, not a show horse.

"At ease, Colonel," said the commander of Far Eastern Air Forces. McGrath was standing at attention. He waited for the general to continue.

"I think you know General Hawkins. He's an emissary from my good friend Mike McCreedy, whom I gather you know as well."

"Yes, sir."

"I suspect you'll recall my suggestion to you four months ago that prior to your reporting to the Director of Policy and Plans regarding the situation in Korea with the 86s you speak to me first. Well, you're in luck. General Hawkins here is representing General McCreedy so you'll be able to report to the two of us at the same time. Saves differing interpretations. Please proceed."

McGrath was prepared. On the walk over to the headquarters building he had rehearsed what he would say should Hawkins ask for the report he'd be giving to General McCreedy.

McGrath spoke for a full twenty minutes. His remarks were rich in content and polished in delivery. It was, Weyland and Hawkins later agreed, an outstanding presentation. Its message was simple and to the point: the F–86s were too few in number to attain air superiority in Korea. And they were lacking in firepower. Six machine guns were insufficient. Consistently outnumbered by the MiGs, the Sabres in Korea could not prevent the enemy from disrupting U.S. air operations in the north.

Weyland and Hawkins listened, asked several questions, and then dismissed McGrath, first telling him to put his report in writing, two copies only—the original to Hawkins, the copy to Weyland. McGrath was to hand deliver the report within twenty-four hours.

"Captain Perkins will get you a secretary," said Weyland.

Hawkins spoke next, directing McGrath to wait outside. The general indicated he would be giving McGrath new orders. Several minutes later Milo Hawkins emerged from Weyland's office. He was carrying a folder that he opened, then spoke to McGrath.

"I have your orders, Colonel." As he read them out loud Milo Hawkins' voice changed from semi-personal to bureaucratic.

"One, effective 21 November, 1951 you are relieved of command of Detachment Q and assigned to the Office of Policy and Plans, Air Force Headquarters, Washington, D.C. to which you will report 21 December, 1951.

"Two, no later than 21 June, 1952 you will report to the Superintendent, United States Military Academy, West Point, New York for a liaison assignment as Adjunct Professor of History."

"West Point?" McGrath's surprise was total. "That's an army school."

"I'm aware of that, Colonel," said Hawkins, who, pointing to his West Point ring, had graduated in the Class of 1925, "and a fine school it is."

"No doubt, sir, but it's the army."

"You're not thinking, Colonel, which surprises me. Fortunately, General McCreedy is, and is way ahead of you."

"Sir?"

"Colonel, the air force, like the army and the navy, needs its own military academy. Congress agrees and has authorized the establishment of the United States Air Force Academy. It's to be located in Colorado Springs and will become operational in three years. It will need a faculty, air force officers with appropriate academic credentials. General McCreedy has decided you're the right choice to head up its history department."

McGrath remained silent, absorbing the news. Still surprised he realized the orders made eminent good sense. The air force needed to staff the school and he was an obvious candidate. General McCreedy had figured this all out, no doubt in advance, and was putting the school together. West Point would give McGrath the opportunity to first see how the army did it.

The more McGrath thought about the assignments the more he liked them. Not as exciting perhaps as MiG Alley, but challenging and rewarding, and a whole lot safer. So he would be going back to the classroom after all. Digesting the thought both then and later, he found it pleasing in the extreme.

McGrath now had but one question of Hawkins, which he put to the general.

"General, if I may, what becomes of Detachment Q?"

"It's dissolved," responded Milo Hawkins. "Its personnel and equipment are to be absorbed into the 4th Fighter Interceptor Group. As of 21 November—yesterday—Detachment Q no longer exists."

"Thank you, sir." McGrath saluted Hawkins, and left the building. He went back to the hotel and changed clothes. In two hours he was due at the University Club. In the meantime he picked up the book he had purchased prior to his four o'clock meeting. Settling into a comfortable chair in his hotel room, he began reading *A Short History of the Great War* by Andrew Merton.

By 6:30, when he realized it was time to dress for dinner, McGrath had reached the end of 1914, at the First Battle of Ypres. Here, at this small town in Belgium, the British stopped the initial German advance. The cost was high. In two months George V's army suffered twenty-four thousand casualties. The enemy's losses were far greater. Moreover, the battle was rich in consequences. It staved off decisive defeat. It also destroyed the British regular army. From 1915 on the army would consist largely of conscripts. More significantly, First Ypres brought the end to mobile warfare. Trenches were dug and by Christmas 1914 they ran across western Europe, 475 miles of them, from the North Sea to Switzerland.

McGrath made no connection between World War I and the war in Korea. In fact, there was a similarity. Across the middle of the peninsula now that the Chinese had been pushed back, miles of fortified trenches had been dug. The ground war was in a stalemate. Territorial gains were minor. Yet two more years of killing were to follow.

At 7:05 McGrath walked into the lobby of the University Club. Martha was waiting for him. He thought she looked lovely. The schoolteacher from Pennsylvania was wearing a cocktail dress of fine silk, lavender in color, elegant in style. With high-heeled shoes, gloves, and a short brimmed hat, she looked like a fashion model. McGrath noticed that he was not the only male in the room to signal interest and approval.

McGrath greeted her warmly, with a kiss on the cheek. She responded simply with an expression that spoke great pleasure at his presence.

"I love surprises, and your being here is just wonderful," she said.

"I'm glad you're glad. Let's go upstairs and have dinner. I have a few things to tell you and there are surprises among them."

Hearing what he had said Martha's face changed to one of worry.

"Nothing for you to be concerned about, my love. Come, let's go."

274

He took her by the arm and they moved to the elevator. Once at the terrace, they opted to eat inside. November meant warm weather no longer embraced Tokyo.

At dinner McGrath told Martha that his tour of duty in Korea was over. He mentioned the conversations with Preston and with Hawkins and Weyland, saying that he planned on drafting his report tomorrow morning and submitting it to the generals by early afternoon.

"What happens then?" she asked, trying, not altogether successfully, to hide her anxiety.

"I have two days in Tokyo and then I take a flight to San Francisco."

"Oh." Martha was crestfallen. She turned her head away, looking down at the diamond ring McGrath had given her.

"I think you better keep that where it is," he said.

Unclear of his meaning, she looked up, her right hand fondling the ring.

"I have two seats on the plane. A friend of mine is the MATS guy in charge here and he says I can take my bride-to-be along. Apparently there are some seats available on the C–54."

Like a thunderbolt, surprise rippled through Martha Dawson's body, from the blonde hair on her head to the lavender nail polish on her toes. Stunned, she said nothing.

"Don't you want to come with me?"

"Oh, yes. God, yes. I most certainly do." She then started to cry, and continued her thought. "But my job, I mean I just can't leave the school. Here you've gone and proposed and I want to marry you but . . ."

"Martha, let me give you some advice a wise man once told me."

"Which was?"

"Ask forgiveness, not permission."

They spent the next two hours at the University Club enjoying dinner and each other's company. They then returned to the Akura Palace where passion and love merged in perfect harmony. The next day, after breakfast in the room, they separated. Martha attended to her affairs, school and otherwise. McGrath wrote his report, submitting it just after lunch. He spent the rest of the day playing tourist, discovering however, that sightseeing was far more enjoyable with a companion, preferably female.

The day before they were scheduled to leave Martha did not appear where they had agreed to meet. This was the Paper Moon, a restaurant they had come to enjoy. Twice and then twice again McGrath telephoned Martha at her apartment, only to have the phone go unanswered. At first McGrath thought something terrible might have happened. Then a darker thought emerged. Martha, he concluded, had decided not to marry, nor to leave with him. She could not make the break, neither from her school nor from her life in Tokyo. She had made a life for herself here in Japan and had found it more than satisfying. She had decided that being the wife of an air force officer, even an academic one, was not how she wished to live.

Sadly, and a bit callously, McGrath adjusted to this line of thought. If she wanted out, so be it. He would be sad but not grief stricken. He had altered his life once before, he could do so again.

The departure lounge at Haneda was large, about the size of a basketball court. Even by governmental standards the room was dreary in appearance. The floor was linoleum, made up of black and white squares that were scuffed, in need of polishing. Rows of red plastic benches and cheap wooden chairs dominated the room, whose walls were painted light gray. Vending machines stood in one corner, along with a water fountain and several trash baskets. The only relief was found on the wall facing the tarmac. Four large windows enabled passengers to see a variety of aircraft.

McGrath stood near one of the windows, looking at the C–54 that in twenty minutes would take him away from Korea and Tokyo, and from Martha Dawson. Thinking not about her, McGrath focused on the future, about what life would be like at West Point.

Martha was doing the same. Rushing into the lounge, wearing a raincoat and carrying two suitcases, she looked about for McGrath. She found him near one of the windows. He did not see her.

Putting her luggage down, she walked over to him, at the same time running her hand through her hair, hoping it looking presentable. Tapping him on the shoulder, Martha spoke as he turned around.

"I love you, McGrath, and here I am, yours if you still want me."

Minutes later, as rain fell from the cloudy sky and made puddles on the concrete, Martha clung closely to McGrath as they walked toward and boarded the C–54.

— The End —

EPILOGUE

Five weeks after arriving back in the States, McGrath and Martha Dawson were married. The wedding took place in Scranton at the Lutheran church her parents attended. It was not a large affair. Mostly family members were present although Roger O'Boyle made the trip from Washington. Surprisingly, and sweetly, so did Laura McCreedy and the general. The reception was held at Scranton's Princess Hotel, which is where the wedding pictures were taken. One of them, a photograph of McGrath and Martha on the hotel's grand staircase, quickly became a family favorite. In it, wearing a dress of lace and silk with a long, regal train, Martha looked extraordinarily beautiful.

Despite misgivings by some at the wedding—the bride and groom, after all, they pointed out, had not known each other for very long—the marriage was a success. In 1953 and 1954 Martha gave birth to their daughters, Anne and Elizabeth. Both children received fine educations and married well. Elizabeth became a schoolteacher like her mother. Anne had a successful career in advertising. Together, as children often do, they greatly enriched their parents' lives.

After several months in Washington, McGrath reported to West Point. Two years on the army faculty sharpened his teaching skills and resulted in an affection for the Corps of Cadets that lasted his entire life.

At times, even when in Colorado Springs, he could be heard whistling, "On Brave Old Army Team."

The assignment to the Air Force Academy came late in 1954. Colonel and Mrs. McGrath moved to Colorado soon thereafter. After renting an apartment that they soon outgrew, McGrath and Martha purchased a house overlooking a lake fifteen miles from the academy. Here they resided for ten years, happy with each other and content with their lives.

Often friends would visit, staying for extended periods of time, especially in the summer. Among their guests was Roger O'Boyle, who came each year. McGrath always enjoyed O'Boyle's company and their friendship endured. Not surprisingly, the Jesuit had prospered in his profession. At his death in 1986 he had just retired as vice president for academic affairs at Fordham University in New York. Another friendship grew strong over the years. This was with Stephen Cardinal Fermoyle. McGrath and Martha visited him in Cincinnati just before leaving for West Point in 1952. The visits occurred yearly thereafter, with the cardinal occasionally coming to Colorado. Traveling without aides, Fermoyle treated his visits to the McGraths as vacations. In time he at last became to McGrath simply, "Father Fermoyle." To Anne and Elizabeth the cardinal was more like a grandfather than a prince of the Church. Indeed, not until well into their thirties did the girls realize how prominent their visitor was. When he died in 1979 Fermoyle was the leading Catholic cleric in the United States.

Of the many visitors to the house on the lake only two were friends from the days in Korea. Edward Brumbaugh, who retired from the air force as a lieutenant colonel, came to Colorado Springs several times, by car or train. Fred Cox also visited. He was the one friend in the air force who rose to very high rank. At one time Cox commanded all air force units in the Pacific and upon his retirement was air force vice chief of staff.

McGrath did well at the Air Force Academy. He built a strong history department, insisting on faculty who could teach and inspire students. Against the wishes of the commandant he hired a female to teach

European history, believing that as the world was co-ed so too should the instructional staff be. Plus, he knew the lady to be an exceptional teacher. Martha, and later his two daughters, were proud of him for this. While at Colorado Springs, McGrath published three well-received books. One was a history of the United States at the turn of the century. One was about Theodore Roosevelt and the Russo-Japanese War of 1905. The third became the authoritative work on the War of 1812. Less successful was a novel he wrote in 1961. This was about a P–47 pilot in England during four months in late 1943. McGrath thought the novel first-rate. Publishers, passing on the manuscript, did not.

McGrath failed to obtain his air force star, remaining a full colonel until retirement. Mostly, this was his own doing. Twice he was offered jobs at the Pentagon and twice he refused. By not serving in Washington, McGrath essentially opted out of promotion to brigadier general. There were in the air force a limited number of slots for one star generals; none of them were reserved for academy faculty. McGrath made a conscious choice to remain an academic, and at the time and thereafter, had no regrets. He liked what he was doing. Moreover, as a triple ace with both Messerschmitts and MiGs to his credit, McGrath had within the air force prestige and respect denied most generals.

On May 11, 1971, at the age of forty-seven, Martha died after a six-month battle with cancer. She and McGrath were then living in Chapel Hill, North Carolina where he was teaching at the university, having left the air force and Colorado Springs in 1965. Her illness was full of pain and both McGrath and the girls thought death a blessing. At the time of Martha's passing he was fifty-one with two teenaged daughters.

McGrath stayed at Chapel Hill for several years, expecting to retire and live out his life in North Carolina. However, that was not to be. In 1975 Lt. General Fred Cox invited McGrath to Washington in order to participate in air force celebrations marking the first downing of a MiG–15 by a F–86. Several events took place including a formal dance at the Mayflower Hotel. There McGrath ran into an old friend from his and Catherine Caldwell's past. At his table in the hotel ballroom he was sitting across from Cynthia Stewart, Catherine's best friend and her designated maid of honor. He recognized her immediately, and she him. They conversed and promised to meet again. Which they did, McGrath taking her to dinner at the 1789 restaurant in Georgetown. Dinner led to more engagements including baseball games and the symphony, and, the next year when McGrath proposed marriage, she accepted. Her only question to him was why he had waited so long. He chose not to reply that it was not his usual style.

Cynthia was a widow, with two sons both grown and living in California. She resided outside of Chestertown, Maryland in a splendid house overlooking Chesapeake Bay, her husband Dan having left behind a considerable sum of money.

Cynthia was an attractive, intelligent woman. She had a grand sense of humor and enjoyed the finer things. More than once McGrath told himself he had been fortunate to find her. Anne and Elizabeth found her kind and generous and in time became quite fond of their step-mother. She in turn cared deeply for them and, without hesitation, financed their college education.

Regarding McGrath, she was simply in love. He had been a late sur-prise in her life, resulting in an affair of the heart she honestly believed women of her age rarely experienced. She admired McGrath's intellect, shared his interests, and treasured his devotion to her. She also found amusing his apparently endless quest for the perfect egg salad sandwich.

Often, while sitting on the porch, reading and enjoying the view of the water, McGrath would look back with satisfaction at the life he had led. He had enjoyed two careers, one in the classroom and one in the cockpit, excelling at both. In his study, on the second floor of Cynthia's house where they lived, remembrances of the former were much in evidence. Books, academic and otherwise, lined the shelves. Hardly vis-ible at all in this library was a single reminder of his time in Korea. It was a model airplane, highly detailed, with a blue nose and blue rud-der, with black and white stripes along the fuselage and wings.

In 1999, McGrath passed away. He was seventy-nine. He was read-ing a book on the porch when life departed. Sadly, he was alone when death came to call. Not so at his funeral, which was held at Arlington

National Cemetery. There, in large numbers, friends and family gathered to honor Benjamin Tyler McGrath. Tears were shed, memories revisited, and eulogies were given. All who remembered and spoke said his time on Earth was about love of country and love of family. It had been, they agreed, a life well lived.